BLOOD FOR LOVE

Chris M. Finkelstein

Crave Books

Published by
Crave Books
3533 Port Charlotte Blvd
Port Charlotte, FL 33952
412-260-8483
crantic@gmail.com

Dedicated to the People of the Book

Contents

Chapter One

Martha's Having a Baby

The underground room was larger than it needed to be. It was four stories down from the hospital top floor, which was the only floor aboveground.

Martha was sitting there, uneasily, with the other pregnant couples. She was a member of LERN, the "Love's Epiphany Requirement Network". LERN was an underground group that upheld the traditions of love, and they were on the top of the NOV's State Enemies List.

Here she was, in their lair — and they were hungry for her blood.

Her husband, Griswolt, did not have a clue.

A group of twenty-three pairs of people, mostly husbands and wives, had spread out on the red-carpeted floor. Some were sitting upright, while others reclined, listening as the instructor spoke.

The instructor had on a slick white ela leather lab coat, sporting a gray leathercloth suit underneath. Her spotless white blouse, tailored to the neck, was fashioned of a more finely woven leathercloth. She had a military posture and tone, which was the norm in the NOV. Her voice demanded attention, and her words could not help but draw it —

"Attention! Please! Attention! We will begin where we left off before the break. We were talking about the application of the Rules of the Temple of the NOV. This is critical! We must not let the heresy of love spread, for it will spread, like a virus, if we do not stop it now at its inception. We are entering into a very dangerous territory here. Twenty years ago, the Temple leadership had no choice but to allow newborns and their mothers a five-year waiver of the DeathBT penalty for the crime of love."

DeathBT, Death by torture. What a horrid thing, and these idiots act like its normal, Martha thought. She was here with Griswolt for the maternal counseling sessions required by the NOV.

Annoyed by the unpleasant subject presented before her, Martha changed her thoughts. She was enjoying the maternity robe that the day's fashion allowed. She looked down at it, pinching a bit of the cloth and rolling it in her fingers. It was produced by loosely looming fine leathercloth threads, and had aquamarine shades throughout its length. Best of all, it was freely fitting — a nice change from the coarse leather outfits she typically wore at work, supervising in the mines. She was sitting cross-legged, belly sticking out front, with her tail peeking out from behind the robe. Her husband Griswolt was fresh from work, still wearing his NOV uniform. It was the usual black splint leather, but since he was in administration, he had a lighter weight jacket than most party members.

Martha appraised the room, barely noticing those around her now. *These walls and floors have the most uneven ferrist coat I've ever seen.*

Ferrist mixes were carefully applied, molten, on to the surfaces of almost all of the well-designed and very complex underground structures that everybody lived and worked in. These multiple underground rooms were first expertly sculpted out below ground, and then coated — forming hard, thick, metallic interior walls, floors, and ceilings.

Our mine supplied the agrist to make this place, Martha was thinking. Ferrist was a mix of iron and agrist. They used a two to three inch coat of it inside all structures because it would stop underground digging predators, and water, from entering the premises. Agrist prevented the oxidation of the iron and expanded it, like foam. Because of the heat involved in the process, they had to do it in stages, which took time.

Aboveground structures were rare and costly, and had one primary disadvantage — D'ot had extreme temperature ranges throughout each day. Heating and cooling costs were enormous, as ferrist was a conductor, not an insulator, in spite of its foam-like qualities. In an underground structure, this was not a significant issue as the temperature stayed the same year round, and only needed a small heat source.

Martha, ignoring the instructor, continued to observe her surroundings. *They keep these walls here polished instead of painted.* She found herself appraising the designs on the walls. They had copper and chrome inlaid patterns of elaborate lines that looked like fine thread-like curls of smoke as it may rise from multiple candles. These appeared to clash with the squared off and geometrically conjoining darker lines that also covered the walls. Together, they struck Martha's perception as smoke being held captive in a cage.

The teacher was now talking about the paradox of love, although she was unaware of it, "The NOV allowed the temporary waiver for the crime of love because babies and children were dying at a rate that was climbing. This was due to failure to thrive, murder by mothers, or as the children grew up, self-destruction. Important research by the now infamous Dr. Re demonstrated that when the mothers were permitted to express and share the superstition of love with their babies and young children, they had a higher survival rate. While this lesser evil is productive, it opens the door to the viral nature of love, and that door must be closed one hundred percent when the child is five years of age. We cannot allow this disease to infect our population. It makes our citizens insane, lazy, stupid, unpatriotic, and serves no productive purpose but to drug its victims and blind them to reality. Males are warned to be the masters over their wives — particularly during this five year period when love is allowed."

Martha took a sideways glance at Griswolt. He always loved that part. Females and males alike were taught that males had a hormone that made them want to be the ruler of any group.

The instructor continued along the same line, "God is wise, and He saw that males fought males for the top of any power structure. It was therefore natural for them to do this in the home. God decided to put males in control of the family because they were already beating and killing their wives in order to be the ruler anyway. God gave his answer, the Temple enforced it, and the fighting over control dropped considerably."

Great, so God allows the bigger psychopaths to run our homes, Martha thought to herself.

The instructor was pacing slowly back and forth in front of the classroom. She had the air of NOV "nobility", however Martha knew the kind well, and was aware that this instructor was an imposter. The NOV top crust came from old families who considered themselves "above" ordinary emotions such as hate and anger. That was for the masses.

The noble ones prided themselves on self-control, eliminating all emotion from their mental state. Of course, that is until one would strike — and then the full fury hidden beneath the calm cool veneer would be displayed in all its venom. There were usually no witnesses when such an event would take place, excepting the recipient of the attack.

She continued speaking, "During the time of this five-year waiver, any *excessive* expression of love is not to be tolerated in the home. It is to remain repressed, although endured. If love is not actively subdued, it will grow, as it is, of course, a disease. You have been warned.

"You know that when the child reaches the age of five years, the NOV separates the mother and child, and each must go to love deprogramming rehabilitation for a period of four weeks. You have all heard about this. It is harsh, and it is a test. If we can still elicit any sign of love after four weeks of love-deprogramming school, we separate the mother and child forever. The mother, being the responsible agent, must enter a one-year incarceration in a love-*destruction* institution, where any and all traces of love will be replaced with a burning hatred of the concept of love through well-programmed torture. Any such mother is of course neutered before being sent home, because they have a tendency to kill babies afterwards."

The instructor gave her head a slow tilt, looking down and left — followed by a grim grin.

She continued, "By the time the mother is set free, if she is to return home, the child must be moved to a foster home or orphanage. These are bad alternatives. You must decide now if you are willing to go on with the pregnancy."

The instructor paused to let the whole thought sink in. She kept a keen eye for any signs of weakness, any sign of love's presence in the mothers. The mothers in the room were fidgety. *Good,* the instructor thought, *They are reacting.* She scanned them as they squirmed on the floor as though trying to get more comfortable.

Martha was feeling it. She was trembling inside. *I have to face this,* she thought. Her fear was familiar. It came from what she had been dreading ever since learning she was pregnant. She had to face what the instructor was bringing to fore. She had to keep the baby no matter what. *I must keep it together. I can do this. I can, and I will pass the test.* Holding those thoughts helped, but she was still quivering. *Tail, don't twitch,* she thought.

The instructor continued. "Let me remind you that any expression of love before childbirth is not protected by waiver, and cause for DeathBT."

She scanned the class again, searching, searching. There was always one there. She went on, "Considering what you must endure, is there anyone present that would like to go with our attendants standing by the door, and simply abort it now?"

Martha saw three mothers get up immediately, scared to death, and one of them was a LERN member. *No — Sandra's going for the abortion!* She wanted to get up and grab Sandra and scream, "Turn around! You can do this!" Martha was suddenly more horrified, because with the pregnancy, the stress, and the emotion, she felt it coming — *no!* She felt a tear developing. She could not stop it. *No!*

Tears in the maternity class were often a sign of an underground LERN member, or simply a predictor of someone who would not make it through love-deprogramming school. "Love-lovers" was an epithet used against them on the news, whenever they were found and arrested. The instructor was keen to watch for any signs of emotion. She received a sweet bonus for detecting a LERN member, and she was good at it.

She abruptly spotted Martha, and was on her like a giant eight-legged trachna. The instructor practically climbed over the ones in her way to get into Martha's face, her tail whipping anyone who did not duck or get out of the way.

Griswolt suddenly noticed Martha's tears and instinctively backed away, with an awful look of shock and concern on his face. He knew what this meant and wanted no part of it.

Martha watched in horror as the instructor came straight for her, and her insides turned a new twist she hadn't felt before. *Is this it?* She asked herself. *Is this the end? What can I do? What? What?* She just stared at the instructor, frozen.

"What's this?" the instructor shrieked, as she reached out with one bony finger and touched the narrow tear trail on Martha's face.

Martha was staring back at her, paralyzed out of numbing fear when a thought arose — *bite your tongue!* In a panic, she bit her tongue, hard. She could not give a twinge of expression as her razor-sharp piercing teeth dug deeply into the tender flesh, releasing a flood of blood into her mouth.

"I bit my tongue!" Martha spat the words out, getting some blood on the instructor in the process.

The instructor recoiled, disgusted. She stood back and looked Martha up and down. "Clean yourself up!" the instructor ordered, then just as quickly looked around the room for anyone she may have missed.

Martha was still shaking inside, but she had the composure to get out a cloth, and hold it to her mouth.

The instructor pulled her own cloth out of her lab coat, and coolly returned to the front of the class. While wiping the blood off her lab coat, she continued, "As I stated before, should a mother fail, for her protection, and the protection of the state, she will be then sent to love-destruction prison for twelve months. This one year imprisonment should be considered a merciful act of the state, because otherwise the penalty for love would be DeathBT." She looked about the room for emphasis.

"To reiterate, DeathBT is a process that is prolonged as long as possible, serving as an extreme example to others for the prevention of crime."

She paused again, and took a breath. "OK, is that all? The ones still here are all staying for this now, correct? Have I given a good warning of what is to come, and the risks involved?"

The group responded affirmatively, most were happy to move on.

"All right then, let's discuss the clinical aspects of your pre and post natal care."

The instructor proceeded to review the issues of hospital admittance, methods of delivery, and protocols. This went on for the rest of the evening, and the class was eventually dismissed.

Martha was glad to be having a child at such an age as twenty. The life span of people of D'ot averaged forty-seven years, primarily because diseases would overtake them. Any one of them was rarely in perfect health on a given day. Body sores with various etiologies, coming from any number of pathogens were common problems. Sores would start under the scales, and spread to the softer skin underneath. Sometimes a D'otian would have a section of scales surgically removed, just to let the skin dry out and heal. These sores would eventually overcome most people in old age, if something else did not kill them first.

Laws, which, in the end, discouraged childbirth, were hardly needed. Conceiving a child was difficult. There was still a relatively high death rate among babies from disease. Females' breasts had slowly ceased functioning over the last five thousand years. It was now assumed that they never worked.

On the ride home traveling westward, Griswolt and Martha were sitting together in the exposed back seat of their contiss-drawn taxi. It was pleasant to ride on the outside of the taxi, facing backwards. This was the way they would typically choose to ride, if weather permitted. The night air was cool, and the lesser moon was out and full. The dark rolling hills to the north lay in contrast to the streetlights and traffic ahead as one entered the NOV's capital city, Justilant. Not only was Justilant home to the central committee of the NOV, it was also the location of Strakna Laboratories. This is where they produced the "hundred-year poison" vaccines for the entire nation.

The homes, being underground, were marked by their mounds a few feet in height, the outline of which typically reflected the structure beneath. The entry door enclosures usually extended ten to twelve feet aboveground, with similar dimensions in width and depth. The entrance was characteristically the tallest structure of a house.

As they approached the city, they would see more and more "aboveground" homes. The wealthy owned those homes. One could occasionally see this type of domicile in the upscale neighborhoods outside the city, as well. The average temperature range was sixty-seven degrees in a day, with the average temperature being anywhere from thirty degrees to as high as seventy, depending on the season and location. It was much more efficient to build underground, and take advantage of the temperature stability there.

To the east, the rolling hills became a harsh landscape of solid iron-based shafts jutting thousands of feet jaggedly into the sky. These were the outgrowths of highly magnetized iron-based vein formations that had been forced vertically up through the ground by opposing magnetic polarities below. The iron shafts were made of a crystalline matrix, and so they were squared off on the sides, and extremely sensitive to magnetic forces. Some were still very active, rising almost fifty feet in a single year.

Not much was said on the way home until Martha spoke first — and then wished she had not. "Thankth for thticking up for me in there," she said with her swollen, wounded tongue.

Griswolt was just waiting — "What the hell was all that about? I've never been so humiliated in my life! You looked like a damn love-lover up in 'ere! You could have gotten us both into DeathBT!"

His voice was as deep as his body was big. He shifted his large frame in her direction, waving his hefty dark gray hands for emphasis. They hit a bump in the road. The metal alloy wheels of most means of transportation had only their suspensions to buffer the roads.

Griswolt's rising voice was a concern to Martha. The taxi driver up front might hear. Griswolt did not know she was in the LERN underground, and Martha had to keep it that way.

"I bit my tongue!" Martha protested.

Many LERN members had marriages with non-LERN members since it served as a good cover. Because of their knowledge of how to love, even covertly, their spouses were generally happier with their marriages than most couples were. They simply did not know why. In some cases, they did know why, or at least had suspicions. Still, they "didn't want to know", or let it come to the surface, because they could not face such a fearful thought.

Griswolt gave a skeptical look at Martha, and said, "You bit your tongue, huh?" he sighed, "When was the last time you bit through your tongue like that?"

Martha realized she did not want to go down this path because it was a loser — and the talking was making her tongue hurt. She retorted, "That inthructor thcared the hell out of me! Weren't you lithening, or do you only look out for yourthelf?" *Owww.*

Griswolt thought about the class they had to sit through that day. *That was really rough,* he thought to himself. *What hell these girls have to go through to have a baby. My baby.* He looked at Martha. She had her scales done for the class, and they looked positively beautiful in the moonlight. Under the full, lesser moon, their polished surfaces seemed to glow with a deep, gray-almost luminescent-blue.

Griswolt smiled. *Our baby,* he thought.

Chapter Two

Trachnas Interruptus

an woke up. He had just celebrated his third birthday yesterday, and his next-door neighbor Rebecca was coming over to visit today, as well. He jumped out of bed and ran upstairs. His mother Martha was in the kitchen, cooking breakfast. The toasted yama bread smelled wonderful.

The kitchen was large enough to have room for a table and chairs. It was the central room of the home, with the home entry stairs coming down into it. From the kitchen, a hallway went to the bathroom and parents' bedroom. From the other side of the kitchen, one could enter the living room. In the living room were the stairs that led down to Jan's bedroom, and a storage room was down there as well. From Jan's room there was also a narrow-staired emergency exit to ground level. The black stove was the newest appliance in the kitchen. The refrigerator and toaster were black as well. The very light green walls of the rest of the house did not extend into the kitchen. The kitchen had tan/yellow paint over a coat of a nonporous ferrist, same as in the bathroom. The well-lit rooms in the home had recessed lighting in all the ceilings. The cabinets were a shade lighter than the walls, the counter top was a finely polished deep green, white, and black striped marble.

Although Jan was too young to care about yama bread's source, his mother was always cognizant of the fact that yama was the only plentiful source of carbohydrates, essential amino acids, minerals, and certain vitamins on D'ot. They harvested yama directly from the ocean in the old days, which was dangerous. Sea creatures would stalk the harvesting areas, particularly along the NOV's coastline. Now they had aqua farms that were free of those dangers. Huge corporations processed yama in many different ways. Differing extracts were plentiful, and people used them as spices, medicines, cosmetics, as well as a multitude of other specialized uses. Yama was part of most meals, in one form or another. Jan looked forward to the butter and suka she would be putting on the toast. He always asked if his mother would put more of the sweet suka on it, and sometimes she would.

Jan also smelled something he was not too happy with — keesh. The slices of keesh his mother was preparing came from an animal that used its mouth to attach to sea creatures when it was in the ocean, or in lakes and rivers. Once attached, it did not matter if the host animal stayed in water or not. The keesh would then suck blood and lymph fluid from its host. It looked like a big, black blob with a pointy tail. These days they raised and harvested keesh from the bodies of elas. Farmers would keep them caged in the keesh farms. Elas were dangerous, long slithering creatures that could support the growth of this parasite without dying. Keesh could be prepared in many different ways. It was a common part of breakfast, because it could be fried quickly, and only needed salt and one or two seasonings. One common seasoning was an enzyme extracted from yama, called "nako". It added a "hotness" to the dish and helped a little with digestion.

Jan did not like a lot of the food they gave him, but he sure loved yama toast and butter. "Can Rebecca come over now?" he asked.

"A little later, Jan," Martha said. "After we eat, OK?"

"OK." Jan stood there watching her slice the keesh, with the frying pan waiting. *What can I do?* He glanced over at Sala, their pet emui. She was sleeping at the entrance to the living room. She was one of the few animals on D'ot that had fur, and Jan liked to touch the light brown and white fur because it was always warm and soft. *Better leave her alone,* he thought. *Sala scratched me the last time I woke her up.*

Jan turned his attention back to his mother. "Can you play music?" he asked her.

Martha sighed, and put down her knife. "What do you want to hear?"

She's going to do it! "Stahs at Night," Jan responded excitedly. He loved that tune. It made him feel happy.

"Well, at least it will keep you busy until I'm done cooking breakfast." She gave his crest a rub.

Jan had a singularly unusual crest. Whereas Aletians had crests with shades that were a bit darker than their natural gray scale coloring, Jan's crest was very different. It had irregular yellow-gold stripes, running vertically on a rather white crest. The crest coloring stopped at the base of his skull and faded into the usual gray as the crest became minimal along the spine, and into the tail. When he was first born, the entire crest, from head to tail tip, was yellow-gold on white. While out in public, people would stare at him, but those who were familiar eventually got used to it.

Martha went and fetched the music player from a drawer, and placed it on the kitchen table. She took the case that came with it, picked out a spool, and inserted it in the player. Then she threaded the metallic string through the guides to the receiving empty spool. She turned it on and the empty spool started turning, pulling the string through the guides. The music started.

Jan jumped up and down, clapping his hands. "I love you, Mama!" he yelled loudly.

Jan's outburst startled Martha. By reflex, fear shot through her, and she ducked. "No!" She quickly spun around, turned the music off, and squatted down to Jan's eye level.

Jan had no doubt something was wrong. "What Mama?"

Martha grabbed both of Jan's shoulders and said, "Jan, please listen to me. The bad police will come and get you, and take me away forever if they catch you say the word 'love'. Do you understand?" she asked with extraordinary intensity.

Jan just looked at her with his big, wide eyes, and said, "No, I don't."

Martha sighed and looked up, as if an answer were up there. She looked directly at Jan again and said, "It doesn't matter if you don't understand why. They are bad police, and they hate the word 'love'. They will hurt you! They will kill Mama. You don't want that do you?" she asked, shaking her head "no" so as to lead him in the same head motion. It worked.

Jan was now shaking his head "No". He said, "I won't say that bad word again!"

Martha responded, saying, "Baby, 'love' isn't a bad word, except to bad people. If you want to tell me you love me, you have to whisper it in my ear, OK? And I have told you many times never to say 'love' in front of Daddy, because he works with the bad soldiers."

"Daddy is bad!" Jan said, with attitude.

"No, dear, Daddy is not bad. You just don't understand. He loves you too, but he cannot say it, even to himself." Martha sighed. *How do I explain this nonsense to a three year old?* Another sigh. "Here, give me a hug, you little blog!" He jumped into her arms with a big smile.

She whispered in his ear, "I love you."

He giggled, "That makes my ear itchy!" He whispered back into her ear "I love you," and now she giggled. She gave him a quick tickle, and went back to finish cooking breakfast.

A little later, she called Jan to come eat. Jan had a good appetite, and cleaned his plate. He wanted her to be happy with him, and she always was when he would finish it all. After they were done, she sat with Jan in the living room and read to him for a while. *It's so nice when Mama can stay at home with me,* he thought.

There came a light knocking at the door.

"Rebecca!" yelled Jan, as he jumped out of his mother's lap. He ran into the kitchen and up the stairs to the entry door. He opened it, and there was Rebecca, his favorite friend in the world. "Hi Rebecca!" he said, come in and let's play! I have a game out for us." Jan then said, unexpectedly serious.

Rebecca, suddenly distracted, ignored his remark for the moment.

"Look!" she proclaimed, as she pointed to a large six-contiss bus passing by on their street.

They both gazed at it. It was unusual to see a bus that big on this street.

She jubilantly exclaimed, "Aren't they beautiful?" Rebecca had some toy contiss figures in her house, and she cherished them.

Jan readily agreed. The fact that such a large animal was not dangerous was intriguing. He knew what was coming next.

"I can't believe they can fly," Rebecca said. "I'd love to see it."

A contiss was about twelve feet tall at the head, and ten feet tall at the shoulders and rear. They were a dirty brown color for the most part, but they were unique in that they had a shroud of loose leathery hide that fell between the front and back legs, enabling them to leap from almost any height, and glide to a landing. A contiss would land by balling up and rolling out of it, unfortunate rider or not. Along with the shrouds, which looked like a skirt, they had vertical, (from the side,) bands of thick-scaled hide that looked like armour running over their shoulders and torso. The bands ran from one side of the contiss to the other, and each band was about a foot or less in width. The bands closest to the neck or tail were narrower than the rest.

After the bus passed, Rebecca said, "I wish I had one," but with the entertainment over, they turned and went inside. Rebecca passed Jan on the way downstairs, sniffing the breakfast aroma that still lingered.

Martha was back in the kitchen again, and catching Rebecca's eye as she was coming into the room, asked her, "Would you like some toast, dear?"

"Yes, please," Rebecca said shyly. She was on the thin side. Her mother Salom blamed it on her appetite, but Rebecca always seemed to have room in her stomach for whatever was available at Martha's house.

The children prepared to set up a game called "Catch the Yeta" on the kitchen floor. Jan said, "Hey Rebecca, look at me!" He took his loose-knitted cream-colored leathercloth security blanket and fluffed it into the air, slowly letting it settle down perfectly on the kitchen floor.

"Wow!" said Rebecca, very impressed. "I don't know how to do that," she said, shaking her head and munching on her toast.

"I'm grown up!" Jan said proudly. They then proceeded to set up the game on top of the blanket.

Martha had gone into her bedroom to do some laundry. Jan and Rebecca had just finished setting up the game, when Jan, hearing something unusual, cocked his head. All of a sudden, there was a rhythmic hard tapping sound. *Tap. Tap. Tap. Tap. Tap. Tap.* Jan turned his head, and saw a trachna on the kitchen counter. He had not seen one before, but simply looking at it, he instinctively knew it was bad. It jumped to the floor. It was shiny, hard looking, and had a lot of legs. *Tap. Tap. Tap. Tap.*

Trachnas were about twelve inches around, and had eight legs. Their legs had exoskeletons, so that the muscle was inside the shell-like leg sections, resembling some bottom dwelling sea creatures. The shell itself was a chrome alloy that the trachnas were able to absorb and utilize from chrome deposits in the ground where they would nest. They used their legs to tear and rip into their prey until it was dead. The legs joined a central roundish body that had no such armour. They traveled in packs. After a kill, they would stay there for as long as the carcass lasted, sharpening their claws against one another, readying for the next kill.

Jan and Rebecca huddled together as his emui Sala unexpectedly leapt into the kitchen, dividing the trachna from the children. The emui was growling at the trachna, and had its head down low, and tail straight up.

They screamed — both he and Rebecca were absolutely terrified. "Mama! Help!" Jan cried out, as he pulled his blanket out from under the game, making a clatter. Jan grabbed Rebecca to bring her with him at the bottom of one of the kitchen chairs. They tried to hide behind the blanket.

The children were horrified as they watched the trachna take one leap at the emui, and immediately lock its huge jaws into Sala's shoulder. It tore and stabbed at the emui with incredible speed. The emui was dead within seconds, and a bloody mess. The children screamed even more. Martha was in her bedroom, down the hallway, and heard them.

What's that? Martha thought. "Oh my God!" she cried aloud as she opened the bedroom door and heard the true intensity of the children's screams. Martha ran down the hallway towards the kitchen.

"Trachnas!" Martha gasped as she found two large ones blocking her way. She ran back to the bedroom to get the gun. "Trachnas!" she screamed again unbelievingly as she fumbled with the lock on the gun cabinet. She knew that Griswolt kept a common metal stick and small sword under the bed for protection, but that wouldn't do for trachnas.

After killing Jan's pet emui Sala, the trachna in the kitchen had become distracted by the footsteps and voice of Martha, as well as the sound of its partners screeching their attack call in the hallway.

Jan and Rebecca were still cowering on the kitchen floor at the bottom of one of the chairs, with the blanket over them. Jan was peeking out from the blanket. Inexplicably, a beautiful soft light above the kitchen table, just above him, distracted Jan. Jan smiled at it, unexpectedly oblivious to the trachna and his surroundings.

He heard a friendly male voice, *"Jan, come up here with me. Remember to hold Rebecca's hand. Come quickly now!"* The voice made him feel safe, and he followed it.

Jan hurriedly grabbed Rebecca's hand, and pulled her onto the chair with him. Then he got on top of the table, pulling his blanket with him.

Their activity attracted the trachna's attention again, and it started tapping its way towards the kitchen table.

The voice said, *"Jan, throw your blanket over the bad animal — nice and easy, like before."*

Jan felt safe now. He went to the edge of the table, and deftly fluffed the blanket into the air above the trachna. It came down perfectly, loosely trapping the trachna for the moment.

Two deafening shotgun blasts from the hallway rang through the kitchen. Martha exploded into the kitchen, spotting the children. She instantly saw the trachna trying to escape the temporary net it was caught in.

"There you are!" With a half-wail, half scream, she lifted her arms high and brought the shotgun butt directly down on the trachna once, smashing its center with a cracking, squishing sound. A red color appeared on the blanket, and the trachna stopped moving so fast, and started twitching. Then she just cut loose, smashing it repeatedly, screaming the whole time, while the children watched with their eyes and mouths wide open.

"Stay where you are, Jan. I'm going to look around." Martha re-loaded the double-barrel shotgun, and went through the house, room by room. She looked under beds and behind furniture.

When she had disappeared, Jan looked to see if the light was still there. "Thank you for helping us." he said.

"Thank you for helping Rebecca," said the voice. *"If you listen to me, you will always be able to help her."*

Rebecca watched Jan as he sat on the table, talking to nobody. After a while, Jan stopped talking, turned his head to Rebecca, and said, "He's gone now."

"Who —" Rebecca started to say, when Martha came back, proclaiming, "There are no more trachnas." Then she looked at the mess in the kitchen, what was left of Sala. "Oh, poor Sala!" Martha said sadly. She stood there looking at the scene, and realized what happened, shaking her head.

Martha went over to the emui laying dead on the floor. She knelt down, held its head, and petted it. "You saved my little boy," she said with bittersweet gratitude. She picked up their dead emui, carrying her upstairs and out of the house to bury her. The children followed her, accompanying her for the impromptu ceremony. They brought a shovel along, and dug a small hole in the back of their property. Martha laid Sala in it, and covered it with dirt. She then placed some big brown rocks over it. "We need to put these rocks over Sala so the wild animals won't dig her up," she explained to the children. Then Martha asked Jan if he would like to say a short prayer.

Jan was happy to, and as they bowed their heads, he said, "Dear God, please take good care of Sala because she was a good emui." They finished with the ending response, "Let it be."

Rebecca said, "I want to go home now."

Martha said, "Sure, sweetheart, Jan and I will walk over with you." They went over to Rebecca's house, keeping an eye out for any more trachnas. "I'll need to call the Hunter's Station about this when we get back home." She paused and then asked herself, "How did they get in?"

Jan just nodded his little head, as if he understood what she was talking about. He could tell it was important though, and it would keep the trachnas away.

Chapter Three

The Dark Cloud

ell, that was pretty good, wasn't it?" Martha asked, with a contented smile. Martha and Salom were in the kitchen, cleaning up after a small LERN get-together. The last of their friends had left a little while ago.

"You would never know that they were all in LERN," Salom said. "So many wonderful people, and they must all hide." She paused, while looking up thoughtfully, "Why is it the way it is?" She wore a light beige dress tonight, and instead of her usual hooded outfits, Salom had adorned herself with a headscarf that almost matched.

Martha knew what Salom meant. *Why do we have to hide such a simple, wonderful thing as love?* Martha asked herself silently. She gave a heavy sigh.

Salom changed the subject. "Hais is still complaining that he doesn't have a son yet," she said. It was not the first time she had mentioned it, for it had been weighing on her mind.

Martha was sorry for Salom. She knew Salom felt guilty for not giving Hais a son, and had been trying for the last four years. Martha had wanted to avoid it, but dove in anyway asking, "Well, how often do you two 'do it'?"

Salom lowered her eyes and bashfully grinned. "A lot."

"Well, if you have sex so often, why aren't you getting pregnant?" Martha asked, wondering if she should see a doctor.

Salom fidgeted. "He doesn't usually do it that way." Salom looked down again, with a wry grin now, peeking up shyly at Martha.

Martha became embarrassed, and shaking her head, said, "Males, they are all keesh, aren't they?" Then they both looked at each other and started giggling, shaking their heads together.

The laughter lowered to silence. Not uncomfortable — comfortable.

Martha was thinking, *the time is right. Griswolt's working late tonight, everyone has left, and the children are downstairs in Jan's bedroom.* Martha's expression became serious. She looked at Salom. "Rebecca's going to be four years old shortly, like Jan. You know we need to start."

Salom's gut tightened. She instinctively stalled. "Start what?" Her instant change of body position to something more — tense betrayed her false question.

Martha put down her towel, looking straight at Salom, deadpan, and said, "You know exactly what. We can't avoid it, we can't run from it — we've no choice but to prepare for it."

Salom lowered her eyes from Martha's gaze. "Love rehabilitation school," she said with resignation — head dropping, and posture going with it. Because there were no males around now, Salom had taken her headscarf off. Martha could not help but notice the deep scar from an old gash that marred Salom's smallish dark gray crest.

Martha became anxious just looking at Salom's weathered face. *My God, she is slumping so much she's going to curl into the letter "Ac",* she thought. *I had better keep this rolling.* "We've got to start practicing for it, Salom. And we also we have to tell the children, sooner or later," she said. *You have to pass!* Martha looked at Salom directly, forcing Salom to return her gaze. "Have you talked to Rebecca?" Martha asked, knowing the answer as she asked it.

"No — I haven't had the time," Salom responded, trying to brush it off. She was now looking down at the scuffed pair of black shoes she was wearing tonight.

"Maybe we should try, now," Martha suggested. "We could bring the children upstairs, and see how they respond, together." Martha straightened up. She liked the idea of finally confronting this. "Maybe it will be better if they are together."

"How can you expect them to understand that they will be made to hate us?" Salom blurted out, now crying.

She can't lose it like this. Salom, please, get a hold of yourself! She'll never make it! Martha's mind raced with ideas of how to handle Salom.

"We need to do this, Salom! We must confront it, be ready, or — we — will — fail!" *You will fail — and you might take me with you.*

Just then the children appeared. The raised voices had drawn them. Jan was wearing his new yeta costume. He was looking at his mother through the big mouth of the head mask.

"I don't hate you Mama," Rebecca said.

Martha took charge. "Jan, sweetie, come over here with Rebecca."

They came over to Martha's side of the table.

She continued, "You know we love you both, right?"

They children shook their heads affirmatively.

"Well, do you remember that I said we had to go away to a special school when you become five years old?" Martha asked.

They both shook their heads, "No."

Martha sighed, and looked at Salom, who was paying rapt attention. Martha looked back at the children. "Jan, do you remember when I told you about the bad police that hate the word 'love'?"

Jan gravely nodded his head, "Yes".

"And do you remember what they will do if they hear the word 'love'?"

Jan thought a second, and with a flash of inspiration said, "They will take us away forever to jail."

"Very good, Jan." Martha said. "But really, they will kill us both."

Salom was shocked. "Martha!"

25

Martha gave Salom a sharp look, and said, "Neither of them even remembered about the school. This is real, and I need to get their attention. We need them to remember, so that we are all prepared."

Jan's stomach started to ache. He pulled his head mask off and said, "I don't want to talk anymore."

Salom butted in, and said, "I agree, Martha. Let's stop this. It was such a nice evening."

Martha would not be dissuaded. "The fact is that this is going to happen, and we all need to practice for it. She turned to Jan. "Jan, the bad police want to make sure I don't love you. They want to make sure that you don't love me. If we can get them to believe that, then everything will be OK, OK?"

"OKaaaaayyeeeeee, Jan said, stomping one foot. He looked at her quizzically and responded, "You want me to pretend that I don't love you?"

"Yes! Yes!" Martha was relieved that he understood *part* of it, at least. "I just want to warn you, so that you are ready. When you are ready to turn five next year, we will have to pretend that we don't love each other."

"Like a game?" Jan asked.

Rebecca was standing there, turning her head back and forth between the two of them, trying to follow.

"Yes, Jan. Like a game." Martha paused. "We will have to pretend to fight."

Jan did not like that. He did not want to hear anymore. "I don't want to fight with you!" He ran out of the kitchen, angry, and into the living room.

Martha started to feel like she was sinking. She looked at Jan running, then Rebecca, and then her eyes landed on Salom. Poor, weak Salom. Nobody was ready. *Nobody's going to be ready. They are going to torture us, kill our love, and nobody is going to be ready.* She looked at Salom again. She shook her head in defeat. *Is Salom going to make it, or not? It's up to me to get her ready — and what about Jan? My sweet baby Jan.* She had a flash in her mind's eye of Jan strapped to the torture chair, receiving extreme jolts of electricity, and she just as quickly chased the flash away. She found herself crying aloud, to no one in particular, repeatedly slapping her hand on the kitchen table, "No! No, no, no, no, no! I can't take it. I just can't. Nobody's going to be ready." Now Martha broke down sobbing.

Jan heard this, and came back from the living room. He and Rebecca instinctively came over to Martha, and stroked her arms, telling her that she would be OK.

But it wasn't going to be OK, and she knew it.

Salom decided to help out, in her own dramatic way. "Listen, I've had enough of this!" she said resolutely. "There's no way out of it. In one year, the NOV is going to take us for four weeks, whether we like it or not. They are going to make us hate each other so much that the love is *gone — gone*! Wiped from our minds." Salom rapped her short stubby fingerclaws on the table for emphasis. "It always happens. We've seen it time and time again." She was staring at Rebecca the whole time. Now Rebecca was looking down.

Martha felt a surge of inspiration. She looked up at Salom, then down at Jan. He startled her with the look he was returning. *So deep for a child of your age,* she thought, as she looked into his questioning eyes. "Not for those who prepare!" she exhorted.

Jan was holding Martha's hand tightly now, and looking up at her as if to say, *Tell me this isn't true, it's not true, is it?*

Martha had the feeling that they had confronted it enough, and said, "I think the children have had their fill for now. This burden won't go away until we get through it. There's no sense in obsessing about it, especially if we haven't practiced yet." She looked at Salom, who returned her gaze, understanding.

"Practicing hate! I can't believe I need to do this", Salom said. "Rebecca, let's go home. I'm tired and we have a baby coming over early tomorrow morning." She looked at Martha and said, "Those people down at the processing plant in Havenworth are idiots. They make you so nervous, you forget things."

Martha knew what was coming. *Salom lost another job. Hais has got to be angry.*

Salom continued, "So they fired me just because I dropped something and it broke. I'm just going to babysit for now, and Jena down the street is dropping her baby off tomorrow morning."

Martha hesitated, but decided, *why not?* "It would be great if Jan could stay at your house instead of daycare. The more he's there, the more sores he gets."

Salom was delighted, and broke into a big, toothy smile, (which could be kind of scary sometimes.) "Oh I was hoping you would ask! Hais and I could sure use the money."

Martha was glad that her decision picked Salom up so much. *It will also help keep that bastard off your back.* "It's settled then, I'll drop Jan off tomorrow morning."

Salom rose, and got Rebecca ready to go. They said their goodbyes, and parted ways for the evening. Griswolt was still late at work. A little later Jan had gone to bed. The evening was hers. This was a good time to study the writings, and to prepare her letter as well. Martha went into the bedroom, reached her hand behind the heavy painting of the NOV Temple on the bedroom wall, and pulled out a big envelope. She went to her small desk in the bedroom corner and had a seat. She opened the envelope, which was filled with various pages and scraps of scriptures and devotions to love. Martha pulled out her favorite ones, and read them. These writings had survived for centuries, and were very rare. Martha's mother handed most of them down to her. She had scribed copies for LERN, but kept the originals. There were twenty-three in all, some just scraps a few inches long. Then she opened a desk drawer, retrieved a blank page of the familiar white metallic paper, and began to write.

LERN advised all mothers preparing for love-deprogramming school to write a letter to themselves before going there. LERN members had to stay away upon the mother's return home, for fear of the spies that would randomly stake out such homes hoping to capture them. The letter was meant to be read upon the mother's return from the school. It existed to remind herself of who she was before the love-deprogramming took place. She was to include loving pictures of her and her child stored along with the letter. She had scenes of normal activities, like eating together, or sitting outside, or playing. Martha had taken pictures with Salom and

Rebecca for this purpose as well. There were quite a few photographs of them hugging and kissing. It took her about an hour to write the letter. It was difficult, but had to be done.

Afterwards, Martha stored everything away back behind the painting. She then went back to her desk chair, sat down, and meditated. She meditated on love. She meditated on thanking the source of love, and feeling it grow. She was an outlaw love-lover, plain and simple. She loved it, but knew she was supposed to give it up a few months before the school started. After she was done, Martha went to bed. Her work in the mines started early in the morning.

Jan went to Rebecca's house the next morning, and almost every day from then on when his parents were at work. There were good days and bad. The bad days were typically when Salom's husband Hais was home. Hais was usually drinking tuba, and it made his breath stink. He would reliably pick on Salom, or insult Rebecca. There was almost never a day that Hais and Salom did not fight. Hais treated Rebecca much better when he took her alone to hognot matches. He would much rather have had a son to bring.

About six months had passed...

Jan was spending yet another day at Salom's house. It was laid out differently from Jan's house, having a living room/kitchen combination. A light beige coat of paint on the walls had black-and-brown-stenciled forms of various animal shapes along the upper part of the walls as they joined the ceiling that used to be white.

"Salom! Where's my rawhide hat?" Hais hollered from downstairs.

"How should I know? I don't wear it!" Salom yelled back from the kitchen upstairs.

Here we go again, thought Jan, looking at Rebecca.

Rebecca pretended not to notice. She was practicing knitting, and she was becoming quite skilled at it, for being only four and a half years old now. "They always yell," she said. "It's no big deal. I think that's just how grown-ups talk. You want to go to my room?"

"No, that's OK," Jan replied. He was working on a puzzle on the living room floor beside Rebecca. Rebecca was sitting in a little chair her size, knitting, just like her mama did. She appeared to be quite pleased with herself.

Hais came upstairs, huffing and puffing. He was wearing his usual attire for hitting the bars. He liked tan suede, and if his color choice varied at all, it went to brown. He usually kept his work helmet on long past working hours, but liked to wear hats in any case. His crest was short and wide, like his body. Aletians prided themselves on their tall crests, and so he was not considered particularly fetching. Alcohol helped, (for the object of his attraction.) He was not faithful in the least, but Salom was afraid to confront him when he came home covered in some other female's scent. This was because he was typically also awash with the stench of alcohol, and that meant a beating if she did not handle it perfectly.

He was still looking for his rawhide hat. The suede hat needed cleaned. "It's got to be here somewhere. I just know you did something with it! You're always hiding my stuff — you don't know how important it is!"

"I saw it last week in the shed," said Salom. Why don't you look out there?"

Hais got angrier. "I've been in and out of the shed all week, you idiot! Don't you think I would have seen it?"

Salom got up, and went outside to check. In a minute, she was back with the hat. "Here you go smartass!" she said. He was not drunk yet, but she knew he would have a comeback. Salom looked at Jan, "By the way Jan, your mom is home now."

Hais was far from beaten. "You think you're so smart. How are you gonna think your way out of love-deprogramming school? It's only five months from now!" He had an evil smile on his face. He knew that would knock her down a peg or two.

"I'll be ready," Salom said with phony confidence. "Martha and I are preparing."

"Oh yeah? How are you gonna prepare for RSE?" he shot back.

Random Sublethal Electrocution, otherwise known as RSE, was the Nation of Vengeance's torture method of choice.

"Oh shut up!" Salom screamed, covering her ears.

He had her now. No time to let up for a true ela. "You know that everyone that goes to jail now has to wear an RSE collar no matter what the crime?" His nostrils flared as he projected another twisted smile.

Jan and Rebecca were still within vision and earshot of the argument. Jan was paying rapt attention, while Rebecca still pretended not to notice.

"Yep, that's right," Hais continued. "Now every regular prisoner gets at least one random shock every week, no matter what they are in jail for." He paused, embracing the idea. "I think it's great! Half the ones in prison are love-lovers waiting for their trials anyway. They need to have their brains fried."

"Why do you hate them so much?" asked Salom, tauntingly.

"I hate them because they're weak! They spread lies and laziness! I hate love! It is a stupid superstition, and the Temple of the NOV is right!" Hais continued with his rant, "Love is like a magic trick, it's fake and empty! There's nothing there, and these idiots spread it to their kids!"

Salom shot back, "You talk about the Temple? Hah! The only time you go is for the child-burnings!"

Hais retorted, "The Temple is right about love! They hate it, and so do I, just like any decent citizen!"

"Well now," Salom thought aloud, "How can you get so angry at something that doesn't exist?"

Hais opened his mouth for his next response, but there was none. Just an empty big mouth. "Oh, just shut up!" he retorted lamely. He needed to regain the attack. "You won't be so cocky in love rehabilitation. They do RSE on you every day there."

Salom's gut tightened. The thought took the wind out of her. *No!* She sat up straight, and said to herself, "I can take it. I can take it. I'm ready for it."

Hais wasn't about to lose the argument. "What about Rebecca?" he gave his evil grin again and they both looked at Rebecca and Jan, and then back at each other again.

Her fear was now replaced with revulsion. Salom's face contorted, "You disgust m —"

31

The words were barely out of her mouth when she received a back-handed smack from Hais to her mouth. He had her timing down to a "T", and was ready to give himself the opportunity to show her who was boss.

Jan jumped, startled. He had seen Hais hit Salom before, but the tension of the moment, and the words he just heard made his reaction more exaggerated.

Salom cried out when he hit her, and she held her face in her hands, now weeping.

Hais looked disgusted, picked up his hat, and left for the bars. The door slammed behind him.

Salom had taken a seat in the kitchen, where she was silently sobbing. Rebecca, distracted for only a moment, was back to her knitting.

Jan was replaying the words he had heard — especially the words about what would happen to Rebecca. *If that electric thing is going to happen to Rebecca, then it's going to happen to me, too — and Mama.* Jan wanted to know more. "Let's go ask your mom what she knows about love habit-shun school," he said to Rebecca.

Rebecca was still just sitting and knitting. She seemed oblivious to everything, including Jan now. She did not answer.

So he asked again, and Rebecca ignored him again. When he asked a third time, she stopped knitting, and looked at him very seriously — announcing, "I don't want to talk about it." Rebecca started knitting again for a few seconds, then stopped and looked at Jan again, "I don't want to think about it." Then she went back to her knitting, but this time a tear developed in her eye. Then there was another tear — followed by another. She sniffed. She would not look anywhere but her hands.

Jan suddenly realized that Rebecca knew what was really going to happen in that school that everyone was afraid of.

He asked Rebecca, "Why were they talking about jail? We're not going to jail — we're going to a school, right?"

Rebecca would not answer. She pursed her lips, and kept right on knitting.

Jan was getting frustrated. "Rebecca, look at me!" he yelled. She would not look.

He glanced over at Rebecca's mom. She was still sitting at the kitchen table — just sitting, staring at her hands.

He tried again. "Rebecca, don't you want to know? Let's ask your mama."

He received no response from Rebecca.

Jan was afraid, and became angry. He was still anxious from the recent drama, and now he was full of questions and getting no answers.

"I'm leaving!" he said, loudly and angrily. He stormed out of the house, almost raging.

Jan was halfway to his house when Rebecca came out of her house, slamming the door behind her. He turned and stopped as she ran up to him.

"I'll tell you," Rebecca said, catching her breath and displaying a very grave expression on her young face.

They went around behind Jan's house. His house had a risen façade. It was not actually functional, but it looked fancy, a little like an aboveground house. Usually, when Jan was behind his house he would make it a point to look up into the sky, because nobody could see him there. He often wondered why they were not allowed to do it.

"Why can't we look up in the sky?" he would ask his dad, and Griswolt would have to tell him the same story again, "The Temple of the NOV has decreed that for God to bless us, we must submit to his judgment of us as deeply inferior sinners. According to the Temple, it is arrogant for us to look up into the heavens, God's home, and therefore, a sin. It is contempt of God. If we do not commit this sin, we will be blessed as a people. The nations we destroyed committed this sin, and look, where are they now?"

When they were behind the cream yellow façade, Rebecca stalled. She sat down, and picked at the clean, rounded, yellow-orange decorative gravel that was there.

Jan was in no mood — "Well, tell me! What's going to happen to us?" Jan asked. "You said you would tell me!"

Rebecca just wanted to be with him, and not her mom — or her dad. She looked at him and said, "I hear my mom and dad arguing about it all the time. I'm sick of it." She looked down and shook her head. "There's nothing anybody can do. They are going to take us away from every-body." She started sobbing. "They are going to put us in jail, and put electricity in us, and hurt us until we forget everything." Rebecca was shaking now, uncontrollably. She stopped talking, and slowly looked up at Jan, still sobbing, shivering — searching for a reaction. Anything.

Jan could not imagine it. His stomach sank into a tight ball, and he retorted, "I don't believe you! What are you talking about? Nobody is going to hurt us! You're lying!" The more he talked, and the more he saw the look on her face, the more his fear climbed. The reality of it was becoming too "real".

Denial was the only option. Jan abandoned his friend, leaving Rebecca sitting there sobbing. He ran around the front of his house, terrified, as fast as his feet could take him, and on through his front door. "Mama — she'll know!" he said to himself with resolve, tight lips and stony gaze.

Martha had been home from her job in the mineral processing plant for a little over fifteen minutes. In that short time she had taken off her light-blue ela leather jacket, kicked off her boots, and was relaxing with her eyes closed on the easy chair in the living room. After a long hard day at work, she would find herself feeling like she was sinking materially through the chair, like melting. It felt good, and was "recharging" for her. She was almost "there" when Jan came inside, slamming the door loudly enough to make Martha's face twitch and wince.

Martha thought to herself, *I'm going to have to talk to Jan about th* —

"Mama! There you are! Jan was out of breath and shaking.

Martha, startled by his appearance, sat forward. "What's the matter, baby? Come here." She reached out her arms and motioned for him to come and sit on her lap.

Jan came across the room and said, "I don't want to. I just want to hold your hand, OK?"

Martha was becoming more concerned than curious now. She leaned forward from her chair, and held his hand. "What's wrong?" she asked with a worried look on her face.

Jan looked up at her. He had "the look".

This is going to be bad, Martha thought to herself, but still not sure where this was going. She looked into his troubled eyes. "What's wrong, Jan? Tell me."

He straightened up, and blurted it out, "Tell me about love re-hapshun school! Tell me!"

Martha pulled away slightly. *Love-rehabilitation school. They must have been talking about it over Salom's house.* She sighed — *I'm really not ready for this now.* Truth was, she had been putting it out of her mind of late. She had to — it just made a day so miserable when she thought about it. She studied Jan. *It looks like he's ready.* Martha gave another sigh. *I'd better let him start with what he knows.* "What did you hear about love-rehabilitation school?"

Jan didn't wait — he knew exactly what he wanted to ask. "Do they shock us with electricity?"

It was the last question Martha wanted to hear. She blinked, startled, and shook her head. She wanted to lie. She *really* wanted to lie. *I am. I'm going to lie to him. I just can't — can't face this.*

Jan was insistent. "Will they shock us like they did in daycare?"

The NOV required that all children be subjected to "Sublethal Electrocution", ("SE",) once, by the time they were four years old. "The fear of God" was the rationale. They used a collar device on the neck, which networked with ankle and wrist electrical bracelets. It produced a twenty-thousand volt shock, at a low enough amperage that would not kill. That was not the only thing it did, though. It was able to produce a five-inch "field" around the collar wearer. This outer field would draw the electricity, as if the outer field were grounded. Thus, arcs would develop in the body, and their blue sparks would exit through the skin to the field around the body. This produced skin and scale wounds. Some of these would squirt blood and bleed profusely if the arc exit point were near a larger blood vessel. While the engineering of the SE system would have been easier had they used direct current, they opted for alternating current instead, because it produced tremendous tetanic spasming of muscles, and the most agony. When in prison, the collars were programmed for "Random Sublethal Electrocution" (RSE.) The number of electrocutions per day or week could be programmed into the collar. Animal studies had shown that random shocks were the quickest way to producing temporary insanity. Love retreated from consciousness in this state. Other variables such as amplitude, pulse width, and frequency were easily programmed into the unit as well.

Jan was still waiting for an answer, but he was bright enough to know that his mother's delay in answering meant only one thing: *It's true,* he thought to himself. He did not want to accept it. *I can run away with Rebecca!* He thought. *Yep, that's what I'm gonna do.* "I'm running away!" he said defiantly.

Martha just looked at him. "My God, if we only could run away!" she said, shaking her head and now rubbing her hands together nervously.

There were rumors in LERN that high-level members were planning a mass escape into the wildlands. They did not yet have the vaccines for those areas. The NOV could barely keep up with the vaccines in their own national territories. The hundred-year self-replicating viral poison did not mutate away after the hundred years were up, as was supposed to happen. The NOV had released it in order to kill all other D'otians on the planet. Because of it, they had wiped out the other three entire race/nations. For one hundred years now, the NOV was the only nation still in existence on D'ot. The process of producing the vaccine involved hundreds of specially guided mutations of yama cells. It took almost twenty years of a steady string of controlled mutations in order to produce the vaccines. This was to the NOV's great advantage. All other nations were caught off guard, and there was no way for them to have the time to produce their own vaccines. The NOV had proven their "superiority", for the final time.

"Yes Mama, let's all run away!" Jan said, so excited at the answer to this terrible problem they were facing. He started jumping up and down, clapping his hands.

Martha was heartbroken, looking at him. *I have to tell him.* "Jan, we can't run away. I would love to, but there is no place we could hide for long. The bad police would find us, and then it would all be over."

She abruptly had a flash of inspiration, and her expression changed, trying to cheer him up in any way possible, "We can get through this, Jan. Everyone you see that is older than you has made it through, and you can too! Then, we will run away someday! I know people who are planning that right now!"

Martha studied Jan, to see if he was buying it, and continued, "So, you see, you just have to hang in there, and you'll get through it — then we will all be able to leave someday and be happy!"

Jan smiled. Then the smile faded. "But we still have to get shocked?"

Martha just sat there, not wanting to say it, when Griswolt arrived home from work, and was coming through the kitchen. Martha gave Jan the look he knew all too well, "No more of this, we'll talk later."

Jan protested, "But I want to know more! I want to —" Martha pinched his shoulder, cutting him off — a sure sign to shut up.

Griswolt walked in, saw the exchange, and asked, "He wants to know more about what?"

Martha looked up at Griswolt, and replied, "He's asking about love-deprogramming school. I don't want to talk about it right now."

It was certainly a subject that Griswolt was loath to walk in on, especially after a long day at work. He just grunted, and went back to the bedroom to change out of his uniform.

Martha was relieved Griswolt had dropped the subject so easily. It would be all too easy for Jan to let something slip about the scope of his understanding of love, and that could make Griswolt suspicious. He was a solid NOV party member, climbing professionally and socially. Any hint of Martha's participation in the LERN would have likely sent him straight to the police. Anything less was suicide, and an ugly one at that, compliments of DeathBT.

Martha whispered, "We will talk after dinner," and sent Jan off to his room. She then went into the kitchen to prepare the leg of splint she had bought on the way home from work. The yama bread was still fresh, and she always had a seasoned yama-extract tea brewed for after dinner as well.

Dinner was pleasant, and delicious, according to Griswolt. He even gave Martha an NOV appropriate term of endearment, "I approve of you," after dinner. She returned the compliment, with her cheeks feeling warm under her scales. He gave her a look that said that they would be staying up a little later than usual.

37

Afterwards, they were relaxing in the living room listening to the radio. Griswolt always needed to check the news, even though it was mostly NOV lies. "Well, I have to know what people are lying about don't I?" Griswolt would answer Martha when she brought up the obvious agenda and bias of the "news". He would go on, "If everybody believes the lies, then they become our reality. It gives me something to anchor to politically, whether true or not."

After a little while, Martha said, "I'm going down to Jan's room to clean up. Do you need anything?"

Griswolt was concentrating on the latest story of a big LERN bust, and just waved her away as if to say, "Don't bother me now."

Martha went downstairs to Jan's room. It was a well-lit room, larger than a child really needed. His numerous posters cheered the room, all very colorful. They were taped to the same light-green painted walls as upstairs. Jan had created most of them a while ago when he was in daycare. She went over to him, as he was busy drawing a picture of a yeta.

The yeta was the "king of the wildlands". A full-grown yeta would stand over ten feet tall when upright. They traveled in packs of two or three, occasionally more. It looked like a big skinny tack, but could walk upright on its muscular hind legs, and it had two front arms that sported strong claws that could grip its prey as it tore into them with its massive jaws and teeth. These were a real prize for both amateur hunters and professional NOV Hunters, but were only found deep into the wildlands. To hunt there, hunters had to wear special masks and environmental hunting suits to avoid the lingering mutations of the hundred-year poison in those areas.

She sat down on the bed beside Jan. He had been quietly working on his drawing, and had calmed down. She took a breath, steadied her voice, and gently asked, "Are you ready to hear what is going to happen?"

Jan did not stop drawing, and didn't look up either. He shrugged his shoulders. "Yes, I guess so." He already knew. He had already begun to dissociate from it.

"If you can fool them, they will only shock children once a week. That's just four times…and they also turn down the electricity for you."

"They said that at day care, and it still hurt, *really* bad." Jan stopped drawing, still looking at the picture.

Martha felt it welling up. *Don't cry! It's the last thing you need right now!* She bit her lip. She did not know exactly what to say next, when Jan piped up.

"Why, Mama? Why do they have to do this to us?" He looked up at her. "Why?"

Oh no! She couldn't stop it. The tears came streaming forth from her eyes, rolling off her face onto the bed. She took one of Jan's leathercloth undershirts lying on the bed and dabbed her eyes with it. "They want to remove our love. They destroy love," she choked it out, barely able to speak the words, sniffing her tears, and gulping her breaths. *Martha, get a grip! You can't even talk?* "They can, and will make me forget that I ever loved you — and you, too."

Jan was scared, but not as frightened as he could be because he truly could not understand. He looked at her, confused. "I love you, Mama. How could I forget that?"

Martha looked at him, with such dear and gentle affection, still sniffing, and then realized the truth. She thought, *the only way to explain this is for me to tell you that they will make you hate me, and me hate you. They will smother your love and repress it with terror, hate and rage, and you will be reborn in the alien womb of the torture rooms.*

He has to be prepared. How do I say it? OK, here goes. She started to tell him, and opened her mouth to start, but the words would not come out. *I can't tell him.* "What can I do?" she wailed aloud.

Jan stood waiting for an answer. So did Martha.

A thought came to Martha. A thought came that lifted her soul for a moment, and she remembered what she had said before — *he doesn't need to prepare, but you do. That's it!* She thought. *I need to prepare! As long as I have things set up here at home, I will remember love for the both of us after it's through, when we are back home together again. Then I'll help Jan to remember!* She felt some relief. "You won't forget that you love me, sweetie. Mama will make sure of that — and I will always love you."

Martha cradled his small chin in her hand with a tenderness Jan had not felt in a while. He looked up at her and smiled, and then he climbed up on her lap, and whispered in her ear, "I'll always love you, Mama."

Five more months went by. It was not spoken of in those months, at least not often, or deeply. Before they knew it, the time had passed.

Both Jan and Rebecca's birthdays were in this quarter, and the date had been set for the next starting class, which was tomorrow. Both of them would be going with their mothers to love-deprogramming school. Martha greatly desired to have a nice last evening together before they were all to disappear for four weeks into the bowels of this beast within the NOV. For now, she had invited Salom and Rebecca to join her family to celebrate Jan and Rebecca's fifth birthdays together.

Martha went to the front door, and opened it for her guests. "Well how do you do, birthday girl? Happy birthday, sweetheart," she said to Rebecca as she gave her a big smile and a bigger squatting hug.

"Thanks Auntie Martha," said Rebecca, smiling and hugging back. Rebecca surprisingly gave Martha a quick little peck on the cheek.

"C'mon in, Salom! It's getting cold out there," said Martha. It looked like Salom was shivering, but that was not unusual for her anyway, especially these days.

"Thanks for having us over Martha, it will help Rebecca to get out of the house tonight," said Salom.

Yes, and I'm hoping this will make it easier on you, Salom, thought Martha. Hais was out and about. They expected him to stop by Griswolt and Martha's house when he came home. *I just know he's going to ruin it,* Martha thought to herself about Hais. She smiled at Salom, "Well let's go downstairs where it's cozy." She proceeded to lead the way to the living room.

Griswolt was in the kitchen putting the finishing touches on a glazed gendra inner layer rump roast that had been cooking in the oven, and it smelled delicious. He had prepared it with a salty injection, and a coat of a sweet yama fraction called "sok". He added butter to the sok, and it looked, smelled, and tasted delightful. He had the hydrogen oven going on high, happy to test their new hydrogen extraction unit.

Griswolt was not ambivalent about this evening, even with the brave front. He was fighting his deep concern for Martha and Jan. He was alone in the kitchen, talking lowly to himself. "Everybody with children has to go through this, and most of them are alive, aren't they?" Even though covert, the effects of Martha's love had manifested, and he was beginning to doubt the wisdom of love-deprogramming school. Griswolt had been gaining a reputation as a softie at work. He sometimes complained, as most husbands did about their wives, that Martha coddled their son too much. "He's turning soft." Griswolt would often say to Martha. "You've got to be tough. Don't be afraid to punish him." Martha would always respond that Jan never did anything worth punishing. He was a good kid, plain and simple. *It just happens sometimes.* Regarding the school, Griswolt was primarily concerned about Jan. He redirected his thoughts, aptly shrugging it off, and loudly declared the rump to be royally roasted, followed with a hearty, "Let's eat!"

Rebecca was ready to eat. She had become so well-conditioned that she now became hungry by simply walking into Jan's house, even if she had no appetite in the first place.

Martha continued the momentum during dinner, keeping everyone engaged and talking. She was very happy, not thinking about tomorrow at all. *This turned out so nice, thank God,* she thought.

As dinner was wrapping up, they heard a loud knocking at the door. It was Hais. Griswolt sent Jan up to open the door for Hais. They both came downstairs, and Hais stopped at the entrance to the kitchen where everyone else was still sitting. He looked like he was swaying a bit. He was obviously observing the aromas of the room.

Griswolt asked, "You want some roast, Hais? It turned out great."

Hais looked at the food, mesmerized by it, but his pride held him back — it was the chip on his shoulder. "No thanks, I ate already." He kept looking at the food, though.

"Well come on over and have a seat anyway, Hais," Griswolt said.

Hais obliged, and sat down on an empty seat at the table. There was a brief uncomfortable silence.

Martha needed to keep the positive track going. "Who wants to play Chino?" she asked, hoping to get the children and Salom into the living room.

"You got any tuba here?" Hais asked Griswolt.

Yes, and I'd like to pour it on your head, thought Griswolt. "Sorry Hais, I ran out last week."

Hais looked at him skeptically. He glanced at the roast again. "Yeah, I'll have a slice of that, if you got extra," he said to Griswolt.

While Martha and the others left for the living room, Griswolt sliced Hais a piece of roast, and added a portion of yama bread.

"So how's work going?" he asked Hais, thinking that small talk shouldn't hurt.

Hais remembered his latest frustration with his economic distress. "I've been working overtime to make up for Salom's last job loss. At least she was babysitting. Now she'll be gone for a month! It's not much, but I'm going to miss that cash. Stupid rotten love-lovers! If they were wiped out, we wouldn't have to go through this! I'd like to find and kill them all! Burn them, that's what I say. Search every home for them, and root them out." Some of the food he was chewing was now spraying out in front of him.

Hais quickly finished his snack, and in short time became fidgety. He kept looking towards the living room, and hearing the laughter in there, got up from the table.

Not good, thought Griswolt. "Where you going?" he asked Hais, but Hais was up and on his way into the living room. Griswolt thought, *oh well, I tried,* and proceeded to clean the table off.

They had already started playing the game, and Salom was in the lead. She was laughing, and then she saw Hais come in from the corner of her eye. She turned her laughter down. They all pretended that he was not there as he stood watching the game for a while, still swaying a bit.

"Oh no, dear," said Salom when Rebecca rolled a zero. "We should let her roll again, since it's her birthday party, too."

"Yeah, that's it. Just let her have another chance. That's what it's all about, isn't it?" Hais said, smiling in his sarcastic way. He was leaning against the wall, now. He generally shied away from joining folks, unless it was fellow drunks in the local pub.

Salom tried to ignore him, but knew he would try again.

"Never mind, I don't want to roll again," Rebecca said, dully.

"No," said Martha quietly. "I like Salom's idea. This is a very special night. She looked up at Hais with great sadness. "They should have whatever they want tonight."

Hais was caught off guard by recognition of something in Martha's eyes — *what the...?* He quickly averted her gaze by looking down. He started feeling woozy. Out of nowhere, he got angry. "You're all weak!" he yelled. He stood away from the wall, defiant, trying to think of something else to say.

Salom saw what was coming, and got up to take him home. *I can come back for Rebecca later,* she thought. "Hais, dear, let's go home and rel —"

"I'm not finished! You all need to hear this!" Hais continued, "We all hate love, but I hate it more than any of you! Salom, you are too soft on this girl, and, well, just look at you!"

They looked at each other, wondering what he meant.

"Come on, Hais," Salom pleaded, this time tugging lightly on his arm.

"You're all weak! Love has done this, don't you see? They shouldn't allow it at all, even if some babies die! Then we wouldn't have to go through with this school!" Hais argued, callously pulling his arm back away from Salom. "You all need to be stripped of your love. It has to be beaten out of you!" His voice was shouting now.

Salom tried once again to get him to go by pulling on his sleeve, and he swung around and punched her, hard, in the left eye.

Oh brother, here it goes. "Well, I'm ready for school, and I'm ready for you!" Martha roared from behind Hais, as she had positioned herself and was prepared for this. With that, she grabbed the last ten inches of his tail with all her might, and bent it hard backwards on itself so the fifth bone was just about to dislocate from the sixth. Hais tried to escape as expected, and she was ready. She bent and twisted it even more and it cracked.

Hais dropped to the floor, "OK, OK, let go."

43

"No fucking way!" Martha shouted, and she barked, "Get up!" as she bent his tail even more. He cried out, and submitted.

Griswolt had just come in to see what the commotion was about, and seeing that Martha had things well in hand, simply stepped out of the way.

Hais tried to say something to Griswolt. "Griswolt, tell this — Arggggg, OK, OK, I'm going."

Martha forced Hais all the way upstairs, and gave him one more hard shove, directly from his fifth tail bone, which elicited one more big "crunch", and sent him flying out the door, falling in the gravel in his ignoble departure.

Hais was groaning on the ground, pain radiating in electrical pulses up his back from the injured tailbone. He slowly got up. Then his face changed. His attitude changed. He wasn't done yet. He turned around to head back to into the front door and was surprised by Griswolt standing there with his arms crossed, feet relatively wide apart.

"Just try it," Griswolt growled. He had enough of this stick and watching Martha at work put him in the mood to do this gendra-ass some violence. *I need to unload some stress too, you know,* he was thinking to himself. Griswolt was a big Aletian. At nine foot five inches, he was fifteen inches taller than Hais, and at five hundred and sixty pounds, he was seventy pounds heavier.

Hais looked up at him and with a wave of his hands shot back, "To hell with you all!" He turned around and started for his house, bellowing all the way, "I wish they could stay away longer! I hope they never come back! I'm tired of paying for those ungrateful keesh!" And so, his last night together with his wife and daughter ended.

Griswolt just shook his head, and went back inside. Martha had already invited Salom and Rebecca to spend the night. *At least I can give them one quiet night before* — her thought trailed off into that blind spot of the invisible mind where such things must be placed — *if they are to remain unseen.*

Chapter Four

Love-Deprogramming School

artha was in a fog. *Perhaps I'm in shock.* She was standing with the other mothers, looking around with her eyes, not turning her head. They were all there at the Temple of the NOV's love-deprogramming school, which was one of twelve such schools place around the country. They were standing outside of the top floor of the building, which in typical fashion was the only floor aboveground. The cold black paint on the building's exterior did nothing to help allay her fear. As the wind swept to-and-fro, she could catch the scent coming from the building. It was difficult to identify. If anything, the smell reminded her of an old hospital for mentally deficient children and adults she had once visited as a child. The sunny day did not have its usual effect. It gave a surreal aura to the moment — a misplaced disparity. It did not belong here, not today.

How can I willingly submit to what they are going to do to him? To me? In spite of herself, Martha was hypocritically looking at Jan. Her son stood motionless and quiet with the other five year olds.

Jan turned his head to look back for her.

I told him not to look back, she thought to herself in frustration. She looked away. She had told Jan to be tough, to act tough. *Show no weakness or it will be that much worse.* Martha's thoughts flitted to the others. *What about Salom and Rebecca?* They had been split off into different groups upon arrival.

Martha knew the drill, sort of. Those in charge were looking for emotional people. They were not looking for emotions like rage. They were vigilant for signs of softness, gentleness, tears — anything betraying love or hope. Lingering looks between mother and child made them easy targets.

When Martha was a child, all love was illegal, before, during, or after childbirth. Because of that, love-deprogramming school had not yet been invented. Love-destruction prison was non-existent as well. Anyone found guilty of the heresy of love was simply executed via DeathBT. The primary concern of the Love's Epiphany Requirement Network was to remain hidden, and had not deviated in time.

The NOV suspected, (but hid,) the fact that a large proportion of the surviving babies had mothers who were LERN members. The simple mathematical construct of this was that LERN members would eventually outnumber the non-LERN members. This was unacceptable. The NOV then developed the plan of allowing love to be used in the child's first five years of life, culminating with love-deprogramming school.

The guards were cold, showing no emotion. They appeared to be NOV nobility by their calm detachment. Martha tried to look them in the eyes, but ended up just staring at her boots. The chief guard exited the building, walked up, and addressed the twelve mothers in this particular group.

"You know why you are here," she said. "Up until this moment you have been citizens of the NOV. You have been protected by the laws of the NOV. That ends for the next four weeks. You are now our property, to bend as we wish. Be prepared. We make no apologies for what we must do to destroy the virus you have in you. We start, now!"

The plentiful group of guards held guns on the mothers, waiting for a reason to shoot. They were only to hit the legs at this stage. The mothers stood there as the guards went from one mother to the next. Martha watched in revulsion as the first mother was held and beaten on the head by the main guard with a flexible metal device called a "bauger", until the screaming mother was unconscious. The mothers were petrified, watching as each one's turn came up. Then the guards then went into faster action.

Two of them grabbed Martha from behind, and a third one came up in her face.

She had already given up. She did not struggle, but she kept a toxic eye on him. *What's the use, fucker?* The guard had no expression as he raised his hand with his bauger. In the last millisecond, Martha caught a gleam of rage in his otherwise dead eye just as the bauger came down at an acute angle, striking hard on the side of her head with it. Martha screamed, still propped up by the guards. The next blow was muffled, and the next — not noticed at all.

Martha awoke with a pounding headache, finding herself in a ten by ten foot cell — her home for the next four weeks. As she slowly regained consciousness, she felt the coldness of the room.

What? Where am I? She realized that she was strapped to a toilet, naked. She woke up in this way — and she was cold in the damp musky room.

"How heavy *is* this thing?" The pounding of Martha's head increased as she attempted to lift her hands to feel what was on her neck, but discovered her arms were bound to her sides. She moved her aching head around, feeling a large heavy object wrapped around her neck. She was barely able to look down at the equally heavy cylindrical devices attached around her wrists and ankles. Her face stared back at her, warped, in the pretty, chromed metal.

"Well, here we are," she said to herself with a resigning sigh. "I wonder when the first one will come." Martha was still slowly regaining consciousness, and pondered the blank white projector screen in front of her. The area was dimly lit with a single small wattage light bulb. The ten by ten foot room she was in was coated with porous ferrist, and looked like it had never been painted or washed. Her space reeked of stale urine and overwhelming body odor. Random screams from various directions startled her. *Look at those stains on the walls — they look like old dried blood.*

She searched down more closely, trying to see the devices on her wrists, and traced their wires to another larger unit mounted on the wall to her right. "I guess — GGGGGGGGGAAAAAAAAAA!" Everything stopped but the pain. Martha's entire body convulsed and her neck arched back, along with her arms and legs, straining as far as the restraints would give. The twenty thousand volt shock lasted ten seconds. She found herself limp, disoriented. "Oh my God, wh — GGGGGGGGGGGG GGGGGGGAAAAAAAAAAAAAAArrrrrrrrrrrrrrgggggggggg —" She convulsed again with the tetanic contractions, her face contorting into a grimace that had the ghastly look of a broad smile, with eyes that wanted to pop out of their sockets. That session was twenty seconds long, and left her gasping. *Just let me breath!* Her arm felt like it had been stabbed by something. She looked down, and saw blood coming from the side of her elbow.

"What have I gotten myself into?" Martha cried out. "How many of these do they do in a day?" she desperately asked the malodorous air, still catching her breath.

A dispassionate male voice came from a speaker in the room. "When set on random, ten per day, up to seventy per week. Sometimes more, depending."

"Depending on what?" Martha asked aloud, still asking herself. *At least the voice sounded reasonable.*

"Depending on if I think you are passing or failing. I have a stake in your successful completion of this school. I am accountable for my record of failures. Failures greatly decrease both productivity, *and* my chances for promotion. You *will* pass my class." What he did not tell her was that he was very experienced, and could "play" a "student" like a finely tuned string instrument. This hot mama was going to pass, but it was going to be his way, and for that, she had to fail — temporarily at least.

What about Jan? Martha thought, and picturing him in the same state, started sniffling. "GGGGGGGGGGGGGGGGGGGGGGGGGgrrrrrrrrrrraaa-aaa aaaaaaaaahhhh!" Her upper lip sprouted blood, snot shooting out of her nose.

"How dare you cry in my presence?" Her torturer revealed emotion, but then he caught himself and toned it down, "You will learn about tears here." He hit her with another high surge.

"GGGGGGGGGGGGRRRRRRRRRaaaaaaaaaaaaaaaaaaaaaggggggggg gggggggggaaagaga," Martha was starting to pass out from lack of air, caused by the spasming. Her muscles were racked with pain. She was barely holding her head up now, in total exhausted agony.

The four by four foot projector screen lit up in front of her, and caught Martha's attention. It displayed a picture of a mother tenderly holding her baby. A recording started. It was a female voice. Like the others there, she spoke in the monotone of the royals, *"Repeat after me, 'This is death. This is death. This is death.' Whenever you receive the electricity, remember this is death. Love is the reason for your pain. Love is the reason for your pain. Whenever you receive the electricity, remember, love is the reason for your pain. What is the reason for your pain? What is the reason for your pain? What is the cause of your pain? What is the cause...?"* and so it continued. Countless words, countless repetitions, countless pictures of loving images would continue night and day, with no let up for the rest of her time here.

Three days squeezed by, shock by shock. Each day, Martha was freed to wash herself. After those ten minutes were up, coarse, hardened attendants would then throw her back on the toilet, and there she would stay, bound and helpless.

Oh God, help me through this! she prayed silently. It did not take long to realize that her torturer watched and listened for any sign of emotion. Any such detection always resulted in a more severe SE. Otherwise they set the system on "Random Sublethal Electrocution, (RSE.) These were more standardized levels and generally not as severe, rarely drawing blood. Therefore, she said nothing but what the recording of the female voice told her to repeat. She watched the screen or looked around the room, listening to the same monotone voice repeating the same mantras over and over again. *It is maddening, yes, but you can still do this,* she kept telling herself silently.

"Love is death. Love is death. This is death. You will die here. Repeat after me, 'I will die here. I will die here. I will die here.' Repeat after me,

'I will die here, and another one will leave in my place. I will die here, and another me will leave. I will die here, and another me will leave. Love did this to me. Love did this to me. The superstition of love. Love did this to me. The superstition of love. Love did this to me. The superstition of love. The Temple protects me from the heresy of love. The Temple protects me from the heresy of love. The Temple protects me from the heresy of love. I am a recovering love addict. I am a recovering love addict. I have a disease, and my cure is here. I have a disease, and my cure is here. I have a disease, and my cure is here.' Repeat!"

"GGGGGGGGGGGGGHHHHaaaaaaaaaaaaaaaaaaasggggggggggghhhhh hhhhhhhh!"

Day seven. Martha was now just an empty lump of flesh. Any slight noise would send her heart rate skyrocketing for a few seconds, then slow down into an uneasy silence. Waiting. Waiting. Waiting. The drone of the female on the recording had become just a blur and all her words and just sounded like distant logic. *Of course, love is evil,* she thought. *Of course it is. How can it not be? It is so clear — I was so foolish.* GGGGGGGGGGGGGRRRRRAAAGGGGGGGGGAAAAAAA-ARRRRR RGG!"

Martha's abdominal muscles were dreadfully raw and painful, and her whole body was throbbing with or without the shocks.

And so, this ritual went on, day by day, the second week coming and going. The female voice kept on, maddeningly, "Love is pain. Love is pain. Love is insane. Love is a lie. Hate love. Hate love. Hate love. Love is death. Love is death. Love is death. Pain is truth. Pain is truth. Pain is truth. Pain is real, love is not. Pain is real, love is not. Say it! Say it! Repeat after me!"

Martha now looked catatonic. She was incoherently staring ahead, no longer thinking about when the next SE would come — just there, period. She was feeling as if who she was really *had* died, and another thing had taken that place in this body of hers. She was dully repeating the words because she would be electrocuted more severely if she did not.

This day, her torturer came in the room, and brought a folding chair with him. He set it up in front of Martha. It was the first time she had laid eyes on him. He was a little taller than Hais, and just as wide. He proceeded to pull some photographs out from an envelope he had in his hand. He was sitting rather close to Martha. She was not looking at him. She was in her own world.

This was his chance. She was a fine looking female, and he was hoping to take this to another level. She had to fail the "midterm" now, in order for that to happen. He picked out a photo of Jan in mid-electrocution, a blue-arc escaping from his cheek, with blood coming down from another wound on his forehead, grimacing with the "smile". He stuck it right in front of Martha's face and said, "Look at your boy!"

Martha's distant vision closed in on the object in front of her nose. A look of recognition and a tilting backward of her open-mouthed face led directly to a gasp — and then the screaming came. From that point on, Martha kept on screaming as if she had gone mad, her screams eventually descending into sobs. The sobs lost momentum as she finally settled into quiet weeping. *Why aren't they shocking me?* She asked herself. She finally worked up the nerve to look at her torturer.

He had a very serious look on his face, and had been waiting for her to see it. "You have failed. You are going to be sent from here to be tortured in love-destruction prison for a period of one year. You have failed. I have failed." He gave a feign sigh, and got up from his chair.

While Martha had thought all emotion was gone, it was right back again, with full force. Her insides fell and fell into a pit that she was desperate to escape. She wrestled with her restraints to no avail. *I'm losing Jan!*

"No!" she raged, straining her neck and head forward against the cervical restraints and was immediately backhanded, hard, by her torturer. He then turned towards his chair to remove it from the room. She stopped crying, and started pleading, "Why? How can I fail now? It's only been two weeks!"

The torturer had picked up his chair, and folded it. He turned, looked at her and said, "You just cried a moment ago. Tears cannot be but a sign of hope, for when hope is gone, tears cannot exist. After two weeks of torture, you showed hope. You need the more intensive treatment of love-destruction prison. You're done here. I've turned your RSE unit off — you'll need to rest for what's coming." Then he turned, and left the room.

Oh my God, what am I going to do? Martha desperately thought to herself. *I was ready. I was taking it — I was ready for another two weeks.*

"I was ready for another two weeks!" she shouted out, hoping he could hear — hoping anyone could hear. *I can't do this for a whole year.* Her thoughts floated in and out of her awareness. She could not imagine having a shred of sanity or identity with a year of this torture. *What can I do?* she asked herself. "I was ready for another two weeks!" she yelled again.

The hell with it, she thought. *I have nothing to lose now.* Martha took a deep breath.

"You know, you really suck! All you had to *do* was shock the living shit out of me, and you couldn't even do *that* right!" She paused, waiting for a reaction. *Is he there? Is anyone there?* She tried again, sneering, "No wonder you're worried about productivity and failures. How many females have you lost? Of all my luck, I have to get the loser of the bunch. You fucking looooooooserrrrrrrrrrr!"

The torturer burst into the room. This was not the response he was expecting. "I make them all pass!" He quickly regained his composure.

Good. He's here. "You've got to be able to do this!" Martha shouted, fearless now. I'll put up with anything, please!" She was looking at him, pleading.

He stood there, staring back at her, waiting.

He's thinking about it, she thought. "I'll do anything," Martha begged, looking directly at him. "Anything."

He still stood there, studying her. *I think she's ready,* he thought to himself. *Yes, she is.*

"There *is* something I can do," he said. "You must sign a waiver for it. It is extreme, but you should then pass. You *will* become like an animal." He paused, "Actually, less than one."

"Anything! Anything! I'll sign!" *Anything to see my son again.*

"Don't you want to know what it is?" he asked, surprised.

Martha paused. *What is it? What — it doesn't matter! I've got no choice!* She looked at him. "It doesn't matter. I've got to pass."

He pulled out a form that he had at the ready, and held it for Martha to sign.

She signed the document and then, as her shoulders and head sagged with resignation, her torturer said, "I'll be right back."

He left the room for what seemed to be about fifteen minutes. He came back with a couple of other male guards. Her torturer began flashing pictures of Jan up on the screen now. These were pictures of Jan's SE's, from different angles. There were close ups and the most horrible scenes of painful contortions of Jan's face when in tetany. All the pictures showed bleeding. They started up the recording of the female's words of hate again, with her endless repetitions about the heresy of love. Then they started the SE's.

The three torturers stood there and watched as she received seven SE's in the period of a half hour. Then when she was an incoherent lump, they unstrapped her from the toilet, and bound her on the sticky floor. They then had their way with her in any and every way, and they took their time about it.

When they had enough, they brought in a big, very heavy female. She wore a black leather mask over her eyes, and was tightly strapped with black leather strips over her body to the point of pain. Her fat flesh bulged out from the tight leather restraints. She brought instruments of pain, and used them to force Martha to pleasure her in any way she desired. Sometimes her only pleasure was to cause Martha pain. Although there was a death penalty in the NOV for homosexuality, there are always exceptions, and she was one of them.

The rule was that Martha had to be bound such that she was always facing the screen with the beastly images of her son's torments. When satiated, the leather female left Martha bound helplessly, laying there sticking to the floor. Then the next guard came in for his turn. When they ran out of rapist volunteers, they tied Martha back in place on the toilet for her standard RSEs. The pictures on the screen went back to pictures of other people in loving scenes. The female voice went on and on…

An hour went by. Then another hour, trailed by the next. Another day, then another followed this, although Martha would not have known it, if it were not for her torturer's shift. He had never taken a day off. In between his shifts, she was put on automatic RSE, with the occasional 'visitor'. Another and another followed another shift, and so it went. Minute-by-minute, hour-by-hour, day-by-day this experience continued, and then her torturer's voice disappeared for a day or two. The other rapist volunteers still came though.

A day came when her assigned torturer walked into the room, smiling. He had indeed taken a couple of days off, making sure there would be replacements. He stood there, observing. The female voice was droning on, *"Love did this to you. Love did this to you. Love did this to you. Love will kill you. Love kills. Love kills everything. Repeat after me, 'I hate love. I hate love. I blame love for everything that has happened to me. This is my vaccination for the prevention of love. This is my deserved punishment for becoming infected with love.' Repeat!"*

Martha became vaguely aware that someone had entered the room and started growling, low. Blood was seeping from her crotch, and her throat was raw and bruised. Her genitalia were sticky and filled with the stench of old blood and infection. Her mouth and face reeked of the leather female's unwashed scent. Her head was down, and her eyelids half closed, but she was looking up in a savage way. She had not cleaned herself in over a week, and just plain stank. She had not eaten either, and so they had been using the tube with food paste to force-feed her.

The female in leather entered as her torturer was still standing there. He looked at the leather female and dryly asked, in his detached way, "You want to go first? You don't leave a mess."

The leather female replied, "No, she's become a biter." She paused, and said, "I think we're done."

The torturer uncharacteristically started laughing in spite of himself, "That's what Dremo told me! Did you see that cut on her arm? He did that when she took a bite out of his pride!" They both started laughing, and then he said, "Well, let's take a look."

He changed the pictures on the screen to the latest ones of Jan being tortured, and Martha looked at the pictures with absolute rage, and started howling at the screen, "Kill him! Kill him! Kill him! Love must suffer! No mercy! No mercy! Kill him!"

Martha's torturer pressed a button on the device he was holding in his hand.

GGGGGGGGGGGGGGGGGGRRRRRRRRRRRRRAAAAAAAAAA AAHAAAAAAAAAA AAHHHHHHHHhAAAAAAAAAAAAAaaaaaaaa aaaaaa!" That shock was one hundred and fifty percent higher than average and lasted thirty seconds. Blood spurted out of both nostrils. Martha spit it out of her mouth too, and growled like a sick, sick animal, back to her catatonic gazing. The growling continued.

The torturer looked at the leather female and said, "What do you think?"

She glanced at Martha with half bored eyes, and said, "I think she's cooked."

Her torturer stared at Martha a bit longer. If she had not reeked so badly, he may have had another go at her. He decided that she would indeed graduate, one day early. "I told her I could do it," the torturer said proudly, gloating over his handiwork.

Chapter Five

The Male Who Could Not Love

nock, Knock.

Griswolt took a deep breath, and then a sigh. *My stomach. Well, she's here,* he thought, as he rose to go upstairs to open the entry door. He had been waiting since early morning, and the day felt like it took forever. Now, it was evening, and Martha had finally arrived. Griswolt felt the drag of gravity on his big frame along with increasing anxiety as he pulled himself up the stairs. He opened the door. There she was, along with an attendant, who looked too young.

"Does she belong here?" the attendant stupidly asked. His hat matched his uniform, but it was too big for his head, which made him look even younger.

"Yes, she does," Griswolt said with a frown. He did not like incompetence, and this guy sure didn't start off right. Griswolt had not looked at Martha but for a glance when he first opened the door. He took a better look at her now. She had a stuporous, starved appearance. Her gaze was distant, and she looked and smelled horrible. She had been heavily sedated and was in a straight jacket.

"I have some documents for you to sign," the attendant said as he reached into his satchel, and pulled them out with the release form. He held them for Griswolt to sign.

Griswolt signed them, handed them back, and said to the attendant, "I think I can take it from here." He turned to Martha, and said, "Come on, sweetie, let's go inside — you're home now." With that, he turned towards her and put his arm around her, ignoring a low growl that was developing in her throat, as she was standing there, semi-crouched.

Martha instantly recoiled at his touch, and her growl became a raving roar. The attendant was ready, and tased her, causing Martha to squat and duck her head down in reflexive fear. For effectiveness, the taser had the same frequency as the SEs used in love-deprogramming school, which was thirty beats per second. This was highly effective at subduing these subjects, as the "tone" would be forever burned into their physical memories. It also emitted a loud, vibrating sound of precisely the same wavelength. The amplified audible tone alone would often subdue these subjects.

Griswolt was still recovering from the shock of this stranger's response. That is what she was — a stranger. The overcast day accentuated her pale looking scales.

Martha's presence was certainly not there. He found himself wondering if the attendant would leave the taser there for a bribe. He took another look at Martha. "What do we do now?' Griswolt asked the attendant.

The attendant looked at him with hardly hidden disapproval, and said, "You didn't read the manual, did you?"

Griswolt was taken aback by this young upstart's question.

There should be a class for husbands for this, Griswolt thought. *I think I'll bring it up at our next meeting.* "I did read the manual!" he retorted to the attendant.

The attendant, remembering the high-scale neighborhood he was in, backed down, and apologized. "I'm sorry sir, I didn't mean to accuse —"

"Save it!" Griswolt snapped. "How do we get her inside?" Griswolt asked as he stepped toward Martha again.

"Stop!" the attendant yelled, putting his hand in the way of Griswolt, who was about to take Martha's arm.

Griswolt stopped, and said "What? What now?"

The attendant looked at him, taking a breath to think of how to say it. "I'm sure you have studied your manual. It's kind of long, and sometimes people miss important things there. One important thing is that you do not touch the graduate upon arrival home. In a few days to a few weeks, she will let you know when it is all right to do so, and even then, you will have — issues. Secondly, you must be as quiet as possible. Move slowly and gently around her." He stopped, and looked at Griswolt. "You do remember this, right?"

Griswolt barely remembered it. He had a hard time forcing himself to read it, or face it for that matter. Suddenly, this kid seemed to know what he was talking about. "Would you help me to bring her inside?" Griswolt asked.

"Of course," the attendant answered. He said, "Martha, we are going inside now, you go first." Then he motioned for her to move. She would not. He pulled out the taser, and just turned the sound on. Martha jumped at that. He said again, "Martha, please go inside your house, or I'll have to use this."

Martha moved. She started for the stairs, and slowly descended them, with the attendant and Griswolt following. When they made it downstairs, they led her to the bedroom, where she just stood.

Griswolt and the attendant left her standing there and went back to the kitchen. The attendant put a big bag of various bottles of sedatives and pharmaceuticals on the kitchen table, along with a surprising supply of antibiotics. Then he told Griswolt, "I can give you a loaner taser, if you like."

Griswolt looked at the taser. Although he had wanted it earlier, now he had an unfathomable feeling of confidence, and changed his mind. Martha looked so weak he no longer considered her a threat. "No, thanks."

The attendant shrugged his shoulders, said goodbye, and then quickly left.

Griswolt went back into the bedroom. "Do you want anything Martha?" he asked. No response. She was gazing off a million miles away. He could smell her from where she was standing. *I have to get her out of that contraption,* he thought, looking at her straight jacket. *How can I do that without touching her? I should look at that manual again.*

He left her there, and went through the house and into the living room. He picked the dark blue NOV Temple love-deprogramming manual from the bookcase, had a seat on their old gray gendra-hide sofa, and started reviewing it. He looked for when and how to remove the straight jacket. He checked the FAQ's and the flowcharts. Nothing. *What about the medications — the sedatives that guy left with me? Nothing!*

"What is this *bilgat* crap? Just like every damn trouble-shooting manual I have ever seen! They tell me everything except what I need to know!" he shouted in exasperation, and then ducked, realizing that he was not supposed to speak loudly. He then thought about the distance that she was from him, even though the bedroom door was open. *She didn't hear me. I've got to get her out of that straight jacket! How is she supposed to sleep with that thing on?* Griswolt spent the next hour or so listening to the radio. He eventually got himself up, and walked back through the house to the bedroom. He peeked in.

Martha had taken a seat in the chair near the right side of the bed. She still had the same alien look. Griswolt slowly walked in. Martha fell into another low-throated growl.

Griswolt stopped.

The growling stopped.

Now what? he asked himself. *I'll talk, really nice and low,* "Martha, sweetheart. Would you like me to take that jacket off of you?"

Her facial expression changed. It became an expression of pain. Not necessarily good, but a change.

She responded! He took a slow breath and offered, "Martha dear, if you stand up, I can take that thing off you."

Martha lowered her distant stare, and instead focused it on their beige and brown patterned carpet about six feet in front of her. Her face and scales looked very dry. She slowly and weakly stood up, keeping her eyes focused to the same point on the floor. She stood there for a moment, winced, and said, "Go slow!"

She talked to me! "You're going to be all right, dear," Griswolt said with a smile. He slowly walked over to her, and Martha started growling lowly again.

"Slower!" she hissed, starting to stoop in a guarded way. She was still staring far through that same point on the floor, but also intensely focused on the one coming closer to her.

Griswolt stopped and waited for her growling to stop again. Then slowly, bending over so he would not look so large, Griswolt made his way across the room to her. Every time she started growling, he stopped and waited. In a few minutes, he eventually made it to her. Her breath was fetid. With time and patience, Martha allowed him to get behind her. She was shaking as if she were freezing to death. He slowly undid her bindings. She continued to growl — but nothing came of it. She smelled much worse with the jacket off.

Griswolt's mind was racing with questions about why she was in this state — they had to wait.

"Do you want to take a shower?" he asked, but she just stood there. "Why don't you lie down on the bed?" Griswolt suggested.

Martha's stare was interrupted as she glanced at the bed. A look of sadness passed for a moment. She did indeed make her way to the bed slowly, sat, and then laid down on it.

Griswolt wanted to do more, but decided otherwise. "I should get out of here while she's calm." He went into the living room and prepared for sleep. He said to himself, "I'd better give her a sedative. I don't want her walking around here tonight."

He went back to the kitchen to get the pills along with a glass of water, and then returned to the bedroom, entering slowly. Martha was lying there on the bed, staring at the ceiling. "Here Martha, will you take these? They'll help you to sleep," he said, as he gradually came to the bed.

Surprisingly, Martha went along with it. As if in slow motion, she sat up, and took the pills. Then she lay back down.

Griswolt breathed a sigh of relief, and went back to the living room. He got himself comfortable on the floor with a pillow and blanket, and fell into a light and uneasy, guarded night's sleep.

The next morning, Griswolt woke up and made one of Martha's favorite breakfasts. It was a soft-boiled splint egg with toast. He was hoping the smell of it would rouse her. He bought fresh splint eggs the day before. Jan would be coming home tomorrow, and if the eggs got more than five days old, they would become increasingly bitter. Jan didn't like that. When Griswolt was done cooking, he went to the bedroom to try to wake Martha. She was still deeply asleep.

"I guess that sedative really worked — oh well, let her sleep," he said, as he put her plate away for later. He went into the living room after breakfast, and started on the manual for a second time. "Hmmm. They say here that I shouldn't try to touch her, even if she is talking, for at least three days. Some take three months! Wow. It says that some may never recover." He stopped and thought about it. *No, she's going to be all right — most of them do turn out OK.* He started thinking about the NOV. Griswolt was sure that this was the right way to go. To aggressively confront the NOV leadership on this would be political suicide.

"I really do think I'll recommend a special class for fathers, rather than this lousy manual," Griswolt said to himself. After climbing up through the ranks, he was an NOV policy maker now, a bureaucrat.

It reminded him, "I'd better call the office." Only the higher-level officials of the NOV were entrusted with electronic communication. It was wise to call in. He had to make his presence known. The bureaucracy making up the higher ranks of the NOV was very competitive, and others would try to take advantage of Griswolt's absence from work.

He went into the living room, picked up the heavy green phone and called his secretary, who connected him with others there. During the call, Griswolt discovered that the NOV was nationalizing a nearby mining conglomerate. After the phone call, he turned on the radio to hear the latest news about it. It was the main story of the day. The conglomerate had been threatening a strike because of the ever-increasing taxes imposed upon it by the NOV. The NOV had just "solved" their problem by eliminating all taxes on them. They did this by nationalizing the conglomerate. Now, instead of taxes, all the profits would go directly into the NOV's treasury.

"Wow! This could be a good opportunity for Martha," Griswolt said to himself. Then he remembered, looked towards her room, and sighed. After his second time through the manual, Griswolt changed his reading material, and found himself going over the latest changes to the intra-party regulations of the NOV. *I have no life,* he thought to himself glumly as he read the dry, mercilessly detailed information. *I'm reading government regulations in my living room. Who does this?* He smiled to himself.

Just then, he heard some movement. He looked up, and could hear Martha exiting the bedroom and heading down the hall to the bathroom. Griswolt sat up erectly — straining to hear, yet feeling like a weight had lifted. He focused his ears on anything he could identify. He heard water running. Slowly, he went over to the closed bathroom door. *She's getting in the shower — yes!* Griswolt cheered in his mind's ear. He then got control of himself, quietly turned, and went back to the living room. He sat down, and resumed his review of the regulation changes. *She's going to be OK. She is.* It was a small thing, but at least it was *some*-thing.

After a while, it occurred to Griswolt that Martha had been in the shower for quite a long time. He looked at his watch. He thought about going back and listening again.

I should have checked my watch when she went in. Maybe it hasn't really been that long. He looked towards the kitchen again, listening for sounds coming from the hallway on the other side. *Going over these regulations sure makes time drag,* he thought to himself. He had his right leg crossed over the other, with the report opened on his forty-five inch thigh, and realized how much he was waggling his foot, which was a lot.

I'll wait another fifteen minutes. Just then, he heard a crash. He was up like a shot, and ran to the bathroom. "The door's locked," he complained aloud, and then shouted through the door, "Martha, can you hear me? Are you all right?" The water was still running. He ran to the kitchen, grabbed a likely utensil, and ran back to the bathroom. He clumsily picked the bathroom doorknob open, and was aghast at what he saw upon opening the door.

Martha was half-conscious on the shower floor, trying to get up, but too weak. She was waving her arms in the air, as if trying to grab hold of something invisible in order to raise herself up. He ran to her and clutched an open hand as it was groping the air.

She immediately pulled her hand back, curled up, and giving Griswolt a chilling look, screamed, "Don't touch meeeeeeeeee!" She focused on him with a dagger-filled eye and threatened, "If you ever touch me again, I'll kill you!" She attempted to exit the shower. Griswolt watched as she got up and staggered out into the bathroom proper, but was weak indeed. As she was turning to reach for a towel, Martha slipped, coming down on her hands and knees, and then falling to her side.

Griswolt was shocked at what he saw from behind. His mouth dropped open. *My God, what happened to you?* His blood went to boiling. "What *happened* to you there?" he shouted. Everything between her legs was red and raw, with a slowly seeping bloody discharge.

Martha looked up, and turned her head around towards him. She was still incoherent, and didn't realize —

Griswolt stormed out of the bathroom. "I'll get to the bottom of this! Someone is going to pay!" he shouted as he lumbered down the hall to the telephone. He called in and asked for his secretary, Mari, and told her, "I want you to get the Office of Love-Deprogramming on the phone, and find out who was handling my wife over there!" Mari said she would check it out and get back to him.

By the time Griswolt returned to the bathroom, Martha had regained her mobility, gotten up, and was now drying herself.

Deciding to leave her be for now, Griswolt went back to the living room, putting the book of regulations on his leg once more. His foot was wiggling again as if it were its job. He could not focus. He looked up, and around at the comfortable room he was in. The NOV was the reason he had such a nice home and lifestyle. "I completely support the creed of the NOV," he said to himself. *Love is a dangerous idea — otherwise — they wouldn't make such of a fuss about it. This has to happen, to keep an orderly and stable society.*

Since he was fighting some doubts about the wisdom of this require-ment, Griswolt continued thinking along the lines of the NOV's side of the debate. There were indeed important points about the serious negative effects of love on civic order. Because of love, citizens would repeatedly refuse to point out family members or others involved in any number of illegal activities — from outright violent crime to black markets, and to organizations like LERN.

With any black market, there was also a "gray" market that blended with the official economy, which had always been somewhat dependent on the gray market. This problem was agreed by all to be unacceptable to law and order. However, upon the successful destruction of these black and gray markets decades ago, the economy had never fully recovered. It did not matter. The NOV finally had the law and order that they coveted so dearly, and the upper crust didn't have it so bad.

Look at what the superstition of love had done to law and order! Still, Griswolt had to keep pushing away the nagging thought that there had to be a better way. *Especially now,* he thought to himself. He could hear Martha in the bathroom, moving around. He got up, went to the bedroom, and picked out a nice thick leathercloth robe she really liked. *No, she's probably still bleeding,* he thought. *Better, just go with some old comfortable clothes for now.*

With the infection rate the way it was, hospitals were a gamble on their own, and even Griswolt did not have the best insurance for the safer hospital in town. He would not take Martha there unless he had to. He left the clothes hanging on the outside of the bathroom door and let Martha know they were there. He would give her the antibiotics later.

The phone rang. Griswolt went to answer it, and it was his secretary calling back. She told him to check for a waiver among the document copies left with him.

He put down the phone and looked in the kitchen. The waiver was there among them. Griswolt returned to the phone, and said, "I found it, thank you Mari," and hung up. He sat down at the kitchen table to read the waiver. The heading read, "Waiver of Sexual Rights." *What the...?* He read the verbiage below, and could not believe what he was reading. "I agree that I will not pass love-deprogramming school unless I submit to 'Sexual Trauma Love Removal'. Without this extreme treatment, my torturer has predicted I will fail. Sexual Trauma Love Removal has a ninety-eight percent success rate…" Griswolt glanced at the bottom of the page and saw Martha's signature. He had the wind taken out of him.

Griswolt looked in the direction of the bathroom where Martha had been stirring, and then at the waiver again. This time, he slowly read his way through the list of sexually traumatic acts permitted. Griswolt let the document fall to the table, and put his face in his hands, energy sinking.

"Oh Martha," he said, lifting and shaking his head, "When I think of how lovely you were the last night before you —" He stopped, lost in thought, and gulped, "You were so radiant that night. You put on such a brave face." He paused, swallowing again. Then Griswolt smiled, remembering, "And when you threw Hais out, that was perfect!" He started laughing, it was a strange laugh — one that he could not seem to stop. He kept laughing, until it became almost convulsive, and he couldn't take a breath. Then the most unimaginable, terrible thing in the world happened — unbelievably, he could not stop what had started sprouting from his long dormant glands, now rolling down his cheeks, and his uncontrollable laughter quickly spiraled into a repetition of choking, spastic sobs. As much as he tried, it would not stop.

As Griswolt was caught in the chain of sympathetic reflexes with this outburst, Martha astoundingly burst in on him, grabbing a knife from the kitchen counter. As she lunged at him with the knife, she screamed, "No hope! No crying! No crying! No hope! I'll kill you! No hope! No cryyyyyyyeeeeeeeeeeeeing!" She cut him on his left arm as he dodged to his right.

Reflexively, Griswolt quickly spun around to his left, and came back at her with his right fist. He punched her straight in the mouth, and with the shock, Martha dropped the knife.

She repulsively spit out the blood from her split lip at him, and started laughing with gleaming, glaring eyes.

He had to do something. Griswolt grabbed her and started shaking her, "Stop laughing or I'll kick your ass!" *That was stupid.*

She smiled evilly at him, going limp like a rag doll, "Go ahead!" She started singing, "I'll kill you in your sleee — eeeeep! Ah hah hah hah hah!"

This is going nowhere fast, he thought to himself, fixed on her crazy grinning face, absorbing her cackling laugh.

Martha abruptly realized that she was being held. She screamed in terror, "Don't touch me!" and pulled away from him with all her might.

Griswolt was startled enough that she did indeed pull herself away from him. As soon as she was free, she looked at him, slightly bent over, pointing one finger up in the air, and said, "Don't touch me," now weakly jabbing the pointed finger into the air for emphasis. She then turned, and walked unsteadily back to the bedroom. It sounded like she was getting back into bed.

Griswolt was standing there despondently. Now *he* was in shock. "My arm's bleeding," he said to himself as he only now really noticed it. He gave a sigh. *I can't really blame her — she's just crazy.* The cut wasn't bad — his scales stopped most of it. "Good thing she cut down instead of up," he muttered to himself. He got a bandage from the bathroom, and taped it on. He then went and peeked at Martha in the bedroom. She was lying on the bed again, on her back, eyes open. *Better leave her be,* he thought.

As Griswolt went back to the living room, he wondered aloud, "Is it like this for everyone?" He had a seat again. He was thinking, *I can't remember anyone saying much at work about going through this.*

Whenever the subject came up around those who had been through it, the usual response was, "Oh, you don't want to know, believe me," like it was — like it was — like it was nothing much. Like it wasn't worth talking about. Some just made it into a "knowing joke".

Maybe I was wrong, Griswolt thought. *Maybe they didn't talk about it because it was too painful to think about. Now that makes more sense.* He started talking aloud, "I need to bring it up at the next meeting. There must be a better way than this." He then remembered Adap, the chief accountant of his division. Adap was another high-level NOV party member. Adap complained loudly about the love-deprogramming school when his wife committed suicide one week after arriving back home. *That's right, Adap was sent to an obscure post in the northwest after that. Hmmm. Maybe I'll be more careful with my words when I deal with this. If I can get my supervisor to agree, we may be able to make recommenda-*

tions for some change — or at least some civility. Griswolt sighed, and took another look at the manual. He flipped it open to a random page, and read:

"If all else fails, give the mother time. She will become more normal with time."

Griswolt looked up, and thought about it. *Yes, time. She'll come around in time.* He gave a half smirk, and said quietly, "If she doesn't kill me first," while shaking his head, and examining his bandage. He looked again, in the direction of the bedroom. *I've got to do something. I can't just wait.* He got up and went into the bedroom.

Martha was still lying in the same position, on her back, staring at the ceiling.

Griswolt entered the bedroom slowly and as quietly as he could. As he approached her, she slowly curled up into a fetal position.

As he motioned to the side of the bed he asked, "Can I sit down here?"

No response.

He slowly sat down next to her, but careful not to touch her. He looked at her broken face, and said, "I honor you and approve of you, and I deeply value you."

For a moment, Martha appeared to become lucid. She looked at him and said, "I need time." When she then turned her head away, he started to reach for her, and without looking at him, she firmly said, "Don't touch me, please."

She said 'please'! Griswolt was uplifted at the thought as he stopped moving. He got up, and left for the living room. *She's going to come around.*

Later in the morning, Griswolt re-heated breakfast and brought it in to the bedroom. He set it next to Martha on a small table. He did not speak. He did not want to do anything that might interfere with what little appetite she may have. He gave her a sedative as well. After he set her meal up, he quietly left the room. Griswolt went back into the living room and laid down for a nap. He was drained by the morning's events.

As he was starting to relax, he suddenly panicked when he remembered that he had cried, and Martha had seen it. "She won't remember," he told himself. *She can't remember, she just can't. No adult male cries! Never! What happened to me? Maybe I'm going crazy too. I'm beat. I don't know how I'll be able to do it, but I've got no choice.* Sigh. *What did she say? No hope? What was I hoping for?*

Jan is coming home tomorrow. Jan! Griswolt could not stomach thinking about it. He sighed. His breathing eventually slowed into a steady rhythm, and he fell into a semi-relaxed state.

He got up about an hour later. He went into the bedroom, and saw that Martha had eaten some of the food he had left for her, and it looked like she was sleeping.

"Are you going to eat any more?" he asked.

No response. He wasn't expecting any. Griswolt took the table away from beside the bed, and cleaned up. Then he went into the kitchen to make himself something to eat later for dinner, as he had no appetite for lunch. Afterwards, he went through a number of magazines, while listening to his favorite daytime shows on the radio.

When dinnertime came, he brought a plate into the bedroom for Martha, and left it there for her. After finishing his meal in the living room, Griswolt spent the rest of the evening listening to the radio, and reading some more. Later, he gave Martha her pills before bed, and just like the night before, she took them without hesitation.

Griswolt went to sleep early. *Big day tomorrow. Jan* — his thoughts drifted off into the night's end.

The following morning, Griswolt rose early and went outside to check the weather. He was standing on the small porch in front of his home's entry. It was getting cooler, but a nice clear day was developing. *Maybe I'll take Martha outside for a while,* he thought. Then he remembered that the manual said something about bed rest, peace and quiet.

Still, I need her somewhat normal for when Jan gets here. They said he would be delivered in the early afternoon. He took a deep long breath and sighed, and caught himself looking up at the sky.

Griswolt instinctively looked down, and then took a couple of sideways glances to see if any of the neighbors caught him looking up. *No, he* thought to himself. *Good.* He peered over at Hais and Salom's place next door. *Nothing to see there. Salom and Rebecca should be back home soon.* He stayed outside for twenty minutes or so. A couple of contiss-drawn taxis passed by. Griswolt thought to himself, *it's so nice outside. No crazy people, and that's something I need right now.* He saw a father and son walking their blog. *I think this is something Martha needs too.* After a while, Griswolt went back inside.

Martha was in the shower. *Great! Maybe she's hungry.* Griswolt went to the bathroom door, and opened it a bit, and asked, "Can I make you something to —"

"Get out!" Martha screamed, as if he were a stranger.

"Woah!" Griswolt blurted as he quickly shut the door. "What do I do now?" He was considering the options as he headed down the hallway. "I know, I'll make some good old toast for her for." Then he thought about it. *She is skin and bone. She needs to eat something substantial. Maybe I'll order some fresh splint blood.* He thought about it some more. Griswolt found himself nodding his head in agreement with his internal conversation. "That's what I'll do. That should give her some stamina," he said to himself. It had to be absolutely fresh, if it was to be consumed raw — which was the only proper way to prepare and drink it. He thought about it some more. *Maybe I'll get some for myself, too. I could probably use it.* He went to the phone, called his secretary and asked her to arrange the delivery.

Griswolt then went into the living room, and sat down to read more regulations. *I need the office to drop off the weekly reports here,* he thought to himself. Martha had left the bathroom and was in the bedroom now. Griswolt waited, and gave her time to get dressed. He put down the regulation changes he was reading, and went to the bedroom. Martha was lying on the bed, still in her robe.

"May I come in?" he asked at the door.

Martha looked over at him, and then went back to staring at the ceiling.

"I'll take that as an OK," Griswolt said. He gingerly entered the room. He eventually made his way over to opposite side of Martha, on the bed. He slowly sat down.

Martha just kept staring deeply into the ceiling.

"You know, it's a beautiful day outside. What do you say I get you a little breakfast, and we go for a walk?" He smiled his most charming smile, waiting for her to hopefully say or do anything.

Martha just blinked.

What's that mean? Griswolt asked himself. "I'll bet it would make you feel more like your old self again, what do you say? Come on," he coaxed, waiting and looking as if she was expected to respond.

Martha turned her head and looked at him, with a questioning look on her face "More like myself? More like myself?" Then her puzzled look faded into an expression more resolute. "I have no self," she said to Griswolt, looking straight at him. As their eyes were locked, she said, "There's nothing here anymore, honestly. Nothing —" Then she looked away, settling her head in the pillow again.

"Come on, Martha, let's go for a walk. You know it will make you feel better. Let's go!" Griswolt said with great fake enthusiasm.

Martha sighed, and closed her eyes. "I'm so tired," she said.

Griswolt felt a surge of hope. *She's responding! She's talking, so keep it going Griswolt.* "You know that when you get your blood moving, you'll feel better."

Martha opened her eyes. "I need to do something." She paused, and stated, "I'll go for a walk," as if it were a new inspiration. She turned her head his way to look at him and said, "A short walk, I need —" She could not think of the words.

Another big response! "Wonderful!" Griswolt exclaimed. "Do you want some toast first?"

"Toast would be nice." Martha replied.

Griswolt felt like his heart would leap out of his chest. *She's acting normal!* He said, "OK, I'll get it for you, and you can get dressed."

"Don't ever tell me what to do!" Martha barked, unexpectedly looking at him as if he was the enemy. She sat up.

Griswolt's heart fell for a second. "It's OK — it's OK. I'm not telling you what to do." He was holding out both hands as if to say, "Slow down." She settled, and he said, "I'm going now to make some toast, OK?"

Martha was simply sitting there now, fiddling with a thread that had come loose from her underwear.

Griswolt took a good look at her wounds. Her bathrobe was partially open. *She looks better today. The bleeding looks like it's stopped. The redness is less,* he thought to himself.

He was glad he had not taken her to the hospital. *We don't need no stinkin' hospital,* he thought.

Griswolt came back with the buttered toast, and saw that Martha had not started to dress yet. *Don't say anything,* he thought to himself. He pulled up the portable table, and set a plate with her toast on it, with a small glass of splint milk. "Here you go, Martha." He smiled at her, and slowly left the room to wait in the living room.

In about forty minutes, Martha came out of the bedroom, dressed for her walk. She looked in Griswolt's direction, and with a sigh of resignation, said, "Let's get this over with."

Griswolt was delighted. *This is great!* "OK, Martha, I'll get a jacket for you." He went to retrieve her purple early fall jacket. He came back, and gingerly helped her to put it on. *She's acting more normally — I hope you're ready for Jan,* he thought. Jan would be arriving in about four hours, and Griswolt was sorely pressed to make things at home better than they were now. *We'll make it work.*

Once outside, they walked down the street to a well-developed small park. It was a simple place where people could gather, sit, and talk. There were benches scattered about, with a few sculptures of NOV and Aletian heroes located at the center of place.

Randomly placed along the park's perimeter were the rock gardens, particularly well done, using imported two and three-foot nuggets of a nice variety of attractive iron-free ores. Iron stains could rapidly age an outdoor place like this in no time. Some of the nuggets would be relatively crude — others were weathered, rounded, and some highly polished. The rock artist always kept the basic shape of each nugget unaltered. By expertly balancing and stacking them, the artist created works of art that would eventually collapse in time. Then, either the same artist, or another, would make another monument from the collapsed group. The true artist could both make a monument that would be imbalanced-looking, yet be poised well enough to stand the test of time.

Griswolt and Martha had a seat on an unoccupied bench. They watched an older couple feeding breadcrumbs to some a few local stray blogs. Griswolt took a sideways look at Martha. *Are her eyes softening? I think she's starting to relax.* He in turn relaxed a bit, and closed his eyes for a little. The wind was soft, and other than the occasional bus or someone riding a contiss on the street behind them, it was relatively quiet. The blogs made a cry for more food after the elderly couple ran out of crumbs. The blogs had their routine down. They knew the marks, so after a quick test, the blogs moved on to find some more productive visitors. Griswolt heard them coming his way, and slightly opened his eyes. He and Martha did nothing but ignore them, and the blogs continued on their day's rounds.

Well, I might as well test her out — this is why I got her out here. Griswolt thought. *How should I say it?* He took a breath. "You know Jan is coming home today?"

Martha's slow transition into relaxation was immediately aborted by her reaction to Griswolt's words. Her relaxing eyes switched into a squinting, fierce look. Her face became ugly, very quickly. She coldly said, "When is *it* coming here? I need something I can hurt. This all its fault! I'll make it pay!"

Griswolt's stomach tightened. *No!* His posture shot up, in a direction leaning away from Martha. "Martha, what are you saying?" Griswolt asked. "You're talking about our son. You remember Jan, don't you?"

"This is *its* entire fault," Martha insisted to the air in front of her. "All *its* fault. All *its* —" and now she was screaming. She bent over on the bench, almost convulsing with her screams. The older couple was startled, and hurriedly got up to leave, glancing cautiously back at Martha and Griswolt.

Griswolt was shocked and crestfallen. "What am I going to do with you?" he asked, mostly to himself as he looked at Martha. No way could he touch her now.

Her screams quieted down, and then Martha caught hold of herself. She looked at Griswolt and said, "This is *its* entire fault." Then she looked off into the distance again. "I want to see *it*."

Griswolt was upset. "Stop calling Jan 'it', please! Please."

Martha continued to look away and said, "I want to see *Jan,*" not in a nice way.

Griswolt's visual reflex was drawn to a new group of visiting blogs. *I think that's all she can do for now,* he thought to himself. *I guess I have to be content with this.* He sighed. *I think I'll drop the subject.*

They sat there for another half hour or so. When it appeared that Martha was starting to relax again, Griswolt figured it was time to head home. Martha didn't seem much to care, and so they started walking back. As they were approaching their home, the delivery of fresh splint blood had just arrived up ahead.

"Great! I forgot about this, but we're just in time!" Griswolt exclaimed. "Hey, we're over here," he shouted from a distance, "Hold up!" He did not want them taking off without delivering, which they would readily do. They would not leave their delivery unless someone was there to sign for it, and they had other deliveries waiting. It would just spoil too quickly for them to leave out, even with ice. Griswolt paid them, and then he and Martha went into the house.

They descended the stairs into the kitchen, and Martha stayed with Griswolt there. He mixed some salt, nako, and carefully added a fresh raw egg into each big glass of blood. It was nice to make it so cleanly that the egg yolk stayed intact, and could be swallowed whole. This was a traditional preparation, and one that Martha loved.

She did finish most of it, and Griswolt had some more for himself. *It's expensive, but what the heck? She needs to get her strength back.* He was very pleased to see her eat. *Things are looking all right for now,* he thought, but then remembered her reaction to Jan's impending arrival. *Worrisome to say the least,* he thought.

Griswolt asked Martha if she would like to go to the living room to listen to the radio. She passively agreed, and he went over with her. When she was settled, he went back to the kitchen to clean up.

The phone rang in the living room, and Griswolt went to answer it. It was his secretary, Mari. Griswolt couldn't believe what he was hearing. The Secretary General of the Central Committee of the NOV had sent his provincial liaison to Griswolt's building. All those in administration were to report for duty. He had one hour to get to work. He slammed the phone down. "Of all the —"

He had Martha's attention. Anyone would have noticed.

He looked at her. *What the hell do I do now? Jan's going to be here in a few hours and she isn't close to ready.*

Martha was looking at Griswolt now, curious.

Griswolt started pacing back and forth, and then into the kitchen. *Think, Griswolt, think!* He was greatly disturbed that he had to go in at all. This was just another surprise inspection, meant to keep the intimidation fresh. His office was in order. He imagined meeting the pretentious liaison officer.

That's it! Griswolt stopped pacing. He went back to Martha. He came into the room rather abruptly, which startled her. He realized his mistake, and stopped. Then he slowly walked in front of her, keeping his distance. "Martha, dear. Can you do something for me?"

Martha had been perking up since the walk and the blood confection. She looked at him rather lucidly, and said, "What?" but still with little emotion and much detachment.

"Can you call me at work after I call you from there later?" Griswolt asked.

"What?" Martha asked.

Griswolt thought a second, and said. "I have to go to work, but I want to stay with you instead. I am going to call you from work in about an hour, OK?"

She sat there a moment, like, well, nothing. Empty. "OK," Martha said.

"After I call you from work, I want you to call right back to my secretary Mari, and tell her that you started bleeding, and you need me at home," Griswolt explained. He looked at her. "Do you understand? I call you, then you call me, OK?"

"OK," Martha replied.

He looked at her, "Do you really promise you will?"

She raised her tone, "I said I would!"

Griswolt thought to himself, *I have no choice. I have to go to work. Once I meet with the liaison, I really don't need to stick around anymore. An emergency will make my exit more valid.*

Griswolt gave Martha her pills in the living room, and he went to change into his uniform. He then said goodbye, gave one more reminder, and left for work. He had a plan. What he had not planned on was Martha's pocketing of her pills today.

Chapter Six

Mama's Not Feeling Herself

An hour passed. Griswolt called, and Martha did indeed answer the phone.

"Hello?" asked Martha, as she put the phone to her ear.

"Martha! Thanks for picking up the phone. Listen, I can't talk long. The liaison hasn't arrived here yet, so I really have to wait. Has anyone called about Jan?"

"Jan!" Martha spat, sounding like a different person.

Griswolt's stomach grinded at the sudden turn of her voice. *Change the subject!* "Listen, Martha, don't call me back now, OK?" he said.

"You want me to call you?" Martha asked.

"No, not yet. I'm not done here yet. I'll call you again, and then you call me, OK?"

"OK." *Click.*

Martha went back to sitting in the living room. She had turned the radio on, and was dully listening to the Temple of the NOV's daily program. Truth told — she was not really listening. She was still just sitting and enjoying the peace of having nobody around. "I'm starting to feel —" she started to say it, but did not know how to finish the sentence.

She searched for the right word. *Safe? No. Peace? Maybe. Good? No. Better? Maybe. Not so scared? Yes. I'm beginning to feel not so scared.*

She took a deep slightly shuddering breath at that last thought. Then Martha took another yawning breath, less tense. Not a sigh. A good deep, cleansing breath. *Not so scared.* With the long extended exhalation came a feeling in her gut of a knot untying. Every time she found the right word or two to describe her deepest negativity, the knot untied some more. She took another breath. *This feels good.* She was smiling slightly, still with hurting eyes. *Do I really feel better now? I guess I do, a little.* Then with her eyes looking off, resentfully thought, *I swore I'd never feel good again. I don't want to feel good.*

Martha's eyes narrowed, *this is all its fault. It shouldn't have come here. It ruined me forever. I can't get even if I allow myself to feel good. I'll never forget what it did to me.* Her face fell to a look of misery. *What they did to me. What animal is that cruel? The NOV is right. The ela is holy because it kills so quickly.* She stared off in a different direction now.

Knock, knock. Knock, knock.

The sound at the front door startled her into present consciousness. *Who's here now?* "Griswolt?" she shouted up the stairs.

Knock, knock.

"I'm coming, I'm coming," Martha said loudly, and went up the stairs. She went to the top of the stairs to open the front door, and standing there was the delivery attendant with Jan.

"You!" she spat at Jan. The reality had not sunk in that Jan was truly coming home that day. Martha was still in a post-traumatic shock, and was the polar opposite of being ready for this. She could not bear to look at him, but did notice that he was covered with scabs, like her, from the repeated SE's in love-deprogramming school. *Good*, she thought to herself.

Jan was just staring straight ahead. He now looked as Martha did on the day she arrived at home. He had a stubborn look to his face. It was stone cold.

The attendant studied Martha, looking her up and down.

"Isn't your husband home?" he asked, looking a bit concerned. He had dropped children off with their "recently graduated" mothers alone before, and twice so far there had been two murders. It was not uncommon. Usually the mother was the killer. Sometimes she would be the victim.

"My husband is dead," Martha coldly replied to the attendant.

Oh well, the attendant thought, *I have to get back. I've got three more deliveries today, after this one and the ones in the wagon. It's not my fault if something happens.* He was not required to refuse deliveries of the children to their messed up mothers. He *could* refuse, but it involved a lot of paperwork. *Documents, yes,* he thought to himself. He pulled out the release documents, and gave them to Martha to sign. As she was signing them, he asked, "Is there anyone at all home inside?"

"No," Martha replied.

"What about any neighbors?" He asked.

Salom! What about Salom? Where is she? Isn't she home? Martha looked in the direction of Salom's house. "She might be home," she told the attendant.

He went over to Salom's house, but nobody answered the door. When he returned to Martha's house, all that was there were the signed documents on the porch at the front door. He sighed, shaking his head. *They should require me refuse to deliver these kids when it's bad like this,* he thought. It did not matter that it was logical to refuse to leave the child there, or that he had it in his power to do so. What mattered was that he could transmit blame to someone else. That did the trick for his reptilian conscience, and he went back to his wagon. He had two children sitting in the wagon in restraints as well, plus the three still waiting back at school.

Martha and Jan had gone into the house. Jan resisted at the top of the stairs, so Martha grabbed him by the back of his straight jacket, and carried him down the stairs, throwing him down that last few steps, with Jan spilling onto to the kitchen floor. As soon as he hit the floor, he yelled, "Don't touch me!" and in his straight jacket, clumsily got up and ran into the living room. Martha immediately followed him into the living room. "You're a piece of rotten keesh," she hissed, and then spat on him.

He was standing there, looking angry and removed. He did not flinch.

I can't stay here with it, she thought to herself. I'll go crazy. *I've got to kill it. I can't live here with it.* Her eyes lit up. *I'll drown it.* She looked

79

down at him. She sneered at Jan and squawked, "You stink! You need a bath!" She went over to him and bent over to untie him. In her confused, frantic state she was thinking, *I can't drown it with this straight jacket on. They will know it was me. They'll give me DeathBT.*

Jan struggled against her, but with the straight jacket on, he could not do much to resist. He screamed the whole time, but she got the jacket off. She threw him back down on the floor when he tried to stand up, and ordered, "Stay there!" Martha ran through the home to run the water in the bathtub.

Now out of the straight jacket, Jan curled up on the living room floor, maintaining his unbreakable mental wall.

Once Martha had the water running, she came quickly back to the living room. Jan was still there, in a ball on the floor. She marched over to him and said, "Let's go!" She grabbed him and dragged him towards the bathroom.

Jan was kicking and screaming, resisting as best he could, but he was emaciated, just as Martha was when she first arrived home.

Ring...Ring...Ring... Martha ignored the phone as she was wrestling Jan to the bathroom. *Ring...Ring...Ring...* She had some strength back, but not nearly what she had before. *Ring... Ring...Ring...* As she pulled him toward the tub, Jan was able to get loose enough to make a run for the door, but she dove for his feet, and caught him, pulling him to the floor. She quickly punched him, hard, in the back, and he stopped for a second. Then she just took hold of his feet, and dragged him to the now full bathtub. She dug her fingers into his arms as she lifted him, and threw him in the water.

Jan was thrashing, and managed to bite her hand deeply. It started bleeding profusely, and now that it was mixing with splashing water, she knew she could not ignore it. *When the police come, they'll find blood all over the place. There's no way they'll believe he did this on his own.*

Ring... Ring... Ring... Martha gave Jan a hateful sneer, and quickly retrieved a towel. He was out of the bathtub now, curling up again on the floor as she wrapped her bleeding hand in the towel, and went to the ringing phone. *Ring... Ring..* Martha switched the phone off.

She stood there thinking a moment, then smiled, and then turned the phone on again. Martha called the Temple of the NOV, and asked to be connected with the child-donation department. She smiled again, *why didn't I think of this before?* "Hello, yes. I would like to donate my child for the next child-burning ceremony. Yes, he just attacked me, and my hand is bleeding. He is very bad, and I think that sacrificing him to God is the best way now. How soon can you pick him up?"

The Temple was always happy to take these donations. All they needed was the consent of one parent. *I'll just tell Griswolt that he ran away,* she thought. After the arrangements were made, she went back to the bathroom. "You stay right there," she ordered. *I don't care what he does, now. He's leaving!*

The Temple of the NOV did not waste time in picking up child-burning donations. They wanted to get there speedily make the pick-up — just in case one or both parents changed their minds. If only one parent donated the child, and the NOV already had that child in its possession, it was very difficult to get the child back. If both parents donated the child, it was damn near impossible. The Temple decreed that the children were holy once donated, and thus Temple property. The Temple had peaks and valleys in donations. When they had bigger numbers of children scheduled for child-burning day, they had much larger turnouts. This meant more donations, and promotion of their important faith. Therefore, they advertised the upcoming numbers on the local news.

Martha went back into the living room. She had a seat on the sofa, and picked up a fashion magazine. She was looking at the pages, but nothing was being read. Her mind was racing with thoughts of the present situation. *They said they would be here in an hour.* Her pulse was still very rapid. *What about Griswolt?* Her face turned grim. *Fuck Griswolt. This is his fault, too.* She continued to pretend to read, even though nobody was there to watch her. *Ring... Ring... Ring...* Martha got up, went over to the phone, picked up the receiver.

"Martha!" It was Griswolt, beside himself in worry.

Martha hung up, and then turned the phone off again. She took a look in the bathroom. Jan was sitting there, still wet, picking at scabs on his arms. "Don't move!" Martha commanded. She went back to the living room to "read".

An hour passed. Where are they? Martha looked at the phone that she had turned off. *Maybe they tried to call.* She went over to the phone, and switched it back on. Just then, a rapping at the front door startled her. She went up the stairs, and standing there were two temple prostitutes who had arrived to pick up Jan.

Temple prostitution was one of the ways for the uneducated to enter the employed services of the Temple of the NOV. There were other career paths for the unskilled — executioners, torturers, maintenance people and guards were common avenues. Once inside the Temple, anyone could pay for the many levels of classes required to continue to be promoted. The faithful were told that anyone could eventually enter the secret inner circle of the NOV. These ones dictated the laws of the NOV, and they were above the central committee. Nobody knew exactly who these people were. When someone was chosen for the inner circle, they simply disappeared without a trace. Since people disappeared all the time, nobody could know who went where, although there were always rumors.

Martha observed the prostitutes. *They don't look like much.* Of course, Jan was still very weak. "Please come in," Martha said to them. *I don't want to touch him unless I need to. I'll let them wrestle with him,* she thought as descending the stairs. With each step, she felt lighter and lighter. *He's going to be gone!* Martha thought with glee. They came downstairs, and Martha signed their documents in the kitchen. She led them into the bathroom.

One of them was smiling, and coquettishly said to Jan, "Come with us, Jan. We want you to stay with us." Jan just sat there, on the floor, looking obstinate. They then went over to him, picked him up by each arm, and efficiently carried him out of the bathroom. He continued to hold himself in a tight ball.

"He's not kicking. Hmmm," Martha muttered to herself. "He doesn't know where they're taking him." She watched as they carried him down the hallway, and up the stairs. She listened for the closing of the door. "Whew," she said. "I did it. He's gone." Martha smiled, pleased. She went over to the living room, and turned the radio back on. It was the news. They were talking about developing new vaccines for new areas in the wildlands. The problem was that whenever they started a new expedition, the explorers would fight among themselves, and the expedition would end in failure. Being removed from the fear of the central authority of the NOV brought out the alpha in all the participants.

"In the next year, we will be able to send our first mission into the far southwest territories. This will give our nation more access to rivers and fish, which are abundant there. In other news, there was small LERN sting in which four members of a local group were arrested yesterday…"

She got up, and turned the radio off. *LERN,* she thought with disgust. *What a lie!* "Those hypocrites left me here, nobody has even tried to help," Martha said with revulsion. *Love is death. Look at Jan —* she instantly sat up, tilting her head. *Jan —* She could say his name now, "Jan." Still detached, the thought of the child was allowed in, because the threat of what he brought with him was now gone.

She looked at a game that Griswolt had set out earlier in anticipation of Jan's return today, sitting in the corner of the room by the radio. She gave a sigh and said, "I don't have to face him now. He'll be burnt, and he won't hurt me anymore, and he won't hurt anym —" She felt a tear develop. *No hope!* She sniffed it up, and there were no more.

The door slammed upstairs. *What? I should have locked the door!* "Who's there?" Martha called out as she was walking to the bottom of the stairs to see what was going on.

"Me!" bellowed Griswolt, carrying Jan in his arms. He had left work early without waiting for the liaison. He had intercepted the temple prostitutes as they were leaving with Jan, and forcefully taken him back from them. Griswolt glared at Martha as he passed her at the bottom of the stairs, straight into the kitchen. He sat Jan down on one of the chairs. Griswolt turned and said, "Now what the hell —" but was interrupted by Martha's pushing him out of the way to get at Jan.

With a scream, she lunged at Jan, pounding him in the face, and grabbing his crest, trying to twist his head as if trying to break his neck. Jan was warding off her blows.

Griswolt reacted by punching Martha on the back of the head, shocking her. Then he grabbed hold of the collar of Martha's robe and pulled her backwards, hard, away from Jan.

As Martha went flying backwards, she twisted and clawed for Griswolt's face, trying to scratch him. Once she got her bearings, she screamed a battle cry and went after Griswolt, punching and scratching at his eyes.

This went on for less than a second or two when Griswolt said to himself, "I've had enough of this," and clocked her hard, right on the side of her head, immediately knocking her unconscious. He caught her as she was falling and laid her down on the floor. He quickly glanced at Jan. Jan was focused on the unconscious Martha lying on the floor, and he had the smile of vengeance on his face and in his eyes.

Creepy, Griswolt thought, and then he went to the bathroom, and opened the brown bag of pharmaceuticals that were for Martha. "There's one in here, where is it?" he asked himself as he fiddled in the bag of pills and such. "Here it is!" It was a paralyzing narcotic, in liquid form, and it came in a dropper bottle. "What's it say here?" He said, reading the label. *"Given the patient's weight, give three drops every twelve hours as needed for sedation. To induce paralysis, give six drops every eight hours."* He went back into the kitchen. He found Jan peeing on Martha, and she was starting to awaken. Griswolt pushed Jan out of the way with a loud "No!" He quickly cleaned Martha off, and proceeded to give her the narcotic.

Griswolt then carried her to the bedroom, and he laid her on the bed. Then he went back to Jan, who was still in the kitchen. *We'll wash her up better later.* He was going to give Jan hell for urinating on his mom, but after getting a good look at the mad expression on Jan's face, Griswolt said to himself, "What's the point?" He simply had Jan sit there while he wiped up the kitchen floor. Then he sat down with Jan at the table. "I'm really glad you're home, son, I know it was tough, but it's over now," Griswolt said, leaning forward to rub Jan's crest.

Jan ducked from Griswolt's attempt at comforting him, but was otherwise relatively calm with his father.

They went downstairs into Jan's bedroom in order to get him into some dry clothes. "I'm going up to make some early dinner Jan, what would you like?" Griswolt asked.

Jan found himself more at ease around Griswolt — the NOV had not poisoned him against his father. Jan asked, "Can I have a splint egg and toast?"

Griswolt was heartened that Jan had an appetite, and was talking to him. "Coming right up, son!" he said energetically, and then he asked, "Do you want to play up in the living room while I make your meal?"

"No, I just want to stay down here for a while." Jan paused, thinking, concerned. "Is *she* going to wake up and eat?"

Griswolt looked at Jan with a sad, heavy heart. *It was so nice before* — "No, Jan, Mama is going to sleep for the whole night."

Jan's face squeezed into itself, "Don't call her 'Mama'!" he spat, with the same ugly look that Martha would develop when speaking of Jan.

Griswolt sighed with regret, his mind again returning to the last night they were all together before love-deprogramming school. *Gone*, he thought, with great remorse and longing. *Gone*. He went up the stairs to the main floor, a little slower, a little heavier, than when he came down.

When he got upstairs, he went into the kitchen to start cooking. After starting up the stove, he received a phone call from Chark, a friend who had connections in the Temple of the NOV.

"What? Salom failed? Oh, really — oh no! — oh, that's horrible — poor Rebecca!" He sighed and said, "OK, thanks for calling." Griswolt hung up the phone.

He went back to the kitchen, cracked and put the eggs in the awaiting hot pan. The steam and spurts of the hot lard crackled immediately. Just right. He sighed, repeating what he had heard Martha say, time and time again.

"How do we stay sane in this world?" Griswolt asked the eggs. They just sizzled their olfactory answer, and that was enough for now. After he was done cooking, he called Jan to come up and eat.

While dining together on their simple meal, Griswolt had a chance to observe Jan better. His sores looked bad, but they would heal. *Why did he get so many wounds?* "I'll bet you're hungry!" Griswolt said.

Jan shrugged, and continued to eat.

Griswolt wanted to get him talking. He smelled badly, even though at first glance the bathroom looked like he had been in the bathtub. The wet clothes Jan was wearing before were a question mark. "Did you take a bath?" He would be sorry he asked.

Jan dropped his toast, and looked down. "She tried to kill me. She tried to drown me." He stopped everything, and his face fell to a heart wrenching expression no child should display.

Griswolt slowly put his hand on Jan's shoulder. "She's sick, Jan. I'm sure she will feel terrible about this when she comes to her senses. I'm so sorry, buddy." *He's not pulling away,* Griswolt thought. *Maybe there's hope for one of them, anyway.* He sighed and looked in the direction of the bedroom, then sighed again.

After dinner, Griswolt got Jan started on putting the finishing touches to the set up of the game in the living room, and then he went back to the kitchen to clean up. While in the kitchen, his thoughts kept returning to the way things were before.

"They have to do this," he tried to tell himself. "It is necessary for national order. We can't let the virus of love loose in society. It breeds traitors. It leads to breakdown of discipline. Discipline is necessary to survival and productivity." He was merely regurgitating more Temple dogma, trying to reinforce his alliance with this system within which he was embedded. Still, it did not make him feel much better.

When Griswolt had finished in the kitchen, he joined Jan in the living room to play the game.

Jan seemed to forget his pain for a while, and he started to relax a little. Driven from his consciousness, however, happiness was not yet permitted to return.

It appeared evident to Griswolt that Jan was loosening up.

"Is Rebecca home yet?" Jan asked.

Griswolt felt another pull of angst. *Rebecca,* he thought. *What's going to happen over there, with her mother being sent away for a year? Who is Hais going to keep when the year is up? Rebecca or Salom? One of them has to go.* He sighed. The person on the phone earlier told Griswolt that the NOV sent Rebecca home today, just like Jan. *I guess Hais was home to bring her in today,* he thought with a shrug. He answered Jan, "Rebecca came home today, Jan, just like you."

"Can I see her?" Jan asked, expectantly.

"No, not today, son," Griswolt replied. *God only knows what it's like over there.* "She had a bad time like you. I'm sure she needs to rest."

"Rest won't work," responded Jan, as he moved a game piece. "It's your turn."

"Sure, son. Here we go," Griswolt said as he rolled the dice. He was pleased with how things were going. He thought a moment, and said, "You know, it's safe to take a bath now since I'm here. We really should clean those sores off."

Jan stopped playing, and looked down. He looked at two wounds on his left arm, and scratched at one of them. Then he lifted his face towards Griswolt, bearing an apprehensive look and asked, "Will you stand by the door?"

"Of course I will," Griswolt said with a big smile. Then he became serious. "I'm going to protect you Jan. Nobody will ever hurt you again. It's all over."

Jan still had that worried air, deficient in trust, but Griswolt's last statement melted some of his anxiety. He gave a shy smile, just a little one. He was starting to feel safer, for now — *there's always her, though,* he thought, and his smile disappeared.

They played the game a few times. They then spent the rest of the evening sitting together in the living room, listening to radio, and occasionally talking about things not too serious. Later, Jan took his bath and then got ready for bed. Griswolt assured him that Martha would be asleep all night because of the medicine he gave her.

In the meantime, six hours had gone by since Griswolt sedated Martha with the paralyzing dose. She had been lucid enough to hold it in her mouth to spit out later, but a lot had still been absorbed. She was able to move her head slightly now, but had been unable do much else. Earlier, Griswolt had propped her head up a bit with the pillows. She had a good view of the room, but her dazed attention was loosely focused on one thing: the heavy painting on the opposite wall. She knew something dangerous was behind the painting, but could not think of what it was.

Had she not been so heavily sedated, she would have found it maddening. Martha stared in wonder at the mystery before her. After another hour, she was able to get up, barely. She wobbled weakly over to the painting. When she tried to think about what was there, her mind would just go blank. She started to move the painting, and the heaviness of the big frame felt familiar.

"There's something here, I just know it!" she said with frustration. Martha pulled the painting out away from the wall, and looked behind it. She found a large pocket attached to the back of the painting. She pulled a few envelopes out from the pocket, and sat down on the bed with them. *I know this,* she slowly thought to herself. *What are they?* She started reading them, and recognized them. *These are love-lover pages!* Martha said to herself in shock. She threw them down in horror. *Why did I keep these? What was I thinking?*

"What's this?" Martha asked aloud as she opened the envelope with the letter she had written to herself. As it opened, the photographs she had taken fell out. "What are these?" she exclaimed loudly in utter revulsion as she examined the photos. She started shaking.

Martha spastically jumped up, put the pages and the letter in the top drawer of her dresser, and pulled out some matches. She went back to the foot of the bed with all the photographs, and started burning them on the floor, cursing at them.

Meanwhile, Griswolt had just come upstairs after putting Jan to bed, and he heard motion in the bedroom. He did not pay it much attention until he heard Martha's voice. He decided to check it out, and went to the bedroom. Upon opening the door, Griswolt smelled the smoke, and then saw Martha being crazy and he yelped, "What are you burning?"

She was sitting there on the floor, with a nice little fire going in front of her made of flaming photographs. The pictures apparently caught fire quite well.

"You go to hell!" Martha barked.

"Well, that's where Salom is going," Griswolt shot back, "She failed love-deprogramming school, and she's in jail now." *Why did I say that? I'm shot — I just can't do this right.* He made his way toward her.

Martha was staring into the pile of burning photos on the floor. "Salom?" she said with a confused look.

Griswolt made his move and grabbed the hand that was holding the matches. He then stomped on the pictures until the fire was out. "What were you thinking?" he yelled in exasperation. He surveyed the carpet. *That burn is there for good,* he thought. He looked at Martha. She wasn't fighting. She was obviously still very drugged. *I'll give her about six more drops before bed,* he thought. *I had better get her to the bathroom first.* She obliged. He went with her down the hallway, and into the bathroom. She was sedated enough that she let him help her so she would not fall. After they returned to the bedroom, he gave Martha the narcotic, and then left her there in bed.

Griswolt would be sleeping in the living room, with the door to Jan's room downstairs just a few feet away. He had hung a bell on Martha's door, so he could hear if she opened it.

He then lay down on the old gray gendra hide sofa, and went to sleep.

Chapter Seven

Let's Run Away!

The next morning began with the ringing of the telephone.

Griswolt got up half-awake from the sofa, gave a good stretch, and answered the phone.

It was his secretary, Mari, calling. She told him that his boss was exceedingly angry that Griswolt had departed the office before meeting with the Secretary General's liaison.

Griswolt had left in a panic the day before, without waiting for the liaison. He had used the excuse that his wife was bleeding at home but in cases like this, there was no excuse. He had to come in to the office today. The liaison would be returning today, and Griswolt still had to meet with and update the liaison about issues relating to his department.

Griswolt did not have time to get Jan re-instated in daycare, as he was obviously not ready for school. "I'll just make sure Martha is sedated enough to last until I get home," he said to himself. He went downstairs to tell Jan he had to leave.

Jan was not happy to hear that Griswolt had to leave. He was just waking up, and rubbing his eyes.

"What about *her*?" Jan asked, with the same change in appearance that seemed to come now whenever he mentioned his mother.

"I'll give your mother some medication to let her sleep all day. I need to trust you to behave, OK?"

"Can I go over to Rebecca's today?" Jan asked.

"Not until I come home, Jan. We don't know how bad it is over there. Rebecca's mother is in jail, and I don't know how Hais is taking all this. It might be ugly, so wait for me." Griswolt examined Jan's response to see if he looked like he would listen, but couldn't be sure.

"I have to go now, Jan. I'll put some snacks out in the kitchen for you, and there is more food in the refrigerator. I need to leave now, though."

After giving Martha six more drops of the sedative, Griswolt then left for the day. Once again, she spit it out after he left the room, but was still absorbing a goodly amount through the mucous membranes of her mouth.

Jan found himself lying in bed, staring at his eggshell colored ceiling, trying to think. He had great difficulty holding onto any solid thoughts yet. His mind could simply not focus on anything for very long. Whenever he had a line of thought for more than a few minutes, it would be invaded by his memories of love-deprogramming school. Each time, he would repress it and think of something else. He was understandably restless, so he got up, and went upstairs to eat.

When Jan was upstairs in the kitchen, he peeked down the hallway at his mother's room. Her closed door still had the bell hanging from it. He proceeded to open the refrigerator, and pulled a bottle of milk out. After retrieving a cup for it, he helped himself to some yama chips set out for him on the stainless steel kitchen table. Unlike the bread, the chips were salty.

"Dad was really nice yesterday," he said to himself. While munching on the chips, he looked darkly down the hallway again and said, "I hope she never wakes up." As his thoughts flitted about, he wondered, "What does Rebecca have to say about that school?" After filling up on the chips, he decided that he had to see Rebecca.

He slipped into some outdoor clothes, and Jan left his home to go over to Rebecca's house As he exited his front door, the brightness of the day caused his eyes to squint. Other than the day before, he had not seen the sun for a month. The sun felt good, though. The days were getting cooler now by the week.

Jan walked up to Rebecca's door and knocked loudly. It felt good to bang something hard with his fist. There was no answer. Jan was feeling disappointed, but had no place else that he wanted to be. He knocked some more.

After a while, Rebecca did finally come to the door, and asked, "Who's out there?"

His heart leapt when he heard her. "Rebecca! It's me! Jan! Open up!" he shouted. His mood instantly lifted at the sound of his best friend's voice.

"My dad said to not open the door for anyone, not even you!" Rebecca called out from the other side of the door.

"Your dad is a gendra's ass!" retorted Jan loudly, repeating what his father had said so many times.

The door opened. "You sure got that right," the little girl responded, but she wasn't joking or smiling. She did not look the same. For a second, Jan wondered if they switched Rebecca with another little girl. She had the same scabs that Jan had, and it made him remember —

"Can I come in?" Jan asked.

"I guess so," Rebecca said lifelessly. She looked Jan over, confused, "You look different."

"So do you." Jan walked in, and accompanied Rebecca into the living room. The place was a mess. Soiled clothes were collecting in various places around the house, and a stench wafted from the kitchen of dirty dishes piled up, old food still on them. Jan did not know why he was there. He really did not want to connect with anyone when it came down to it. Still, he was hoping for something normal to happen.

"Where's your mom?" he asked.

Rebecca's face turned to ice. "She's not coming back. She failed school, and now they are sending her to jail for a year." She sighed, and then barked, "I'm glad! I never want to see her again! I hate her." Rebecca paused, as if thinking of more to say, "I hate my dad, too. He said he's going to keep her when she comes back next year. They'll send me to an orphanage." Her shoulders sank as she confessed, "He doesn't want me." She looked at Jan and bitterly said, "He would keep me if I was a boy!"

While Jan waited for her to finish talking, Rebecca hesitated another moment, and then exclaimed, "I hate him, and I hate her! In fact, I hate all grown-ups. I'd like to throw them all in the fire! They all stink!"

Jan understood what she meant. "They *do* all stink!" he replied. "All their stupid rules..." He could not find the right words to express his frustration with the fact that adults did such horrible things. His face went into a deep frown when he told Rebecca, "My mother tried to kill me yesterday." As much as he hated his mother now, he still could not comprehend that she would attempt such a thing. He could not even begin to let *that* one go.

Rebecca measured him for truth, and then she expressed surprising empathy, responding, "*Your* mama?" She was truly shocked at the incongruent picture in her head. Then she thought about it and decided, saying, "Well, now you know what they're *really* like."

"Yeah. Hey, where's your knitting stuff?" Jan asked, thinking about how much she liked to knit, and how he had enjoyed watching her do it in her peaceful way.

"I don't know. It's not where I left it. It doesn't matter anyway," Rebecca sighed, "Nothing matters anymore." She was trying hard to reach a scab that was on her back.

Jan said, "Here, let me," and went to scratch her back for her, and she leapt away, angrily squalling, "Don't touch me!" She turned and faced him and said very seriously, "Nobody touches me, understand?"

Jan understood. He looked at her. Everything was different now. Everything.

They both had a seat on the sofa in the living room. "Well, what do you want to do?" she asked, sounding as if she did not feel like doing anything.

"I don't know. I just want to stay away from my mother. I don't want to be around any grown-ups!" Jan answered.

"Me too," Rebecca replied. She looked around at the mess and said, "You know, my dad wants me to clean the house today. You want to help me?" Her father had told her that he wanted the place to be clean when he came home from work. A month's worth of slovenliness was there, awaiting Salom's homecoming, but now she was not coming home. The default fell to Rebecca.

It was not the first thing that Jan felt like doing, but at least it was *some* activity. "OK, I'll help. If it isn't done, you'll get beat for sure."

Jan and Rebecca started cleaning the living room. It felt good to focus on something — it took his mind off the hurt.

They spent the entire morning cleaning up the mess of Hais. After clearing out the living room, they tackled the kitchen. When they finished that, they went around the other rooms in the house, picking things up and cleaning whatever needed it.

"My dad will be coming home tonight. I just know he'll still complain," Rebecca said with a sigh. Without Salom around, she instinctively knew he would vent on her now. "I hate everything. I want to run away."

Jan brightened up with the idea. "Yes, let's do that. What a great idea, Rebecca. I know! We can go live at the old box factory! I heard my dad say it was shut down a long time ago."

Rebecca looked at him with unexpected inspiration. "Do you really think we can?" she asked hopefully.

"Anything is better than this!" Jan responded. "Let's get some food to take with us." They then went foraging for food. Jan said, "I'll go back to my house to get more food and clothes."

Jan went running back to his house, opened the front door, and went inside. He slowly made his way down the stairs, and took a quick look down the hallway at his mother's bedroom. The door was still closed. *Good.* He then gathered some clothes, put them in a bag along with some cans of food, and started up the stairs when the bag fell open, and a few of the cans fell tumbling down the steps.

"I hope that didn't wake her up," Jan whispered to himself as he nervously looked down the hallway again. He started re-packing the bag. He heard some movement in his mother's bedroom and hurriedly left for Rebecca's. When he returned to Rebecca's house, she looked different. She appeared decidedly panicky.

"I don't want to do this," Rebecca complained, "I changed my mind. What if they catch us? Then what? Will they torture me again?" She was quivering in fear now with the prospect of the two of them leaving on their own. "The house is clean now," was the last reason she could come up with to stay home.

Jan, deflated for a moment, refused to be defeated. "No! You have to go with me!" He was not going to do this alone. He wanted his friend with him. This was the perfect answer. "Please, we need to escape from the adults. *Please!*"

Rebecca was not budging. She had already started to put her things away.

I have to do something. Jan thought. "What about your dad, Hais? Do you really want to live here alone with that jerk? He has only you to pick on now, and you know you'll get the beatings he can't use on your mother!"

Rebecca wasn't listening. She had made her mind up. "It's better than torture," she replied, as she continued to unload her bag.

Still not to be dissuaded, Jan responded, "What about a year from now, when your mother comes home, and they send you away?"

That got her attention. She stopped. Rebecca's expression went from stubborn to sadness. She had learned in love-deprogramming school that tears were an invitation to more pain, so there were no tears to match the great, deep sadness she held right then. She looked at Jan, scratching a scab on the back of her hand. "They're going to throw me away then. What's going to happen to me, Jan? What?"

"So let's go, now!" Jan responded, hoping that he had won the debate.

The decision was tearing her apart. She had to make up her mind now, and after mulling it over again, she did decide.

"OK, I'll go," Rebecca finally said with resignation. She began to put the clothes and food back into her bag, and Jan helped. After they were packed, they headed out the door. The old box factory was about a two-hour walk down the road they lived on. They had barely started their trek, when they were startled by footsteps running up from behind.

It was Jan's mother, in a sprint, with a wild look in her eyes. Before they knew it, she was upon them. Martha snagged Jan first, before he could get away. Then with him in tow, she snatched the back of Rebecca's coat collar. She started shaking the both of them. Rebecca looked terrified, shocked at Martha's appearance. Jan tried to get away, but Martha had a solid grip on his arm. He swung at Martha with his free arm, but she head-butted him so hard that he was dizzy for a moment. Then she dragged them both home, screaming at them all the way.

"You think you're going to run away, and leave me to explain why you are gone? I don't think so. Your father will be certain I killed you now, and then they'll send me off for DeathBT. I just bet you'd like that!" Martha gasped with sudden realization, and said, "That was your plan all along!" She gave Jan an extra hard yank on the upper arm she was dragging him with, causing him to cry out. Martha continued her ranting, and after throwing Rebecca back into her home, she hauled Jan back to their own house.

Once they were inside, Martha carried Jan downstairs by the arm. In the kitchen, she threw him to the floor, and yelled, "You stay right there, or I'll kill you!" She quickly went to the hall closet and pulled out a set of Griswolt's disposable handcuffs he had from work. Returning to the kitchen, she tied Jan's wrist to the stove handle. "That should keep you in one place," Martha said contemptuously, and then she went to the bathroom.

Once she was gone, Jan stood up from his crouched position. *If only we would have left sooner, I wouldn't be tied to this stove like this.* In his frenzied state, his mind ran wild. *She's going to come back and kill me right here. I saw it in her eyes.* He started looking around for some kind of way to escape. *I've got to do something!* He kept searching. He came up with an idea. *I know!*

Jan then proceeded to grab anything he could reach that would burn. He took the towels and the bread on the counter, and put them on the stove. He turned it on, and they quickly caught fire. *I need more,* he thought. *I know!* He then started to take his pants off, to burn them. This was difficult, because of his tail, and the fact that he had one arm tied to the stove. Because of his condition, the plan was simple and insane. *She'll have to get us both out of here, and I can run!*

Chapter Eight

Shadow of Love

As Jan was wrestling with his pants, he heard Martha come out of the bathroom.

Martha entered the hallway, and she smelled smoke. "What the hell?" she yelled, and rushed to the kitchen. She ran to turn the stove off, and then turned the exhaust on. "I'll kill you!" she screamed. The items on the stove were still burning in flames, but she nonetheless proceeded to start punching Jan, who could not escape.

With his tied arm extended upward toward the stove, Jan tried to curl into a ball, to live through yet another beating. When Martha stopped punching him, she poured water on the fire to put it out. Then she turned her attention to Jan again and started shaking him. When she saw blood coming from the wrist that was bound to the stove she stopped.

Jan looked up at her, dead on, and said, "Everything you learned about love was a lie! I hate you! I wish you were dead! I wish you died when I was born." He stopped, thought, and spat, "I wish I never *was* born!"

Something about his eyes and words stopped Martha cold. *What am I going to do? He's here, and there's nothing* — she was becoming disoriented. She staggered and leaned onto the kitchen counter, her adrenal glands exhausted. "I can't stand up. I can't think," she said, rubbing her eyes. *There's got to be an answer, there's got to be another way.* Martha looked again at Jan, who was sitting there, tied to the stove, staring back at her, fearlessly.

"What am I going to do with you?" she said towards the wall, dazed now, baffled by this impossible yet inescapable situation. She could not live with him, and she couldn't kill him. *What did he say? Everything I learned about love was a lie.*

Martha's mind drifted to the documents she had found in the bedroom. *I need to burn them!* She looked at Jan again — he was still cowering, yet defiant. She had no answers. Her exhaustion was overwhelming. "What can I do?" she wailed, looking up.

Jan was squatting now, watching her. Studying her.

The idea of the letter she found kept replaying in her confused mind. *They are all lies! I need to burn them all!*

Before she knew it, Martha was heading down the hall. She marched into the bedroom, went to the top drawer in her dresser and pulled all the papers out. Then as she frantically went to the spot on the carpet that she had previously burned, her adrenaline petered out and with it went the pressure that kept the blood in her head. She started to pass out. Martha collapsed to the floor, spilling the papers on the floor in front of her.

It only took a few seconds to regain consciousness, but Martha was absolutely drained by the morning's events. She lay there prone, hyperventilating on the carpet, head lying sideways. When she tried to get up, she got dizzy, and then fell back down again. There was a paper in front of her face. Martha weakly reached for it, and the words of the ancient Platacs came into focus:

"...the epiphany of love does not come easily in this world. When it does, the daggers thrown at us by our world would completely destroy it if possible. Once lost, it is just as difficult to find as the first time. Only our connection to God makes it possible to remember love again, but the true God is not welcome here..."

The act of reading the words could not but have had their effect on her, before soundly rejecting them. Still weakly lying on her side, she plopped the page face down on the floor. *It sounded so real — that's why*

I was seduced, she scornfully thought. Her rambling feelings continued. She lay there — gazing at that page, as well as the others sprawled out on the floor before her. She started entertaining the idea, tempted by the thought and remembrance of a quick release from her pain. *A little pretending for now might be better than this. Even if it is fantasy, it did make me feel better before. There is nothing else — I have nowhere else to go — but to go back there?*

Little did Martha know that she had already begun to relapse. After considering the forbidden idea a little more, she thought, *still, what could it hurt — I can always burn them after I look at them. Maybe I can find a clue — an idea, something —*

Martha was eventually able to get up from the floor. She gathered the pages, and lay down on the bed, organizing them. She found, and began to read, the letter she had written to herself before entering love-deprogramming school. It seemed as if years had passed. As she looked at the gentle handwriting and words before her, she said, "Another person wrote this," shaking her head.

"Hey, untie me!" Jan yelled from the kitchen. "I need to go to the bathroom!"

Martha went cold. She stood up. "You wait until I'm ready!" she screeched. She took a breath. *Calm down.* She sat back down, and started to read:

"Dear Martha,

I know how hard it must be for you to begin to look at this letter. You are probably frightened. I don't know what you have had to endure, but you've got to remember that the passing of time always helps anyone who has gone through the school. Remember your favorite picture —"

Martha was thrown into the thought, dreamily wandering her mind for her favorite picture. She felt the distant glow of it within her bosom, and somehow knew that the memory was there in that warm feeling.

Without warning, there was a crash in the kitchen.

"Dammit!" Martha exclaimed as she jumped out of the bed, and ran to the kitchen.

Jan had pulled the big jar of suka off the countertop, and it had smashed on the floor. He was yelling at it, calling it stupid and ugly, when Martha lit into him, pounding him on the head and back with closed fists, as he curled up once again. This time, however, he did not hide his face. He kept staring at her, gritting his teeth with tenacity and rage.

All of a sudden, Martha felt light-headed again, and nauseous. She stopped, grabbed her stomach, and ran to the bathroom, where she started throwing up. "What's happening to me? Who am I?" She cried as she watched the water of the toilet swirling its contents away. The room was spinning around her. She plopped her butt down on the edge of the bathtub, and bent over, elbows on her knees, face in her hands.

Jan was still shouting from the kitchen.

"What can I do?" Martha asked once again, shaking her head. She paused. The recent thoughts of the bedroom came back to her.

"I need to read that letter," she declared aloud. She felt better just thinking about it. It gave her hope, however unreal and taboo.

"What about Jan?" she asked herself. She thought about it. *Doing something nice might work.* "Doing something nice?" she responded aloud to herself, incredulous at the thought. *It couldn't be any worse.* She allowed the outrageous idea to linger in order to contemplate it more fully. Through desperation and force of will, she saw herself doing it.

"Yes!" Martha said aloud, with sudden inspiration. She went back to the kitchen, where Jan was squatting, wrist still tied to the stove, stretched up above him.

"My arm hurts," he complained. Jan was staring at the floor now. The mess from the broken suka jar was sitting there inviting retaliation.

Martha studied him. He appeared different to her for some reason. She looked at his wrist, and the blood had dried now. She actually found herself feeling some small pity for him. She was on an impossible mission: she was going to try to be nice, while something inside her was screaming for revenge. Martha slowly walked closer to Jan. She gradually reached out her hand, and the gently touched tips of her fingers to his tied arm. She calmly told him, "I want to untie you, and I want you to go into the living room. I'll put some music on for you there OK?"

Jan did not look up, but he didn't reject her, either. "OK," he said stiffly. "I still need to go to the bathroom."

Martha was surprised to see Jan cooperate, and it gave her some hope in her new approach. "Can I trust you to be good, and to be quiet while I go to my bedroom and read?" she asked, as steadily as she could. She desperately wanted to finish reading the letter now.

"Don't hurt me or grab me," was Jan's answer.

Should I do it? Martha thought to herself. *I'll try.* She went to the other side of the kitchen, and took some scissors from the cabinet. She came back and cut the disposable cuff from Jan's wrist. The wound on his wrist was not bad, and now was not the time to deal with it. She waited as he went to the bathroom. He did his business, washed up, and when he came back, they both went into the living room. Martha retrieved the music box. She was going to play the music he liked, but she paused and asked, "What would you like me to play?"

Jan was not ready to play nice. "You know, and what do you care?" he spat.

Martha had to fight the urge to scream and pound on him again. She took another deep breath, and put his favorite recording of songs on the player.

Jan was sitting on the chair beside the sofa, against the wall. He did not know how to handle this change in Martha. It did not make any sense to him. He had a blank look on his face.

Martha turned and observed Jan sitting there, returning her look with an evil eye. The cheerful music that was now playing was unfortunately not reflecting the present environment. She still found herself torn between the thought of attacking him versus the vague feeling that her escape magically lay in the letter in her bedroom. "Will you stay here and be quiet, while I go back to my bedroom?" Martha asked.

Jan then averted her eyes, and now stared at the opposite wall. "I told you already!" he said, with aggravation in his voice.

Martha swallowed hard, and said, "Thank you." She then went back to her bedroom. She left her door open to hear anything that Jan may be doing. She had a seat on the side of her bed, picked up the letter, and continued:

"...Remember your favorite picture —"

"What was it?" she asked herself. The warmth of the memory inside returned once again, but she could not place it. She said to herself, "Maybe I should look through the photo —" Martha abruptly remembered that she burned the photos the other night. She sighed, and read on:

"...Remember your favorite picture, and hold it in your mind. If it is too painful for you, just sit and think of anything good..."

"Good? What can possibly feel good?" Martha complained as she threw the letter down on the bed in disgust. "How stupid I was to believe this crap," she bitched. "I give up! Where did Griswolt put the matches?" She rose and started searching around the room, and then it dawned on her. The picture came through as clear as day, rushing into her mind like a warm breeze.

"Yes," she exclaimed, as she became overwhelmed with a feeling of fullness and warmth with the whole remembrance. She could smell the water —

The picture was one of Martha, Griswolt, and Jan on a friend's boat at the local lake. The day had been a sunny and warm. Griswolt and Jan had been fishing, but had not caught much. In the picture, they were all laughing at something the friend had said, as he took their picture. He had captured the happiest, most perfect smiles on all three of their faces.

"It *was* perfect," Martha found herself saying aloud, vision distant. She felt a twinge of regret when she remembered that she had burned the photograph. She continued reading the letter and found her body relaxing. She became slowly aware of the "something else". Her letter went on:

"... before love-deprogramming school, you had to use your discipline to meditate. We use love and love uses us at each other's request. We use love to become aware of our invisible minds, and put them at the service of our souls, which point to our home in heaven. LERN requires this discipline because minds trapped in a world in which everything dies are lost indeed. Now, Martha, you need to do the pinch exercise, and meditate."

"The pinch exercise!" Martha said to herself. "I remember." She found herself feeling better, clearer, and hoping for more. She went to the chair against the far wall of the bedroom and had a seat. She pinched her arm, hard enough. Then she focused on the part of her "self" that did not feel the pain. Martha repeated the mantra for this exercise, "There is a part of me that feels no pain or fear, and has no body. It is my soul. I am aware of my other self now, and the love that comes from there. It is my life. It is my future."

Martha did this with eyes closed, and continued for a while, and a hint of a smile developed. She stayed with it for over an hour, finding herself surprisingly free. Then her eyes popped wide open, and she exclaimed, "Jan!" Her expression changed to one of empathy, followed by shock, "I can't believe how I hated him." She was suddenly changed by the appearance of familiar presence within her.

She realized a schizoid shift, as she switched in a flash to another personality, the real Martha. "It feels — weightless. I — I remember —" She was still sitting very still, calmly, letting the love grow in awareness.

Then she remembered another part of the exercises, "I have to look with love on Jan *now*. I can't believe how I treated him, I need to focus." Martha then closed her eyes again, becoming aware of her invisible self again, and from that place, looked on Jan in her mind, loving him. "Oh Jan," she said to herself, with heavy remorse. She got past the remorse, and just loved him. Her emotions abruptly switched again to resolution for the job ahead of her. *I told him I would remember love for the both of us.*

Martha got up from her chair and left the bedroom, heading for the living room.

Jan was still sitting there listening to the music. He was looking at a scab on his leg he was busy scratching. He was aware that Martha had come to the living room, but did not acknowledge her.

Martha looked at her own ugly scabs, and started losing her peace. *I can't lose this feeling so soon. Love, stay with me, please! I must act now!* Martha slowly went over to the sofa next to Jan and had a seat. *Maybe if I can get him to look at me, he can see that I'm calm now.*

"I feel much better now," Martha found herself saying very gently. "Thank you for giving me time to relax, Jan."

Jan continued to sit and pick at himself. He had been tortured for a month, and terribly abused by his mother. He was not ready to respond just because his crazy mother decided *she* was.

Dismayed by the lack of communication, Martha was desperately trying to hold on to the awareness of her love. It was all too easy to be sucked out of this state. Still, she knew it was the only way to waken Jan. She also knew it would fade away into the minutes and hours ahead, and Jan's state appeared impossible to overcome. Martha continued to try. "Those scabs need to be cleaned better," she said to Jan.

There was no response from Jan.

Maybe if I touch him, Martha thought. The chair Jan was sitting on was close to the sofa. She slowly leaned over from the sofa and reached for Jan's arm, gently touching it. "Jan," she said as softly as she could, "Can I —"

Jan pulled his arm away, and yelled, "Don't touch me!" He started curling into a ball on the chair. He put his hands over his ears.

Perplexed, but not dismayed, Martha rose from the couch and slowly came over to Jan. As she approached him, she squatted down to be at his level. *I must catch eye contact with him,* she thought. She tried again, this time she attempted to touch his hands. Very, very softly, Martha said, "Jan, I am going to touch you just a little bit, and I promise I won't hurt you." With that, she slowly reached out her hand and placed it on his.

Jan was still on high guard. He did not know what to make of the change in Martha, but was now trained to hate her. Her touch, far from comforting, was now interpreted as painful — but he did not pull away. He froze, as he was now confused, and did not know what was coming next. It didn't look like a beating, though.

Martha was relieved that he did not pull away. She held her hand very still. Still, she had to do more. "Jan, when I was in the bedroom right now, I remembered love —"

"Love!" Jan screeched, and grabbed hold of her right arm, biting it with his sharp front teeth. He jumped up and hid behind the sofa. "Lies, lies, all lies! I'm going to turn you in to the police!"

Martha screamed when Jan bit her, and would have reactively punched him if he had not jumped away so quickly. The arm was bleeding badly. *Now I've got two bites on this arm. I'll kill him!* Martha thought as she ran to the kitchen to get a towel to compress her bleeding arm. The other bite had opened up again as well. She wrapped them tightly, and while doing so remembered her mission.

"What's the use?" she said to herself with a sigh, and plonked down onto a kitchen chair, pressing the towel on her arm. She remembered the bedroom experience, and thought, *you've got to stay with it Martha. Don't lose sight of the love. You've got to wake up Jan! You can do it.*

"I *can* do this," she told herself with renewed resolve, and went straight back to where Jan was hiding. "If I can do it, he can do it." *We must.*

Jan was still hiding behind the sofa, close enough to the end of it to peek around and see if Martha coming back. He ducked his head back behind it when she returned.

Martha entered the living room, and slowly made her way to the sofa. She quietly knelt down at the end from which Jan had been peeking. Out of nowhere, she decided to pray aloud. "Dear God, help me to find peace with my son, Jan. Help him to remember us." She knelt there in silence for a minute or so. She thought to herself, *tell Jan about how you feel.*

She considered it, and said, "Jan, I am so sorry about how I treated you, the things I've done here." Martha said. W*hat else?* Martha continued, "They made me crazy in that awful school, and I just wasn't myself. Please, please forgive me," she begged. After a short silence she said, "Jan, I feel different now, and I know what I've done to you is terrible. I promise I won't be mean to you anymore."

There was no reaction from behind the couch.

Martha bent a little closer, to where she could see Jan's face. He was staring at her, still defiant. *Was there something different in his eyes this time?* Martha moved right up to the space behind the sofa, on her knees, holding her eye contact with Jan.

"I am so, so sorry, sweetie. They hurt Mama in school, really, really bad." She paused, looking at Jan dearly, looking past his hate to what they had before. She hoped it was there, in spite of the distrusting look on his face, and continued, "They hurt Mama, just like you. They, they —" She was choking out her words now, and could not speak clearly. Her mind became flooded with the memories of the tortures she had endured, as she also recalled the awful photos of Jan being tortured.

Martha became lost in this, breaking down and weeping. She folded up in her kneeling position. Her head was almost touching the floor, face in her hands, as if trying to contain her deep, uncontrolled sobbing.

Jan stirred from behind the couch at the scene before him. It may have been because he felt that she couldn't attack him in this weakened state of hers — he came closer to the edge to look at her.

Martha heard him move, and turned her head in Jan's direction. His eyes were emotionless, but they did not have the hate in them that was there before. She said, "Mama's so sorry," as she raised her upper torso, still kneeling, keeping eye contact. Between sobs, she looked, pleadingly at Jan, and asked, "Could you please forgive me — and — could you — come out?"

She crawled a distance away from the end of the sofa to give him some space, and waited hopefully. She continued to wait as Jan stirred, restless now, behind the sofa.

Jan did eventually crawl out, confused, but he had to come out *some* time. He slowly stood up in front of her, looking at her, waiting for, what, he did not know —

He was not expecting her next request.

Martha looked at him with great sincerity, and said, "Jan, I need to show you that I'm OK now. I really am. I need my little boy back, and only you can give him to me." She paused, holding her gaze. S*hould I try?* She tried. "Jan, dear, is there any way — could you —" She stopped. *He'll never do it, I'll scare him away.* She ignored the thought and asked him anyway, "Could you — could you give me a little hug? I really, really need one right now."

Jan looked down from her pleading expression. He gazed through the floor as in a trance, rubbing his right toes in a circle on the floor. The conflict was clearly evident, and he answered, "I can't —" He paused, trying to find the way to say it, "— but *he* can."

"Who, dear?" Martha asked, wiping her eyes, sniffing up the tears.

"The little boy that used to live here." Jan slowly stepped towards Martha. He did not appear afraid.

Martha gave a choking gasp at his response, and looking at him with great sympathy, said, "Yes, yes, please, please, let him come to Mama!" while holding out her arms, still kneeling.

Jan hesitated. "Don't look, look over there," he said, pointing to the living room entrance.

Martha, heart leaping, obliged, and looked away.

Jan slowly came to her. Putting his arms up over her shoulders and onto her back, he gave Martha the most delicious hug she had ever felt in her entire life. She let loose a torrent of tears, sobbing spasmodically, as Jan laid his head on her shoulder, patting her back slowly and rhythmically. He stared off into the distance, as if still in a trance, showing no emotion. This went on for a while, then Martha did look at Jan, and with a tender smile said, "Thank you Jan, thank you. I'll never forget this as long as I live."

Then as she was looking at his wrist, she said, "I think it's time to take care of you. Let's clean you up."

Considering that Jan and his mother were both still physically and mentally tramatized, weakened, and trying to heal, the rest of the day was filled with simply showering, dressing wounds, and then resting.

After they had tidied themselves up, they took a nap together in Martha's bedroom.

They were awakened by Griswolt's voice, as he was shocked by the scene before him upon entering the bedroom. At first glance, he thought they were both dead.

"What the —" Griswolt loudly exclaimed, and both Martha and Jan opened their eyes. Martha smiled contentedly at Jan, and lovingly stroked his arm.

Jan sat up rubbing his eyes and said, "Hi Dad." Then he said, "I'm hungry."

Griswolt was still standing there with his lower jaw dropped open, the tips of his tongue loosely hanging out. He had come home early because his meeting at work had concluded. He had been enormously apprehensive on his way home, not knowing what to expect. He had called home a number of times from work, but there was no answer, as Martha had turned the phone off. He just stood and stared. In fact, the scene before him was so surreal, he felt disoriented. When he realized that it was "safe", he walked toward the bed quickly, as if everything were normal. It wasn't, not yet.

Martha shot up in bed and said, "Don't!" She stuck her finger pointed up in the air again.

Jan dodged Martha's arm, and putting his hand on it, said to her, "He's OK."

Griswolt stopped dead in his tracks. "Can I come and sit with you two?" he asked awkwardly, like a school kid.

Jan said, "Sure, come over with us!"

Martha kept a keen eye on Griswolt and warned, "Just don't touch me, I can't —" and she looked at Griswolt with confusion in her eyes. She didn't understand why she couldn't let him touch her, and now she did not want him touching Jan, either.

Griswolt made his way slowly to the bed, and sat on Jan's side. He gently rubbed Jan's crest, rattling Martha, and shaking his head said, "You both look great. How —" He stopped, and then continuing said, "This is wonderful. Thank you both, you are amazing."

Martha broke her gaze, and looked away. *Why can't I handle this,* she thought to herself. *I thought everything was going to be all right, but now —*

Griswolt didn't care about the rejection. It was so nice to see them together, like normal. Well, normal enough.

Jan looked at his mother and asked, "Can we eat soon?"

Martha started to get up, and said, "Well, let's see what we have in the kitchen."

Griswolt said, "No, let me get dinner for us. I'll take care of it." He did not want to change anything he saw there. He turned and left the bedroom, happier than he had been in quite a while.

Griswolt prepared a quick dinner, and they all gathered in the kitchen to eat. This was their first official meal together, and he relished all of it. *I thought they were lost forever,* he thought to himself during dinner. *It is so hard to understand — it's like a miracle.* During dinner, Griswolt asked Martha, "So what happened today? How did things change so quickly?"

Whenever Griswolt would speak, Martha would get a shiver down her spine to the tip of her tail. It would twitch, and she could not control it. His male voice triggered it. She would essentially snap her replies at him, if she responded at all. She could not tell him the truth, which further complicated things. After a while, her tone lowered, and she became more civil.

Jan was comfortable now, and was more responsive. He still, however, held onto the detached demeanor somewhat.

When dinner was over, Griswolt retired to the living room. Martha had offered to clean up after dinner, which he welcomed. Jan stayed in the living room with his dad and played a game of "Stack" with him.

Martha joined them later, but she sat by herself on the chair, reading a magazine.

"I see you tended to Jan's wounds," Griswolt said to Martha gratefully. "Thank you."

Martha looked at Griswolt with a pursed half-smile, but then quickly avoided his gaze. The evening went on in largely the same awkward manner, and at the end of it, Jan went to his bedroom. A little later, Martha went down to say goodnight to him.

Chapter Nine

A Bright New Night

Jan had just settled into his bed when his mother came in from upstairs.

Martha walked over to the side of his bed. She sat down on the side of the bed, proceeding to give him a goodnight hug, kiss, and saying, "Goodn—"

Jan bolted up out of bed, screaming, "Don't touch me!" He was standing on the floor on the other side of the bed now.

Martha, startled by his reaction now, rose and quickly told him, "It's all right Jan, I won't touch you. I'm sorry I surprised you. I understand, I still feel like that now —" She hung her head and continued, "— with your father." Then she lifted her head, and catching his eyes said, "We're going to get better, I know it. We will be happy again." With a smile she said, "Goodnight, Jan."

Jan was standing there, his heart still pounding. *Why did you just scare me? You won't hurt me now, I know it — why am I still afraid?* He did not return her "Goodnight" gniteerg. He stood there in his red and yellow dotted pajamas, waiting for her to leave.

Martha knew that he only needed a little more time, just as she did, so she simply went upstairs for the night.

After he lay back down in bed, Jan's heartbeat began to slow. He started thinking about the day. He was not so afraid now, but was still extremely conflicted. "Love is death, isn't it?" he asked himself.

Why does it feel so good, then? He thought about how scary yet nice it felt to hug his mother earlier today, and how he did not feel as frightened and panicked as before. He could not understand why his fear came back so fast — *and what about love?* "If love is bad, why does it make things better?" he asked to the dark room.

"Love is bad only to the dragon," the voice said.

"You!" Jan said. "I remember you!" You helped me in the kitchen!" Jan suddenly felt very safe. The voice seemed to come from inside of him, but it was the gentlest adult male voice. It felt good — expanding comfort, pleasance, came with the presence of the voice.

"Can I ask you something?" Jan queried.

"What would you like to ask?" the voice responded.

"Can you tell me why I was afraid of Mama tonight?" Jan wanted to know. He felt that the voice would somehow know something about this.

"It was the dragon," the voice answered. *"The dragon is driven to hate and fears love. The school made your dragon stronger, and brought it close to the center of your mind. It would have stayed there for a long time if it were not for your mother's actions. She saved you from your dragon today."*

Jan was confused. "How did she save me?"

The voice said, *"She made you remember love. The dragon cannot stand the thought of love. When you accepted it, and chose to forgive your mother for a moment, the light of that decision arose from your true center, weakened the dragon, driving it back into the far edges of your mind."*

Jan became concerned, "Will it come back?"

"It did tonight, when she startled you in bed. As long as you walk this world, the dragon can return," the voice replied. Then the voice said, *"God protects the center. Relax and sleep child, you have won the day. Well done, Jan!"*

The voice then appeared to fade away, and Jan curled up on his side, eyes closed and relaxed, smiling. He stretched, gave a yawn, and drifted off into a pleasant night's sleep.

As Jan's body was slowly releasing, he slipped deeper and deeper, and became barely aware of a whispering in his ears. It sounded like many voices, male and female, all whispering unintelligible words. The whispering then fell silent at the reappearance of the voice.

In the dawning of a dream, Jan found himself in his kitchen, and the voice was above the kitchen table, in a diffused extremely white light, very reminiscent of when he had been a toddler confronting the trachna. Although the voice sounded like it was coming from his own thoughts, it also seemed to be part of the lovely light suspended softly before him. Jan was standing on the chair, pondering the light — so bright yet soft, so gentle — so purely white.

"How could I forget you?" he asked the light, knowing that someone was there. "Who are you?" Jan asked the light.

The voice spoke, and it said, *"I am the Guide, Jan. Please take my hand."*

Jan wondered about this. He was thinking, *what hand?*

Then he saw it. A hand slowly appeared in the light, and Jan found himself wondering why he hadn't seen it before. He knew that somehow it was there the whole time.

"Take my hand, Jan," the voice repeated.

Jan slowly reached his hand out to the light, feeling the opposite of a chill as his hand crossed over into it. The gentlest expanding warmth filled his hand as he continued, tentatively grasping the hand presented to him. The remarkable warm feeling traveled up his arm, and his heart deeply accepted it. From there, his whole body seemed to be filled with this wonderful presence, inside and out. As he felt the glow of this, his vision opened. He saw more in the light, starting with the hand, then the arm, and then before he knew it, the experience changed. Jan was holding the hand of what seemed like an angel standing next to him, beside the table now, in the kitchen.

Jan looked closely at the hand. Each scale was glowing, perfectly smooth as glass, and rounded — the scales together appeared countless in number and depth. The Guide patiently waited as Jan intimately examined hand and arm, which extended from the brilliant white robe he was wearing, and then Jan's attention was turned to the whole. The robe looked as if it were woven from threads of light. He looked up.

The Guide's face was stunning, glowing. His shade of color appeared to alternate between white light and random striking pure colors of the rainbow, depending on each instant's perception. All of the Guide's scales were translucent over what appeared to be light underneath. His body scales projected thin prism-like rainbows of color around their outlines as well. They appeared to be scales within scales, like mirrors within mirrors. It was all very mesmerizing to Jan.

"You are so beautiful! How? What are you?" Jan was in absolute awe. *His scales — what is it? Each one looks like a star, as deep as the sky, but they're small, here in front of me. So beautiful, so strange — so perfect.*

"What am I?" The Guide responded, *"I am your future. I am everyone's future. I come to those in the world who the Author has chosen for special uses. Everyone has a special use. Some of these are especially critical to the timing of the plan. You are one of these. I am here to teach, and you are here to learn."*

"What do you want me to learn?" Jan asked, still in a state of awe. He would do anything for this person — just to have his presence.

"You need to learn many things, but for now, you need to learn about the dragon," The Guide said. *"Here,"* he said, *"Let me show you something"*. Then he reached over and pinched Jan in the arm.

"Ow!" Jan said, surprised, as he backed away.

"Now then," the Guide said. *"Did that hurt?"*

"Yes!" said Jan, as he was rubbing his arm.

"Tell me now," the Guide gently challenged, *"How can your arm hurt if this is a dream?"*

Jan was standing there, rubbing his arm. *He's right, you know*, he thought to himself, *this is a dream.* As he continued rubbing his arm, he realized that it didn't hurt at all. He had been hoodwinked — by himself. He unexpectedly felt foolish.

"You see Jan," the Guide continued, *"This is a part of you that is not part of the world of harm. You need to become more aware of this part of you, if you are to be brave in the world of harm. When your dragon rises, you will forget this part of you. When you forget this part of you, your dragon rises, because of your world. We must protect your memory by binding the dragon. We should do this tonight."*

Jan was nodding his head. For now, he only understood that he did not want the dragon, and that the Guide knew how to keep the dragon away. "What is the dragon?" he asked, a little fearful of the answer.

"It is that. The fear you feel when thinking about it. The dragon is a place of bad memories inside you and everybody. It needs you to be afraid, because if it can make you afraid, you become bound to it."

"What do you want me to do?" Jan asked the Guide.

"Please hold my hand again Jan," the Guide requested.

Jan took hold of the Guide's hand.

The Guide continued, *"Now, Jan, I want you to think, as clearly as you can, about the love-reprogramming scho —"*

Jan recoiled at the thought. He let go of the Guide's hand and said, "No! I won't go there!"

The Guide slowly squatted down, and looked Jan eye to eye.

Jan was quite easily mesmerized by the empathetic eyes and loving expression on the face of the Guide. "I love you," Jan found himself saying.

"I know," said the Guide, returning the love as Jan's heart warmed. *"Trust me in this, Jan. You will understand when we are through. Can you trust me for a little while longer?"*

Jan diverted his gaze. *Should I? I don't want to think about that school. But —* "Will you be there with me all the time?" he asked.

The Guide broke into a loving smile, *"Yes, I will, the entire time you stay with it, I will be with you, Jan."*

Jan was ready, "OK, then, what do you want me to do?"

"Hold my hand," the Guide said, having a seat beside Jan.

Jan held the Guide's hand, and then said, "Now what?"

The Guide replied, *"I want you to return your mind to the first thing you can remember about the love-destruction school."*

Jan felt a flash of fear when he remembered taking his one last glance at his mother in front of the school when the guards knocked her unconscious. He saw her slumping body being held up as she was attacked. After a moment, Jan realized something, and said, "I don't feel anything right now. I thought I was afraid. She's not there now — she's safe here at home."

The Guide answered, *"You can do this. You are a child, and your mother has exposed you to much love. That fact makes it easier for you to talk to me than it is for an adult to talk to me. Love flows more purely in children for a while in the world. It does not last. Each painful experience builds the dragon. The dragon cherishes each pain, and saves it. It is true that the dragon and I cannot stand in the same place at the same time. Keep me with you, and we will do this together."*

One by one, the Guide and Jan went through Jan's horrific episodes in love-deprogramming school. As each fearful episode was handed over to the common observation of Jan and the Guide together, the Guide's presence erased any trace of fear associated with the memories. Memory by memory, Jan's load was lightened. *It didn't hurt this part of me at all!* Jan realized. He was thinking, *is this real?* Then, out of the blue, he saw his torturer's sore-riddled face right in front of him, and it scared the daylights out of him.

Jan sprang up in bed, wide-awake, with his heart pounding in the dark. He was sitting, bracing himself up with his arms, and panting for breath. His chest was still seized with fear. *It's OK* — he thought to himself, *there's nobody here.* He started to relax, and wondered about the Guide. He heard the Guide's voice again.

"Jan — it's all right Jan. I'm here with you. I'm always here." the Guide said in an easy, soothing manner.

The Guide was reassuring, and Jan started to relax. He felt the gentlest warmth again that came with the voice of the Guide. In his dark bedroom, Jan began to notice a soothing glow coming from his chest. It was both inside him and outside him. The glow grew to about the size of his chest, and he could not stop looking down into it.

The Guide said, *"Remember what I've said. When you bring me with you, you can look at any frightening thing, and it won't scare you. We need to continue. Don't be afraid, Jan."*

Jan knew what he meant. He now understood that his memory of the torture room was still there, inside, untapped, full of dark potential. He knew what the Guide wanted, and Jan did not want it.

He said to the Guide, "If I look in there, I'll die!"

"That is your dragon talking. The only thing vulnerable is the dragon. It wants your pain to remain hidden. If we look at it together, it can't control you any longer, and your mother won't frighten you anymore. Please, look, and I will be there with you."

Jan trusted the Guide, but still —.

In the end, he seemed to have no choice. He had to do it.

"OK, I'll try," Jan said with a sigh.

Jan resumed his focus on the glow coming from his chest to get more secure, and then thought of the school. He was drawn to his most fearful memory of the school. His torturer had just come back from a break, and had found him crying. Jan's torturer punished him for this by giving him a double dose of electricity. His ugly face was in front of Jan's face, delighting in Jan's misery.

"I don't feel anything!" Jan exclaimed. "Look at him! He can't touch me, nothing can touch me!" He looked at the image, and said, "You can't touch me, can you?" The image of the torturer faded from his mind.

"Why aren't you afraid?" The Guide asked.

Jan answered, "Because when I look at the dragon with you here, I can tell that it's not real, because you are *more* real. *You* are what's real, not what happened!" He hesitated, waiting for the words to describe how he felt. "I feel so strong!" Jan started laughing.

"Yes, Jan. You have begun to discover what you really are. You cannot be hurt, but in the world, your body can be hurt. This fact is what you will learn. Our Author created us safe forever and ever, but souls in your world are blind to this. During childhood, they soon forget their invulnerability, because that was not what they came here for. I cannot tell you why, it is too much for you to bear for now.

"When you look at love, you become blind to the dragon's temporary, but powerful, existence in the world. You cannot both carry love and remember pain in any given instant. Painful memories and revenge are the only things the dragon has, aside from its hosts' cooperation. It is impossible for the dragon to see the only true light, because the dragon does not exist in truth. The dragon does not come from eternity, and cannot understand or see any of this — but you do and you can."

"I feel wonderful! I can really feel love everywhere!" exclaimed Jan. Then, with the Guide's help, he continued to look for other painful memories of the love-deprogramming school, and the fear went away with each one. Then they proceeded to search for any other bad memories. When they were through, Jan was told that his dragon would never be completely gone while in the world. For many souls, it would stay attached long after leaving the world, keeping those souls trapped, blind, lost and confused, outside of heaven's gate, until they were led to choose again.

Jan, bright boy that he was, asked, "What about the good memories? Where are they?"

"Ahhh," said the Guide, pleased with the question. *"They are accepted by the white dragon, which immediately adds them to your treasure in heaven for safekeeping. Each soul has developed talents and skills made in to survive in the black dragon's realm. We steal these talents from the black dragon after binding it, and the white dragon is built from this, in the service of heaven."*

Jan smiled at that. He could not comprehend much of what the Guide had said, but understood that his good memories would be safe in heaven.

When they were finishing, the Guide made a request, saying, *"I want you to help Rebecca tomorrow. She needs you to lend her a hand with this, but she does not know. She cannot see it. Remember to do this."*

After they were through, Jan was exhausted. The voice of the Guide faded, and after some pondering of the night's wonders, Jan fell into a deep, pleasant sleep.

Chapter Ten

Another Candle

The next morning Jan woke up, and speedily ran up the stairs to greet a brand new day. He felt better than ever.

"Hi Dad!" Jan said happily to Griswolt as he sprang into the kitchen. Griswolt was finishing his breakfast while Martha was taking a shower in the bathroom.

"Good morning, son," Griswolt responded with gusto. The word "miracle" came to mind again as his eyes followed Jan hopping up on a chair at the kitchen table with him. *His scabs look much better today,* Griswolt thought. He reached over the table and rubbed Jan's crest affectionately. "What would you like for breakfast?" he asked, knowing the answer.

"Toast!" Jan announced, "With butter and suka!"

"Coming right up!" Griswolt said. He shortly rose and got it started, thinking, *my family — just yesterday I thought that they were gone forever, and now look* — life was good again. He made the toast and had a seat with Jan at the table.

While he was eating his toast, Jan asked, "Can I go over to Rebecca's house?"

Martha had just come into the kitchen from the bathroom. Before Griswolt could answer, she appeared concerned over Jan's request, asking, "You're not going to try to run away again, are you?"

Griswolt's head shot up, and said, "What?" However, he was ignored.

Jan looked at her and said, "No, that was — different. It's all different now, better!" He paused, turning his eyes to a thought. He looked at her again and directly said, "You saved me yesterday, Mama," and he got out of his chair and went to her to give her a hug.

Martha responded with a big smile, returning the lovely hug. She looked him over with a sad smile, "I'm still so very sorry about how I treated you, Jan." She gave him a once over.

"You — you do look different today, don't you?" she said to the beaming, smiling Jan, who was still looking up at her.

Jan was waiting for her answer, "Can we go?"

"Go wash up after you're done eating, and we'll go over to Rebecca's together," Martha replied.

Griswolt had risen and was starting up some eggs for Martha now. He was pretending not to be observing them, but he certainly was. He did not want to interfere with any of this wonderful change. It made no sense, his puzzlement amplified by his inability to put any reasonable pieces together that might explain their reunion.

After Jan's bath, they both went over to Rebecca's house. Rebecca answered the door. She did not look like she was recovering well, and found it revolting to see both Jan and Martha holding hands.

"Hello Rebecca," Martha said as she and Jan entered the house. She squatted down to get closer to Rebecca, and asked, "How are you doing, dear?"

Rebecca stepped back as Martha reached out to touch her arm. Her face changed from just dismal to stern. She was wearing the same, too-tight gray suede overalls she had on yesterday. Rebecca averted Martha's caring gaze by dropping her eyes to the floor, arms crossed. She did not answer.

Martha looked at her in sympathy. Still squatting, she pulled her outstretched hand back. "Is there anything I can do for you, Rebecca?" she asked.

"No," was Rebecca's reflexive response. Rebecca did not look up, but said, "I want Jan to stay with me here — we won't run away." She still held the same facial expression.

Jan had been soaking this all up. He knew where Rebecca's attitude was coming from, and it frightened him a little. He did not ever want to go "there" again. He felt badly just looking at her. Rebecca did not look any better than yesterday, while *his* whole world had changed overnight. "We'll be OK, Mama," he said to Martha. "You know I won't run away now, don't you?"

Martha stood up, and said, "Let's all go inside for a bit, and we'll see." They went down straight into the living room. Martha looked around. The place was clean enough. She glanced at Rebecca. *I really don't have anything good to say to her, and she won't hear me anyway.* She looked down at the two children with eye-ridges pursed, "I suppose it will do Rebecca good to have some company here for a while. Jan, I want you home for lunch. Why don't you bring Rebecca with you?"

Rebecca, still not looking up, slightly turned and tilted her head. The stern look on her face broke. Her thoughts turned toward a distant memory.

"OK, Rebecca?" Jan asked, "Will you come over for lunch?"

Rebecca stirred, and started picking at a scab on her shoulder. "OK, I guess."

Martha smiled broadly, "Well, it's settled then. Jan will have a guest for lunch." She looked around the immediate area again, and said, "All right Jan, I'm going to leave now. Be good!" She knelt down to give Jan a hug, and glanced at Rebecca, but Rebecca just backed away. *Sigh.* Martha then went up the stairs to leave the house.

As soon as the door upstairs had opened and closed, Rebecca un-crossed her arms. "How can you stand her?" she hissed at Jan.

Jan was taken aback by Rebecca's behavior. He thought about how he completely agreed with her yesterday. "I feel different today, that's all," he said. "I feel better."

Rebecca looked at him. She looked confused. "You — look better." She paused to think about it, and then said, "And you look happy. Why?"

Jan was about to tell her about what happened the day before, and realized that love-deprogramming school graduates were very conditioned to report any love activity to the police. *I was going to turn my mother in myself just yesterday. I have to show her, not tell her,* he thought to himself.

Trying to think of something else to say, Jan changed the subject and asked, "Did you find your knitting stuff yet?

Rebecca frowned. "No, my dad said that my mother threw them away," Rebecca replied. "What an idiot! I hate her! She's ruined everything!" Rebecca sniffed.

Jan came closer to her, and she jumped back.

"Don't touch me!" she screamed.

Her reaction startled Jan, and he stepped away from her. "OK, Rebecca, I know," he said, nodding his head. He thought about it. "If there was a way for me to help you feel better, would you want to try?"

She looked at him suspiciously. "I don't want to feel better. I need to remember that —" Her thoughts trailed off as she tried to define the reason she did not want to be happy again.

Jan was perplexed. *How can I make her happy when she doesn't want to be happy?* "Are you sure you don't want to be happy?" he asked.

Rebecca fidgeted, and said, "Oh, I don't know. Maybe someday. A long time from now."

Jan was not to be blocked this easily. "Why not now, with me?" he prodded.

Rebecca looked at him. He looked so happy when he arrived. She did want to feel like that. "I guess it's better than the way I feel now," she said. "OK, what do you want me to do?"

Jan then realized that he did not have a plan. He let his instincts guide him, making it up as he went along.

"Let's sit on the floor," he decided. He went over to the middle of the living room floor and Rebecca followed him. They sat down on the floor, facing each other. Jan tried to remember how the Guide helped him. He said, "Take my hand." He reached out one hand, and waited for Rebecca to take it.

She looked in fear at the outstretched hand of Jan's. It might as well have been on fire. "I can't do it," she said in dismay.

Jan leaned over and took hold of her hand.

Rebecca snarled, and grabbed his hand firmly, trying to bite it, but Jan was too quick, and she only snagged it, drawing a thin line of blood along the back of his hand.

Jan yanked his hand back, and jumped backwards. When he saw her getting up, he ran behind the big overstuffed chair in the corner of the room, hiding out of her view. *I'm getting tired of this,* he thought.

Rebecca was shocked at what she had just done. "What's happening to me?" she wailed up to the ceiling. "I can't control myself!" She looked over in the direction of where Jan was cowering behind the chair. *He's afraid of me, she thought. I am a monster now.*

"Jan," Rebecca called out, "I'm sorry! I didn't mean to — I won't do it again."

Jan was still ducking down behind the chair.

Rebecca tried again. "I won't do it again, Jan. I don't know what happened."

Jan was frightened now. He had seen the crazed look in her eyes, and it reminded him of the school. It was still too fresh. "How do I know you won't bite me?" he asked, still behind the chair.

"I'll be OK, I promise!" Rebecca responded. "Come out, Jan, I'm OK now. Please?"

Jan warily came out from behind the chair.

Rebecca tried to produce a smile. "Let's sit on the couch and try again."

Jan was not so sure of this, and asked, "Are you sure? I don't know now."

"I don't want to be an animal," Rebecca said, with a sad look. Then she looked up at Jan and said, "I think you were helping me."

Jan looked her over. She seemed safe enough now. He took a deep breath, "OK." He smiled at her. "If you get scared, just let go of my hands, all right? — if you get scared." He wiped the bit of blood from his hand onto his pants.

She timidly looked at Jan and said, "I'll sit in my knitting chair instead of the couch, and you can hold my hands there. I think I'll be all right there."

So they went over to her little chair, and Jan knelt down in front of her to be at her level. He slowly and wordlessly reached out his hands, and Rebecca hesitantly received them. They looked at each other, and Rebecca slowly settled from her erect defensive posture into a more relaxed state. They stayed this way, and Rebecca started to finally smile.

Jan realized something, and his face grew very sad.

Rebecca could see it, and asked, "What?"

Jan took a deep breath, and letting out a sigh, said, "You're going to go away forever when your mama comes home." Shaking his head he said, "I'm going to miss you."

Rebecca's expression changed. She showed a look of recognition on her face, which then changed to an expression of great loss. She stood up, and unexpectedly wailed, "I miss my mama!" She started crying, very hard.

Jan stood up with her. Without thinking, dropping all guard, she fell towards Jan with both arms over his shoulders, crying, head and tears, on his shoulder.

Jan simply held her while she cried. Slowly and gently, he patted her on the back, just as he had done with his mother. Jan found himself staring off — once again — into that place which had become all too familiar. Love — and all that came with it, was all he had to give — and it was exactly what Rebecca needed.

Chapter Eleven

Recall

The passing of time did help. Jan had been back in school for a month, along with Rebecca. Martha had returned to her job over two weeks ago, working at Mineral Processing Plant 11B. Other than fending off questions about love-deprogramming school, things were getting back to normal. She was finishing up for the day, when two NOV police, accompanied by her manager, came looking for her. The manager pointed her out, and one of the police said, "You are under arrest for committing the crime of love, and of being a member of LERN."

Martha was shocked. "What? That's ridiculous! Where did you hear such a thing?" she pleaded frantically.

They simply handcuffed her and escorted her out of the processing plant, and into the rusty awaiting police wagon. When they arrived at the station, they had Martha sit in a heavily guarded brightly lit white room with others waiting to be processed on any number of charges. Some were ordinary criminals, but a few were obviously LERN members. In the interest of self-preservation, she stayed away from the other LERN members.

After a few hours, they called Martha's name, and took her to a small dark room that held a table with two opposing chairs. The guard told her to take a seat. There was a device on the table, which had some wires attached to it. Two males came in, the interrogator and his assistant.

A feeling of helplessness would not do. Martha stiffened up, and was ready to fight. "What's this about?" Martha demanded.

The primary interrogator had a seat opposite Martha. "One of your neighbors has identified you as a LERN member, and has given us good reason to believe her intimate knowledge of your activities," the interrogator said.

Martha realized her worst fear — the fear that Salom would talk. "Salom? Are you talking about Salom?"

"Yes," the interrogator replied. "Your neighbor failed love-deprogramming school. She has stated that you are a LERN member."

What am I going to do? Martha was not revealing the chill running down her spine, or the fear that gripped her guts. "That's the craziest thing I've ever heard," Martha retorted. "I hate love-lovers!" she said with disgust.

The interrogator looked at her, in a bored way. "You all lie. I've never seen one that didn't." He sighed, shaking his head. "I don't have the time. We have a simple, quick way to get to the truth. Hold still."

He made a nodding gesture to his assistant, and the latter proceeded to attach the wires from the device on the table to Martha's forehead and wrists.

Martha looked at the device and wires with obvious distrust, and the assistant ordered, "Don't move." The assistant appeared to be making adjustments to the device, and finally looked at the interrogator, and said, "She's ready."

The interrogator took a handful of photos out of his briefcase. "These are photos of your son's "lessons" while in love-deprogramming school. I want you to look at each one closely."

One by one, he held them each one in front of Martha's face, long enough to get a reading. As he did so, he kept a keen eye on the display of the device sitting on the table.

Oh my God, Martha thought. *He's going to try to make me cry. I won't!* She sat stoically, cold as ice, as the pictures were shown. *It's just the past — it's just the past. Focus, Martha, focus!*

The interrogator stopped. "That's it," he said. He glanced at his assistant giving him a look. Then he said to Martha, "The machine doesn't lie." He looked back at the assistant, and said, "Go get a guard, and bring him here." The assistant departed. The interrogator had been through this enough times. There was always trouble when he gave the news. Still, he could have a little fun before the guard arrived. She didn't look like *that* much trouble. He looked at Martha, and said, "I am sorry, but you have failed. You will be sentenced to DeathBT for the crime of love."

Martha did not hear any words past the "I am sorry —" She jumped up from the chair, tearing the wires from her arms and head. "No! You're all wrong!" she shouted. She started pacing back and forth in the small room like a wild caged animal. *What can I do — how can I escape?* She desperately searched for any means of escape. She looked at him, just sitting there, on the other side of the table. He was leaning forward, hands on the table, poised in an alert posture. *Is he enjoying this?*

Her fear switched to rage. *Be smart, do it right.* Martha took a breath, marched up to him, and in an instant, she pulled a dagger she usually had hidden in her belt and nailed the startled interrogator's right hand to the table with it.

"There!" Martha screamed, "Is that the love you want to see, mother fucker?" Snarling, she backed away from the table.

The interrogator shrieked, and pulled the knife out using his left hand, just as the guard was entering the room with the assistant.

The large guard was outraged at the scene and immediately grabbed Martha from behind. The interrogator was already making his way around the table to get at Martha. When he reached her, he punched her in the stomach with full force, causing her cry out and double over in pain. When the guard held her back up for another go, the interrogator instead stared at her blazing eyes glaring back at him. He paused a moment, as she was catching her breath from the first blow. He stalled.

"Let her go," the interrogator said, still gazing into Martha's incensed glare.

What? thought Martha.

"What?" both the guard and the assistant said in disbelieving unison.

The interrogator tilted his head to the side, and then he looked down at his wounded hand, supporting it with the other. He looked at the guard and his assistant. They were still waiting for a reason. He then shrugged his shoulders, sighed, and said, "She gave a good answer." He turned his attention back to Martha, and reiterated, "Good answer."

Martha was simply stunned now. She was still catching her breath.

"Can I keep that?" the interrogator asked, pointing his good hand to the bloody knife lying on the table.

Martha, still in shock, looked at him and stammered, "Yes — of course."

The assistant led Martha back out of the building, and Martha left for home. It was nighttime now, and she took a bus. It was a small bus that only had two contisses pulling it.

On the way, she fell into a deep depression. She found herself openly staring at the people around her. *There's no end to this. Why does it have to be so bad? I can't stand it — I can't stand these people on this bus. They are all so miserable looking, and why not? We're living in hell here. My son... his world...they are doomed to this horror.*

Then she remembered her only hope. *The escape. Yes. It's coming and I will be there! We will leave with them.* She felt a little better pondering the great escape LERN had been planning. Details were sketchy because they were on a "need to know" basis. All she had heard was that LERN was working to infiltrate the NOV's sole vaccine producing laboratory in order to escape into the wildlands.

There had been a primary laboratory for eighty years, with a second, backup lab in Justilant. After the primary one became contaminated beyond repair, they only had the backup lab to rely on. Plans had been made for a new one, but with the economy the way it was, and the anticipated dissolution of the one-hundred year poison, the investment did not seem to be a priority.

The wildlands made up most of the planet. Just the thought of freedom lifted Martha's spirits. *How long? How long?* The vaccines were very difficult to develop, thus their great potential when withheld by enemies. She did not understand the process, but she knew that it took twenty years from start to finish in order to produce a batch of vaccine from the beginning. She sighed again, leaning her head back for the ride home.

By the time Martha arrived at home, it was rather late, and Griswolt was there. When she came in, he was in the living room with Jan.

Martha had fallen. She really did not want to talk to anybody, and said nothing when she had come inside. She simply went straight back to the bedroom to change her clothes. Then she took a shower, which was unusual in the evening.

Griswolt could hear her taking the shower. She had come home unusually late. He got up, and went to the bathroom to investigate. Opening the door, he asked, "Where were you tonight?"

"Just leave me alone, I'll tell you when I'm ready," Martha coldly said from the shower.

Griswolt felt challenged. She had been getting better, but this was wrong. He had to make a stand. He raised his voice, "Tell me now, I want to know!"

Martha was in no mood. "I said get out!" she screamed.

Griswolt was taken aback by her caustic response. "I'm really getting tired of this," he said under his breath. He backed out of the bathroom, and walked down the hall, muttering, "She's pushing it too far. This up and down crap is starting to get old." He grumbled his way back to the living room to continue with a book he had started.

Jan was on the floor, reading. The homework load this year was demanding.

Griswolt looked at Jan, thinking. Martha had been cold to Griswolt since coming back from love-deprogramming school — but with Jan it was different. It was obvious that Martha and Jan were getting along very well. Griswolt had a flash of resentment. He missed the "old Martha". Only Jan was privy to that side of her now. *Maybe I'll send Jan to see what's going on with her.*

Griswolt said to Jan, "After your mama gets out of the shower, would you go and ask her about her day today? Can you find out why she was late coming home?"

Jan looked up, and said "OK. I thought she was going to be coming out here pretty soon."

Griswolt took a furtive glance in the direction of their bedroom, (which he still was not permitted to sleep in,) and said, "No, I don't think she's in a hurry to do that. She won't talk to me, and I need to know why she came home so late."

Griswolt had recently begun to entertain his own thoughts of escape. *I am going to start looking for another place to live tomorrow. I may as well be ready, I certainly can't put up with this forever. It's as if she's back to where she was a month ago. I'm sick of it.* He looked at Jan, and leaned over and rubbed the gold striped crest on Jan's head. *Those kids are going to start giving you a rough time over this crest of yours,* he thought in sympathy. "You need to go to self-defense school," Griswolt said.

Jan looked up at him with his big innocent eyes. Griswolt gave a sigh. *I can't leave. You're gonna need me around, son.* Then he thought — *maybe I can take you with me.*

After Martha went back into the bedroom, Griswolt waited a short while, and sent Jan to the bedroom to check on her.

In a half hour or so, Jan came back. He plunked down on the big chair, and looked at the awaiting Griswolt. "She's sad," he said.

"Of course she's sad, she's always that way now," Griswolt grunted.

"No, it's worse now," Jan said. "She wasn't even friendly to me." Jan knew how differently Martha treated him compared to Griswolt. He didn't know why she was so cruel to his dad now, but she obviously was. "I don't think you should bother her tonight," Jan opined.

Who is this kid to give me advice? Griswolt thought. "I'm going to get to the bottom of this! I want her to come out and tell me what her problem is," he said to Jan, with feigned authority.

They both stayed in the living room for another hour. Martha was still in the bedroom. Griswolt worked up the nerve to go back to the bedroom to pursue his quest for an answer. He opened the door, and Martha was lying on the bed on her back, eyes closed. "What's the matter with you tonight?" Griswolt asked, upon entering the room.

Martha took a deep breath, and gave a long sigh. "It's just — everything." She sighed again. "I really don't want to talk about it now — maybe tomorrow." *You're the last one I want to be around right now.* She sighed again. *My God, I was seconds away from being convicted of committing love.* Then she realized — *thank you for saving me.* Her next impression was — *how can stabbing someone in the hand be saving?* She paused in her thoughts. *Thank you, anyway, just in case.*

"You were gone all day and night, you're acting like this, and you're not telling me anything!" Griswolt said roughly.

Martha was startled by his voice yanking her from her thoughts. In spite of that, she was finding herself a little calmer now. *Just tell him,* she told herself.

She opened her eyes, lifted her head up from the pillow, and glared at Griswolt. "I was almost convicted of being a LERN member today," she blurted out, "OK? Leave me alone, I'm so sick of all this! Just leave me alone."

Griswolt was aghast. "You? In LERN? Where would they get a crazy idea like th —" Then he remembered Salom. She was capable of saying anything, just to stop the torture for a while. "Was it Salom?"

Martha gave a thought of Salom going through her own hell, and started sobbing, saying, "Yes — yes, it was Salom." After a few more sobs, while Griswolt was formulating his next question, Martha continued, "It's over now anyway, they let me go."

Griswolt was relieved. His breathing loosened. "I'm so sorry you had to go through that —"

"Yes, *had* to!" Martha yelled, sitting up. "I *had* to go through it because I *have* to live here with the insane, evil NOV!"

Griswolt bristled at such words. It bordered on criminal language against the state. "You're upset because of today, don't talk like that. Give it time," he responded.

"Just get out!" Martha screamed, throwing a pillow at him. "I told you to leave me alone!"

Griswolt, having his curiosity satisfied, went back to the living room where Jan had fallen asleep. He carried Jan downstairs and tucked him into bed. Then he went back up to his place on the sofa for the night.

The next morning came, and Jan woke and went upstairs to find his mother in the kitchen, preparing some breakfast for the three of them. She had called in to her job to tell them she would not be coming in. They understood, considering. They were just happy that she wasn't taken away forever.

"Good morning, Mama," Jan said, as he hopped up onto a chair at the kitchen table.

"Good morning, Jan," Martha replied. "I want you to have a raw egg with your toast every morning now. We need to get more weight back on you."

"Yuk!" Jan said. Raw eggs were too strong tasting and slimy. Worse yet, they reminded him of the names that they were calling him in school now. "Egghead," he said aloud.

"What?" Martha asked.

"Oh, nothing," Jan replied. The kids in school had been saying that his crest looked like a broken egg. *Rebecca likes my crest, though.* Jan smiled, thinking about her.

Griswolt came into the room. He was showered and dressed for work. He had smelled breakfast earlier as it was cooking, and was looking forward to eating before leaving for the day. "Mmmm. That smells good!" he said as he leaned over Martha's shoulder to take a look.

"A little space please!" Martha barked.

Griswolt grumbled, and said, "I hope you're making some for me!" He started to glance at a report he had in his hand. He was still a bit groggy, having not slept well.

Jan was observing as Martha's pleasant demeanor changed with the introduction of Griswolt's presence. It was as if she hated him now. He realized that it was her dragon. *Her dragon rises whenever Dad comes near.*

Even though she had already intended to make Griswolt's breakfast, Martha sighed as if he were asking for some heavy task, and asked, "How many?"

"How many?" Griswolt asked, yawning and still rubbing some of the sleep out of his eyes.

"How many eggs, you idiot!" Martha snapped.

Griswolt, startled and angered by her attitude first thing in the morning, shot back, "Fuck this!" He departed the kitchen with impulsive resentment, and left for work without saying anything else.

When she heard the door slam, Martha turned the stove off and just stood there, both hands on the stove, holding up her slumping body. "I don't know," she said. "I try — but I can't."

Jan was sitting there, soaking this all in. He felt badly that his mama was always angry with his dad. He wanted to help, but wasn't sure how. "What can't you do, Mama?" he asked.

When Martha turned her head towards Jan, he could not help but see the deeply unhappy look in her eyes. "I can't stand your father, and I don't know why. I want to be nice to him. He has been so good to me." She paused. "To us." Martha looked away, and was thinking aloud now. She said, "I wanted this morning to be pleasant. Why is it, as soon as he appeared, I got angry? Now he's gone, and that angry person in me is gone. But I know that when he comes back, that other person in me will come back. I don't know how to make it stop."

It's her dragon. Jan just blurted it out, "It's the dragon."

Martha's expression changed as if someone had splashed cold water in her face. "What — where did you hear about the dragon?" She had scripture that mentioned the dragon, but there was not much to go on. The NOV preached the black dragon, but it was just superstitious propaganda.

"Daddy raises your dragon," Jan said, matter-of-factly.

Martha was now in no little shock. "How do you know about the dragon?" she asked again.

"I don't know, I just do," Jan replied, then continuing, "The school raised my dragon, but I looked at it, and it went back down." He nodded reassuringly, "You'll feel better when you do." He did not know how else to say it. He didn't want to talk about the Guide for some reason, so he just left it at that. He never told anyone, not even Rebecca, about the Guide. There was no good way to describe him.

Martha just stared at Jan, a little spooked. *What an unusual kid,* she thought. For some reason, she became frightened at the thought of the dragon, and resented Jan for bringing it up. "Mind your own business.

You don't know anything about this. Finish up your breakfast, you still need to get dressed for school," she said.

Jan obliged, and in short time was off to school. Martha was left with the day all to herself. She started it by taking her morning shower. Afterwards, she inspected the new scales coming in where the burns had been before. She was still taking antibiotics for the infections that were always looking for an entrance.

Martha had been to a few LERN meetings since school, and was given helpful new copies of other writings as a recovery gift. She retrieved her expanding collection and went into the living room to study them. She poured over them, looking for references to the dragon. All she could find there was that the dragon was the same for everyone, yet different. Most were Aletian translations of Platac scriptures, and this was one of them —

"...the dragon, for it has lifted the vilest portions of the hidden realm to the light of life that it may become the life. The great dragon desires life, but has no awareness of light..."

Martha put the scriptures down, and stared at the opposite wall. "I don't understand," she said to herself. "Jan said that Griswolt raised my dragon." She thought about it. "I have this dragon?" she asked herself. She took a frustrated breath. "Jan's just a child. He was talking nonsense this morning. I need to ask Jen the next time I see her." Jen was a LERN member that had a wealth of ancient literature, along with copious access to others with scriptures of their own.

Martha then did her LERN meditations. She focused on love, and when finding it, she felt it grow inside her. *It is incomprehensible that other people get along without this,* she thought. She had as much time as she wanted, and spent a couple of hours "floating".

Later in the day, Martha listened to the radio. She turned it off as usual when the propaganda got too thick. "How can intelligent people take this junk seriously?" she asked herself.

Martha decided to prepare a nice dinner for Griswolt and Jan for when they came home. "I know, I'll just think nice thoughts about Griswolt all day," Martha said aloud. *I've really got to get over this. Griswolt won't take my problem forever.*

136

In the early afternoon, Jan came home from school. He was in a hurry to finish his homework, so he stayed in the living room doing it while Martha worked on dinner.

When Griswolt arrived from work, he was still angry about the morning's episode. The day at the office was no picnic, either. He was on guard when he came downstairs and into the kitchen. Dinner smelled wonderful, but he wasn't about to do anything but relax, if he could. He said nothing, and went to the bedroom to change his clothes.

By the time he came out of the bedroom, Martha was putting dinner on the table. "Jan, come and eat!" Martha called out. She looked at Griswolt, who was just walking through the kitchen. *Be nice.* "Griswolt, are you hungry?" she asked, as sweetly as she could.

Griswolt looked at her, trying not to betray his distrust. "Yes, I sure am," he replied.

"Well, have a seat, we are almost ready," she curtly responded.

She's ordering me, Griswolt resentfully thought. *Oh well, I'd better have a seat.*

Jan came in from the living room, and they sat down to eat. Try as she may, Martha was finding herself annoyed by Griswolt's chewing sounds. "Could you try to eat like a D'otian, and not like a gendra?" she asked with a terse tone.

Griswolt had had enough. She was taking another potentially enjoyable moment, and turning it into an attack. He looked at her and said, "Why don't you shut the hell up, and let me eat in peace?"

Jan tightened up, anticipating something bad.

Martha threw her fork at Griswolt, got up, and ran out of the kitchen yelling, "I'll leave you in peace! This is the thanks I get." She ran down the hallway to their bedroom, slamming the door behind her.

Yeah, I'd like to give you more than thanks, bitch, Griswolt thought to himself, as he continued to munch on his dinner.

Jan had lost his appetite, but Griswolt made him stick around and finish most of his plate.

Later in the evening, Jan was thinking about what happened during dinner. He wanted to help his mother. Not knowing exactly what to say, he went into her bedroom anyway. She was lying on the bed, reading a magazine. "Can I come in?" he asked.

"Yes, love," she responded, "Come up here in bed with me, Jan."

He hopped into bed, and snuggled with her. They lay there for a while without saying anything.

Eventually, Martha put down the magazine with a sigh. "I'm sorry about ruining dinner, Jan," she said. "I tried. I really, really tried. I prepared all day for it. I don't know. I feel like this will never change."

Jan was thinking. *How can I tell her?* "I think it will change when you do what I did," he said.

Martha turned over in bed, facing Jan, and asked, "What did you do, dear?"

Jan had mixed feelings. *Should I tell her? She won't believe me. Oh, well.* "I was with someone who loves me, and he helped me look at my dragon, and it went away."

"What? Who?" Very alert now, Martha propped herself up on her elbow.

"The Guide," Jan said, plainly.

"Who's the Guide?" Martha asked, suspiciously.

"He comes to me in my dreams, and talks to me in the day some-times," Jan said. "He always helps me, and makes me feel good — like you do."

Is he crazy? Martha found herself thinking. *Did love-deprogramming school drive him mad?* She dismissed the thought. "Oh, Jan, that's just your childish imagination," Martha said.

I knew she wouldn't believe me, Jan thought. However, he was as persistent as usual, "Just try this, OK? I know you will feel better if you do this, Mama."

"What? What do you want me to do?" Martha responded with a sigh.

"Just look at me and let me love you," Jan said. "Then, when you are ready, tell me, and I will take you there."

Martha shook her head, "Take me where?"

Jan confidently said, "I'll tell you when we are ready."

Martha was still lying there, facing Jan. She was lost, and her son seemed convinced that he had the answer. *What am I doing?* Martha thought. She looked into Jan's deep eyes. He was focusing on her with care and tenderness.

Jan instinctively started stroking her forehead, lovingly tracing the start of her crest, following down to the ridges above her eyes, and trailing his fingers along her left ear.

"That tickles," she giggled.

He smiled, *I love you so much,* he thought. He said lowly, "I love you, Mama."

"I love you too, sweetheart," Martha responded, feeling her body relax into the loving comfort of the moment.

Jan continued his slow stroking of her forehead, and said, "I'll stay her with you, but you need to look at your dragon now."

Martha was not sure what he meant. "How can I look at the dragon?" she asked suspiciously, somehow afraid that he did have an answer.

"You have to look at your own dragon. You have to remember what happened at the school. I'll be here with you, OK?" Jan said.

Martha blinked. "What does the school have to do with the dragon?" she asked.

"The school raised our dragons." He paused thoughtfully and then said, "I think the dragons were there already, but the school made them very strong."

Martha became anxious. "I'm not going to do that," she said firmly, feeling the tension rising further. "I need to forget it all, I want to bury it."

"But it's still there. You can't see it, but it is there. It makes you fight with Daddy," Jan said. "You have to look at it like I did. You need to have love with you when you do. It was scary at first, but then I laughed," he said, hoping to sell her on the idea.

Something about what Jan was saying, crazy as it was, made some sense to Martha. *Should I? It's not getting any better with Griswolt.* She lay her head back down, and closed her eyes.

Jan continued stroking her forehead, and waited.

Martha went back to feeling the comfort of the loving son she had, trying to help her now. She felt she was ready, and found herself first remembering the stench of the school. Then she was drawn to the face of her torturer. She was surprised that the memory of him did not bother her so much now. *Maybe Jan was right about this,* she found herself wondering. She started thinking about the horrible photos of Jan. Then she found herself remembering the sexual trauma rapists.

Her pulse quickened, and in no time she was curling up into a ball, grunting — heart pounding. She sat up in bed with a loud "No!" She looked at Jan, who was startled by her spontaneous reaction.

I can't do this. "Look at me, I'm trembling," Martha complained to Jan, shaking her head. "I can't do this. You don't know. Nobody knows what I went through."

Jan looked at her. *She's done for now, I think.* He sighed. "Can I sleep with you tonight?" he asked.

Martha broke her line of thought, and looked at him. She rubbed his head and answered, "Sure, you stay with me tonight. I'm tired of sleeping alone anyway."

It was getting late, so they turned out the lights on another day, and went to sleep.

The next morning Martha called in sick again, just so she could work on herself. After Jan and Griswolt left for the day, she spent the morning studying and meditating. She tried to find out more about the dragon, but other than the day before, she could find nothing practical. There was nothing there about the dragon that she could really understand.

I still feel as if Jan was on to something yesterday, she thought. Jan had said that she needed to have love with her when she looked into her memories of the torture room. She chuckled. *I'm taking the advice of a kid. But what else can I do?* What was there left to do with this unworkable situation?

OK, I'm going start with growing my love. She had a couple of LERN methods to do this. One was the "Love Shower", in which she imagined being in a shower of water made of love, and as she returned the love to God, it would grow. It took about a half hour to build up steam, but it was effective. Martha soon found herself forgetting her troubles, and "floating" with the presence of love. It made her surroundings seem less real.

Now's the time, she thought. She forced her mind to recall that awful room — the torture room. *OK, so far so good, I guess.* Then she recalled the face of her torturer. His ugly, fat, sore-riddled face readily came to mind. She looked at it — at him. *The love is leaving,* she thought. Tension was creeping in to replace the love being lost.

Martha focused on the "Love Shower" again, and it replaced the tension. After re-tuning to a solid love channel, she continued with her attempt. *I have got to find my dragon, if there is such a thing — I must continue.* This time her mind took her to the aching of her limbs that she experienced when tied to the toilet. Then she recalled her experience of being bound in excruciating positions while being repeatedly raped. *They did it over and over, it never stopped, the pain — I never had a chance — stay with me,* she found herself silently talking to the love that was with her. *Please stay with me.* She heard her own inner voice saying, *you are here now, this memory is past — the past has no power here.* She found she was able to retain the awareness of love's presence while the stark terror of the torture room seemed to fade from any discernable physical tension. As she did this, she felt better. Lighter.

Martha started to feel good, and ready to continue. She was surprisingly confident now, and found herself able to face anything from the torture room, without losing the presence of love. *I understand!* She thought. *The whole ordeal, all of the horrible things that happened to me, this is the dragon!*

She went to work with confidence. She sat there and asked herself if there was anything left in the dragon. Every time she asked, another negative memory would appear, and she would stare it down, with love at her side. Martha's mind eventually took her past the torture room, and carried her to other painful episodes in her life. She looked at those memories too, feeling lighter and more confident with each success. After a few hours of this, she was simply exhausted from the mental exertion, and took a nap.

She awoke an hour later, feeling like a new person. The room looked brighter, and she was looking forward to Jan and Griswolt coming home. She kept repeating, "I feel wonderful!" throughout the day. "I'm going to make the best dinner!"

Martha went into the kitchen. "This room is filthy!" she declared to the kitchen. She went and got her cleaning supplies, and started working on it, beginning with the floor. While cleaning the kitchen, Martha thought about the choices for dinner. "Griswolt loves tenderloin of splint," she said with inspiration. She called the local grocery to have one delivered, along with some fresh bread, yama extract spices, and some yama wine. *This evening may turn into a romantic one,* she thought with a smile.

Martha had it all planned out. She could not wait for Griswolt to come home. "I miss him so much," she thought, as if she had not seen him in a year. "You've been so good, I know it has been hard for you," she said aloud to her image of Griswolt.

When Jan came home later in the day, Martha greeted him with an enthusiasm that set him back a moment. Then he realized that it was real, and his mama was truly home now. The tenderloin was roasting in the oven, and had a tantalizing smell. Jan was in the living room doing his homework when his dad came home.

Griswolt descended the stairs and came into the kitchen pretty much like any other day. Martha was in the bathroom when he arrived. He noticed the smell of the cleaning detergent Martha had used on the floor and cabinets, and realized that the kitchen was sparkling. Then he took a peek in the oven, and saw the tenderloin, looking and smelling fantastic. "Harrumph," he grunted. "Another meal to ruin with your company today," he said to an absent Martha.

He then went into the living room to see Jan. "Hello, son," he said. "How was your day?"

Jan looked up from the homework he was doing on the floor. "It was really good!" he replied. "I can't wait till dinner. Mama's in a good mood today!" He was hoping with all his heart that they would not fight today.

Martha came out of the bathroom and checked on the roast. Then she went into the living room where the other two were, Griswolt now sitting on the sofa. "Hi Griswolt," she said with a smile that took him by surprise. "I made a nice dinner for us tonight."

"So I see," said Griswolt, warily.

Martha went right up to Griswolt and shocked him by bending over and giving him a hug and a kiss on the cheek. "I am so sorry for the way I have been, dear," she said to an astonished Griswolt.

He in fact tightened at her touch. *She puts me through hell for a solid month, and I'm supposed to act like everything is normal?* Then he realized what he had just thought. The horrible month she had subjected him to was not remotely close to the month of hell in the torture room she had experienced. *Still —*

Martha sensed the obvious emotional distance that Griswolt had. It did not dissuade her. She smiled pleasantly and said, "I'll go back to my cooking. You two can have fun in here."

They both watched this new person walk out of the living room and into the kitchen. Griswolt looked as if he were in a trance. He kept staring towards the kitchen after she left. He looked confused.

Jan silently watched the scene, studying his father's reaction. "I think she's getting better," he offered to his dad.

Griswolt blinked and shook his head, as if Jan just woke him up. "We'll see, he said." It was too good to believe. *Nobody changes overnight,* he thought to himself.

The dinner was actually quite nice. Martha tried to make small talk, but Griswolt just passively went along with it. *Something's going to go wrong,* Griswolt kept thinking to himself.

After dinner, while still at the table, Martha brought out the yama wine, chilled and ready to go.

Griswolt felt like he was being trapped. *Maybe she wants to get me drunk so she can kill me,* he thought.

Martha could see that she was getting nowhere with Griswolt. *I know what he likes,* she thought, and she got up to rub his shoulders from behind. "Here dear, you look so tense. Let me —"

Griswolt jumped out of his chair as she put her hands to his upper shoulders to massage them. "Don't! Just don't," he barked, shaking his head. He backed away from the table, and moved to another part of the kitchen. He looked at her in confusion and anger. "How — how do I know you won't stab me?"

Martha looked at him, and was tempted to respond in kind. *Because if I wanted to stab you I would have done it already, you idiot!* These thoughts and others came immediately to her mind, but she was keeping them to herself now. *I won't let my dragon rise,* she thought to herself.

Martha took a deep breath, and said, "I'm feeling much better, Griswolt, and I wanted to share it with you."

Griswolt believed her for a moment, and then spat out, "Share it with yourself! I've been living without it for a month now. I don't need it now, and I don't need you!" He left the kitchen in a huff, and went back to the bedroom, as he had not changed out of his uniform yet.

As soon as he was out of the kitchen, Martha found herself fuming. "Of all the ungrateful — I *should* have stabbed him," she said, gritting her teeth. She found herself looking at a knife on the table, and got a mental flash of grabbing it, and running into the bedroom to stick it into Griswolt. Then she realized the dragon had indeed been raised. *Shit! I've lost it. Help me, please,* she prayed silently. The dragon started to subside.

It was then that Martha realized, *Griswolt has a dragon of his own.* She muttered, "With what I've put him through this month —"

She looked at Jan, who had been observing the entire episode. "Jan, what do we do about Daddy's dragon?" The absurdity that she was asking a child crossed her mind. "I can't tell him about love, so what do I do?" She was not really expecting an answer, but she received one.

Jan looked at her thoughtfully. "Dad's been pushing his dragon down, because if his dragon rose, you both would be crazy, and something even worse would happen here." He paused to think and said, "Now that your dragon is smaller, his dragon can rise without fear of disaster. His dragon can get even now."

Martha stared at Jan in amazement. "How do you come up with these things?" she asked incredulously.

Jan shrugged his shoulders, "It just makes sense. I see it," he said. He went back to picking at what was left on his plate.

Martha studied him. He seemed to know what he was saying. *I took his advice, and it helped me today,* she thought. "Do you have any idea about how we can bring Daddy's dragon down?" she asked.

Jan thought about it. "Love," he said. "You can use love for Daddy, since he can't use it for himself." He chewed on another bite. "It won't help right away, but it will help." Jan mused a bit more, and then he said, "His dragon will come back at you at first. Then he'll stop the dragon, because he really loves you." He looked at Martha and smiled. "He'll love you again, and his dragon will get weaker."

Martha was sitting with her mouth agape, in a daze. She gazed at Jan, who was still nibbling, wondering. He made so much sense — it seemed so simple. Was it true? *Am I just listening to the simple ramblings of a child? It seems so right. What else can I do?*

"Jan, I need you to help me with this, OK?"

Jan looked up at her, "Sure Mama, I already know what I need to do."

"What's that, dear?" Martha asked.

"Give him love," Jan said, and he smiled at her, "Just like you."

Martha's heart warmed. "You are one amazing little boy," she said with a smile as she tenderly rubbed his crest.

Jan looked pleased. "I'm going to go see Dad," he said, and he hopped off his chair, and went back to their bedroom.

Chapter Twelve

Salom, Interrupted

he past year had gone by much too quickly for Rebecca and Jan. Martha had a difficult time of her own, still upset over Rebecca's recent departure.

It was a day off work. Martha was in the living room, listening to some NOV sanctioned music on the radio. She did not care to expend the energy on the music player. Jan was at school. He would not be seeing Rebecca there anymore. Martha sighed one of many since Rebecca's departure a couple of weeks ago. Jan was still very depressed at the loss of his best friend. Rebecca's mother Salom had returned home a week ago, but Martha was giving Salom time to settle before she visited. To be truthful, she resented Salom for Rebecca's unfortunate departure.

"Salom, what —" She could not think of the words — no one was there to hear them anyway. She tried a few endings — "why would you come back, knowing what was going to happen to Rebecca?" That was a good one, but a line she would never use. "What kind of person are you now? How sane are you now?" Martha was emotionally drained from attempting to sort out the meaning of a little girl that she dearly loved, being sent off to — God only knows. She would have done anything to keep Rebecca with her own family at her young age, but NOV law prohibited it.

Then there was Hais. He had to make her cry on her last night home. What a bastard, Martha thought. She remembered Salom again, now stuck with Hais. *I really should do something. After all, it's been a week since she returned.*

Martha brightened up with a simultaneous statement, "I know! I'll bake a cake, and invite her over. I'm sure she's ready to get out of there for a bit." She had just purchased the latest cake mix that had a new highly refined yama fraction. It was supposed to produce the lightest and fluffiest cake.

After preparing it, Martha spent the rest of the morning and early afternoon cleaning while the cake was baking in the oven. Hais was not home, so this would be a good time to go over to Salom's house. When the cake cooled down and was finished, Martha went over to see if Salom might want to come out. She went to Salom's door, and knocked. She waited for a while, and knocked again. There was no answer. "Salom, it's me, Martha!" she called out towards the door. *Do I hear something inside?* Then she heard footsteps coming up the stairs. Salom opened the door.

Martha was prepared for something bad, but nothing like this. It was not Salom. The wretch in front of her did not even seem to recognize Martha. "Salom, it's me, Martha," she said with care.

Salom stood there, staring at Martha's chest. "Martha?" she asked as though to herself.

Martha bent down to meet Salom's gaze, and with a smile said, "I wanted you to come over to my house. I've baked a cake for you."

Salom's face gave way to a slight smile. "Cake?" She took a furtive glance at Martha's eyes. "For me?" Then she looked at Martha again, with heartbroken eyes, and said, "Martha?" Salom was bent over, as if she was ducking, and she was covered with scars upon scars. Her weight was that of a child.

A noisy four-contiss cargo wagon came by, and it startled Salom. She showed a fleeting look of dread at the loud sound as it passed.

Martha reached out to hold Salom's hand. Salom began to pull back, but Martha insisted, and Salom did let her hold her hand. "Why don't you come out of the house for a while? You've been in there for a week now, you know."

"It's been the best week of my life," Salom said slowly.

Martha could hardly imagine a week with Hais being the best week of her life. "What about Hais?" she said.

Salom's face got ugly. "I'll kill that keesh if he touches me!" she shouted. She got into an aggressive posture, with her hands semi-clenched, claws at the ready.

Martha thought to herself, *Well, I guess that answers that question.* "So come over, please?" she asked with a charming smile.

Salom looked at her, then at Martha's house.

"Is there anyone over there now?" she asked.

"No," Martha replied.

Salom looked deep in thought. "Ok, I'll come over."

Salom then followed Martha over to her house. Salom was lifeless in her walk, and did not bother to cover her scarred crest with a hood or scarf, as she had always done before. When they arrived, Salom was keen to look around at first. She acted as if she believed someone was hiding somewhere there. Martha had decided to not bring up the prison at all. She tried to lift Salom's spirits, but it was a difficult task. She could not talk about prison, or Jan, or Rebecca, so she talked about Griswolt, and then asked about Hais. "So how is Hais treating you?" Martha asked.

Once again, Salom instantly changed. "Hais? I'll kill that stick!"

Well, I guess Hais is definitely off limits, Martha thought.

Just then, Jan came home from school. He would come home from his new school about thirty minutes before his mother, so there was no more need for daycare. When the door opened upstairs, it made Salom jump, and she went into a stiff defensive posture, still sitting at the kitchen table.

Jan came romping down the stairs as usual, but stopped cold when he caught sight of Salom's intense stare focused directly on him. He walked down the last few steps more carefully. She looked scary. "Hello, Salom," he said, testing her out.

"What's *that* doing here?" Salom shrieked, looking frightened and cornered.

Jan stopped dead in his tracks. He looked at Martha, who defensively moved in between him and the raving eyes of Salom.

Martha was startled by Salom's sudden change from bad to worse. *I've never seen a look like that,* she thought.

"Salom!" Martha said with a raised voice, "You are not in prison anymore! You can relax."

Salom turned her attention to Martha, and with an incredulous look, said, "Relax? I'll never relax again as long as I live! And it's all because of those," she spat, pointing past Martha at Jan.

Jan was still standing there, at the entrance of the kitchen. He knew he was safe with his mom there, but wasn't sure whether to continue through the kitchen or not.

"Come on, Salom. It's not the children's fault. It's the stupid laws we have," Martha countered, trying to bring some logic to the situation.

Salom took her gaze away from the direction of Jan, and worked on forming a smile on her face. She looked at Martha, and said, "You're right. You were always right." She kept the smile frozen on her face, and turning back to Jan, said in a syrupy sweet voice, "It's all right, Jan. You surprised me, that's all. Why don't you come closer, so I can get a good look at you?"

Jan gave Martha a skeptical look, and really did not want to get any closer to this crazy lady. He just wanted to get around her, so he could get to the stairs that went down to his bedroom.

Martha was thinking about how to handle this, when Salom, whose eyes were riveted on Jan, said sweetly again, "Come here, boy. Have a seat on Auntie Salom's lap, and let me take a good look at how big and handsome you are now." Her voice became very high pitched at the end of her sentence, and was the definition of creepy.

Martha was obviously concerned. She said, "Wait, Jan." She looked at Salom and said, "Salom, I want to help you, but I don't think you're ready for children yet."

Salom looked pleadingly at Martha, "I just want to hold him, I just—"

Martha interrupted, and said, "I don't think Jan wants to do that right now, Salom. Why don't we give him, and you, more time?"

Salom's face became contorted. She boiled at Martha with insane rage, and started screaming, "You're love-lovers! I know it!" Then she lowered her voice, and repeated, "I know it." She glared at Jan. "I'll report the both of you love-lovers. You'll both fry!" Then she started laughing hysterically. "You're going to fry!"

Martha panicked, "We are not love-lovers anymore! Get out! Get the hell out of here!" She pounded her fists on the kitchen table in right front of Salom, and Salom cowered.

"I said get out!" Martha roared as she grabbed Salom's blouse by the shoulder and lifted her out of her chair. "I want you out now!"

Salom gave a shriek as if she was injured. Martha, undeterred, escorted her up the stairs and out of the house.

When Martha came back downstairs, she found that Jan was still standing in the kitchen. "Come over here with me," she said to Jan, while motioning towards the table. When he came over they both had a seat and she said, "I want you to listen very carefully to me."

Jan recognized her grave expression, and was paying attention.

"Jan, you must stay away from Salom," Martha said, tapping her thick, light red polished fingerclaws on the table.

"I don't want to be around her anyway," said Jan.

"No, Jan. It's more important than that. She can't think right now. She may try to hurt you, so it's important that you do not trust her. Don't go into her house, even if she says she needs help. And lock the door behind you when you come home from school, all right?"

Jan promised that he would. After that, he went downstairs to change out of his school clothes.

Later, Martha told Griswolt about Salom, and Griswolt was concerned as well. They agreed that until Salom returned to an ordinary life, she was not to be trusted.

Jan, on the other hand, was not very concerned. He did take precautions, and always locked the front door when he came home, but that was about all he needed to do. Over the next few weeks, he had other things on his mind. One of those things was a new kid that just moved back into the school district. He heard that his name was Barab, and that he picked on smaller kids when he was living here before. Barab was two years older, but had been held back in school twice. This new kid had been targeting Jan's unusual crest. Today, while in the school's cafeteria, he did it again. Barab laughed at Jan, calling him a clown-freak.

Jan did not know how to take this new kid. He had become accustomed to receiving simple stares from other children and adults. Once Jan was with the same class for a while, the kids would stop paying attention to his crest. He could only hope that the new kid would stop, too. He noticed that Barab was really limping on his bad leg today.

Just home from school, as Jan opened the refrigerator — he heard something in the hallway. He turned to see a shadow coming his way and his heart jumped and started racing at what he saw. It was Salom, coming into the kitchen. He looked for an escape and ran into the living room, shouting, "How did you get in here?"

Salom followed him, smiling with incongruently hateful eyes. "I found Rebecca's keee-eee-eey," she answered in a screechy high voice. As soon as she said that, she got a forlorn look to her face, as if she had lost something. "Rebecca," she said into the air. She looked at Jan, "Do you have Rebecca?"

Jan had run to hide behind the sofa once again and yelled, "No! Rebecca went away! Go away!"

Salom became more confused. She said, "Rebecca? Rebecca, come out of there!" Then she proceeded to pull the sofa away from the wall. Jan tried to get away, but she was able to grab him. Skinny as she was, she was still much bigger than Jan. She was holding him from behind, screaming, "Stand still!"

Jan stomped on her right foot with his boot, and she yelped and loosened her grip. Jan ran through the kitchen and down the hallway to his parents' bedroom.

Salom immediately went after him, but stopped in the kitchen. "Here, this will do," she said to herself as she took hold of a heavy meat-tenderizing hammer. "Rebecca! Come here, Mama will punish you if you don't come —" she called out, now making her way down the hallway to the bedroom door that Jan had locked. She started banging on the lightweight door with the hammer.

Jan was terrified, and had gone to hide under the bed. *What am I going to do?* he asked himself fearfully. *A sword!* He found a short sword of Griswolt's sitting next to a metal stick. He grabbed the sword with both hands, the tip up in front of his eyes, and waited under the bed.

Bang! Bang! Salom was using the big black hammer to break through the door. In short time, she had a big enough hole to reach in and unlock the door. Once in, she started looking for Jan. "Rebecca," she said in a stern tone, come out right now!" Then her voice became eerily sweeter, "It's time for your punishmeeeee-ee-eent." She went around the room, checking the closet, and then she turned and looked at the bed. Salom got on her hands and knees, and saw Jan under the bed, sword in hand.

Jan was alarmed when her eyes met his. He displayed the sword defiantly and yelled, "Stay away! You're crazy! I'm not Rebecca — I'm Jan!"

Salom crawled over to the foot of the bed, and swung the hammer at his feet, keeping away from the sword. Jan was kicking at her, and his bootlace became caught on the hammer. In a flash, she yanked hard on the hammer, pulling his foot out from under the bed. She grabbed his foot and pulled him out violently. Before Jan could react, Salom was able to jump on him, snatching the sword from him, then throwing it behind her.

Jan fought, but she had him. He was struggling to get away. "Let me go!" he yelled, futilely.

Salom flipped him over on his back, and quickly sat on his chest. "Now I've got you, you bad girl," she laughed with an evil grin and glistening eyes.

Jan froze, eyes wide in terror as she lifted the hammer high, focusing on his forehead, and said, "You need a scar like mine to straighten you out," and suddenly her expression changed. It changed to one of shock. The hammer fell dead out of her hands, bouncing off the floor right next to Jan's head.

It was then that Jan saw the sword tip extruding from her abdomen, and blood started spilling out from the spot. As she slumped, he saw

Griswolt on his hands and knees, eyes wide open. His look was fierce. "Dad!" Jan yelled in wonder.

"Fucking bitch!" Griswolt barked, and he got up and kicked her dying body off Jan. He turned his attention to his son. "Jan, are you all right? What did she do?"

"I thought it was over, I was dead!" Jan got up and wrapped his arms around Griswolt tighter than he ever had before. "Thank you, thank you, thank you!"

Griswolt was only now coming to grips, and the whole thing was dawning on him. He said, "It's a miracle. My boss sent me home early today — I was the only one."

He paused, surveying the scene. "We need to call the police and report this," Griswolt said. "Let's get you out of here." He looked down at Salom and shaking his head remarked, "We're never going to get that blood stain out of the carpet."

They left the bedroom as it was, and Griswolt called the police.

Chapter Thirteen

Cleansing Day

ill them before they sin!' That's what my dad always says," Rebecca proclaimed, as Jan and his parents were getting ready to attend "Cleansing Day". She was getting along better with Hais now after accompanying him this past summer to the hognot matches.

Martha had been complaining all morning about having to attend this monthly event. Apparently, the local NOV Temple had seven children ready for today's burning. The higher the number they had, the more attendees, and thus higher collections.

Because of WADD, (Witches Against Delinquent Daddies,) there was steady pressure on the various police districts to increase the numbers of child donations. A great competition had evolved between police departments to accomplish this mission. The numbers were published in the local news, thus calling to task the police departments that were lagging behind.

After all, it was a noble cause. It prevented delinquents from living long enough to either kill, commit crime, or become fathers, (or mothers.) This stopped society from breeding more of the same self-destructive people. It was easy to prove in all measures that lives were saved because of this. WADD had been able to increase the child-donation numbers by encouraging random police checkpoints on the roads. Since arguments often arose when traveling, they were able to get parents to donate their children more readily in those situations. Numbers increased.

Martha responded to Rebecca's statement, "Well we know that your father loves to repeat temple dogma, but I still think it's terrible." She looked at Griswolt, hoping for him to give in, and not force her and Jan to attend the event this month. She could sometimes wear him out.

Griswolt had been trying to ignore her, but instead said, "Why can't you get it through your head that I must show up with my family, especially today? This is where I get to show that I am respected by my family. This makes me promotable in the department. You know what that means — more money and prestige for all of us."

"Its politics," Jan chimed in, understanding his father's need to do this. It was plain to see that Griswolt did not like going there anymore than they did. He was busy shining his new and bigger slick black dress shoes.

Martha glanced at Jan with a curious look, and went back to buff polishing the scales on her arms and legs. She had her perfume on, and it made the event seem more familiar.

"We're going to be late to the temple today," Rebecca said. "Dad is setting up tack traps this morning. He's in a bad mood — that's why I came over." Tacks had been getting into her house lately. They were small, typically not harmful, but they hid, were dirty, and spread disease.

"How is Hais doing these days?" Griswolt asked, not sure if he wanted to hear the answer.

Rebecca looked away, "He came home from the bar with someone new last night." She paused. "He still wants to kill Jan because of what happened to Mama. I try to talk to him but he won't listen."

Jan chimed in, "Dad didn't have a choice! It's not fair, and your father shouldn't blame us."

Rebecca just shrugged her shoulders. She was torn over the whole thing, because it was the reason she was saved from the NOV orphanage she had been placed in.

Griswolt changed the subject, "I would like to get there early, and get a good seat with the others."

"Yoicccech," said Martha in disgust.

Not to be deterred, Griswolt said, "Well, the bus stop is sure to fill up, we had better get going."

They all left the house, and Rebecca went home. As they were walking by Hais's house on the way to the bus stop, Griswolt smiled and waved at Hais, who was going back to his shed for more traps. Hais just stopped and glared at them. Griswolt and family continued on to their way.

As they were walking, Jan asked a question, "Why is does he want revenge Dad?"

Griswolt shook his head and said, "Hais is having evil thoughts, and wants to get even. This is an evil world, son — you can't have "getting even" without evil, and you can't have evil without "getting even"."

Griswolt sighed, and said to Martha, "You know, I've been waiting for Hais to cool down, and he's showing no signs of it. Maybe I should have him killed before he kills one of us."

Martha was shocked, "I'm surprised you would even think about taking such a chance!"

"Exactly," replied Griswolt, "But what else can I do? What's the alternative? Must we always be on guard for when he thinks he can attack?"

Martha gave a big sigh. They were about to get in line for the bus. "Just give it time, OK?"

Griswolt growled, "I don't know. It's a hell of a way to have to live."

They boarded the bus, and took the short ride to the temple.

The usual repertoire of choir and prayer occurred in the beginning of the service. The collection for the service took place right before the sacrifice. Then they brought the children out, all shackled to one another. They were dressed in refined black ela robes, (very expensive,) and there were seven of them. They were mostly boys, as usual. The children were rarely very dramatic during the spectacle. They were always drugged, for convenience and predictability. The posture of most was a bit slumped, as if they had accepted their fate. Fear was still evident as some were visibly shaking, eyes wide.

The children were ushered up to a pit that was circular and very wide — about eighty feet in diameter, and twelve feet deep. It was rounded and tapered, so that the congregation could have a good view. It was also acutely angled at the edge, like a bowl, so the children could not get out once thrown in. Most of the interior of the bowl had small holes in it, with small hydrogen fueled flames coming out of them. The sides were steep enough so that when the first children were thrown in, the rest of them were simply pulled in by their common bindings. Then they all slid to the center, and the pressurized fuel was released, causing giant flames. In less than a minute, the screaming would die out and the smell of burnt protein would fill the air. The congregation stood in silence as this occurred, some quietly humming hymns to themselves, others praying, the rest just soaking it in like sadistic iron drawn to a suffering magnet.

Jan's reaction was similar to his mother's. They would just look away, or down, or close their eyes. It was difficult to cover their ears in public, or their noses. Over the years, they could not but become desensitized, albeit never completely.

Martha let go a breath as if she had been holding it forever. *It's over. Thank God,* she thought to herself. *I can't stand this. I have to find out more about the escape. We must escape, or we will be like everyone else here.*

It usually took half a day or so for the shock to wear off Martha, not that anyone noticed. She would just hope that she would feel better.

They were quiet on the way home. It had been a nice summer. Fall was coming, and the air was getting cooler. The insects would be trying to get in the house again, like every year.

Chapter Fourteen

Predator High

an was finally and gratefully into his senior year of school. He was not going to college. With great difficulty, Martha had arranged a job for him in the mining industry, as her father had done for her. Griswolt was agreeable, considering his private opinion that Jan would not make it in Griswolt's field. His was an aggressively competitive environment, and Jan would have needed to start as a trooper, just as Griswolt had.

At eighteen years of age, Jan was becoming more adult looking. He was now just over nine feet tall, and was filling out as well. Jan had been told that he was looking more and more like his father Griswolt, who was still a few inches taller, much heavier and more muscular. Jan had his mother's eyes — big, deep, and translucent green. He also had her temperament, for now.

Jan was sitting in the last class of the day, history class, listening to the teacher.

"Stop it!" he heard his buddy, Buz, say to Sak, the guy sitting behind him. Sak had killed a pladis, and was rubbing it on the back of Buz's neck when the teacher wasn't looking.

A pladis was a nasty little worm-like insect that had hundreds of legs. It had poison in the tips of its many feet, which left red marks on D'otians. These would tend to become infected. Their primary food sources were dead animals or other insects.

"I said cut it out!" Buz complained to Sak, as he turned around in his chair to glare at him. If he made a loud scene, he would likely get into trouble as well. Sak just snickered, and looked back over to his right to make sure Barab was watching and enjoying this as well. Barab was relishing the show immensely. He had returned to this school again last year, after being forced to attend elsewhere for the previous four years.

The teacher, Mr. Rachnard, was busy up in front of the class talking about the round black/white symbol behind him up on the wall. It was the symbol of the Temple of the NOV. Jan's attention was on the teacher again. The symbol reminded Jan of a slowing swirling whirlpool.

Mr. Rachnard was saying, "We all know that the obvious meaning of the black/white symbol. It represents the black dragon chasing, penetrating, and succeeding in attacking and possessing the white dragon. The white dragon, being empty and weak, is under attack by the black dragon for all of time. The reason that the white dragon is able to replace the tail of the black dragon is because of the laziness in the tail of the black dragon."

Jan was getting more and more frustrated with Sak's treatment of Buz. He flicked his heavy pen in the air towards their metal chairs, hoping to make a noise that the teacher would notice.

It didn't work and Sak picked up the pen, smiling at Jan, and slipped it into his pocket, once again glancing over at Barab for approval.

That was lame, Jan thought, disgusted with himself, and Buz.

Mr. Rachnard was still at it, "The return of the Black Dragon will be the return of our salvation. He will rule with an iron fist and annihilate the lazy, the stupid, the love-lovers, and all the useless people in our society. We will finally be purified, and go on to live great lives for all who he allows to live."

The teacher paused for emphasis and said, "The Black Dragon was perfectly ruthless. His name was Ido the Great, a grand conqueror and leader, and he ruled with fierce vengeance against any who challenged him. His armies had been decreasing their momentum in the expansion of his empire. They had become soft. Mercy had begun to creep in to his campaign. Therefore, he went into battle, with the front lines of his troops. He did this to show them how to focus, how to show no mercy to the enemy. Ido died in righteous rage as he slaughtered the males, females and children of Platacs. His own armies had been decreasing the slaughter there because they had been seduced. They grew fond of the people of that enemy nation. Ido showed them their weakness when he martyred himself as an example to follow. His was the motto: 'No mercy to the non-Aletians! Victory is great!'"

Jan was distracted again by Buz's weak protests to Sak. "Why doesn't he do something more than just complain?" Jan asked himself.

A voice popped up behind Jan —

"Fuck this!" It was Huto, a friend of Buz's. Huto got up, ignoring the teacher, and marched over to Sak.

Sak stopped what he was doing and looked at Huto, with a look like "What the hell do you think you're gonna do?"

Huto responded to Sak's expression with a hard openhanded ear slap to the side of Sak's head, the blow promptly knocking Sak out of his chair. Huto was one big guy.

His attention drawn to the action at the back of the class, the teacher stopped talking and called out Huto, and sent him to the principal's office. Huto left the classroom with a cocky look, glaring back at Sak.

Mr. Rachnard started to continue when Jan said to himself, "I can't stand any more this crap." He waived his hand to the teacher.

"Yes, Jan?" the teacher asked.

"Mr. Racknard," said Jan, "Regarding the NOV Temple symbol up on the wall, since both sides are equal and balanced, how can one be more powerful?"

"Why, that's just common sense, Jan. It's the good sense God gives us that allows us to see the true meaning of such things," the teacher responded. He stopped, looking around the room for a moment.

That's it? What typical NOV shit, Jan thought — *and look at him — he's happy and satisfied with his answer. What a stick. Should I mess with him? Hmmm. Oh, what's the use? He'll bend heaven and D'ot to support his position.* Jan decided to drop it, and just make it through class. The school day was ending soon.

The teacher went on, "The Nation of Vengeance is the sole authority on D'ot now. In ancient times, we had been part of a worldwide attempt to instill law and order. Ido was able to convince all four of the races to agree to separate into their own nations, and he expanded the Aletians' land into theirs as well. Borders were drawn, however Ido shrewdly resolved to keep the Tomaks joined with his nation because he could use them to his advantage.

"Wars stopped for a half-century, and then they slowly started battling again. Ido eliminated the green demons from his land, and our successful conquests rose dramatically. Then the other countries followed suit as well, banning the green demons from their lands as well.

"However, the totally corrupt Platacs would not give them up, and suffered the consequences. They were weak, and easily beaten. Some people today think the green demons were a superstition, and never existed. Look up at that wall over there,"

Mr. Racknard pointed to the west wall. Up there was a small poster, a copy of something used as a symbol six thousand years ago. It looked like a hand, its green scales were very pointy, and there was a big "X" over the entire picture. He continued speaking, "Thanks to Ido, we do not need to worry about the green demons anymore, they are extinct.

"Eventually, the fierce Nahabs, the thieving Platacs and the treacherous Tomaks could be tolerated no longer. Ido's descendent Agrimon almost succeeded in wiping them all out, but they kept breeding. It took us five thousand years to finish what he started then."

"As you all know, we Aletians came up with the final solution, and annihilated them all over one hundred years ago. We now have expeditions going into these lands, but progress is slow because of the specialized vaccines needed to live in those territories. In any case, the poison out there keeps getting thinner and thinner, and we will someday be able to start new colonies all over the planet without vaccines!"

"Fat chance for that," Jan muttered under his breath. He had heard through LERN that even with the new specialized vaccines, the NOV colonists had failed. They had been sent out into the far southwest old

Tomak territories. Once away from the fear of a rigid central authority, certain ones would inevitably try to take over control of the colony. Fighting would always break out, ending in mutual slaughter of the colonists and their families, who would be on differing sides of various arguments. The few that survived were usually executed by the NOV for either their success of killing the others, or for their failure to thrive as a colony. This type of disaster had happened on four occasions. Very few people knew about the NOV's top-secret development of other vaccines that were meant for the old Platac territory as well, which was south-southeast. Being next to the ocean, it held great yama reserves, and there were plenty of wild keesh and fish to be harvested there. These would fetch a much higher price than farm-raised stocks.

The bell rang, and the school day was over. Jan and Buz headed out together quickly. They both knew that if they did not get rolling, Barab and his gang would mess with them on the way to the buses.

In the hallway heading to the buses, Buz saw Tama, a girl that he had a crush on. He was not the most confident kid in school, and Jan was always encouraging him to engage her. Buz was smaller than Jan was, and skinnier. Jan, amused, watched Buz as he stared at her walking in front of them.

"Go say hello," Jan said, elbowing Buz, egging him on.

Buz dodged Jan's jabs, looked at him in a panic, and harshly whispered, "Shut up!"

Jan did get some humor out of the situation. He knew that Tama was a LERN member, but of course could not tell Buz about it.

Once they were on the bus, Rebecca and her friend, Ferta, were already there, so Jan and Buz sat across the center aisle from them. Eventually Barab, Sak, and a couple more of their gang came in. Barab and Sak took a seat behind Rebecca and Ferta. They immediately tried to talk to the girls, but the girls of course were not interested in the least.

"There's a party tomorrow night, what do you say?" Barab asked Ferta, who was looking at Rebecca.

"When I want to get drugged and raped, I'll let you know!" retorted Ferta. She was a large gal, and would probably have been able to hold her own against Barab.

Sak looked at Barab for his response, as if his hero were just insulted. Barab took his time thinking of a good comeback. "Why would I want to be seen with a gendra like you?" he sneered.

Ferta just shook her head, realizing that she would not get any peace until she got off the bus. Moreover, what he just said did hurt, even coming from Barab.

Barab turned his attention to Rebecca now. He leaned over and touched her neck, and said, "What about you, sweetheart?" He was smiling sadistically, knowing that Rebecca could not stand him. It made it all the more amusing for him.

Rebecca pulled away from his touch, and now Jan, who was glued to the entire thing, chimed in, "Leave her alone! She doesn't want to talk to you!"

Barab looked across the aisle at Jan with great distain, barking, "Mind your own business, egg head. I'm just talking, that's all." He turned his attention back to Rebecca again. "You sure are a pretty thing. I bet your mama was real pretty, too."

"Ugghh! Just shut up and leave me alone," Rebecca responded, moving as far away from Barab as she could, while still staying in her seat.

Buz nudged Jan and said, "Tell him off! She's your girlfriend!"

"She's not my girlfriend — she's —" Jan said to Buz, as he got up, and stood in the middle of the aisle. Jan had Barab's attention now as he challenged, "I said to leave her alone!"

"Or what? What are you going to do?" mocked Barab, eyeing Jan now.

Jan didn't have a quick answer. He looked back at Buz, who was clearly not impressed with Jan's performance as hero.

"I'll report you to the school! It won't be the first time, and you know it," said Jan, with his arms crossed.

Barab looked at him with simmering rage. "You little tack. You probably *would* do that." He leaned towards Jan and threatened, "You know what I'm going to do with you the next time I get you alone?"

Jan stood there with his arms crossed, hiding his fear. *What have I gotten myself into?* he asked himself silently.

Barab studied Jan for another moment, and said, "Fine!" He leaned back, arms behind his head, half-smiling. He gave Jan an evil stare as Jan, satisfied, turned to return to his own seat. Barab could not afford any more "reports" like this if he could help it. He had already been removed from this school twice. He really wanted to get into mining school, and needed to keep any bad reports to a minimum now.

When Jan sat back his seat, Buz was smiling in approval.

In a short while, they arrived at Jan's bus stop. Jan, Rebecca, and Buz got off the bus. Buz said, "Great job with Barab in there, Jan. I think he's getting the message."

"I don't think that's the end of it," replied Jan. He looked at Rebecca. She was glowing.

"Oh Jan, thank you! You're my hero!" With that, Rebecca went right up to an unready Jan, and planted a big kiss on his lips, surprising Jan, and astonishing Buz.

Buz said, "I'm out of here," and immediately left for home. Such public or even private intimacy was alien to him, as well as most citizens. Still, on the way home, he could not get the image out of his head. He wondered what it would be like if Tama, the object of his affection, did something similar to him.

Rebecca was still holding on to Jan just as Buz left. *She looks different,* Jan thought. *She's looking at me like I'm a steak.* It made him feel — uncomfortable — *what is that look?*

Rebecca did indeed have a different shine in her eye. Something about the episode on the bus had stimulated her. After all, she *had* been laying hints on Jan of late. Indeed, for the past year, her attitude towards Jan had been changing towards something more — close. Now, still holding onto Jan, they were looking into each other's eyes. Rebecca move to kiss Jan again, more slowly this time. As her lips touched his, he began pulling away.

Rebecca stopped, and became embarrassed. She looked down and said, "Oh I — I don't know what came over me!" She smiled and lifted her head, letting go of her hold on Jan.

Jan was a little shocked. *I didn't see that coming. I wasn't ready.*

"Rebecca," he said, "I can't do that — why would you think — it's too —" He paused, "It's so different. You're acting different, and it's weird."

He doesn't get it, Rebecca thought. *What an idiot.* Suddenly Rebecca felt angry.

"You're the one that's weird!" she retorted, and feeling awkward, she departed for her home. On the way home, she wondered if he was gandy. The NOV had no place for such. As a minority, they were targeted and removed from society. Homosexuals were not given DeathBT, but were summarily executed. Female gandies hid more easily, and were somewhat tolerated, if not used, by the NOV brass. They could sometimes obtain waivers for use in the temples and the torture rooms. Applying for the waivers was obviously risky. This was, after all, the Nation of Vengeance.

Jan stood there, watching Rebecca walk away. Even though they were going the same direction, he let her get ahead of him. He was confused. *I love Rebecca, but I don't feel that way about her. Why don't I feel the same with her as the other girls? Why? I don't know why, but it would be a mistake. It would change everything. I would lose her — she would become someone else.*

He heard the Guide chime in, calmingly blending in with his mind's ear, *"What you would lose would be the relationship you now have. It would become conformed to something more common in this world — though all relationships have their unique harmonics. It could become binding to the point of lifetime acceptance and devotion, or eventual rejection of the obligated relationship. The outcome cannot be but be one or the other, and either one can result in love or hate. This can be extremely hard, and actually not necessary, considering love is there already. The freedom to choose is there now, but changes dramatically if you have offspring. New sets of lovingly obligated relationships form."* Jan knew what he said was true.

After a while, Jan continued home. It was less than three blocks down the road from the school bus stop. He passed by some kids picking on a smaller kid across the street, but he just let it go. One confrontational involvement was enough for one day.

When Jan made it through his front door, and into the kitchen, it was like entering a different world. His mother was home early, and was baking some fresh yama bread. She occasionally did this, and Jan loved the smell of it. There was some music playing, and Martha greeted him with a smile and a hug. It was as if the harsh world outside the house was left behind, and something closer to heaven waited inside. He felt warm and good.

"I'm going to get my homework done fast today. I want to study your writings tonight," Jan said to Martha, as he took a seat in the kitchen. "I think I know who some of the LERN members are in school. I know two for sure, because of our meetings. I want to ask for copies of what they may have."

Martha had begun to introduce Jan into the LERN meetings she attended. She was not keen on him initiating such contacts on his own, considering the consequences. "I don't want you talking to anyone yet, Jan. You know it's too dangerous," she warned.

Martha had not yet told Jan of the secret signal they would give each other. It was simply the scratching of the left thumb, followed by the scratching of the right thumb. The code would change every so often because the NOV would eventually discover it. The NOV in turn would use the signal to trap as many as they could before it was exposed that they had the code.

Jan opened the refrigerator and retrieved some gendra cheese. With that and a slice of bread, he pulled his books out onto the kitchen table, and proceeded to study for an impending math test. By the time dinner was ready, he had gone through his homework.

He and Martha had an enjoyable dinner, and Jan dominated the conversation by obsessing on retrieving more writings from Martha's friends. She was happy that Jan had such a strong interest in LERN. She deeply felt that he would be able to contribute to the cause.

After dinner, Jan was ready to do what he really wanted to do — go over the writings again. Griswolt would be out late tonight, so Jan could study them uninterrupted in his parent's bedroom. Martha refused to let him take them out of her room, so he had started copying them by hand. Jan had a hiding place of his own, behind his bed.

At school the next day, Jan's last class was third level mathematics. The test was tough, but he got through it all right. He had begun to notice lately that the teacher, Ziba, had been studying him. It made him feel uncomfortable when he saw the intensity of her eyes. Jan was accustomed to people staring at his crest, but this was different. *It seems as if she likes me,* he thought to himself. *So why does she stare?* After class ended, he went to meet up with Buz before they headed to the buses.

Since Buz was coming out of chemistry class, they left by way of the smaller, back stairway. Buz said, "I'm meeting up with Huto tonight after dinner. You want to come over?"

Jan had other plans, and replied, "Let me see what's up when I get home, I've got a ton of homework." Huto was Buz's old friend, anyway. As they rounded the fourth floor turn going up the steps, they heard the floor door open behind them, with a few students coming out.

"Well, look what the emui dragged in," exclaimed Barab with sinister delight. "Grab them!" Sak and two others dashed after Jan and Buz, who had already begun running up the stairs. Sak got there first, grabbing Jan, and pulling him down by the ankles. Buz was still running up the stairs.

Barab didn't care about Buz for the moment. He wanted Jan. The others were holding Jan down, while he struggled to get free. Barab walked up the stairs with his distinctive limp.

Buz stopped running about twelve steps up, and did not know what to do. They were not after him now.

Another group of students came through the door. Huto was among them. Huto saw Buz, took a look at the situation and stormed over to Barab — fists clenched, and barking, "Let him go, now!" Huto was with a couple of his friends from the hognot team, and Barab responded with, "Shit!"

They released Jan. It was then that Ziba and another teacher came into the stairway to see what the commotion was. Barab and his gang took off up the stairs past Buz.

Jan was brushing himself off. "Thanks a lot," he said to Huto.

"Don't expect me to bail you out next time," Huto said, and then he looked up at Buz, and said, "You OK?"

"Yeah, I'm good. Thanks buddy, I don't know what would have happened if you hadn't shown up," Buz said, shaking his head.

"Don't mention it — we're still on for tonight, right?" Huto asked, and then he looked back at Jan with no little scorn. He thought Jan was a wuss, an emui. He did not like seeing his old friend Buz hanging with Jan. It made Buz look weaker than he usually looked.

"You bet," said Buz.

Ziba recognized what just took place. She glanced at Jan, and then back at the teacher who was with her.

Jan looked at her, anticipating that she had something to say. She did.

"Jan, would you come to my office after school tomorrow?" Ziba asked. "I would like to go over some of your math with you."

Jan was confused as to why a meeting was necessary, but said, "Sure, should I bring my books?"

"No, I have some other ones for you," she replied, rather furtively.

It was Jan's turn to study *her* now. *Her smile looks real enough,* he thought. He replied, "OK, we'll see you tomorrow," and smiled back at her. When he did, it almost seemed as though her eyes sparkled for a moment.

Buz said, "C'mon, Jan, we're going to miss the bus."

So they went on their way, and did indeed miss the bus. Their homes were only a thirty-minute walk away, so they started following the smallish but well-maintained brick road that ran along the school there. There were a number of housing subdivisions nearby and they passed many of the mounds of the homes while on their walk. In this area, they used plain uncolored gravel over the homes and yards, and most were fenced. Eventually it became sparser for a while, with a few businesses or construction sites along the way.

"You should come over tonight," said Buz, as he gave a stone a side-armed throw up ahead and watched it bounce.

"I dunno," Jan replied, "I don't think Huto likes me much."

"He's just jealous 'cause you ace every test, and he's struggling to get into Party Management College. He wants his dad's life, enough income to qualify for two wives, and the lifestyle that comes with being a party boss. That's why he wears that neckcloth all the time. He thinks it will help, somehow." Buz knew Huto well because they grew up as neighbors before Buz moved into Jan's neighborhood on the east side of town.

They had walked about halfway home. Jan and Buz were passing a parked buckboard loaded with scrap and did not see as Barab, Sak, and another guy popped out from behind it. Within seconds, they were on Jan and Buz. Barab noticed earlier that they had not made it to the bus, so he and his posse got off early in hopes of ambushing Jan and Buz as they walked home. He was right.

Because of the element of surprise, Barab managed to snag Buz because he was the closest, while Sak and the other guy caught and were holding Jan.

Barab had Buz down on his back, pinned by Barab's much heavier frame. He looked at the other two holding Jan, and ordered, "Hold him — I'll get to him next!" They were at a construction site, and there were piles of sand around them. Barab grabbed a handful, and started shoving it into Buz's mouth, choking him.

Jan saw something out of the corner of his eye as he struggled to free himself from both of his attackers who each had a tight grip on both of his arms.

"You're going to kill him!" Jan yelled at Barab. "Let him up! He can't breathe!"

Barab paid Jan no mind and continued holding his hand over Buz's sand-stuffed mouth.

Jan violently yanked the guy on his left towards him, and managed to head-butt him sharply in the nose and right eye. Startled, his grip loosened, and Jan immediately stomped on Sak's shin and foot, causing Sak to release his hold momentarily so that Jan could break free, and Jan ran to what he saw in the sand.

It's there! Jan rejoiced as he pulled a shovel out from the sand and came out swinging it wildly at the pair, who immediately backed off. Jan ran over to Barab who was just becoming aware of this, and cracked him hard with the shovel on the side of his turning pulpy face. Then he smashed Barab repeatedly on the head and back, until Barab — screaming, cut, and bleeding, jumped up and ran to the others. Jan was raging, screaming, coming right after them and still swinging the shovel. They were all running. After it looked like they were really gone for certain, he stopped, and remembering Buz, went back to him. Buz was sitting up now, spitting out the sand and choking.

They could still hear Barab, screaming, from further away now, "You wait, this isn't over! I'm going to get you! I'll get even —"

"I can't believe it!" Buz said, still catching his breath in between coughing up and spitting sand, "I thought I was dead meat." Then he looked at Jan and realized, "You saved my life." He looked like he was trying to process it. "You saved me! You watch — I'll tell Huto about this tonight, and he'll change his mind about you — he'll have to!"

"Right now I don't care," Jan replied. "I'm just glad it's over. Let's go home."

He took the shovel with them, just in case.

Chapter Fifteen

Growing Pains

he next school day was rather uneventful. After math class, (which was in the middle of the school day this day,) Ziba asked Jan to come up to her desk at the end of class. "Are we still on for the end of the day?" she asked, expectantly.

"That's my plan," Jan replied. "Can I ask what this is about?" he asked.

"I would rather wait until then," Ziba replied, smiling.

Jan spent the rest of the day wondering what she wanted. *It can't simply be about math,* he thought. When Jan saw Buz later, he said, "I won't be coming home on the bus today, I'm meeting with Ziba."

Buz was puzzled, and mused on the reason asking, "What's she want, anyway? You get good grades."

Jan just shrugged his shoulders and said, "I don't know, but it seems important to her." They parted ways for their respective classes. Eventually the school day ended, and Jan went to Ziba's classroom.

He knocked on the door, and Ziba called out for Jan to enter. He came in, and she was at her desk working on some class work. She looked up, motioned to the chairs in front of her desk and said, "Please, have a seat,

Jan." She put down her pen, and looked at him. For a short while she did not do anything but sit and smile at Jan.

Jan didn't know what to do, so he just smiled back. He noticed she was scratching her hand.

"Do you know what this means, Jan?" Ziba asked as she saw Jan glancing at her hands.

"Do you mean your hand itches?" Jan asked.

Ziba laughed, and stopped scratching her hand. Then her demeanor became more serious. "I noticed that Rebecca and Tama are friends of yours. I know Tama very well." She searched Jan's eyes for any expression of recognition.

Jan fidgeted in his seat, "I thought we were going to talk about math," he said.

Ziba looked disappointed with Jan's response. "We'll get to that in a bit," she said. "I have been watching you, Jan. Do you ever feel like you are different from the others in this school? I mean, *really* different?"

Jan wondered where this was going, but he bit, "Yes, I feel very different. I feel like a fish out of water. I don't like it, but I'm about to graduate anyway, so it's no big deal."

Ziba paused. She picked up her pen again, tapping it lightly, looking for the right words. "Why have you chosen Tama and Rebecca as friends?"

"Well," Jan thought aloud, "Rebecca has been my neighbor since I was a baby, and Tama —" He realized that the only reason he knew Tama is because of LERN meetings. It was the only thing they had in common.

Seeing the perplexed look on Jan's face when it came to Tama, Ziba moved in for the kill. "Well, what is it about Tama?"

"She's pretty," Jan lamely lied. "That's all."

"That's all?" Ziba responded with a kind smile. She said, "Surely there's more to it than that," testing Jan's response. This had to be done very carefully. "Where did you first get to know her? I can't see anything you two have in common, or am I missing something?"

Jan had a flash of intuition. *Is Ziba really headed there?* Jan asked himself. *Does she know about us? This doesn't feel like an interrogation.*

He studied her. *What is it about her? She seems so calm, comforting. Loving. Loving?*

Ziba just sat there, quietly waiting on Jan to make the next move. His reaction to her deeper questioning about Tama told her that Jan was holding back, but she waited patiently.

Jan was beginning to entertain the thought that she may be in LERN. Either that, or she was searching out LERN members for arrest. *No,* he thought, *she doesn't look or act the type to be with the police.* He answered her question. This time, he gave her a clue, and wanted to see her reaction. "I met Tama at some meetings."

Ziba took a deep, happy breath, and slowly let it out. "What kind of meetings?" she asked.

"You tell me," Jan replied, with a smile on his face, waiting expectantly for her response.

"Are they meetings where you can be yourself?" Ziba asked.

"Yes, unless myself is a keesh," Jan replied, jokingly.

"Are the meetings secret?" Ziba asked further.

This time Jan got a bit frightened. She suspected, and she was feeling him out. *As far as I know, this is a trap.*

He started to rise to leave. "I don't think I want to talk any more, I need to get going," he said, hoping to get out fast before he regretted it.

Ziba had already determined that Jan was in LERN, and did not want this moment to escape her. This unique student was leaving, and he may not give her another chance. "I'm one of you," she blurted out.

Jan stopped, shocked that she would take such a risk, but he had to make sure. "One of who?" he asked.

Ziba walked around her desk, came up to him, putting out her hands, and asked, "May I?" Without waiting for an answer, she took hold of his hands to make the smallest of love circles.

Jan's face dropped, and he followed her lead, looking into her eyes, as she was to him. *This is interesting,* he thought, *I'm in a love circle with my math teacher.* He was already familiar with this because of the meetings. He willingly joined her for a while, feeling, enjoying the love grow, and appreciating her more than he had expected.

Ziba spoke first. "You've done this many times, haven't you?"

Jan looked into her eyes. He saw the love there that couldn't be spoofed, and said, "Yes." They smiled at each other for a while. It was the first time he had made contact with someone new outside of the meetings. It felt good, but neither of them had really come out and said it straight yet.

"How do you like the meetings?" Ziba asked.

"I really like them a lot," Jan replied. "I'd like to find more writings to study, but they are hard to come by."

Ziba laughed, and slapped his shoulder. "I knew it! I can sure spot you kids! You probably attend meetings on the south of Justilant, hmmm?"

"Why yes, I do," Jan replied.

"That's why I've never seen you at a meeting. I prefer the ones on the north side of town. You should visit sometime." Then Ziba looked puzzled. "Why don't you know the sign?"

"What sign?" Jan asked, curious.

"The LERN sign," Ziba said. "I would assume that your mother or father is a member. Weren't you taught?"

"I don't know what you are talking about," Jan replied. "My mother taught me everything about this so far."

"Well, you are old enough to know, and you need to know, in order to be safe, now that you are meeting others. Here, when I scratch my left thumb, and then scratch my right thumb, that's the sign for now." Ziba showed him, and then they sat and talked for about an hour. When Jan told her he loved the Platac writings in particular, she went to her desk, and pulled out three complete pages for him to read while he was there. "When you have more time, you can come back and copy these," Ziba offered.

Jan was delighted at the new scriptures before him. He loved the Platac knack for writing. The text flowed with gentleness and was inspiring in its poetic language.

They eventually said their goodbyes, and Jan went home, in very high spirits. *Ziba is great,* he thought. *I am so glad this happened.*

It was getting darker, and he walked fast to get home. Jan was just about home when the school detention bus passed by, and as he was looking at it, he saw a familiar face — Barab, staring back through the bus window with an intensity that made Jan's heart "hiccup". *No — not again!* The bus stopped, and Jan started running. Barab had Sak and two more guys with him. One of them was tall, a very fast runner, and he caught up to Jan first, grabbing him and throwing Jan to the sidewalk. The others got there ahead of Barab, who was slowed down by his limp. They were all holding Jan down.

Barab was not smiling this time. He had a bandage on the side of his head from Jan's shovel treatment the day before. Barab was raging as he approached them, roaring as he kicked Jan hard in the side. "C'mon guys, he ain't just for me!" Barab yelled as they all proceeded to kick him in the head, face, back, and stomach.

Every time Jan tried to get up one of them kicked his arms or legs, and he was back down, covering his head and shouting. He kept kicking and yelling, but he was eventually exhausted. He gave up, hoping it would be over soon, as he curled up, trying to cover his face and head from the blows. Blood was streaming into his eyes now, and the pain from his back and stomach was intensified with every kick he received.

Barab stopped kicking, and stood above Jan now. He was panting from the exertion, and his blood was boiling. He was in the "predator zone". He pulled out a long knife that had a saw-tooth edge. He said to the others, "Hold him down, don't let him move," and ran his fingers along the edge of his knife.

Jan glanced up and trying to escape, started kicking at Sak, who was holding his feet. *They're going to kill me, right here!*

"Hold him down, I said!" Barab shouted, pointing his knife at Sak and the ones pinning Jan to the ground. They all quickly immobilized Jan, and with the combined weight, he did not stand a chance.

Barab got down on his knees, and ground the side of Jan's head into the sidewalk with all his weight, and put the knife against the side of Jan's neck, getting ready to saw through it.

Jan could smell Barab's putrid breath when he yelled again at the others, "Hold him still!" whilst Jan was still squirming and screaming, trying to get free.

They did not hear an older neighbor approaching, out walking his pedigreed blog. He saw what was happening, and yelled at them to stop, and they simply ignored him. Then the neighbor called out Barab's name, and Barab stopped for a moment, looking over at the neighbor.

"Shit! He knows me!" Barab looked down at Jan, breathing heavily, and sneered, saying once again, "This isn't over, punk." Then he rose and gave Jan two more kicks to the stomach, causing Jan to start vomiting, and there was blood in it. They all then ran off down the street. The blog was screeching at all the action.

The neighbor ran over with his blog in tow and helped Jan up. "Are you OK?" he asked.

Jan got up and dropped back down. He started crying, sitting there on the sidewalk in the dark, spitting blood. His stomach — and the head he almost lost were killing him.

"They're gone now," the neighbor said. He then helped Jan up again, and down the street to his home. When they got there, Jan dragged himself inside.

When Martha saw him come into the kitchen, and saw the blood he was coughing up, she panicked. "Oh my God! What happened to you? We need to get you to the hospital!" As she was helping Jan to the living room to lie down, he passed out. His face was so swollen he was difficult to recognize. Martha wiped off the blood — there was so much of it because of the cuts to his head and neck.

Three days had passed, and Jan had not regained consciousness. His mother and father spent as much time as they could at the hospital, but it was Ziba who was there when Jan awoke.

"Where am I?" Jan asked himself, groggily looking around. He recognized the bed he was in as clinical, and there were electronic devices in the room. "This looks like a hospital." He looked to his right, and saw a figure sitting there. As his vision cleared, he could see it was Ziba. "Where's my mother?" Jan asked.

Ziba was happy to see him awaken. She had come after school each day to see how he was doing. "Your mother was here all day, and just left for the night shift. She will be so happy to see you when she comes in tomorrow. She's a very lovely person," Ziba said, with a kindly smile. "I met her two days ago, here in the hospital. You're lucky to have her."

"Luck?" Jan said. "Did luck get me in here?" He was remembering now. Barab. He winced as he recalled the attack. He became aware of the pain in his side and head. He found himself becoming angry.

His nurse came in. She smiled at Ziba, and when she saw that Jan was awake, she looked shocked and excited. "You're awake, handsome!" She looked at the teacher, and asked, "When did he wake up, Ziba?"

Ziba responded, "Just a few minutes ago, Rachel. He seems all right."

The nurse walked over to Jan's bedside, and checked his vitals. "You poor thing. Nobody deserves this — nobody." She stroked his crest in a caring manner that was unusual from a stranger. "Your swelling is almost gone." The nurse's touch felt good.

It was evident that Ziba and Rachel knew each other well. Jan had been given a hypnotic sedative. The drug was to help with both the physical and the mental pain. Still, he was gaining more alertness. The nurse was an eyeful. *Was her name Rachel?*

Rachel was outstandingly pretty. She appeared to be very young for the job. She had a reddish tint to her crest, and she apparently liked lipstick and fingerclaw polish that was deep red as well. She was a bit on the smaller side, but had bigger breasts than almost any female he had seen before. *Why is she so happy to see me awake?* he thought to himself.

"Here, let me make you more comfortable," Rachel said as she leaned over Jan to reposition his pillow. She didn't mind rubbing her breasts lightly against him. "OK, you just relax, and I'll check back later," Rachel assured him with a sweet smile, and then she left to continue on her rounds.

She made him feel better, but as soon as Rachel left his room, Jan became aware of the pain, and negative thoughts began to slip into his mind. He began thinking aloud, "I'm sick of this. I think LERN just weakens me. I would have been able to fight those guys off if I were tougher, if I had trained, like Dad said. I should have been on the watch for them."

He was becoming angrier with himself, his mother, LERN, the world — and then the thought of the Guide came into his mind.

"Fuck the Guide!" he shouted furiously, leaning forward and shaking his fists in the air, forgetting for a moment that Ziba was sitting there. "Where were you?" he yelled in his white hospital room, then fell back, anger giving way to depression.

Jan's words caught Ziba's attention. "What did you say?" she asked.

"Nothing," Jan sighed.

"I'm serious, what did you just say?" Ziba insisted.

Jan sighed, and perhaps it was the drug, but he decided to tell her, "Sometimes this guide talks to me and gives me advice." He paused, looked at her, and sighed again. "I don't even think he's real now, and he sure didn't warn me about this," and then looking up into the air and clenching his fists again, barked loudly, "Didn't you?"

Jan looked back at Ziba, who looked lost in wonder at the mention of the Guide. Jan went on, "I'm sick of all this, I'm sick of everything. It's never going to change. I wish Barab would've finished the job. Fuck 'em all!" He unconsciously probed the bandage that covered the saw wound on the side of his neck.

"What? Barab did this?" Ziba got up, and now she was angry. "That waste of air! We should have never let him back into this school." She looked at Jan with no little intensity. "I'll take care of Barab!" she said. Then she settled herself, came over to the bed, and patted Jan on the head. "I don't know why, but I feel that you are one special guy. I know Rachel well, and told her how much I think of you. I told her to take good care of you." She lightly rubbed his crest now. "Don't let this get you down. You will heal, and you will get over this in time, mark my words." She then gathered the bulky green bag she had with her, and put a book she had been reading into it. "I really must go now Jan. The doctors have said that all they could find were some small internal contusions, and a few bruised ribs. Nothing was broken — you'll be fine."

Jan, still gaining his awareness, observed Ziba as she was leaving. She looked like she was about ten years older than his mother was. He was thinking, *Ziba's OK. I'm glad I know her.*

After Ziba had gone, Jan started scratching his left thumb, then the right, thinking about what she had said about the LERN signal, when he gradually realized Rachel had returned and was watching him from the room entrance. Her vision was zeroed in on his hands, and he stopped immediately.

Rachel smiled at him with a sideways smirk, and asked, "So how are you doing, big guy?" as she strolled over to Jan to check his pulse again.

She holds my hand so warmly, Jan thought. He smiled, grasping her hand a bit more boldly and said, "I'm doing fine, now that you're here." *This isn't like me — it's this buzz juice they have me hooked up to.*

He could see her ears turn a bit red on the edges now.

She's really something else. Jan noticed that she had almost no sores, very unusual. *I wonder if she's using that new vitamin extract bath,* he mused. It was new, and very expensive. She looked like she pampered herself well.

"How's the pain level?" Rachel asked, as she looked at his chart.

"It only hurts when I'm awake," Jan said with a small grin. Rachel gave a chortle, and Jan started laughing too, but when he did, it caused extreme pain. He bent over because of it, making it worse, and he went into a temporary abdominal spasm.

"Oh brother," Rachel said, "Why didn't you tell me? You need a boost of this."

She went over to the cabinet, retrieved a medication, and prepared it for injection into his IV. "This will make you feel better for sure," she said.

"What is it?" asked Jan, who had picked up a natural distrust of hospitals from his father.

"It's something we give all the time for —" she stopped and glanced at him, "For what you've been through." Then she stopped a moment, turned completely toward Jan, and said, "I know what they did, and I'm sorry." Then she looked down, sadly, and said, "Every day I see the things this world dishes out." Then she drew a long breath, let it out slowly, and said, "Oh well, let's get you feeling better." She then injected the drug into the IV, and he shortly started feeling that "floaty" feeling again.

"What is that you gave me?" he asked.

Rachel said, "It's a hypnotic. It will help you to relax, and she patted him on the tummy.

"It sure does," Jan replied a little incoherently, as it was taking effect quickly. He watched her as she moved the chair back into its place, and started cleaning the room a bit.

"That's a sweet tail end you've got," he said as she bent over to pick something up, not even surprising himself at his boldness. He didn't care.

Rachel turned and smiled with a measuring look. She said, "That's the drug talking, but sweet, just the same. Thanks." It didn't stop her from bending over again.

As he continued to fall deeper into the drug-induced trance, he could have sworn she came over to his bed and kissed him on his cheek before she left.

In the morning, Martha and Griswolt were on their way to visit Jan. They were both on a tight schedule, so they took a taxi. They were sitting on the outside, in the back, as was their long time habit.

"You treat Jan too softly, I have said that for years now," Griswolt baited.

Martha just gave Griswolt a sidelong look, and with a smile, said, "Don't start, we've been over this — if you want to train him, go ahead." She snuggled up to Griswolt, taking his arm and hugging it warmly. Then she said the same thing she had had said many times, "He's just a good kid — it happens sometimes."

Griswolt sighed, and never did have a good comeback for that. *Which is why I hear it so often,* he thought. He swiftly had another thought, "It's because of love." He waited, wondering if there would be a reaction.

Martha usually clammed up shortly after love was mentioned, but she would say something now — "What do you mean?" she asked, stiffening a little, and paying a higher level of attention.

Let's really test her. "Well," Griswolt said, "You must admit that they never quite got all of the love out of you thirteen years ago. I see remnants of it, but I just don't say anything."

Martha, heart rate increasing just a bit, continued listening. She let Griswolt talk, giving her time to come up with a believable denial.

Griswolt continued. "It's not like you are trying to do it, but it does slip through, and that's why Jan is so soft." He was unexpectedly sure of what he had just guessed, which surprisingly frightened him. *Why? She might tell me the truth. What truth? No, why would I think that was the truth? That's ridiculous!* Griswolt abruptly decided to change the conversation before Martha could answer. "I'll get him trained," he said with finality.

Glad that he had dropped the subject, Martha started thinking about how close he was to the truth. *Maybe, maybe he would accept the fact that I am in LERN,* she thought. As the escape was gaining more reality for them, she would catch herself feeling guilty for leaving Griswolt out of it. Abandoning him, in spite of her love for him left her with a guilt-ridden conflict that was difficult to deal with. Still, she put the thought of telling him out of her mind. *I have to think of the others, I can't risk their capture,* she thought.

The rest of the ride to the hospital was pleasant. They were upwind of the primary smelting plant of Justilant, and the air was sweet.

That same morning, Jan felt a little better upon awakening. He was less frustrated and angry as the day before, but yet could not shake it.

The doctor came in, checked Jan over, and told him, "I believe your damage was primarily superficial. No organs appear to be seriously damaged, and we know there are no fractures." He paused and examined Jan's face, probing it. "The swelling in your face has gone down amazingly well, but I am going to keep you here one more night, just to see how your internal organs react to bodily movement. I do want you up and walking around today."

As the doctor was leaving, Martha and Griswolt came in together. After they were there for a few hours, Rachel started her shift. She had already become friendly with both parents for the few days that Jan was unconscious, and they were all delighted that Jan was awake and looking much better. Jan was able to get up, and walk around with them, dragging his IV along.

Jan told them, "The doctor said that I need to stay another night."

Griswolt responded, "That's only because I have insurance. I want you out of here before you get a disease."

"Oh, Griswolt, said Martha, "Be polite." She was referring to the nurse Rachel, who was walking with them. "Besides, you don't know what might be damaged. Let's keep him here in case something happens."

Rachel was quick to agree. "Yes, it's best that we be careful with this guy," and she looked at Jan with an expression that said she was very happy to see him stay.

Griswolt had to get back to work for another late night, so he was about to leave. "I'll be here to pick you up tomorrow," he said to Jan.

Martha stayed on for a few more hours, and they ended up back in Jan's room, but she was to be at long meeting later.

Jan told her, "Mom, thanks for coming. When I'm alone I get so pissed off at everything. I feel like everybody is out to hurt us, kill us, rob us — the NOV, neighbors, students, *FUCK!*" He threw his hands up in dismay.

Martha had nothing, but she tried, "Jan, I have something to tell you. The escape —"

"The escape?" Jan barked. "I don't want to hear anything more about the stupid escape. The only escape from here is death — period." Jan started falling into his funk again. "You've been talking that gendra shit for my entire life," he said, crossing his arms.

"The escape is real, Jan, Ziba told me," Martha insisted, speaking more soothingly now. She didn't want to upset him, but she had real reason for hope, and wanted to give him some of it. Especially now. She walked over and gently touched the row of stitches on the side of his head. "This will heal, Jan, and so will you. I love you." Martha bent over and gave Jan a kiss on the forehead, but had to leave to get to her meeting. A minute later, she was gone.

Jan was now alone, and he got bored, so he spent some time walking up and down the hallways of the hospital, still pulling his IV stand with him. As he walked down the various hallways, the odors went from chemical to outright nasty in some areas. One hallway smelled like something was rotten, another area smelled like old stinky people. He noticed the new, shielded ultraviolet lights in all the hallways. His dad had heard about those on the news. Some big shot sued the hospital because his wife died of an airborne infection she contracted while there. He dug up evidence that hospitals did not install them because they made a lot of money treating those infections. The doctors themselves were amazingly unaware of all this. The ultraviolet lights sure didn't get rid of the all the smells though.

Jan was back in his room in time for dinner. He was still in a bitchy mood, and the food was stale tasting. He was feeling some pain returning because of all the walking he had done that day. After eating, Jan decided to read a magazine that his mom had left there for him, and was planning to do that until he went to sleep. In the evening, they lowered all the lights in the hospital rooms automatically, but he was still able to read with a small light beside his bed.

A little later Rachel came in to check on him. "How's it going, Jan?" she asked sweetly. She came over to check his pulse again.

Jan immediately became aware of the perfume she was wearing. *I hadn't noticed that before.* He answered her, "I was doing better this morning, but I was walking around a lot today, and I'm a little sore now, but it's not bad," he replied, enjoying the attention — and the perfume.

"Well, there's no need for that," she said, and got an injection ready.

"I really don't think —" Jan started to say.

"Nonsense, there's no need to suffer, and you'll sleep better before you leave tomorrow," Rachel said, as she injected the drug into Jan's IV.

After she wrote something into his chart, she asked, "Well, are you feeling better now?"

"Much better," Jan replied, smiling dreamily at her.

"Well, let's get this IV off of you now, I don't think you need it anymore," Rachel said. She removed the needle, dressed the puncture, and put the IV stand in the corner of the room. She turned to Jan in the dim light and asked in a low voice, "Would you like a massage?"

Wow, Jan thought, *this is great!* "I would love it," he said, and started rolling over onto his stomach.

"Wait," Rachel said, as she came up against the bedside, "Let's do the front first." She pulled his gown off while rolling him over on his back.

He was utterly naked, and because of the drug, could not care less. Jan saw the look in her eyes. *Rebecca gave me that very same look.* Somehow, it was welcome, coming from Rachel.

Rachel leaned over, rubbing against him, and stroked his head. Her ears were turning redder by the second, and Jan noticed that her crest was becoming more red as well. Jan could take a closer look at her amazing crest now. Along the top of her crest, she had a small natural split, dividing the peaks into right and left mini-peaks. The fragrance of her perfume combined with a steamy musk she was now emitting, and together were tantalizing.

She worked on his arms and chest, leaning over, and looking into his eyes, kissed him on the forehead, then the cheek, then, pausing, kissed him fully on the lips.

Jan found himself aggressively returning the kiss.

She gave a hungry smile at that.

Rachel then rose up, and slowly unbuttoned her blouse, exposing all four of her beautiful breasts. The lower pair was as large as an average female's top pair.

Jan never saw anything so captivating — he was hers.

Rachel then slowly reached over, rubbing her nipples lightly against his bare chest, and after turning off the reading light, climbed in. She had thirty minutes before the shift change, and did not want to waste a minute of it.

Jan fell into a hypnotic sleep after Rachel departed for the evening. She left so quietly he did not know she had gone. He fell asleep very, very happy.

Deeply, profoundly into slumber he fell, and he dreamed —

At first, Jan dreamed of Rachel. She was radiant, like an angel, float-ing in front, and a little above him. She was filled with a beautiful light. She was pointing to her left, and he looked in that direction.

When Jan did so, he immediately found himself in what seemed like outer space, but the stars were sparse. Rachel was not there. There was a door in front of him, and it was about four feet by four feet square, suspended in the dark nothingness. He felt like he had a choice to make — whether to open the door, and go through it, or turn back. He intuitively knew that this was important — there may be no turning back, once he had gone through the door. There was no pressing need to go through the door, but he was curious. Jan took the risk. He opened the door, and climbed through it.

Instantly, he found himself in the whitest, brightest light that he could have ever imagined. As intensely bright as it was, it was the most comforting thing he had ever felt. It actually held love, and Jan found himself repeating in absolute awe, over and over again, "The light *is* love, and the love is light! They are the same! This light is love. It's love, and it's light! They are the same thing —" As he basked in it, he saw that it went everywhere, and he could see it in every direction, even behind himself, without having to look. Jan had never felt such ecstasy in all his life. "This is wonderful!" he shouted.

Then a thought occurred to him. He looked down. He had no body.

"Where's my body? — I'm losing my body!" He panicked, and instantly, with that thought, he felt a gravity-based "suction", pulling him — pulling him back down, down, down, and into his body. He found himself sitting up in his hospital bed, heart racing, hyperventilating.

"Wow," Jan said aloud, "That was a vision! It was more real than this room."

He looked up with wonder — he could feel it —still holding the opposite of a shadow in his mind, "The light was love — amazing." He sat there for a while, calming down, and then laid back down to finally fall into a deep sleep.

The next morning was truly the beginning of a new day. Jan awoke refreshed, and the day carried the exhilarating feeling from the revelation of light he had experienced the previous night.

He had to wait until after lunch to be released. He had hoped to be able to leave before Rachel arrived for her shift. When he thought of her, he had a block. *How can I repeat what happened between us last night, after I saw the truth about her in the vision? She's an angel, like Rebecca. It doesn't feel right —*

"It is a difficult thing to communicate." It was the Guide.

Jan was surprisingly happy to hear the Guide. "Did you see what happened last night? Was that awesome or what?" Jan exclaimed.

"You made the right choice last night, and Love was revealed to you," the Guide replied — *"And yes, I was there and enjoyed your joy immensely."*

Jan thought about it, and asked, "Does love make you soft?"

"Well, it certainly does not harden you," the Guide answered.

Then Jan had a small epiphany, actually, an aftershock of the night before. He said, "It's because we're not supposed to be here, isn't it? The writings say we are blind and lost. We're supposed to be in heaven."

"Yes," the Guide responded, *"Before the beginning, love was not created for a world that would die — but this temporary world, outside of heaven — this impossible world of survival is nonetheless starving for lack of it. You are the ones that can still bring it."*

Jan remembered the previous day, and said, "I'm sorry I said those things to you yesterday."

"I know," replied the Guide, *"Apology accepted and appreciated."*

Jan went back to pondering the what the Guide had said. He had to put the issue of Rachel out of his mind for now. The doctor came in, gave the final examination, and Jan was released. They called his father, who was to pick Jan up from the hospital. As he was gathering his last few items, Rachel arrived.

Rachel came into the room and said, "So I hear you've been released." There was an uncomfortable silence. She piped up again and smilingly said, "I'm really glad you were able to stay last night."

Jan smiled at her and said, "Me too. It was — really nice."

"Really nice? That's all?" She calmly sauntered over to Jan and put her arms up around his neck. Looking into his eyes, she said, "Here's some more 'nice'," and closed her eyes and pulling his head to hers, proceeded to give Jan a full, long, wet kiss. He put his arms around her and rolled with it.

She was already getting steamy, and Jan, whose eyes weren't closed, thought to himself, *My God, her ears are already getting red! I must be crazy —"* He found himself pulling away from her.

Rachel opened her eyes and looked at him. "Is something wrong?" she asked.

"No, no. Of course not. It's just that — I don't know how to say it." He looked at her, with sorrowful eyes, and said, "It's just that you are so beautiful, and I — I don't feel right treating you that way."

Rachel stepped back, and her posture straightened. "Is this a joke?" She started tapping her foot, trying to compute this. She had never been rejected before.

"I loved you last night," she said, with a distressed look in her eyes.

Jan said, "I love you today more than last night. That's the problem. I love you, Rachel, more than you know. I saw you in a vision last night, and you were an angel." He paused, and looked through her eyes and miles past. "A beautiful angel." Then he stepped toward her, and took her hands. "I want to know you, and be with you, but I can't picture doing that with you again — at least for now."

They were still looking into each other's eyes.

Rachel's face, which had become strained, relaxed with a sudden realization. She tilted her head to the side, evaluating Jan, and with a wry smirk said, "Love-lovers — they come in all shapes and sizes."

Jan was startled. "You know?"

Rachel just smiled her lazy smile, took Jan's hands, and scratched his left thumb, then his right, and said, "What do you think?"

Jan grinned and started chuckling, "Well I'll be. That's great! Where do you go?"

Rachel said, "We attend the meetings in North Justilant, like Ziba. That's where I met her." Then she looked excited, still holding his hands. "You must come! Come to our next meeting, pleeeeaaaasssssseee." She waited for a response from Jan, who was still processing all this. "I'll introduce you to the best people — there's a lot going on now. I have many friends there."

Jan perked up. "Do they have many Platac writings?"

Rachel looked puzzled. "What's a Platac?"

"Something tells me you're not into the studies," Jan joked.

"Oh, no. I just love the people. I get a lot of theater dates there," Rachel replied. Then she looked at Jan innocently, and said, "Would you take me to the theater sometime?"

Jan smiled at her. *What a lovely* — he thought. "Anytime, sweetie, anytime." *How could she have gone through life so untouched by the world?* They spent a short time talking, and eventually Rachel had to go on her rounds.

Griswolt finally arrived at the hospital. They left and went home, using a one-contiss taxi. On the way, Griswolt lectured Jan on the need to learn more self-defense. He also said that Barab had been expelled from school, and would not be allowed to return.

"Why don't you train me, Dad?" Jan asked when the subject of martial arts came up.

Griswolt just gazed at Jan with a pitiful look, and while rubbing his shoulder and laughing, said, "Because I would knock you on your ass. I would hurt you, because that's all I've been trained to do. I haven't been trained to teach." They agreed that Jan would start after his injuries healed.

He looked at his son. *What's going to become of you?* Griswolt thought about it. *He is so soft, like his mother.*

"I'm worried about you, son," Griswolt said. "You aren't ready for the real world, and here you are, about to graduate."

"Well, I'll be in mineral processing with Mom," Jan said. "It should be OK there."

Griswolt shook his head. "There are assholes like Barab or Hais everywhere. You've got to be tough with them from the start. Never take any shit from anyone who isn't above you."

Jan nodded his head in agreement. They spent the rest of the trip talking about the choices of martial arts classes in the area, and about a few "easy attack moves," that Griswolt knew by heart.

Chapter Sixteen

Rachel's Secret

"**W**ell, how much longer?" Rebecca asked Jan, as they rode the six contiss bus to the north side of town. It was an interesting ride until they left the city limits. They were both dressed in the typical black or dark gray leather gear, with Rebecca adding a dash of white accessories. Her lipstick was a bright shade of red — she had been choosing redder lipsticks since meeting Rachel.

The landscape gave way to an assortment of fewer and fewer homes sitting between the increasingly isolated sand dunes— a preview of the desert that lay further north.

In an hour and a half, they approached the area of the estate of Professor Kalep, an archaeologist who was one of the oldest members of LERN. Dr. Kalep came from an aristocratic family that once owned the mines in the northlands. It was a miracle that his family was not simply murdered by the NOV when they nationalized the most of the mines. This good fortune was because one of the Kaleps, his grandfather to be exact, was the brother to the wife of one of the NOV's most powerful senators. The wife had blackmailed her husband into having the government pay the

Kalep family what the mine was actually worth. This was unheard of in those days.

Jan and Rebecca had become regular attendees of these meetings in Dr. Kalep's home for the past three months. Jan had been able to obtain copies of wonderful new additions to add to his personal collection of scriptures. He continued to be fascinated by the grace found in the Platac writings in matters of life, philosophy, and, of course, love.

As Jan and Rebecca entered the house, they were attracted by the buzz going on around Dr. Kalep in the great room, which was just ahead beyond the large, ornate foyer they had initially entered. He was pronouncing, in his deep theatrical voice, "My grandfather lived to see this day, and it is a shame that it has taken so long, but it is now at hand." He *had* to be openly talking about the escape, and the buzz of the forty or so people standing around there increased.

Jan said to Rebecca, under his breath, "See, I told you, this group *is* close to news about the escape."

Rebecca was just as hopeful about the escape as Jan was. There had been many rumors about it lately — expectation was in the air.

Rachel came running up to them as soon as she saw them. "Oh, I'm so glad you two made it!" She gave Rebecca a friendly hug, as well as Jan. Rachel was excited about something and said, "Jan, there's someone I want you to meet. You'll just love him!"

Jan smiled, and turned his head towards Rebecca.

Rebecca knew the look. He was going to be off for the evening, delving into long conversations about everything from the escape to boringly understanding the nuances between differing translations of the writings. She had become friendly with Rachel, although Rebecca was still wary of Rachel's sudden friendship with Jan. She could see that all the males drooled over Rachel. *God, I wish I had a body like that. I wish I had anything like that.* Rebecca and Jan had visited Rachel's apartment after the last meeting, and Rebecca decided then that she really did like Rachel. The bubbly Rachel had so many fish in the sea that Rebecca decided she was most likely not a threat regarding Jan.

Jan went on his way throughout Dr. Kalep's mansion. Rachel introduced him to Lep, a lead technician in Strakna Laboratories, the only remaining vaccine producing facility in the entire NOV. Lep had been in LERN for over four years. He was young for his position, but had been covertly positioned by LERN into the top-secret Platac territory vaccine project. Jan took a liking to Lep quickly upon meeting him.

"Lep's a real joker," Rachel said, nudging Lep.

"Naw, not me. I'm the most serious guy in the world, just ask my mom," Lep replied.

Lep was looking at Jan's crest.

"Go ahead, hit me, I'm used to it," Jan said with a grin.

Lep took another look at Jan's crest, and said shaking his head said, "Nope, too easy." He laughed, and then asked, "Does it glow at night?"

Jan mirrored, "Nope."

Then Lep took a glance at Rachel's crest and said, "I heard Rachel's does sometimes, though!"

That cracked Rachel up, and as they were laughing her ears started turning redder, making them all laugh even more. After they settled down, Jan asked, "So Lep, you work in the lab. What's the latest about the new vaccines?"

Lep became serious. LERN had developed him. They managed to place him in the vaccine lab because he was a young and gifted microbiologist. He had been trained to say nothing about LERN's progress, but it was becoming exceedingly difficult as LERN approached fruition of their plans.

"I'm sorry friend, that's on a 'need to know' basis." Then he leaned in close to Jan and Rachel. He whispered, "We are closer than you know. You've got to stay in touch now, because when it happens, it will happen swiftly, with no second chances."

Rachel then looked across the room of conversing people and said, "Oh there's Dr. Scrib, he just started with our group. This will be his first love-circle meeting, and I told him I would hold his hand." Dr. Scrib was a loner, and was painfully shy with females. He studied self-help books about this, but to no avail. His mother was wealthy from old money, and held the inheritance over his head like a heavy weight. The few females he had brought home did not suit her. He was one of the few D'otians who had to wear glasses, was of a medium height of about nine feet, and was rather lean. Rachel went over to Dr. Scrib to say hello, and shortly thereafter Dr. Kalep called everyone for the commencement of the love-circles.

To do this, they all divided into manageable circles of up to ten people. Even numbers were preferred. Holding hands, they were to simply stand in silence, each locking eyes with the ones on the opposite side of the circle. Each person focused on sending love to the others, and receiving the same. Each one did this by perceiving the "holy self" of the other. Their core belief was that life came from love. The goal was to fill the circle with love to overflowing. There was no set end to these sessions. Those in each circle intuitively knew when they had had enough, and the hands would break their hold on one another when the time was right. When they were done, there was an otherworldly, greatly expanded feel to the group. A feeling of peace, comfort, and easy openness would exist that was not quite so evident before.

After all the love-circles had been completed, they continued to gather into groups, talk, and plan. A secret group of LERN leaders, however, did the real planning.

At the end of the meeting, they all parted ways. Jan and Rebecca caught the next bus going to all the way to the south side of town, along with a few others who lived in the city.

The evening was cool, and it had been raining during the meeting. Rebecca snuggled up to Jan, and said, "I wish we could always be like this."

"Like how?" Jan asked, as he put his arm around her to warm her.

"Like how we all got together tonight, as if there were no worries — and our love circle tonight, it was grand." She sighed, closed her eyes, and fitted herself a little more snugly with Jan.

Jan looked down at her. He smiled because she appeared so comfortable, so content. He raised his eyes, and noticed a large miner, still in his mining outfit, coming home from work on the bus, staring at them with a scene playing in his head. The frown on his face said that it was a dark scene. Public displays of intimacy were a target for assholes.

Jan's pulse shot up, and he reacted with rage. *Nobody fucks with me anymore!* Jan was now pretty tall for his age, and about three hundred and ninety pounds — lean and mean. Jan jolted himself upright, projecting forward, startling Rebecca. His jaw was jutting out, his hands poised to tear this guy a new asshole and he roared, "WHAT?" at the one staring at him, ready to jump and pound the shit out of him if he said almost anything.

The miner quickly looked away, ruffled and frightened by this large youngster's reaction. He did not look back, hoping to avoid the impending beating he now envisioned.

Rebecca, startled, felt a flash of fear — of Jan. She hadn't seen him do anything like this before. She kept silent until it was over. "You scared me," she said, after Jan settled back down.

"I'm just sick of it — he thought we were weak," Jan replied, eyes locked on the miner. I'm tired of backing down, being beaten down. I don't care anymore — my freedom is more important than my life."

"What did he do?" Rebecca asked, glancing again at whom Jan was now staring down.

"His eye wasn't right," Jan replied, frowning. "I felt great a minute ago, and he stole it from me, just like all these fuckers here will if they get half a chance." He waved his hand but the others on the bus were now intentionally looking away from him, even the few love-lovers. Then he settled down, and sat back.

Rebecca snuggled up again, and said, "Well, forget about it now, it's over, right?"

Jan was still staring at the miner. "I've got to be ready for him. People like him are like elas. Always looking for a weakness, and they will always strike. If he sees me relax, who knows? I can't relax now."

They departed the bus at their stop. As they walked down the street to their homes, Rebecca took Jan's arm again and held on to him closely. It felt so warm to be with him. She took a forward look towards her home. Her father Hais had a new girlfriend living there who was a jealous, vindictive thing. When they stopped in front of Rebecca's house, she turned to Jan and said, "Thanks for a great evening. It was so nice," and she put her arms around Jan, and went to kiss him.

Jan, caught off-guard, returned her kiss with an abbreviated one.

Rebecca looked at him and sighed. She had accepted that it wasn't a rejection. She knew he completely loved and accepted her, and that is why she was so in love with him. Still —

"You are so bizarre. Are you sure you're not gandy?" she said, taunting him.

Jan gave her the look that said, "Give me a break." He sighed, "You know, I've told you before. You are too beautiful for me to use like that."

"And you are a sicko!" she teased, tickling him. She still loved him as much as he loved her, and that seemed to be enough for now. Rebecca looked at her house and sighed. She hated to end the evening by walking into there. Her drunken dad's new drunken girlfriend constantly threatened Rebecca with the fire. Rebecca would be eighteen years old shortly, and finally free of that threat.

Jan laughed at the insult and tickle, and said, "I do love you Rebecca." Then he glanced with distain in the direction of her home and said, "We'll find a way to get you out of there." He had discussed the issue at home, but could not budge Griswolt to let Rebecca live with them. "That's all we need, an unapproved pregnancy!" would be Griswolt's immediate response.

They said their goodbyes, and Jan went home for the end of an evening that, considering all things, left him feeling a bit more complete.

Another three months later, guests began gathering at Jan's house for his and Rebecca's graduation party.

People were beginning to mingle, and Rachel had arrived unusually early. She was not her chatty self, and seemed self-absorbed with something. She found Jan in the living room.

After saying her hellos, Rachel motioned Jan over to an empty part of the room.

"What's the matter, Rachel?" Jan asked her when they had a little privacy.

Rachel looked at him, her eyes opened wide to almost twice their size. Jan took hold of her hands and said, "My God, you are shaking! What's wrong?"

"I'm — preg — nant," Rachel said — machine-like, just to get the words out. She was clenching Jan's hands now, looking up at him for some sign of help.

Jan's jaw dropped, and he felt the blood draining out of his face. Here, on the eve of freedom, he was to have this bomb dropped in his lap now, tonight. *Oh brother. Is it mine?* There was always hope that it wasn't. So he said it. "Is in mine?"

Rachel released her grip on him. "Of course it's yours! What do you think of me?"

I thought you seemed really experienced, Jan thought. *Better not say that. Damn. I just wanted to have some fun tonight.* "Listen, Rachel," he said, "I won't run from this. Let's talk about this after the party, though, OK? Maybe tomorrow?"

Rachel sighed. At least he wasn't rejecting her, which was her main fear.

Rebecca just arrived and was still in the kitchen. Jan froze, realizing that the other shoe hadn't dropped. He looked at Rachel in no little panic and said, "Don't tell anyone for now, OK? Especially Rebecca?" He followed with, "Can I not *deal* with this tonight?"

Rachel wanted to "deal" with it for the rest of the evening, but she held back for now. She could be sociable tonight, it was after all Jan's graduation party, and it could wait — for a little while, anyway.

Rebecca had said hello to Martha in the kitchen, then came walking up to the two of them in the living room. She studied Jan, and said, "You look like someone just told you that you didn't graduate. What's up?"

"Nothing," Jan replied, with a voice that was a bit too high.

Rebecca could tell he was ruffled. She looked at Rachel, who had slipped into "social mode", and was her usual exuberant self again. *No clue there,* Rebecca thought. She looked over those who had arrived, standing in the living room.

Most of the guests were LERN members, but they were always careful about their conversations if they were not at an official LERN meeting. Lep and Dom showed up next. Jan had become good friends with Lep, but had not yet met his friend Dom. He had heard that he was a goofy guy, but very smart with gadgets. Dom worked at the vaccine lab with Lep. Dom was a short and wide fellow, and tonight he wore an unusually loose large yellow leathercloth shirt over some baggy green gendra hide pants.

Before he got a chance to talk with Lep and Dom, Jan saw that his buddy Buz was walking into the living room now, and that gave him the chance to move away from the girls.

"Hey brother," Jan said to Buz, "How about we get started on the tuba?" Getting drunk seemed like a very good idea before. It was an even better idea now.

"I'm there, buddy," replied Buz. They went into the kitchen, where Martha was preparing snacks for the guests. Jan pulled out two big glasses, and proceeded to fill them both to the brim.

Martha turned and saw the size of the glasses, and said, "You two had better be careful! The night is young, and you don't want to get sick tonight."

If you only knew, Mom, Jan thought. *I've got to tell somebody or I'll explode!* He remembered Lep and Dom, got another two glasses out, and filled them as well. Jan wanted to retreat to his bedroom downstairs to get away from the adults at the party for a minute, and to avoid both Rachel and Rebecca as well. He called his buddies to come join him, and so they followed him downstairs.

"Dude what is *up* with you?" Buz asked, as they walked into Jan's room.

"I just want to get drunk, drunk, drunk," Jan said, shaking his head.

The others could tell that something was bothering him, and Lep said, "Yeah, Jan, why so stiff? This is your graduation party, bud! Let's party!" He started doing a little jig, and Dom joined in.

Jan grinned at Dom. He just met him, and took an instant liking to him. "So you two work together?" Jan asked, trying to be friendly.

Dom said, "No, we don't work together. He's the slave master, and I am the slave!"

Lep shoved Dom, and said, "Yeah, right. If I could get you to work, you might be able to say that. You've got to show up for work, *and* stay awake to be a slave!" They all laughed.

Realizing they all had to talk above some rattling coming from the wall, Dom asked, "What's that sound?"

"Oh, that's coming through the vent down here. It just started last week," said Jan.

"I can fix that!" exclaimed Dom, suddenly looking like he *really* wanted to do it, right now.

Lep chimed in, "Hey, I have an idea — let's get blasted instead." He fed Dom one of the sour looks he'd give when Dom was being an idiot, or otherwise odd.

Dom said to both Jan and Lep, "Here, let me show you guys something, ya got a magazine?" Jan got one for him, and Dom carefully tore a page out of it. He went over to Jan's desk, and started folding it in strange ways. They all stood where they were, watching him. Then Dom asked, "Is anyone coming downstairs?" Negative. Dom stood up with the folded metallic page, and lightly threw it like a weightless dart, right in front of them. It glided as perfectly as a shooting star, point first in the air all the way to the opposite side of Jan's large bedroom, where it bounced off the wall, falling.

They had all been transfixed on it as it traveled so smoothly through the air.

Buz warned, "You'd better not let any of the adults upstairs see that!"

Any device made to fly was expressly forbidden by the Temple of the NOV. The air was God's territory, and had to be honored. Flying was for God and his angels. Indeed, for millennia, the Aletian religiocracy went out of its way to exterminate all animals that flew. The earliest temple priesthood prophesied that they were an abomination, and they were told by God that they would be blessed if they eliminated them from the planet. This was is why all animals, excepting a few insects, now simply crawled, walked, or swam, "as God intended".

Lep said, "You should see Dom's apartment, he has all kinds of flying things in there! He has some big ones that can only fly outdoors — we have to go way up north to fly those."

Dom beamed at that. Lep had recently included him in on the escape, but never mentioned that LERN was behind it. Lep trusted Dom completely and had given him details of the escape, all the way to the river. Dom was also the mechanic for his uncle who owned an oversized cargo-stagecoach. It wasn't utilized much anymore, and he had access to it at any time, along with six contisses to pull it. They were going to use it to steal one of the vaccine lab's modular units, along with all the supplies needed to build a specially designed one, and operate it in the wildlands. For weeks now, Dom had been working on the jumbo stagecoach for the escape.

For the moment, Jan had forgotten Rachel, but when the dilemma returned to his mind, his face changed, and his posture slumped.

"What *is* it with you tonight?" Buz asked again, looking exasperatedly at Jan.

Jan gave a sorrowful expression towards Buz and said, "I got Rachel pregnant."

Lep and Dom looked at each other in disbelief, and Dom blurted out, "You got a piece of that?"

Lep smacked Dom upside the head and said, "This is serious!" Then he looked at Jan and grinned, "But it *is* awesome. Every guy I know wants to be with her."

It was a little noisy with the rattling sound coming from the vent in Jan's room. They were however able to hear someone making choking sounds in the stairway. Buz peeked around the corner, up the stairs, and said, "Rebecca!"

Jan's bowels gave a mini-implosion. He heard rapid footsteps running upstairs, and took off after her. "Rebecca, *stop!*" he called out but saw the last of her at the top of the stairs heading into the living room. Jan ran upstairs, ignoring the guests, and followed her through the house and into the bathroom, where he saw the tears streaming down her face. He closed the door behind him.

"Get out!" she shouted, as Jan tried to comfort her. "Don't you dare touch me!" She was livid, furious, jealous, and dejected.

"It only happened once, in the hospital, I promise!" Jan pleaded, but Rebecca heard nothing but her own mind reeling from this unwanted reality. He tried again, "I was all messed up, they had me drugged, and I didn't know what I was doing, you've got to believe me, please!"

"I knew I couldn't trust that red-crested emui!" Rebecca spit out. She was pacing back and forth now, in the bathroom with Jan. She stopped and looked at Jan with vengeance, "You son of a bitch! I'm going to report the *both* of you for unapproved pregnancy!" Then she stopped pacing and became despondent, and looked at him pleadingly, "What's wrong with me? Why not *me*? Why *her*?" looking to Jan for an answer.

He had none. There was no good answer. *I have to get Rachel to explain things for me.* "Go talk to my mom, she always makes you feel better." *What?*

"Sure, I'll go talk to your mom, and tell her what a keesh she has for a son! Let me out of here!" Rebecca was adamant.

Jan opened the door, and they walked out of the yellow bathroom together, raising the eye-ridges of a couple of guests that had now been waiting for it.

Rebecca went into the kitchen, where Martha was hard at work, preparing more snacks and drinks for the guests. Rebecca had no one to go to. *Nobody,* and that was the problem. Jan and Martha *were* her family. *All my dreams — gone,* Rebecca despondently thought. Her plans for herself and Jan, together, with Martha as her surrogate mother, all shattered. She had not realized how much she had hoped to be a part of this real family until now, one that supported each other, instead of tearing each other down.

Rebecca was so, so hungry for that simple goal, and now it was gone like a breath, because of a baby that was not hers — one that should have been. She was so terrified of rejection that she did not tell Martha, but sat there in the kitchen, waiting for something to happen to take her mind off the heart in her chest, pounding with suppressed rage. It did give her time to calm down a bit. *I have nowhere else to go,* she kept thinking.

Still, Rebecca was a survivor if nothing else, and there had to be a way to keep Jan. Because she had never gotten her way in the world, she was also flexible. Also, considering the winds in her life, it was a wonder she was not completely broken by now. Perhaps she was.

Jan had gone into the living room, where Rachel was hanging out. She was chatting with Lep and Dom now, but was keeping watch for Jan. Their eyes met as he walked into the room. There were twelve people in the living room now. Ziba had arrived, along with a few "professor" friends from the local college. She and Jan had become quite close over the last half-year. She would not have come, if it were not for the fact that Jan's parents had a phone there. All LERN committee members were on high alert.

Ziba diverted Jan's direction of travel by calling him over to introduce him to her friends. She was always anxious to introduce her new young "find" to her sphere of influence. After a warm hello, Jan excused himself, and went over to Rachel. *Come to think of it, Rachel has gained weight.*

"Listen, I need to talk to you," he said lowly, "but not here."

Rachel was dying to talk to Jan. "Where should we go?" she asked.

Rebecca was still in the kitchen with Martha, and Jan did not want to go through there to get to the bathroom or his parent's bedroom, so the only option was downstairs in his bedroom. Once there, Jan remembered Dom's offer to fix the rattle behind the ventilation duct.

As soon as they were alone, Rachel asked, "What are we going to do?"

"I have no idea," said Jan as he paced around the room. "One thing I know, you have to talk to Rebecca. She heard me telling the guys about it down here, and she's pissed." He stopped pacing, slumped, and held his face in his hands. "She is so upset — I can't believe this all just happened!"

Rachel had recently become very familiar with Rebecca. Looking at Jan, her face showed that she did indeed realize the impact on Rebecca. She could see the way that Rebecca looked at Jan, as well as Jan's connection with Rebecca. Her social acumen also allowed her to predict that their relationship was one that would hardly become truly romantic. Jan and Rebecca had been dear friends for too long. She actually pitied Rebecca, learning of her past and present oppressive history over the last six months. Rachel's own mother died during childbirth, so she never had to go through love-deprogramming school, but like Rebecca, she too grew up without a mother. Her older sister raised her with her father.

Rachel took a couple of steps closer to Jan, and started rubbing the top of his shoulder. "I'm truly sorry that Rebecca was hurt. I want to be friends with her forever, and I don't know if that will happen now."

Jan accepted her comforting, and looked at her, concerned.

Rachel moved in front of him, and put her arms up around his neck, hugging him.

Jan caressed her back, looked lovingly into her eyes and said, "We can't do this. I'm sorry, but you have become too special to me."

Rachel broke her hug, and stepped back, putting her hands on her hips. "Would you kindly tell me what the hell you are talking about?"

Jan thought to himself, *OK say it right, and don't mess it up.* "Do you remember in the hospital? The morning after? Do you remember what I said about my dream?"

"Oh, I don't know," Rachel responded, tapping her foot. "You had a dream about me, and it messed you up." She looked at him with a hurt expression, "I thought you'd get over it."

Jan said, "Listen to me, I hear and see things. I never told you about the Guide. I hear him sometimes, and I believe he is real. I've seen him in my dreams, and he glows. When I look at Rebecca, there's something about her that's glowing, and only I can see it. It's, it's — holy." *There, I said it.* Jan continued, "I have this 'thing' holding me back. I know that if Rebecca and I become romantic, we'll lose what we have now, become ordinary or worse, and I don't want that to happen."

He looked at Rachel, and asked, "Do you understand?"

Rachel said, "Yes, I can understand." She managed a smile, and shaking her head, said, "It sounds reasonable, but what does that have to do with us? I didn't grow up with you."

Jan was relieved that Rachel got it. "I didn't tell you about my vision that night."

Rachel tilted her head to the left and asked, "What, when you saw me in your dream?" She crossed her arms because she sensed something hard to handle was coming.

"It was a dream that led to a vision. When I saw you, you were the bridge from my dream to the vision I had afterwards." Jan paused, remembering. He looked up, "You were an angel, glowing, floating, and you pointed the way to the one-way door. Then I had the most wonderful vision of love and light!" He smiled broadly thinking about it, and stared off a million miles. "It was the brightest light you could imagine." He looked at her, "And you were part of the whole thing — you sent me to it."

"The holy light?" Rachel was intrigued now — it was legendary in LERN tradition. "The love light! You saw the love light?" she asked, and now she was staring into his eyes, trying to imagine it through his. Her posture relaxed.

"Yes! I was in it, it was all around me," Jan said. Then he redirected his focus. "The thing is, your part in the beginning of the vision has become part of the whole experience now. I can see your angel-self when I look at you — just like Rebecca." He was looking at Rachel with pleading eyes, hoping for any chance she may understand.

Rachel crossed her arms again, shaking her head, tapping her foot again, and looking at Jan with confusion, "You are so fucked up."

"Tell me about it!" they both heard from the stairway.

Rebecca came strolling in, much calmer now. She had been listening to the whole thing from the stairs, just like before. She knew Jan, and also knew that Rachel was just as fucked as she was regarding this dude. He would never abandon his child, though. Rebecca had to accept this new understanding if she was to stay close to him — and she had to stay close to him.

Rebecca had a smirk on her face, and she looked at Rachel. "You're finding out how impossible this guy is," and now *she* was shaking her head, looking at Jan as if he was some pitiful thing.

Rachel said, "Oh Rebecca, I am so sorry for all this! I didn't know Jan had a girlfriend."

"He's not my boyfriend," Rebecca said indignantly, "He is my *best* friend!" She slithered up next to Jan and took his arm.

"Yeah, right." said Rachel, tilting her head to the side again, testing Rebecca.

"No," said Rebecca. "I heard what he said to you — he says the same thing to me, 'you glow as brightly as the brightest star,'" Rebecca was now dramatically waving her hands, mockingly imitating Jan.

They both looked at each other and started laughing. "He *is* so odd," Rachel said, shaking her head as they both analyzed him. "Most guys come up with that crap to get into our pants, and he uses it to stay out of them!"

Rebecca busted out laughing at that one, because it was the ridiculous truth.

Jan had enough of this and said, "Hey, I'm standing here, you know." Actually, he was just happy that they weren't at each other's throats.

Rebecca got a look of inspiration, and said to Rachel, "Hey, whatayasay that the two of us go out tonight after the party? You can watch me get drunk, and we'll talk about this guy all night long!"

Jan was aghast. Now *his* mouth fell open.

"Excellent idea," said Rachel, happy that the both of them had obvious power over Jan for a change. She patted her belly and said, "No tuba for you, though!"

All of a sudden, they heard someone tearing down the stairs. It was Lep. He shouted in a panic, "There you are! It's happening!" He looked wide-eyed and terrified.

"What? What's happening?" asked Rachel.

"The escape! It's on! Tonight — *Now!*" Lep was hyperventilating. They all looked at each other and ran upstairs. Ziba had already departed with her friends immediately after the phone call. The only ones left besides Jan's mother were Rebecca, Rachel, Buz, Lep and Dom. Jan did a quick take on Buz. He didn't know anything. Jan knew that they had to get Buz out of there. Martha was back in the bedroom.

Looking at Buz, Jan realized he would not see him again. *I can't tell him. One loose cannon could blow the whole thing — decades of planning.*

Buz was a little drunk. Jan said to him, "Listen Buz, my mom wants everyone out before my dad gets home — he's been in a bad mood lately."

Buz said, "OK, sure. Let me have one more —"

"No," said Jan, "I'm sorry to do this," and he looked at Buz, sighing and thinking, *I have to say goodbye with a lie?*

205

Buz was not so drunk that he didn't know something else may be happening. Too many people left at once, and there was suddenly too much tension in everyone still there. In any case, it was obvious he had to go. "OK, buddy, we'll see you tomorrow, all right? No more school!" he yelled up to the ceiling.

Jan looked at him regretfully, "Sure — we'll see you."

Buz lumbered his way up the stairs, and left.

Martha came out of the bedroom with luggage and went down to the storage room, and they all followed her. They retrieved some big pre-packed luggage she had stored for the occasion. When they got back upstairs, Martha said to Rachel and Rebecca, "You girls are to come with me."

"What about me?" Jan asked, not knowing exactly what was next.

"You're coming with us," Dom said with a big grin, and he looked at Lep. They had arrived in one of his uncle's small wagons, parked outside.

Lep chimed in, "We could use you at the lab, and we were talking about it. We need help loading everything."

Jan looked at his mother, not knowing what to do.

"Go with them, Jan. They need you, and we'll all meet up at the rendezvous." Martha was looking at Jan as if she was unsure of her decision. It almost appeared that she was hoping he would resist.

Jan did decide to go with Lep and Dom. "Well, what are we waiting for? Let's go! We're going to be free!" he shouted, realizing that the time for talk was over, and now was the moment for real action. It was do or die.

Martha slowed the emotional momentum. "Let's pray. I want to say Milchexidike's Prayer."

They all stopped their bustle. If they ever needed a prayer, this was the time.

Martha had them all hold hands in a circle.

"Our Creator,
King of Eternity,
Holy is Your Thought,
Love's Kingdom comes,

Love's Will be done,
In Time, as it is in Eternity.
Give us this day, the fruits of your love,
and forgive us our loveless thoughts and deeds,
as we forgive others their loveless thoughts and deeds against us,
and lead us not into loveless desires,
but deliver us from lovelessness."

"Let it be," they all chimed in. A little quieter now, they departed the house and went their separate ways. Martha left the front door unlocked, just in case a retreat was called, and someone had to get back or hide inside quickly. She deeply regretted leaving Griswolt like this, but had been hardened and disciplined by the years of planning.

After they all departed, there was someone still on the road. Buz had not gone home. He had started walking towards the neighborhood where Tama lived. He would occasionally walk by, hoping to get a glimpse of her. However, while he was on his way, he saw her with a group of others in a rental bus as they passed by him going in the direction of Jan's house. It looked like it was loaded with boxes inside as well as on top, behind the contiss driver.

"Where are they going in that thing?" he asked himself. He decided to walk back, since there was no point in going any further. As Buz was approaching Jan's house from a distance, he saw Martha and the two girls getting into a taxi and leaving. He went over to Jan's house, and knocked on the door. Since there were strange goings on, he decided to see if the door was locked. When he saw that it was not, he went inside to find the place empty.

"Something's going on," he said, "And I'm going to find out!" Buz then went out and was fortunate to hail a taxi right away. "I need to meet with someone traveling up ahead, so I need to hurry. There will be a good tip for you if we catch up," he told the driver. The driver willingly accommodated him.

Chapter Seventeen

Exodus

hile Jan's graduation party had been going on, something entirely different was happening a half-mile down the road. Sak, the skinny, nervous pet of Barab was waiting for their gang to find a place to get hammered for their own graduation celebration. They were to meet in an unlit part of the block — no witnesses for their gathering. He was wearing a full-length weathered black jacket over his usual thin black leathercloth shirt and trousers.

As Sak was standing there, blowing on his hands because of the night coolness, waiting, he spotted four figures walking his way. "I wonder where they all got together," he said to himself, thinking they had left him out of something. As they came walking his way, he looked at them with confusion, because their outlines in the night did not show the big outline of Barab. "I guess Barab is coming later," he said to himself.

As they approached him, they unexpectedly started running.

Sak looked past them to see what they were running from. As they came into full view, he saw the one in front, and fear shot through Sak's gut like a knife. He turned and bolted in the opposite direction, but it was much too late. They had the momentum, and they had him on his back on the ground in seconds.

Kran, the one in the lead stood there, towering above Sak, and smiling quite broadly. "You piece of shit, I got you now," he said through gritted teeth, "Your buddy Tans won't be meeting with you tonight." They all started snickering. "Now tell me about the other night, the one with my sister! What did you do to her, and how did she get those bruises?" He had his heel on Sak's chest now, and there was vengeance in his eyes. "You were the only one there! She told me it was you!" Kran hissed, as he dug his heel into Sak's chest.

Sak was thinking, *Barab, he always has to beat on them, that fucker!* He had been out with Barab the previous week, and Barab's favorite method for a successful date truly was to drug a girl and rape her. Sak had finally decided to join in, and their first conquest together was Kran's sister. They both had taken turns on her, but Sak was the only one she remembered. She was not supposed to remember anything, according to Barab.

Just then, they all heard footsteps coming up in the dark. There was the familiar limp. Sak's heart leaped. *It's Barab!* Barab was already nine feet and two inches tall, and weighed over four hundred and twenty pounds.

Barab lumbered into the area, unaware of what lay ahead. At first, he thought that his gang had someone down on the ground, and was robbing him. When he got close enough, he stopped.

All heads were turned in his direction and Kran yelled "Back off! This doesn't concern you, unless you want what he's going to get." Kran looked down at Sak.

Barab glanced at Sak, and back at them. He put his hands up, "No sweat, guys, I don't want any trouble." He then started backing up slowly.

Sak was mortified. "Barab!" he pleaded. "Do something!"

Barab looked at him, and said, "Hey, it's not my fault your mouth gets you into trouble," as he continued to back up.

Sak exclaimed, "What? You fucker! I — " and was not able to finish as he had just gotten kicked in the mouth by Kran, who had turned his attention back to Sak, now that Barab looked like no trouble.

"You know," Kran grunted, between kicks, "I was going to kill you." He kicked him a few more times, and then he continued, "But after seeing your buddy bail on you," he kicked Sak again, "I kind of feel sorry for you." He looked at his friends. They knew it was their turn. He stood back, and watched as they unleashed their own rage at the world on Sak — but they did not kill him.

The quartet left Sak there, laying by himself in the cold. He stayed like that for about twenty minutes. His head was bleeding, and his neck was screaming at him. His stomach was starting to loosen up, but he could not take a deep breath without a stabbing pain in his right side. He agonizingly rose up, with a deadly eye, and it was set on the object of his betrayal — Barab.

"All the garbage I took from that piece of shit," he said with clenched teeth and grim malice on his mind. Sak was only with Barab because he thought he would protect him — this was the thought he could not allow to rise.

Sak limped home, resolute, his ribs tearing at him, and he retrieved something that he and Barab had built together and he had been sitting on. It was a homemade bomb for whatever they may have decided to blow up. Sak was good at making bombs. It also left a poisonous, potassium chloride-based substance behind in the air as a deadly by-product.

He marched one neighborhood over to Barab's house, and banged on the door. Sak waited, stiffened and in shock from what he had just gone through. The loss of his imagined safety of the gang was much worse than the beating he had just received.

Barab's older brother, the tyrant of the single mother family, answered the door. "Barab's not here, punk," he said to Sak. Looking Sak over, he sneered and spat, "What happened to you — and what's that?" as he noticed the two-foot canister sitting next to Sak.

Sak responded with a mighty shove, for Barab's older brother was even bigger than Barab. Barab's brother was drunk, and not ready for such a surprise, he tumbled backwards, continuing all the way down the stairs. Sak walked into the small upper foyer, and heard the mother yell out from below, "What's all that racket, you bastard?"

"Good," Sak said to himself, "That drunken bitch of a mother is home," and he pushed a couple of buttons on the bomb, and forcefully flung the bomb at Barab's brother who was getting up from the bottom of the stairs. Sak then tore out of there, slamming the door behind him. He did not get far before he heard the muffled belowground explosion behind him as he continued running his ass off, holding his stabbing right side.

It was dark, and he then headed — *where? Where can I go? I can't go home. Barab will go there first.* Sak was still in shock, but the pain from his ribs was becoming much worse since the run. He walked towards the city in the dark, but that was changing. The night sky was starting to peek through the heavy clouds, and the larger moon was full. The lesser moon was close to full, so it looked as if it might become a relatively well-lit night later. As the clouds continued to pass and go, Sak was not very comfortable with the exposure of the moons, and tried to stay in the shadows.

"I'll get a job in the mines out west," he said to himself, as he walked on, trying to figure out where to spend the night. He had a little money on him. He was thinking about joining in the mines the hard way.

His now ex-idol Barab wanted very badly to be a miner, but was determined to take the path his deceased father had, through the Miner's School. The problem was that although the tests were not demanding, Barab still was unable to pass them. Unless you knew somebody who could get you in, or went through Miner's School, the only other way was to start out in the areas close to the wildlands as an apprentice. This meant becoming a "plebe" in a "fraternity" which sent plebes to do the deadliest tasks. Many died in those mines, so they would take anyone who would work. Sak continued to walk, hoping to make a decision before he reached the city. He was able to thumb a ride about halfway, but it actually took him a bit out of his way. He caught no other rides after that.

Deeper in the city, at Strakna Laboratories, Jan and Lep had dropped off Dom at his uncle's place, and were now entering through security to prepare for the arrival of Dom and his oversized stagecoach, along with the six contisses that pulled it.

The dozing night guard sat up when he saw Jan and Lep coming through the front doors. "Hey Lep, what brings you here tonight?" He took a furtive look at Jan. "Who's the guest?"

Lep responded, saying, "We've got a late night delivery. There was a delay earlier, and I'm the one who has to receive it." He looked disgusted. "I should be at a friend's graduation party tonight, and I'm stuck here doing this!"

"Too bad," the guard said. He looked Jan over. "So who is this fellow?" he asked again.

Lep had been thinking about his alternatives for this lie. He opted for, "Oh, he's my buddy, Jan. We're going to the party after this, and he offered to lend a hand to speed things up."

The guard made a thoughtful frown. Then he raised his eye-ridges and said, "Good thinking!" He wanted to get back to his "magazine". He thumped his hand on the desk and said, "Well, you two had better get a move on."

They both passed by him and walked down two long hallways to the elevators.

Taking the elevator down to the seventh floor, they immediately went to the back of the building to where the freight elevators were located. Jan and Lep then took the freight elevator all the way up to the first floor loading deck. When they opened the big doors at the top, there was Dom, with his big grin, waiting.

Jan was impressed by the setup that Dom had. The stagecoach was triple the ordinary size, and had doors in the back for loading material goods, or people, depending on the job. It was quite roomy inside the cabin, and had storage capacity above the cabin as well. Dom had changed the suspension and under carriage, sealing it. It was backed up against the loading dock, ready to go.

"What's that thing?" Lep asked as he was surveying the stagecoach. He pointed to a big box that appeared to be bolted into the top of the cabin. It was almost as wide as the cabin, and looked heavy.

"Oh, that?" smiled Dom. "I scouted out the rendezvous point, and outfitted this baby for anything we might run into. You better hope we don't need that one." He had a mischievous grin on his face.

Lep gave him a funny look, but then their attention was drawn by two guard contisses coming their way to check out the scene. There was a heavy fence separating the guard contisses from the stagecoach and the driveway. The fence otherwise surrounded the entire complex of Strakna Laboratories.

Jan had never seen guard contisses this close. They were fifty percent bigger than ordinary contisses, darker in coloring, and they were making Dom's contisses very nervous. Jan went over to the fence to take a closer look at them, when Lep snapped, "What are you doing? Get away from them!"

Jan stopped and turned. "Why?" he asked Lep.

"They are mean as shit, that's why!" Lep responded. "Dom's contisses are spooked enough as it is."

Jan took another look at the huge beasts. He knew that they could not be mounted or ridden — they were only good for guarding territory. He turned to Lep and asked, "What do you feed them?"

Lep looked at the contisses, and glumly said, "The kind you ride." Then he perked up. "Well, let's roll! We've got a big job ahead of us."

They all took the freight elevator down to the top secret fifth floor. As Lep and Jan were gathering items, Dom busied himself with dismantling the connections of one of the precious Platac-territory vaccine production modules. They worked hard, for about two hours. The freight elevator was big. It looked like they would be able to make it in one trip.

"Well, that's it," said Lep, smiling at the packed and loaded elevator, "We're ahead of schedule!"

Dom chimed in, "There's something I still want to do."

Lep said, "You still want to do that, huh?"

"Do what?" asked Jan,

Lep looked at Jan and replied, "He wants to go down into the bottom of this place and tinker." He was looking at Dom and shaking his head. "We still don't have the time, Dom."

Jan agreed with Lep and said, "No! Let's just get the hell out of here! What about the guard?"

Ignoring Jan, Dom argued, "You just said we're ahead of schedule! Don't worry about the guard. Lep, you know he's sleeping by now, and there's nobody here! It'll only take a minute."

Lep studied Dom. "It *is* a good idea, if it'll work."

He made his decision, "Go, fast, and take Jan with you just in case. We already have the elevator loaded, but I'm betting I'll find more things to take while you guys are down there."

Lep was the boss here, and so it was settled. Dom and Jan took the freight elevator down into the lowest level of the building.

On the way down, Dom told Jan what he was planning to do. "First," said Dom, "I'm going to bypass the safety systems and turn up the heat on all the new vaccines they are making for the wildlands. It will destroy most of those vaccines, so they won't be able to come after us for fifteen to twenty years." He paused to smile at Jan, proud of his idea. The old freight elevator was rumbling pretty well under the weight of the load they had with them.

After seeing that Jan understood, Dom continued, "Then, I'm going to lock up the hydrogen supply, then drain all the hydrogen out of the storage tanks down there. It'll take them at least ten to twenty hours to figure it out and fix it all. By then, half of all the main vaccine batches in this place will be mush." Still grinning, Dom nodding his head, "That'll set them back a while — and the main batches will be their priority for the next ten years, giving us a twenty-five year head-start at least!" Dom thought he was part of some new super revolutionary group.

Jan was rolling Dom's words over in his head. "Did you say 'drain the hydrogen'? That sounds dangerous."

Dom replied, "They have special pipelines built for that in case of emergency." He paused, and looked thoughtful, "I don't think they have ever had to use it."

Jan looked at him, eye-ridges coming together. "I hope you know what you're doing."

"Me too," said Dom, as the doors opened and he began to make his way through the huge, dimly lit area first.

Jan could only follow as Dom traversed his way between stacks of large piping, electrical conduit, and plumbing to one section of the sprawling space down there. Dom pulled a couple tools from his kit, and turned five different-looking valves with them. After he was done with that, Jan followed him over to a big electric panel with buttons and lights.

Dom paused, studying the panel. He looked a bit confused, and then he said, "Ah Hah!" He went over to the right side of the panel and opened it. He pulled down on a big red lever. They heard a whooshing sound, like air escaping, and the place started cooling down immediately. Dom looked at Jan, apparently quite pleased. He said, "Here we go," and pushed a green button on the panel that was labeled, "Ex-Out". They waited. Whatever was supposed to happen didn't, based on Dom's melting look of expectation, and he said, "Hmmm." He was rubbing his chin and studying the panel.

Then they heard it. A loud metallic creaking sound rang out, and Jan noticed the sound was coming from some big pipes above them. The pipes looked like they were bulging. He pointed to the pipes and yelled to Dom, "Does that look right?"

Dom looked up, and his face became frozen. He quickly looked at the panel again, and pushed another button. He looked at Jan, panicked. "We've got to get out of here, now!"

"No shit!" yelled Jan. They both ran the obstacle course of piping back to the elevator, and took it up to the fifth floor. It seemed like it was taking forever. As soon as the doors opened, Dom called out "Lep! Lep!"

Lep came running around a corner. "Hey, keep it down!" he said.

"Something went wrong," Dom said. He looked down. "I think there might be a problem."

"We've got to get out now," yelled Jan.

"But I was about to get —"

"Now!" shouted Jan.

Lep ran and jumped into the elevator with what he could carry, and they took it up to the waiting stagecoach. They all scrambled, filling up the cargo area inside the stagecoach, and piling everything else on top against the railings. Dom had also removed the inner seats for the mission. The biggest item to haul was the vaccine module. Along with a portable power supply and accessories, it took up most of the cargo area.

The stagecoach had already been backed up to the loading area, so the task went quickly enough.

As they were loading the last of the supplies, they heard a 'pop' deep below the floor of the elevator. A breeze started coming up, and Dom looked at Lep with obvious fright and said, "I'm going up front to the contisses. You guys hold on."

Lep hopped inside the stagecoach, and Jan climbed on top, behind the driver's seat. He was in charge of the cargo on top. It was then that he smelled the hydrogen. "I smell —"

"I know!" Dom yelled in fright, and as he gave a crack of the whip, the contisses started for a run immediately, and they were off. They were headed for the rendezvous point at the river, but had to travel through the south part of the city first.

Jan's heart was racing. They made it out onto the main street, and the stagecoach was able to gain some speed. Jan looked backwards at the vaccine lab, wondering what was happening down below, when suddenly a blast came roaring out of the loading area they had just left.

"Yah!" Dom bellowed, as he cracked the whip again.

Lep yelled from down below, "Did you hear that? Dom! What did you do?"

Then there were multiple crashing, booming explosions, and from the street they could see the entire top of the first floor of the lab disintegrate into a fire ball, pushing high up into the sky. Flying particles reached them, pelting store windows and pedestrians as well. Lep climbed up from the back of the moving stagecoach, and went up beside Jan, looking back at the cloud of destruction where the lab had been. His face looked like he had seen a ghost.

"Dom, the entire lab is destroyed! Do you know what this means?" He looked at Jan with severe gravity and said, "Most of the population here will die, and it's our fault. It will take at least twenty years to start producing vaccines again from scratch, just for themselves."

Jan put his hand on Lep's shoulder and said, "There's nothing we can do now. We've just got to get to the river." He looked around at the people moving about — people traveling, working, shopping, planning — and a feeling of remorse took hold of him, but not for long —

Alarms sounded in the city. The boys still had a half hour's travel to the rendezvous. Swiftly, the police were out, as well as the NOV troopers. Lep climbed back down below to keep an eye on their precious cargo.

"I never heard *that* alarm before," Jan commented to Dom, as they passed police buses and fire wagons traveling the opposite direction towards the vaccine lab. "Just act normal, don't drive too fast."

Dom was obviously panicked. His face and body would freeze with fear every time they passed a police officer or trooper. *We've got to get out of the city,* Jan thought to himself. *That's the first thing we need to do.*

A few minutes from the river dock, Martha and others had gathered at the city cemetery. Over two hundred escapees had already arrived in the cemetery, and more were amassing at the river. They heard the explosion from within the city, and saw the flash and dark cloud it produced rising slowly in the night sky, accentuated by the city lights. Then they heard the sirens.

"This is all we need," Martha sighed.

"What kind of alarm is that?" Rebecca asked.

"It's the National Emergency call to arms," Martha replied. "All NOV personnel must report immediately. Shit, they'll all be out now. We've still got to wait for everyone to gather here, and run to the river at the signal."

About fifteen minutes later, down at the river everything had been going according to schedule. The cemetery group was to remain separate until the last minute in order that they may more easily escape if something went wrong at the dock.

Over three hundred LERN members had arrived at the dock, with more arriving by the minute. They were all hurriedly loading supplies onto the boats. There had been minimal security tonight. The two guards and a few workers on duty had been bound and gagged.

A young stranger happened upon them. He had been walking rather aimlessly, and found himself strolling along an unpaved road that hugged the edge of a very high cliff. He had been able to see the river almost two thousand feet down below from the edge of the cliff at its peak. The road continued for a half mile or so, steeply downwards, ending at the dock which LERN had chosen for their departure. It was the last dock before the wildlands to the south.

The youth had come to the river, contemplating suicide by drowning himself. He would have jumped earlier from a greater height, but was not ready for the irreversible commitment of that route. His plans began to change when he saw the gathering of people at the dock. As he was arriving, he hid behind the wagons that were gathered and was close enough to hear what was going on.

"These people are going into the wildlands somehow!" he said to himself. He came out of the shadows.

"Please take me with you!" he said to the first ones he walked up to. "I can help, please!" he begged.

The biggest one there, Winoni, walked up to him and asked, "What are you doing here boy?" Winoni barked to some of the people standing around, "We need to speed this up! Help those folks with the big trunks over there!" Then he turned his attention back to the kid. "Well?"

"I was just walking down here, and I heard you are all leaving for the wildlands," he replied. "Please take me with you, I can help!" He started coughing.

"What's your name?" asked Winoni, considering it. After all, what was there to lose now that they were escaping? *This kid really wants to go with us, we do have the room, and I'm going to need miners.* He asked him again. "What's your name, son?"

"Sak," the youth replied.

They heard gunfire cracking from the graveyard. "Shit!" said Winoni, "That's bad." Then he turned his attention to those still loading up. "Move it faster, and release those boats that are full!"

Meanwhile, at the NOV headquarters in Justilant, Griswolt, no longer having military rank, had been deputized with everyone else there. They all departed with groups of troopers sent to the south side of town.

Griswolt was fully armed, like the others. They were accustomed to the unremarkable arrests of LERN members, but now it was different. The ones captured tonight were packed to the gills with supplies one would take when going hunting. They also had many more supplies with them that could not be explained. The NOV command had quickly assumed that there was a conspiracy afoot that was connected to the explosion at the vaccine lab. Griswolt and his particular group of fifty NOV troopers and deputies were on a search and destroy mission — kill anything that looks like an enemy during the martial law that was now in effect.

Griswolt was sitting near the officer in charge, and overheard that the NOV had just now captured another large LERN group traveling in a convoy. This time they found fifty-three LERN members, all stocked up with survival supplies. They were presently interrogating them, but had no significant information yet. Griswolt's group was ordered to head down to the city cemetery, because they were not far from it, and some activity had been reported there.

"OK, let's move!" the officer called out to his convoy, and they headed down there with increased urgency.

After they reached the cemetery, the officer in charge sent eleven troopers and three deputies out to scout ahead and report back as the remainder policed the streets in the area. Griswolt was among those who went scouting.

As Griswolt's group crept quietly into the cemetery, they began to hear noises coming from the southwest. They crouched, and continued until they saw the outlines of people in small groups in the distance. "There are at least one hundred of them," Griswolt said to the lead sergeant.

The sergeant was looking through binoculars. "They don't look armed."

They slowly made their way forward, hidden by the dark, but not for long. The clouds were giving way again, exposing the full larger moon and its little sister. They had some tombstones to hide behind.

More gunfire was picked up north of their position, behind them. They immediately heard some frightened voices coming from their right, much closer than expected.

That sounded just like Rebecca, Griswolt thought to himself, and then shook it off as nonsense.

The sergeant had no choice. The moon was lighting things up, and the people they could hear were so close, he knew his group would be spotted at any moment. He motioned to everyone to head slowly in the direction of the voices.

As they came closer, they could hear the voices more clearly. The sergeant signaled to stop. They all stopped and listened for an instant, using more tombstones for cover.

"He's not supposed to arrive for another ten minutes," one of the people said.

Martha? It can't be! Griswolt was in shock. It couldn't be Martha's voice. *It —*

"We've got to wait, they've got the wildlands vaccines," a different voice said.

Griswolt and company were mesmerized for a minute by the conversation that was taking place. The idea, the thought, of an escape of love-lovers into the wildlands with vaccines was unimaginable. Griswolt was still in disbelief when the last cloud passed, and the full light of the moon revealed the group they were hearing in the night, only about fifty feet away. The troopers were still hiding behind various tombstones.

There she is! Martha! A love-lover! How could I — Griswolt was stunned, he could not reconcile what was about to happen. He looked at Martha with what seemed like tunnel vision. *She always wanted freedom. Martha, don't leave me. Don't go, I love you.*

He then said to himself lowly, "I love you?" with a surprised, bewildered look on his face. Then with a flash of recognition and inspiration, screamed, "I love you!" He didn't care. What was life in this fucking world without her? The troopers around him were looking at him as if he was crazy.

Martha and her group, startled, looked into the direction of Griswolt's voice, and saw the shadows of the troopers moving about the tombstones.

The lead sergeant called out, "Attack!" and immediately headed to Griswolt to check him out while the others started moving and shooting in the direction of Martha's group.

Griswolt screamed, "Martha! Run!" and immediately emptied a number of bullets into the lead sergeant's gut, dropping him. Then he started gunning down the other troopers ahead who were unaware of what had just happened, given the gunfire going off now. One by one, Griswolt was able to shoot all eleven of them with his automatic weapon, disabling or killing them all.

Martha did not run with the others. It might have been guilt over abandoning Griswolt, but she was sure she had heard his voice. Rebecca and Rachel stayed behind with her, hiding behind a big gravestone. She saw Griswolt start to run towards them after the shooting was over. She heard him shouting the words she had never, ever expected, "I love you!"

Martha started out to meet him, but Rebecca grabbed her, and with Rachel's help, they held her back. "I love you Griswolt!" she screamed.

It was then that the gunfire resumed. The officer in charge of the group had arrived with his troops. Martha's sudden hope was crushed as she watched Griswolt fall to his knees. He was only twenty feet away, and started crawling towards Martha. Their eyes finally caught in the now bright moonlight. "Martha, I love you," she could hear him gasping, still crawling. One more shot. Griswolt dropped, blood trickling and glistening from above his right eye in the moonlight.

"Noooooooooo! No, Griswolt! Griswolt!" Martha cried out, frantically trying to get away from Rebecca and Rachel to get to Griswolt. She had no strength. She knew it was over, but she couldn't leave him. Not now.

They pulled her away, hard. A group of armed LERN members came running up from behind them, and started shooting into the area of the troopers. "Get out of here now! The boats must be released now or never. Go! Now!"

Rachel grabbed Martha and looked her hard in the eyes. "We are going to die here too! Do you want that?" She shook Martha's body roughly, and then shoved her in the direction of river and screamed, "RUN!"

I have to run, Martha sobbed to herself, *I have to stay alive — for Jan,* and she started running, harder than she had in years. They were all carrying luggage and boxes, which did not help. *When is Jan going to get here?* Her thoughts were running as fast as her feet. *Oh my God — Griswolt.*

The river was less than a three-minute run away. When Martha and the girls got there, over half of the boats had already left, and the rest were being released. The explosion at the vaccine lab had the NOV on their highest alert, and they were covering everything. The NOV had not yet come to understand what was happening, but was getting information fast.

Rebecca exclaimed, "Look over there! There's Buz! What's he doing here?" They all turned to see.

Then Rachel said, "Oh, that's it. Look at who he's watching! It's Tama! He must have followed her here."

Martha was in no condition to care. With her timing distorted now, she asked, "When is Jan going to get here?"

Before anyone could answer, the ones organizing the departure came up and said, "What are you doing? The troopers are coming! Get on the boats *now*!"

Martha and the girls ran down and boarded one of the cargo boats, carrying what they had with them. The ones in charge were cutting the last of the boats loose. The armed ones who went to fight suddenly appeared, running back from the cemetery screaming, "Let's go! Let's go! Let's go!"

With everyone boarded on most of the boats, Jan's group had not yet arrived. The able bodied went down below to help with the rowing to speed things up. They were holding up the last cargo boat for the vaccine lab equipment. Any other empty boats were cut loose to float downstream so the NOV could not follow. Gunfire was coming their way, and the armed LERN members returned the fire.

"We can't wait for the vaccines! We've got to go now!" one of them said to Raspar, the one in charge now.

Raspar, the one who took over after Winoni's valuable boat had departed, now said, shaking his head, "Well, at least we won't give *them* the satisfaction of killing us." He gave the signal, and the last boat was released.

Jan and company were only minutes away.

These people should have been on their way to freedom, but now found themselves on their way to a poisonous death. The word spread quickly among the boats. The river current was in their favor to distance themselves from the dock. The first NOV troopers on the scene were firing their weapons, but they did not have anything that would sink a boat from any kind of distance. The escapee's on top of the boats could not resist, and they all start screaming, "Fuck you!" at the NOV troopers, along with other choice epithets.

Jan and his companions had been able to move quickly once they were outside of the city limits. Their relief was short lived however.

"Look! There are more police!" said Dom, twisting around to read Jan's reaction. Jan was still sitting behind Dom, on the big metal box that was bolted onto the top of the stagecoach.

Jan had been noticing the same thing. "They should be thinning out this way," he said to Dom, wondering about it.

They heard multiple cracks of gunfire in the distance in front of them. "Shit!" said a frightened Dom, "Did you hear that? That's where we're going! Shit!"

"It should be coming up anytime now." Jan was referring to the road to the river. Once they were past the cemetery it would be only a couple more minutes to reach the river. "There it is!" he said, pointing ahead to the cemetery on the left. They slowly realized that there were a large number of police wagons there, Dom exclaiming in a horrified voice, "Do you see that?"

Jan's attention was riveted on them. His slowing heart rate immediately reversed itself. "Just keep going, slow down a bit when you pass them. There are other people on the road here too. We don't look like love-lovers."

"Like what?" Dom was stiff as a board. Sitting at attention, he drove the stagecoach past the troopers. The few troopers there were standing and talking, waiting for their next orders. A couple of the troopers stared at the stagecoach as Jan and Dom passed. They both gave a sigh of relief as they passed without a problem. Once they were past the troopers, Lep yelled from down below, "What was that all about?"

"Pipe down," Jan said towards his feet. He looked at the police wagons lined up, with few police or troopers. "Where are the troopers for all these vehicles?" he asked himself. They heard more gunfire. This time, he was sure it was from behind the cemetery, towards the river.

"Hey you!" called a voice from behind, and it was one of the troopers. "Stop!"

"Shit — we're gonna die!" squeaked Dom, who was frozen again. He stopped the contisses.

Jan made his way to the back of the stagecoach's cargo top, and heard much more gunfire now, still coming from behind the graveyard.

Two troopers came up, hands on their guns. "What are you boys doing out here tonight?"

"Oh," said Jan, "We're moving our stuff to a new apartment." He paused. "Why were all those guns going off?"

"You mean you haven't heard about the vaccine lab?" the other trooper queried.

Jan looked at him, and said, "What — no! What happened?"

The trooper looked like he did not believe Jan. Lep was not making a peep inside. Dom was still frozen, looking straight ahead.

"What do you have here?" the first trooper asked, walking slowly along the side of the stagecoach now. He bent over, and looked at the unusual undercarriage. "Strange," he commented, reaching out his hand to touch it. They were relaxing because these kids were obviously going to be no trouble, especially if they were love-lovers. The other trooper walked along the other side, and since the windows were sealed and blinded, could not see anything inside.

Jan followed them along the top as they slowly walked up to the front of the stagecoach. *Oh God, they're going to talk to Dom.*

"What's your name?" the trooper on the left side of the stagecoach asked Dom.

Dom opened his mouth to speak, but nothing came out. He looked as if someone just shoved a huge snowball down his pants, and simply stared at the trooper with his mouth open.

All of a sudden, there was a sound to the rear of the stagecoach. The vaccine module was releasing some pressure inside the interior cargo space.

Both troopers went back to see what it was, and Dom found his voice. "Yah! Yah! Yah!" he bellowed at the contisses, cracking his whip, and Jan blurted, "Fuck!" and ducked, because he knew what was coming next.

Crack! Crack! Crack! Crack! The guns went off, and one of the troopers ran back to get a wagon.

Dom was over half speed within thirty seconds, driving the contisses hard. The first police wagon had taken off after them, with others to follow.

The stagecoach was bouncing now, and Jan abruptly shouted, "Turn left!" Dom cried "Whoa!" and the contisses were able to slow down enough to barely make the turn, tilting on the right two wheels, and bouncing it's right rear off of the parked police wagon stationed at the corner.

Two officers jumped out of it, then back in again, and started after them.

"Yah! Yah!" cried Dom again, cracking the whip, and they were headed full steam ahead for the river.

The sky was staying clear now, and they could see as they headed down to the dock that there were more police wagons ahead. Dom had the contisses running on full steam, and couldn't turn back even if he wanted to.

"Where are the boats?" Jan yelled, as they saw nothing sitting by the docks on the river.

"They must have had to leave already," Dom shouted back.

"The boats are gone?" Lep shrieked from underneath. "What the hell's going on out there?"

"What are you going to do?" Jan yelled to Dom. The road was becoming rougher and everything on the stagecoach was rattling or banging.

"There's a road up ahead, if we can make it past them," Dom hollered back.

Two police wagons were closing in behind them now, with more following. They were smaller, and they only had two contisses each. The bumpy road made their weapons useless as they fired. They would have to get closer.

Jan saw them, and said, "Can we go any faster?"

Dom yelled, "Not once we start uphill!"

The troopers already at the dock were not yet aware of the stagecoach coming their way — they were busy firing down the river at the escaping boats.

Dom bore to the right as they approached the river water. They sped past the police wagons at the dock, and in seconds, the troopers down there saw them, and were firing upon the boys as well. Jan saw an old gravel road to the right of the dock, going up along the edge of the hill it followed and said, "Oh no."

That was exactly where Dom was now heading. "Hold on," he yelled, "Yah, Yah, Yah!" and with another crack, they hit the first ruts in the narrow old road. It went up steeply and was close enough to the edge of the cliff in parts to see the river below to the left.

"What the hell is going on out there? I'm taking the blinds down!" Lep yelled from below.

"Knock yourself out!" Jan yelled down to Lep. *We're fucked, anyway.* He was busy now trying to keep things from bouncing off the stagecoach. Where are we going?" he yelled to Dom.

"I don't know yet!" shouted Dom.

"Well, they're catching up to us," Jan hollered back. There were four wagons coming after them now. The stagecoach took a really big bounce, and when it landed, the front wheels both broke off, leaving the front dragging.

"Shit!" yelled Dom. "I *knew* I should have bought factory!" The contisses kept rolling. The gunfire was a great motivator.

They were bouncing more than ever, and as they approached the crest of the hill, there was another huge bounce, and Jan yelled, "The back wheels broke off," as he watched the wheels rolling back towards their pursuers. The road came close to the edge of the cliff, and Jan could see the river a quarter mile down below them now. He could see the boats up ahead. "I can see the boats!" he yelled to Dom.

"Damn!" Dom bitched. "Do you see those mounted troopers over there to our right? I don't think we can outrun them!" Then he said, "Jan! Unlatch all of the latches on that box you're sitting on!"

Jan yelled, "What is this?"

Dom screamed, "Just do it!"

Jan started unlatching the heavy latches on the box.

"Leave the middle one latched!" Dom yelled. "Shit! Shit, shit, shit!"

All of a sudden, mounted troopers on contisses appeared in front of them coming from the opposite direction from over the peak of the hill. A bullet went through a box of syringes from the right, and others were whizzing by or hitting the side of the stagecoach. Jan looked to the right and the mounted troopers numbers had increased, now coming even closer.

Dom saw them too. "Unlatch that last latch, and hold on!" Dom yelled, and when Jan did, he was knocked backwards onto his back by what came out.

"What the hell is that?" Jan yelled while still on his back, as the box's contents were expelled from their container.

"I said hold on!" screamed Dom.

Jan's next question was an incredulous, "What are you doing?" as he felt the stagecoach make a hard left at full speed toward the edge of the cliff, with a multitude of bullets hitting the stagecoach and whizzing by as well.

Then there was nothing. Nothing but weightlessness, as Jan lay on his back looking at the sky — and very aware of the side of the cliff rushing by in the wrong direction. The weightlessness was accompanied by terror, as they were now in a free fall.

Lep was screaming like a little girl down below. As Jan rose and held onto the big latches of the anchored metal box, Dom was still guiding the screeching contisses, and they had their leg shrouds stretched out, starting to glide in the air. This was causing the back of the stagecoach to drop, and boxes started falling off. Then the thing that came out of the box completely opened up above. It looked to Jan like a humungous, rectangular leathercloth umbrella. It caught the air, the stagecoach lurched upwards, and suddenly Jan could feel his weight again.

"We're flying!" he cheerfully yelled to Dom.

Dom hollered back, "Actually, we are gliding!" Dom then shouted, "Come up here, and grab the contisses and guide them the best you can!"

Jan jumped up and took over the reins. Then Dom went back to the gliding device he had made. He grabbed the weighted ropes dangling from each side of it, and headed for the boats. "We just might be able to land this thing!" Dom yelled.

"Where?" Jan hollered.

"On a boat!" Dom shouted.

Lep had just climbed up from the back, holding on to everything for dear life. "What the fuck?" What? What's happening?" He was in shock, and looked delirious.

"Just relax, buddy, it's all downhill now," said Dom, grinning, luxuriating in the wind rushing by them.

They were coming upon the group of boats now, and Jan spotted one of the empty ones that were floating freely. It was spinning very slowly behind the rest as it followed the current. He called out to Dom about it, and Dom agreed to aim for it.

"This is the greatest moment of my life!" Dom beamed, as he continued to steer the gliding hulk towards the boat.

Jan and Lep looked at each other. Neither was convinced completely, yet. The contisses were screeching their lungs out.

As they made their approach, they noticed two things. One was the roar of the crowds on the boats as they greeted their arrival. The other thing was the realization of just how fast they were really going as they approached the boat. The boat, being unguided, had a slow rotation to it, greatly complicating Dom's inexperience. As they came within fifty feet, Dom swiftly pulled down hard and far on the ropes, and the glide stalled, but the momentum and lift that the contisses provided caused the forward travel to continue.

Jan pulled back on the reins. For an instant, they had a perfect hover above the boat, and dropped down onto it, in an oblong orientation.

Lep was sitting, wide eyed, beyond speech. Dom was grinning from ear to ear, and the crowds on the boats were cheering a cheer that nobody had ever heard before. It was the cheer from free people, for something wonderful.

The boat was leaning slightly to the Jan's right. Dom didn't seem to be concerned, until the left side of the boat unfortunately bumped hard, into a big rock abutment. Jan was watching Dom as his smile faded along with the level of the boat. The river current was pulling down on the right side of the boat.

"Hold on!" Jan yelled. The stagecoach tilted and skidded to the right, and along with the boat, conspired to tip the boat acutely to the right and spill the whole stagecoach and team into the river. The contisses were screeching again, but quickly gained their rhythm, and began paddling quite efficiently. While Lep was screaming again, Dom seemed quite composed as the stagecoach leveled out.

Lep looked at Dom with astonishment, "This thing floats?"

Dom said, "Hey, I like to plan." He started laughing, and then decided to jump up and do a quick jig. Jan laughed, and Lep managed a grunt. Then Jan and Lep sat down just because they simply had to. Lep sat up front with Dom, and Jan headed to the back of the stage-coach/boat…flying thing.

The contisses were paddling furiously. Dom guided them towards the other boats they were fast approaching.

Jan was sitting on the back of stagecoach now, arms propped behind him, legs spread, leaning back far enough that his tail came out perfectly between his legs. It reached almost to his feet, as he studied it, still catching his breath. Then he looked up. He was not facing forward, at the boats of cheering people in front of them. He was looking backwards, up river. *Nobody is going to follow us where we are going. We are free.* He listened a moment. *It's going to be quiet out here,* he realized. *No city lights. No NOV.*

Neither Dom nor Lep were talking now either. They were all feeling rather knocked out, exhausted, thankful, and now, finally, they had a chance to soak it all in.

Chapter Eighteen

Closure River

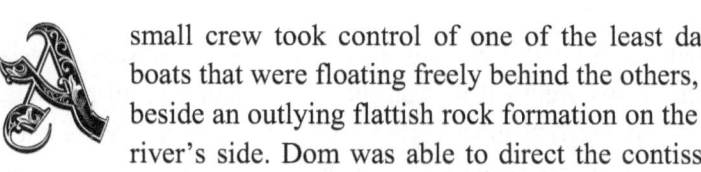 small crew took control of one of the least damaged vacant boats that were floating freely behind the others, and secured it beside an outlying flattish rock formation on the left, (eastern,) river's side. Dom was able to direct the contisses to drag the stagecoach "boat" ashore at that point. From there, they unloaded all the vaccine equipment and supplies from the stagecoach and carried them onto the awaiting cargo boat. As they did this, the other boats slowed down to wait for them.

They brought the contisses on last of all. Dom had mentioned his concerns regarding them, primarily the fact that eventually the contisses were going to get hungry. Contisses preferred to eat blogs or tacks, but fish would have to do for now. Two of the boats ahead had already begun casting nets to catch fish, and more were setting up their own nets. Altogether, over two hundred contisses had been loaded onto the boats. The escapees did bring ample food, but it was prudent to use as much wild food as possible, and preserve their stores.

All the people, over six hundred of them, were making a tumultuous noise. There were happy sounds and raucous laughter, as they were all in high spirits. One of the groups brought a sound system along, and their

231

boat blared illegal music as they traveled through the night. The newbie captains were now guiding the boats with the river's current, and the volunteers doing the rowing below the deck were dwindling in number, as their job was done for now.

Jan and Dom took one of the onboard lifeboats to go and find Jan's mother and the girls. Lep wanted to stay with the vaccine equipment. Jan and Dom paddled their way from boat to boat. As they passed the boats, the people cheered for them, occasionally yelling, "What *was* that?" in reference to the amazing gliding stagecoach they had observed.

As they approached the fourth boat, Jan sputtered, "What? — Buz? Look! There's Buz! Hey Buz!" He was waving his hand wildly as he anticipated Buz's reaction.

Buz heard someone call his name, turned, and seeing Jan and Dom approaching in the lifeboat, started waving and yelling himself. They pulled up alongside his boat.

"Boy, am I glad to see you!" declared Jan, smiling from ear to ear. "I can't believe it!"

Buz laughed and said, "Well, sometimes it pays to obsess! I was wondering where Tama went off to, and then I saw that you all had left, so I followed." He paused, "I'm sure glad I did. They are all goners back there since the vaccine lab is gone." Then he gave a hurt look at Jan, "Were you going to just leave me there to die with the rest?"

Dom chimed up, "No, that was me!"

Buz took a strange look at Dom, then back to Jan, and Jan tried to explain, "We didn't plan to destroy the lab, Buz. Dom here just got creative, and something went wrong. We didn't mean for anything like that to happen." He paused, and with satisfaction said, "I'm really glad you made it, buddy. You don't know how bad I felt to lie to you tonight, but the NOV —"

"— DeathBT, I know," Buz admittedly interrupted. He looked back up river, and gave a sigh. "I understand — you couldn't risk it. I get it — it's OK." There was a short silence, and then Buz chided, "So you're a fucking love-lover! That's why the girls like you!" He gave a questionable smile at Jan, and then leaned over to lend him a hand to come up on board. "Your mother is here, down inside helping."

Dom had been securing the lifeboat, and came on board too. He said to Jan and Buz, "What's all this love-lover stuff?"

Jan looked at Dom, puzzled. Surely, Lep would have told him that it was the escape of LERN. "You know this is a LERN escape, right?"

Dom didn't believe him, "LERN? No way! Love-lovers? Ughhhh! No — you're kidding, right?"

"I'm not joking, and there's no escape for you now, buddy," Jan laughed as he slapped Dom on the back. Zak looked at Dom and shrugged his shoulders. Zak was not sure how emotional the reunion below deck would be, so he avoided it by staying up on top.

Jan and Dom made their way downstairs, and there was Martha, busying herself with Rebecca and Rachel, doing triage on packages and boxes that had been hurriedly dumped there during the escape. They were looking for hunting, fishing, and cooking equipment for now. There were other people below deck as well, gathering useful items for the rest of the evening.

Wow, she doesn't look very happy, Jan thought when he saw his mother.

Martha turned her head to see whose footsteps had just come down the stairs. The box she was carrying dropped out of her hands when she realized who it was.

"Jan!" she screamed as she ran over to him, and she wouldn't stop squeezing him.

"Hey, what about my turn?" Rebecca remarked, as she and Rachel followed Martha's lead.

They got into a group hug, as Dom stood there looking awkwardly at them. The ever-social Rachel said, "Come on, Dom, you can join in!" She could see that he would not easily do this, but no male could resist her charm. She grabbed Dom by the arm and pulled him in with them so that he had no choice.

After they released each other, Dom was smiling oddly, as if he had been hit in the head with Cupid 's bow. Dom thought to himself, *that was scary, but — OK, I guess. Love-lovers, I dunno. Wait until I see Lep, I'm gonna nail him good!* Dom continued smiling, and now he was chuckling to himself.

Martha's face fell again as Jan looked at her.

"What's going on? What's wrong?" he asked.

Martha, with an anguished look said, "Jan — your father — died tonight." Then her face broke into an ugly spasm as her words turned into choking sobs, "Griswolt — Griswolt — gave his — life — for us." Clearly distressed, she looked at Jan and told him, "All three of us would have been shot." Martha put her face in her hands, "I abandoned him, and he died for me-e-e-," and started crying, hard, with deep, deep sobs. "He wanted to come with u-u-u-u-us! He could be here right now, alive!" she wailed, and was now crying hysterically.

They all waited awkwardly for Martha to slow down. She eventually did, then looked at Jan again with a very intense yet forlorn expression and continued, "Jan — he said that he — loved — me-e-e-e —" and she broke down again into a torrent of tears.

Both of the girls were caressing her shoulders and back, Rebecca saying, "Martha, there was no way you could have changed this. You couldn't risk the escape — all our lives."

"I could have trusted him!" Martha wailed, and she started crying again.

Dad's dead. The thought was beginning to be absorbed. *He's gone.* Jan felt Martha's grief — they did after all abandon Griswolt.

Jan hung his head, not knowing what to say or do as he juggled his opposing cerebrations — *I never did give it much thought — why? It was something we had to do — Dad couldn't know, could he? He said he loved her? I can't believe it — he said he loved her.*

Dom had become clearly uncomfortable with the scene as it had been unfolding. He said, "Hey Jan, why don't we head back to the vaccine boat?"

Jan looked at his mother, then at Dom. "No, I think I'll stay and help out here for now."

Dom shrugged his shoulders and replied, "OK. Well, I think I should get going." Then he looked at Martha with sympathy and said, "I'm sorry to hear about your husband, Martha." She was still sobbing, so he backed his way out of the group, went up the stairs, and headed on back to Lep and the vaccine equipment.

The occupied cargo boats, thirty-six in all, slowly made their way down the river that night. Most of the boats were loaded on the top deck with three wagons and six contisses, meant for the land travel ahead. There was no hurry now, indeed, they did not want any nighttime accidents. Some of the escapees slept, others could not, and simply hanged out up on deck talking. Some just worked all night. The boat crews took turns piloting and sleeping. The plan was to travel until daylight, and then gather everyone together for a meeting on land. Cleaning up after the contisses was easy — they just dumped it into the river.

The next morning was pleasant, with low winds, and sunny skies.

"Over here!" called Winoni. He was a big Aletian, standing at nine feet and four inches tall, and weighing in at five hundred and ten pounds. Winoni was a Chief Smelt Engineer who could manage anything from mining ore to refining to smelting it, machining, and producing many of the everyday tools and items that these people would be needing. He had brought his entire library with him, and the New Aletians were very fortunate to have him. He was not in LERN, but his wife had told him about the escape. She knew he was tired of all the NOV rules, laws, the harsh punishments, and the constant intimidation. *"Anywhere would be better than here, even if I am stuck with a bunch of love-lovers!"* was his reply when she brought it up.

"No! I said over here!" Winoni was now hollering at the pilot of the next boat that they were now attempting to anchor against the shore.

Jan rubbed his eyes, and took a look around from the edge of the boat. There was nothing but the river and the landscape of the hill to the right, looking west. On the left, it appeared that the terrain was more flat, and lower. Looking back to his right again, to the hillside against the river, he saw a number of holes of various sizes in the ground, particularly at the bottom of rock formations. *What's living in you?* he pondered, as he looked at one particularly big hole, silently black and hollow, halfway up the same hill.

They had already tied his boat to the shore. Jan got off his boat, and casually walked over to Winoni and asked him, "How are we all going to gather?"

Winoni looked at him, "I can't remember any more names for now, so I won't ask you. We're going to gather over on that flat spot over there." He pointed over to his left.

"What about predators?" Jan asked.

Winoni said, "You see those guys?" He was now pointing to one of the boats already anchored. "A few of them are official NOV Hunters from the Hunter's Stations, and the rest are professional private hunters. They seem to know what they're doing. They've been preparing to scout the perimeter." Then he paused, looking Jan over. "They're looking for volunteers, if you want to join 'em."

Jan looked over at them and saw that they were indeed in their hunting gear and they were departing their boat now.

"It looks like they're leaving already," Jan said to Winoni, and continued with, "I'll think about it." Then he had another consideration, "How well armed are we? Is there any chance I can get a gun — for protection?"

Winoni answered, "We have plenty of guns, *and* ammunition to last for years, and my crew can make bullets from raw materials in no time. You were supposed to bring your own though, you know."

"I'll check with my mom when I get back to her," Jan said. *If we were supposed to bring our own guns, I'm sure she would have brought ours.*

Jan went strolling along the shoreline, observing everyone that had come along. There were so many people, from all over the country. He talked with some, and then moved on to others that had come ashore. He recognized Ziba and her friends.

"Oh Jan! Come here, I want you to meet Jasma! I've told her all about you!" exclaimed an exuberant Ziba.

Oh boy, a nest of old ladies, Jan thought. Little did he know that he was about to meet the most powerful LERN leader who had made it through the escape alive. "Hello, it's nice to meet you," he said to Jasma.

Ziba chimed in, "Jan, Jasma has the largest collection of Platac writings that exist. I asked her if you could study them, and —"

"And I would be most happy to share them with you, my dear." Jasma said with a delighted smile. She came closer to Jan, and staring at his crest, asked, "May I?" Before he could answer, she reached up to touch it.

She ran her fingers along Jan's crest and said, "Your crest reminds me of something — something I remember reading —" Jasma now held a puzzled expression.

"What was it?" asked Jan, quite curious now.

"So many things I have are just loose pages — and the Platacs could be quite cryptic." She paused, then said, "I'll dig it up, and show you later." She could not take her eyes of off Jan's crest after that. Then she said, "Ziba tells me that you can hear someone you call the 'Guide'. Would you tell me about that sometime?"

Jan felt a bit of embarrassment, thinking, *why did Ziba talk about that? They're all going to think I'm nuts!* Then he replied to Jasma, "OK, if you promise not to tell anyone about it, we'll talk about it sometime." As this conversation was going on, most of the people were on land now. Jan looked around at them and said, "People wouldn't understand, they would just think I'm crazy."

Jasma did understand, and said, "Fine, Jan, whenever you are ready, I truly would like to hear what you have to say."

Jan turned his eyes to the left, and unexpectedly barked to their astonishment, "What the *FUCK*?" He had recognized Sak, and immediately dashed out of the females' presence, heading for Sak, who was now working for Winoni's crew, broken rib and all. Jan surprised Sak, grabbing him and violently throwing him to the ground.

"Hey, Hey! Hold on there! What's going on?" Winoni bellowed, running over to Jan and Sak. Sak was gripping his broken rib, and staying in a guarded position on the ground.

"How did he get in with us?" Jan demanded to know, pointing his finger at Sak.

"He asked me when we were loading. I could have just tied him up with the other dock workers, but he begged me to take him with us," Winoni answered — "Why?" — and now *he* was eyeballing Sak.

"He's a no-good, back-stabbing piece of predatory shit, that's why!" Jan barked as he went to lunge at Sak again.

Winoni and the others held him back. "Whoa there, son!" Winoni said.

"I was in a coma for *three* days because of him and his gang, look at these scars!" Jan showed him a two-inch scar on the side of his head, and the one on his neck. "They tried to cut my fucking head off!"

Winoni sighed, shaking his head, and looking at Sak. "Well he's with us now. What are we supposed to do, throw him to the yetas?" Winoni countered. Sak was now getting up, brushing himself off, while still holding his right side with one hand.

As far as Jan was concerned, "Yes, throw him to whatever. He's bad news, and he *will* cause problems here."

Sak spoke up. "Listen Jan, I know you hate me, but you don't know what just happened. Look at me. Barab left me to be beaten by Kran and his gang. He betrayed me!" Sak was looking for sympathy. He was not about to let these good folks know that he also bombed Barab's house, murdering his mother and brother. "I came down to the river to drown myself, and I ran into this. A new chance for a new life!" He paused, looking on an absolutely unbelieving Jan.

Sak continued, "Give me a chance, Jan. I'll show you, I've changed. I want to help here."

Winoni was studying Jan and could see he was hardened in his position. "We'll just keep you two apart for now, and see how it goes, OK?" Winoni suggested in his deep husky voice.

Jan just sighed. What else could he do? These people were not going to send Sak to his death. They did not know him.

"Whatever," Jan replied, and then he turned to Sak and said, "You stay away from me and my family." Then he left them and went up to where the others were all gathering. He was thinking about his last words. Martha and Rebecca were certainly family. *What about Rachel? She has to stay with us, she's having my baby. She's family now, too.*

They had all heard gunfire over the hill for the past ten minutes or so. Jan mused — *I guess the hunters are doing their job. Good.*

The crowd waited for the hunters to clear the area and come back. When they did, they were carrying five dead splints, and six of the hunters were dragging a fully-grown yeta. The hunters were all smiles. "This is the easiest hunting I've ever done," one exclaimed. "We're not going to starve out here!" They put their bounty, already gutted, over by their boat, to finish cleaning and butchering later. The meeting then started, with hunters standing guard around the perimeter of the immediate area.

Jasma was given the honor of being the first to address the crowd. She stood up on a small, conveniently flattened boulder, and after the initial greetings and congratulations, she said to them, "I know you all have not yet been told of our plans. Well, we have old maps of this area — they were developed over one hundred years ago when these areas were still populated. We are heading for what was a major city of the Platacs, near the ocean. Their living structures were known to have excellent construction, so we may be able to find places there suitable to clean out and move into. We will eventually need to leave the boats, and travel by land to get to our destination."

She went on to say, "Dr. Kalep's advisors feel that we should start our land travel sooner than later, but we won't be deciding where or when just yet. We do know that we will be on this river for about one month. Dr. Kalep and his partner Dr. Brader believe that the closer we get to the ocean, the more risk we have of being attacked by a molick or other large sea creature." Although Dr. Kalep was an archeologist, and Dr. Brader a chemist, they had consulted other appropriate professionals on board, and felt that they had good advice to go by. Although their relationship had been kept ultra-secret before the escape, all was out in the open now. Most who knew them were aware they were gandy all along, but this was not a big problem within LERN. Prior to the escape, non-LERN folks also knew about Kalep and Brader, but feared Dr. Kalep's powerful connections, and would not dare to go against him.

They were primarily concerned with a molick attack on the boats. A molick was a humongous fish that had hands with opposable thumbs — on arms with very bony pointy elbows. It was also known to produce a ghastly haunting smile from its eerily looking face when hunting, capturing, and picking its meal apart — always a live one.

Jasma concluded her small announcement with, "My son, Asa, and I are looking forward to a wonderful, loving life out here, and I am just so pleased to be with all of you — out here, free at last!" Everyone cheered, and then Jasma told them all that it was time get into lines to receive their "wildlands" vaccines.

"I hope we're not too late for the vaccines," Jan muttered to himself. He went over to where Lep and Dom had set up shop, and asked, "Do you guys need any help?"

Lep said, "Here, take these to those two other tables," and he gave Jan two boxes of syringes. "Make sure you bring the needles back!" Dom yelled to another group that was leaving with some vaccine supplies.

After everyone had received their vaccinations, they all re-boarded the boats, and headed downstream again. There was not much for Jan to do for the next few hours, so he found a fishing pole, and started fishing alone from the back of the boat. It was not long before he saw a big ripple in the water.

"What was that?" Jan asked aloud. The thing was at least seventy-five feet long. "That has to be an ela," he said to himself, studying the slithering swimming style it had. Jan had heard that they could not get into the boats. He saw it lift its nose for air, and go back under. "Our guns!" Jan said aloud. He put the fishing rod down, and went below where Martha and Rebecca were helping to prepare something for the boat travelers to eat for the day.

"Hey mom, did you bring our guns?" Jan asked.

Martha stopped what she was doing, and said, "I have them over there," pointing her knife to a table on the other side of the cargo area. "They're under that table."

Jan went over to see what they had, which was a shotgun, a rifle, and two pistols. "None of these will stop an ela," he said.

"An ela?" Martha responded. "Did you see an ela?"

"Yeah," said Jan, "It looks like it's following us. I heard they can't get into the boats."

"Would you bet your life on that?" Martha asked. Then she said, "We need a bigger weapon than those on this boat."

"Here, I got what you need!" Bill Standish, a long-time LERN member, had a state-of-the-art Mach3b automatic assault weapon. It was their biggest model, and carried bullets that weighed a quarter pound each. He could barely lift it.

Jan walked over, and asked, "Can I hold it?"

Bill said, "Sure. Actually, you can just have it. I don't know how to use it, or even lift it. My brother-in-law is an NOV Hunter. He helped himself to whatever they could grab at the armory, and gave it to me for the trip."

Jan was amazed at this person's generosity. Then he said, "I guess we are all family now," grinning at Bill. He looked at Martha and asked, "Can I give him one of our guns?"

Martha turned and looked at the weapon Jan was carrying, and said, "Of course, he can have any one he wants."

Bill chose the shotgun.

"Want to watch?" Jan asked as he turned to go back up on the deck.

"No thanks, maybe next time," Bill said. He had not been able to sleep yet, and was heading back to the bunks, which were located towards the rear of the boat within the big space they were now standing in.

Jan went back up to where he had been fishing, but the ela was not there anymore. He sat down and studied the weapon. "This thing is marvelous!" he said to himself. "I can't wait to use it." He fired off some practice rounds, and it felt as if a contiss had kicked him in the shoulder. After a while, he went back inside and took a nap, having had restless sleep the night before.

Later in the evening, Jan was out on the deck with Rebecca and Rachel. Martha was resting below. It was much quieter now, and the air had developed a light mildew smell. Clouds began to cover the sky, and it became very dark. They were talking about the baby.

"I was thinking seriously about having an abortion," said Rachel. "I still can, considering where we are. There is at least one doctor here."

"There is no good reason here to interrupt the flow of life," Rebecca said, continuing, "If anything, the one inside you has all the reason in the world to be born into our new life!" She had become fond of Rachel, and with the turmoil of the last day or so, a bond had developed. They were becoming comrades. Rebecca knew Jan so well that she believed there was no way he could have an affair and be able to hide it. Besides, Rebecca was not actually interested in having a baby of her own right now. "We will be a family, and we'll all help with the baby," she said to Rachel.

Jan was distracted, mesmerized by the dark hillside. "Do you see that?" he asked the girls, as he pointed into the night at a spot offshore. "See all of those shiny things? Those are eyes. We are going to eventually walk off of these boats and into *that*."

They tarried a bit longer on the upper deck. Others had gathered there as well, and they were all talking about the trip. After it had become very late, Jan, Rebecca and Rachel went downstairs to sleep for the night.

The fleet of boats continued in the same way for three long, relatively quiet weeks. There was plenty of work to do for most of the travelers. Fishing, cleaning, cooking, eating, feeding the contisses, and more cleaning took up the days of most people.

The only real concern regarding predators was that the elas were increasing in number in the river. Still, it held true that the elas could not raise their heads high enough to be able to come close to getting into the boats. The travelers did become more cautious, using the rowboats or lifeboats less often because of a couple of ela scares. The people were becoming weary of consuming fish, and the contisses were not eating as they should have. They would occasionally stop and hunt, but really could not spend the time, as they all wanted desperately to get to their destination, the Platac city further south.

Three weeks had passed, and they were getting closer to their destination.

Dr. Kalep and his supporters made a strong appeal to go on land now, as they would be getting close to the ocean within a week. They were becoming more concerned about the big ocean creatures that could swim up river and wreak havoc with the boats. The group could not afford to lose even one boatload of people and supplies.

When word got to Jan's boat, he thought about it, and then he heard the Guide say, "*It would be better to stay on the river for the next three days.*"

When it appeared that no elas were nearby in the water, Jan got into a lifeboat, and rowed up to the command boat. This boat carried the leaders of LERN. On his way over, he was gratified to see how clear the river water had become. The stench of the NOV's sewage and industrial dumping had dissipated over the past couple of weeks.

When Jan boarded their boat, he found Ziba, Dr. Kalep, Winoni, and Jasma with her son, Asa, all on deck. They were all standing there outside, talking and planning. There were a number other people mulling about on the deck as well.

Asa was a few years older than Jan was, and he stood lean and tall — nine feet and six inches to be exact. Asa was dressed in tight thin ela black leather with silver buttons and accessories. He liked to wear an unusual headdress that was a replica of ancient ones worn by the earliest Aletian kings. He thought it made him look knowledgeable and deep. It had long shiny strands of well-preserved thin pale yellow nerves that had been stripped from elas. The strands were tough, numbered in the hundreds, and the entire thing fitted his head snugly, with the strands falling down just past his shoulders.

When Jan came walking up to them, Ziba said, "Jan, what a nice surprise! I believe you have already met Dr. Kalep."

Dr. Kalep studied Jan for a moment, just as he always did with people. "Hello, son, I've seen you at the meetings, and working around the boats here. Great job with the vaccine lab!" He looked at the others and said, "Do you see the innovation that hope of freedom brings? They flew!" He smiled and extended his hand, which Jan shook.

"Hello sir, thank you," Jan replied. Still on task, Jan looked at Ziba and said, "I heard that we are going to depart for land today. I think it's too soon."

Dr. Kalep looked shocked, and Ziba got nervous. She said, "Jan, dear, we have been debating this all night. Dr. Kalep and his advisors insist that this is the safest way."

Dr. Kalep, bristling at the contrary opinion, asked, "Are you an expert in these things? What makes you think that we should stay in the river, vulnerable to any creature big enough to tip us over for a snack?" He put his hand on his stomach. He had stomach problems, worse than most others with similar ailments. He had a stock of concentrated yama enzymes, which helped with his digestion, but he was going to run out eventually. The only two medical doctors here had not brought much in the way of enzymes, but they did have pharmaceuticals that could give relief. He preferred the enzymes, and they were expected to be easier to reproduce at their destination than the pharmaceuticals.

Jan glanced at Ziba and Jasma with a look that said he knew something, but could not say it. They both appeared to understand that something was up, but said nothing.

Jasma had been waiting to tell Jan something she felt was interesting and perhaps important. She had found the Platac scriptures that she mentioned to him earlier. In them was a definite reference to an important figure that had a "white crest", and it said something about liquid gold. Like others, she felt that there was something quite special about Jan.

Jasma spoke up. When Jasma talked, people had to listen. She had funded over half of the supplies for the escape, and she had many loyal friends. "Perhaps we should wait an extra day," she offered.

"This has already been settled!" countered Dr. Kalep. "We've been over this again and again. It's settled! We are deboarding this afternoon, once we reach the bend in the river."

Jasma said, "You don't understand, Dr. Kalep, we have reason to believe that Jan has certain — gifts."

Now Jasma's son chimed in. Asa was unsure of this Jan character right from the start. Now his mother was calling Jan "gifted". Asa did not like that at all. He walked up to Jan and said, "You're nobody! You don't belong here. Go back to your boat with the little people."

Jasma was shocked at her son's behavior, and barked, "Asa!"

Asa just returned a snide look to his mother, then gave Jan a sneer, and backed off. He was not interested in LERN, however he had no choice but to follow his mother into this blunder, as he called it. He certainly wanted no part of the workload.

Jasma said to Jan, "I believe it has already been settled, Jan. These people do know what they are doing, and their best advice is to get off of the river before a tragedy befalls us." She paused, wanting to change the tone, and attempted to help Jan mix with the others. "Here, let me introduce you to Commissioner Cush and his wife, Ushu," Jasma offered. Asa left the group and went on his way.

Commissioner Cush was not a LERN member, but his wife Ushu was. The only reason Cush was here was because his other wife was as treacherous as an ela, and was extorting him because of bribes she discovered Cush had regularly been receiving for legislative favors.

He had been eavesdropping in on his LERN wife Ushu's phone calls, and found out about the escape. Cush kept it to himself until the night of the escape. He had a hoard of gold coins that he brought to the wildlands, knowing it would be useful eventually. He could not imagine Ushu abandoning him, leaving him alone with the shrew wife. He blocked Ushu from leaving when the call of the escape came, which he had also intercepted. Cush confronted her with his knowledge of the LERN escape, and insisted that she take him with her. Now, here he was — another non-LERN stowaway.

Cush was not very friendly to Jan. When he asked Jan about his background, he discovered that Jan's father, Griswolt, was someone he had seen a number of times, as Cush had oversight of Griswolt's superiors. Cush appeared to dismiss Jan as lower class, and went on over to another group there on board to continue his own planning.

When Jasma and Jan had a private moment, she whispered, "Jan, dear, I want to show you something I found last night. Follow me," and she led him down the stairs below the upper deck. Jan followed as Jasma went to her private room, and when they got there, she caught Asa getting into her hard alcohol. "Asa! Get up on board, now!" she demanded.

Asa scowled, and angrily stared at Jan, demanding, "What's *he* doing here?"

Jan was staring right back asking himself the same thing about this bilgat freak with the weird hat and shit attitude.

"Well, it is really none of your business, but we have studies to go over," replied Jasma.

The last thing Asa wanted to do was be around love-lovers talking their nonsense. He left and went back up on the upper deck.

Jasma poured herself a drink, and asked Jan if he would like one. Jan declined, as it was early in the day. Jasma retrieved some papers from her beautifully sculpted cream-colored gendra bone desk. Her posture changed, and she was now behaving very secretively and her voice turned to a whisper — simply out of habit.

"Here, I found this Platac scripture," she said, and handed it to Jan. Jasma elaborated, "My great grandfather was able collect these from the confiscated homes of Platacs purged from the NOV a hundred years ago. It may be my imagination, but it reminds me of your crest, and of what Ziba said about you."

The page of metallic paper was very small, just about eight inches long and four inches wide. The sentences were incomplete as the left side was torn off, but the words there read:

"...will be known by the sign
...molten gold running down like
...his spotless white crest. He will bring back the
...and the dragons of D'ot. He will follow a guide, he
...and we will be reborn, free, for a generation.
...will come. All souls will sleep
...this world, to stir our sleeping souls, in preparation for..."

Jan was puzzled. "And you think this applies to me?" he asked Jasma incredulously. "It doesn't make any sense," Jan said as he, by habit, copied the words down on another piece of blank paper lying there on the desk.

"I don't know, but I can spot a D'otian with destiny written on him, and I must say I see it in you my dear," Jasma said as she once again reached up and stroked Jan's crest, letting her fingers run along the outlines of the irregular vertical yellow streaks. Her eyes fell on his, and Jan saw the same hungry look he had learned to recognize. Her hand ran to his big shoulders, and then lightly down his arm. "You know," she said, purring like an emui, "I can help you out here. I can help find the perfect place for you."

Oh, no, not you too, Jan thought. He wisely and gently took her hand, holding it, and answered, "Thank you, Jasma. I don't know about all of this, but I think I have some similar writings of my mother's that I want to compare to what you've given me."

His statement brought the conversation back to the intellectual side of Jasma. The amazing possibilities did indeed intrigue her. After a bit more conversation, Jan eventually departed. His mission to convince them to continue on the river for a few more days had failed. He went back to his boat, and told those there to get ready to depart the boat soon.

Chapter Nineteen

Land Ho!

t was about mid-day, and those in the lead boats had all the others stop. They had found an ideal place to deboard the boats, and start traveling by land, south-southwest. The river continued directly south.

"This should not happen," the Guide said. *"You will begin to lose people to the wild animals tonight."*

Jan just sighed, "They wouldn't listen to me," he said.

"Now you know how I feel," replied the Guide.

Jan had asked Martha for her original Platac scriptures. The reason Martha had them at all was because her great-great grandmother's husband was a Platac, and writings had been handed down through the generations. Martha's great grandmother and child should have been executed by the NOV along with all the Aletian half-breeds at the time the one-hundred-year poison was released, but she looked very Aletian, and was able to survive because of that. Some of her fellow siblings were not so lucky, and had been rounded up in horrible ways, executed, and discarded as cheaply as possible. When the numbers became overwhelming, the Aletians simply dumped them alive, into spent quarries and then buried them, thousands at a time. Some of the captors had started digging them up shortly afterwards to use their skin for lampshades and such, but apparently, there was a limit to what some Aletians could accept, and the practice ceased. What scriptures Jasma held was from one of the unfortunate ones.

Jan was thumbing through his mother's old pages. They were well preserved because they were made of very thin agrist paper, which lasted almost forever, as long as it was not torn or otherwise abused. Martha's collection had expanded, and there was a lot to go over, then he found a similarly worded scrap of paper that looked interesting —

"of the White Dragon. His crown will be of...
thin rivulets, with no other markings on...
laws of old and the green animals...
will hear God's Teacher...
Then the end of all who walk this world...
for ten thousand years. The White Dragon will again return to...
the end of D'ot, Judgment Day."

Jan could not understand it, but it did look similar to Jasma's piece of scripture. He held his handwritten copy to the right, and then the left of his mother's torn paper, side by side. His face fell with astonishment. The words seemed to make a little more sense now —

"...will be known by the sign of the White Dragon. His crown will be of ...molten gold running down like thin rivulets, with no other markings on... his spotless white crest. He will bring back the laws of old, the green animals... and the dragons of D'ot. He will follow a guide, a servant of God...and we will be reborn, free, for a generation.

Then the end of all who walk this world...will come. All souls will sleep, bound to D'ot for ten thousand years. The White Dragon will again return to... this world, to stir our sleeping souls, in preparation for ...the end of D'ot, Judgment Day."

"I still don't understand anything about this! It's all just a bunch of symbols, and I've seen a lot of that in other writings. It's all gibberish!" Jan complained to himself, frustrated.

With sudden motivation, he put his mother's scrap of scripture in his pocket. "I've got to show this to Jasma," he said to himself. He wanted to catch Jasma before she had her belongings moved from her boat. Jan found himself rowing the lifeboat back over to Jasma's boat. He got there, and she was on the upper deck, coordinating plans with Dr. Kalep and others as usual. It was so nice to be out in the open, in the sun, without fear.

"Jasma, I found something!" Jan exclaimed, as he walked hurriedly up to the small group.

Dr. Kalep did not look happy to see the young upstart who had countered him earlier. Jasma, on the other hand, had all the time in the world for Jan. "What did you find?" she asked, curious and surprised at Jan's unusually excited demeanor.

"I found this," Jan said, and he pulled out his mother's scripture, along side of his copy of Jasma's parchment.

She accepted the two pieces of paper, and held them side by side, as Jan had handed them to her. "Well, I'll be!" exclaimed Jasma. She studied it some more. "This is fascinating — I'll be right back!" She handed the papers to Jan, rushed downstairs and in a few minutes came back with her original piece of paper. Jasma said, "Here, give me your mother's scripture," and when Jan handed it to her, she held them side-by-side. The tear in the pages matched perfectly! Where did your mother get this?" Jasma asked, shocked and intrigued.

"Mom said it was handed down from her great-great grandmother. She was married to a Platac back then." Jan answered.

"Really?" exclaimed Jasma, very interested now. She surveyed him with this new information and said, "You know, you and your mother *do* have lighter scales than average, come to think of it. You must have Platac blood in you."

Jan shrugged his shoulders and said, "Probably, a little bit. My mother said some of her relatives from back then were found and killed, and some weren't."

Jasma quickly copied down Jan's piece of scripture in her notebook, and said she would study it further. Jan had to get going to help unload his boat, so he said, "I'll see you all later!" and headed back.

The contisses and wagons were unloaded first, then the supplies onto the mostly-covered wagons. They were not happy to have lost Dom's stagecoach, but his contisses would still be put to good use. Dr. Kalep and company appeared to know where they were headed. When everyone was ready, they all left in a caravan of six hundred and thirty people with just over one hundred wagons. A small brave group volunteered to guide three of the boats downstream to the mouth of the river as it emptied into the ocean. They planned to anchor them at the same city that the others were heading to by land, which was next to the ocean, according to the maps. Boats would be a necessity there.

They had many, many supplies to bring. Winoni had brought a mini-smelter, which was extremely heavy. It had its own wagon to haul it, and he added two of Dom's contisses to the team of six he already had. They traveled along a nice flat stretch, with few boulders or iron formations to get in their way. The hunters spread out around the perimeter of the caravan, sporadically shooting into the landscape at anything that looked like trouble. They would then go out in small groups, and bring their catch back for skinning, cleaning, and butchering on one of two wagons and crews dedicated to the task.

When it appeared that they were reaching dusk, they set up camp by lining up the wagons in rows and columns. This gave the hunters a tighter, smaller perimeter to protect. Tents were dispersed in between the wagons. With the camp almost one hundred percent armed, a predator might get through, but it wasn't getting out.

"What about the crantics?" Jan asked one of the hunters. Crantics had not yet been seen, and the hunters were particularly concerned about the crantic's stealthy stalking abilities. Crantics were the big, big, cousins of emuis. Their fur was very beautiful, and valuable back in the NOV. The hunters were vigilant, though, and were hoping they could stop one before any disaster happened.

After setting up camp, some musicians started playing, and the crowd cooked some of the meat that had been collected throughout the day, as well as a large amount of fish that had been caught while on the river. With the yama bread that was constantly being baked in the fifth wagon ahead of Jan's, it all worked very well.

There were multiple portable hydrogen stove fires going. More and more people were reveling in their ability to mingle and do, say, and sing anything they pleased. Around some of the fires, there were people who could play the hama, or the oblate, and this provided the means for all to join in and sing the old songs around the many fires. *This is great,* Jan thought, as he surveyed the happy gatherings.

"It won't stay this way for long," the Guide said. *"The lights and noise they are making will draw unwanted visitors to the area tonight."*

Jan realized that the Guide was right. He decided to take a quick walk around the camp, asking the various groups gathered to keep it down, telling them that their loudness and fires would attract the animals. Nobody was listening but the hunters, who agreed wholeheartedly with Jan. The people just wanted to cut loose for their first night on land together. Everyone had waited so long for this. Jan returned to his wagon.

Rebecca and Rachel wanted to walk around the groups and fires in the night to meet people. Rebecca was getting a little tipsy on some tuba, which had been brought by one group of college students, and was also being brewed by Winoni's group now. Jan brought his rifle along, just in case of a surprise predator attack. He wanted to really test his new Mach3b, but it was just too heavy to haul around for no good reason.

"Just smell the air!" Rachel exclaimed, "It's so clean out here, away from the city."

Rebecca was obsessing about the yama supply. "We *need* to get to the ocean, and learn how to harvest yama. Otherwise, we'll run out of hydrogen and electricity — and we need it to eat." She knew what it was like to go without yama, as her dad Hais had not cared for it, and she had often gone without it. The absence of yama as part of her diet had led to the presence of more bodily sores and other digestive difficulties when she was younger.

They eventually ran into Winoni, whom Jan had taken a liking to. Winoni was starting to stress about what lay ahead. He had been drinking tuba, and felt like unloading. "I am responsible for bringing technology along for this group," he said to them. "I need to get as many people as I can to learn how to use the mining equipment that we've brought. I need to train them to mine, refine, and I need to build a full-size smelter as soon as we can. Things are going to break, and we need to replace those things as soon as possible. We can't just run down to the store for parts you know. We need to make them all now, from start to finish."

Winoni was actually looking forward to the challenge. He was a credentialed expert in all aspects of production, and could reproduce just about anything, but he needed help. He wanted to show his stuff, and have these people realize how fortunate they were to have him there. He wanted to make his mark, and was concerned that it may just turn out to be a smudge.

Rebecca piped up again about the need for yama, and Winoni was very happy to see that at least one person understood the importance of harvesting and utilizing fresh yama as soon as possible. They had a huge stock of the dry, dead yama. It was good for a lot of things, but it wouldn't produce hydrogen. Their electricity generators, as well as stoves and heaters, depended on hydrogen, and they needed live yama for that.

They suddenly heard screams and gunfire at the back of the caravan. Jan went running back along with some others, and when they got there, they saw a dead yeta and one dead colonist, with his head missing. Hunters were gathering, one of them had killed the yeta, but it was obviously too late.

The hunters went out into the dark to find the other yetas if possible. Jan went with them, figuring his rifle might help along with the other firepower. There was a large group of hunters, along with helpers similar to Jan out there. While Jan and the hunters were outside camp looking for the yeta's companions, they heard more screaming from the camp again, along with gunfire coming from the same area.

Seeing nothing in the dark with their flashlights, the hunters returned to camp to see what the shooting was all about. As it happened, while they were out, a swarm of trachnas had attacked a tent, tearing a young couple to shreds, along with their four-year-old child. By the time Jan and the hunters arrived, the surrounding people killed some of the trachnas, while others had indeed escaped. The camp had become quieter, but for where the killings took place.

A small crowd had gathered there, including the LERN leaders. Rebecca and Rachel had come, and when Jan got through to see what had happened, he was horrified at the sight and said loudly, with exasperation, "This didn't have to happen."

"What do you mean?" Dr. Kalep asked, in a challenging way.

"I told a lot of people here to keep the noise and lights down, we were attracting this disaster," Jan replied, and he took it further, "and we shouldn't have left the boats so early in the first place."

Dr. Kalep bridled at Jan's remarks. His stomach growled. He was appalled at having his decisions questioned, particularly from an unknown youth. "We could have just as easily been attacked by a molick!" he countered loudly and derisively, as if Jan were a student in one of his classes. "In any case, we can't turn back now, and we only have five or six days of travel to go." Kalep paused, looking into the crowd around them, and back at Jan. "Who are you anyway? What do you know?" He was clearly frustrated with this young kid's continual challenge to his authority, now using hindsight as a challenge. The audacity was infuriating.

"I say we head back to the boats tomorrow. It will only cost us a day or two," insisted Jan, sabotaging any attempt for a graceful exit on the part of Dr. Kalep.

Now Dr. Kalep was overtly outraged. "You are nobody!" he shouted, hoping to put Jan in his place. "Why don't you go back to your family like a good boy?"

Ziba was there for this, and she spoke up. "Jan is not 'nobody'! I know Jan, and I believe he will show himself of great value out here."

"Yes, I agree," Rebecca offered, and then blurted out, "He can see things before they happen."

Jan cringed when Rebecca said that. They all looked at him as if he were crazy, when Jasma added her opinion. "There is a lot about this new person that I have found very impressive. I believe he has abilities that will become more evident with time here." Jasma could not say anything about the scriptures because they were simply so subjective — even threatening to some of those standing there, considering what the writings implied. She needed to keep some credibility, and she knew that.

"The plan stays as it is!" Dr. Kalep roared.

Winoni stepped in, and said, "I go along with Dr. Kalep, he has the team of experts with him, and they all have decided that this is the best way to travel now."

Cush was there, and saw a power play happening. He opted for the side of the obvious winners and said, looking scornfully at Jan, "This 'Jan' — he has no specific schooling, no credentials — all he has is his opinion. Why are we even listening to him? Everyone here has opinions, why give his uneducated opinions even this much attention?"

"I agree!" Asa was joining in now. He knew how these things went, and he did not want to be upstaged by Jan. He had learned in boarding school that he had to keep pushing, confronting. He had to fight to rise in the pecking order that was going to develop. Sure, he had his mother, Jasma, who everyone knew and respected. He also realized that the respect for her would not be transferred to him forever. Asa had to push his way into leadership starting now, if he was going to do it at all. It should not be difficult, as he *did* bring his posse. He had told them to stay away from his mother Jasma for now. Out of sight was out of mind.

Jan could see what was happening. He sighed, telling them, "I've had my say. I'll go along with what is decided." He then walked away, feeling a bit depressed. *Nobody listens.* He imagined the Guide looking at him with disappointment, and then he remembered that disappointment for the Guide was impossible. The Guide just seemed to accept outcomes, and go from there. *No reprimands. Perhaps some chiding.* Jan chuckled to himself.

Rebecca accompanied Jan back to their campsite. Jan insisted, "We should all sleep up on the wagon tonight, even if there's not much room on it."

About half took his advice. During the night, pladises made their appearance, and after some noise, the rest of their group came up from their tents and found a place on the wagon to sleep. Pladises could not crawl up onto the smooth metal wagon wheels that easily and really could not detect the wagon's occupants' scent from the ground anyway.

The hunters took turns at watch, and Jan had volunteered for that as well. "I hope I can try out this Mach3b," he told Buz earlier, but the northern end of the caravan was the only section to see any real action that night — two yetas. They also bagged a good number of blogs — for the contisses. They had set traps around the caravan and that was proving productive as well. Nobody had seen and killed a crantic yet. Crantics were apparently too intelligent, or just plain cautious.

The next day it was more of the same. That is, if the same meant gunshots going off throughout each hour of the day. It was getting hillier, and the hunters were becoming busier. They started spotting very big boulders now that had fallen down the increasingly hilly terrain, and they were becoming more numerous. This all meant more predator hiding spots, caves and nests, unseen in the rough hillside. Nobody had been lost to the predators since the first night.

On their third day of land travel, they started spotting old Platac home mounds that stood up from the sand and rocks, and these excited everyone. Dr. Kalep, being an archeologist, was thrilled by the fact that a few of them were aboveground, and they had a unique construction that was unknown to him. They did not go inside any of structures. There were too many dangers in them, and not enough time to dig into one. There still had been no more fatalities, but the pladises were causing numerous infections. The colonists were running into more flying insects, which was rare up north. These were scavengers, not parasitic, and primarily went after the food.

The caravan was approaching a point at which they could save a day's travel by going directly over the hillside coming up ahead. Dr. Kalep convinced the others that this was the thing to do. He justified it by saying that the best goal would be to arrive at their destination as soon as possible. They could then finally stay in one place and defend it. They had been lucky so far. They made their decision in favor of Dr. Kalep, and the announcement traveled throughout the caravan.

Jan heard it, and once again, the Guide said something contrary to the plan, *"Don't go over the hills, many will not make it. You are much better going east around the hills, but it will take longer."*

Jan said, "Oh brother. You know what they'll say. They don't want to hear from me."

"It will be different this time. Bring your gun — the big one," replied the Guide. *"Do not mention me."*

Jan did what the Guide suggested. He brought his Mach3b. *What the heck, I might as well get a chance to finally bag something.* The lead wagons in the caravan had stopped to discuss whether this was the right spot to start over the hills. Jan walked up to the group that was with Dr. Kalep, they were still making plans. Ziba and Jasma were there, with Dr's Brader and Agnew as well. They had picked a shady spot at the bottom of a slightly leaning iron shaft, about fifty feet from the caravan. These shafts were ranging widely in size, from one hundred to one thousand square feet in a horizontal plane. Jan was determined this time to change things.

Jan did not waste any small talk. He looked directly at Dr. Kalep and said, "It is suicide to head into the hills. We won't be able to stop all the predators, especially at night. We need to go eastward, around those small hills there." Piles of big boulders were nearby them. Jan wondered about the risk, and said, "Anything could be behind those boulders right there."

Dr. Kalep gave Jan an exasperated look and retorted, "The hunters have already cleared this area! Stop telling us how —" He was rudely interrupted when Dr. Agnew who was standing next to him was violently snatched by a ninety-foot ela. The ela had slithered up amazingly fast from around the corner of the iron shaft, and grabbed Dr. Agnew firmly by his side with its enormous jaws. Before anyone could say, *"Fuck!"* it curled its pointed poisonous tail up high in the air, and then instantly thrust it straight down, penetrating the skull of the good doctor. Copious amounts of poison gushed out of the top of his head as the ela injected it, and Agnew was dead instantly.

Crack-crack-crack-crack-crack-crack-crack! Jan cut loose with his Mach3b. He nearly cut the ela in half with the quarter-pound bullets he had just unloaded, and his right shoulder was screaming at him. The half with the head was spastically jerking around, biting at the air, and the tail was jumping like mad, too. The group moved in a wave in the opposite direction.

Jan looked at the visibly shaken Dr. Kalep, who was now holding his chest and stomach, staring at his dead friend. Dr. Brader was in shock, along with Jasma, and Ziba, who was actually the first to say, "Fuck."

Jan shook his head. "I think you should consider what I suggested, Dr. Kalep," he said, "It could have easily been you." He gave a nod to Ziba and Jasma, and then he walked back to his wagon.

Shortly thereafter, they received word that the plans had changed, and that they would be going east, around the hills.

Two days later, after much the same routine, accentuated by some "too-close" encounters with the local wild residents, the group came upon another choice they had to make.

Commissioner Cush along with Dr. Kalep wanted to go down into, and through a valley in which they could replenish their fresh water reserves. Jasma and Ziba usually saw things eye to eye. In this case, however, Ziba saw the danger. Jasma wanted fresh water like the rest of them.

"I'm tired of rationing my water!" complained Cush, when discussing the subject with others from the lead wagons.

"I can't wash my baby the way she needs," a young mother said.

The dilemma was that the hunters felt that they would be easily trapped by yetas and other beasts if attacked by a group of them in the valley, especially near the water. The predators appeared to be getting more numerous as they continued their trek. The caravan had no choice but to head into more hilly terrain, in any case.

Jan began walking around, as the caravan had stopped. People were becoming more edgy. The goal was so close, but they were tired of traveling, and craved a place to stop and settle down. Many had to walk during the day, because either they were guarding the caravan, or they had to take the weight off the wagons so that the older contisses could keep their pace. Buz was busy wooing Tama. Lep had all but disappeared — always busy nursing the vaccine module. Dom was seen occasionally, usually fretting that Lep wanted him back soon. It apparently had become a full time job to keep the temperatures stable in the wagon.

As Jan walked up upon the discussion, Dr. Kalep became agitated at Jan's arrival. "Oh, no you don't," he said to Jan as he walked up.

"What?" replied Jan, not really asking, because he already heard about the decision they were trying to make.

"You always show up like this — at times like this," Dr. Kalep said in an exasperated way. Winoni looked on with amusement at this young upstart.

"That usually means something is going to happen that shouldn't," joked Jan. He smiled at Dr. Kalep, but Dr. Kalep did little more than smirk at him, and shake his head.

Dr. Kalep had gone from a deep distrust of Jan to a moderate dislike of him, along with disconcerting flashes of actual respect. Kalep did have his love-lover training, after all. He did not realize that he feared Jan. Kalep surprisingly said, "Well, Jan, let's see what you have to say, you're going to do it now that you're here anyway." They then filled Jan in on the details, with emphasis on Kalep's side of the argument.

What they did not know was that Jan had a dream the night before. He had seen the same terrain that they were in, but he had risen high above it. The path went east, towards the southern end of the river as it joined the ocean, and the path he saw was alive, like a slithering ela forming the letter "S" over and over again.

Now, Jan looked around and noticed that the way he had seen in his dream appeared hilly and dangerous from ground level. They could not see the flat, clear, and safe path because of small hills hiding the "S" curves, but he knew that they were there.

"Take the way over there, to the left of the side of this hill, but don't go into the valley," Jan said.

Cush threw his cup down, and said, "Blast this insolent young commoner! It won't be any problem at all in the valley! Just look at it! It's all clear!"

They all looked down into the valley, and Cush did have a good point. "I'll tell you what," Cush said. "Let us rest here a while, and we'll send a group of scouts down to the valley to see. It should take them half an hour to reach the stream down there."

"Great idea!" said Dr. Kalep, looking around for takers.

Jasma said, "It sure would be nice to have them bring some fresh water back," looking for Jan's reaction.

Jan just shrugged his shoulders. He didn't know. All he was sure of was the path they *should* take.

Since nobody protested, it was decided that a group of six hunters would be sent down to scout the area and bring back some water. Then they would listen to the hunters' report. They approached the hunter's caravans and the ones there were not happy about it, but they did provide six volunteers to scout. Jan went back to his wagon, near the end of the caravan, to get his gun to help cover them.

The group of scouts went down the steep hillside into the deep valley, towards the distant stream that ran through the bottom of it.

Jan traveled back to his wagon, hoping they would be alright. He got his big gun, and was heading back when he heard screaming up ahead. They were shooting from their location, and there were a few shots fired in the valley.

He ran up to the others, and looked down the hill. All six of the scouts were already being devoured by a pack of at least ten crantics that came out of a cave far below. The planning group could not see the cave opening from their vantage point above, because the lair was below, on the same side of the hill that they were on. Jan fired at the crantics along with the others that were shooting, but the distance was too great, although they scared the crantics back into their lair. Thus far, crantics, being shrewder than realized, had perceived the caravan as very alien and therefore too dangerous to approach.

"What can we do?" Jasma cried out, looking at Jan. "Can anybody help them?"

"Only by going down there," replied Jan, looking at Dr. Kalep.

Dr. Kalep averted Jan's gaze, and looked at his feet. Nobody was about to go down there now, not even to retrieve the bodies — or what was left of them.

They all shuffled about a bit, but eventually prepared to go back to their wagons to continue the way Jan had advised. Winoni came up to Jan and said lowly, "You know, I'm beginning to think you're not full of hydrogen." He smiled, and patted Jan on the upper back, which, reckoning Winoni's size, knocked Jan off his balance for a moment.

Jan just smiled, and they walked together as far as Winoni's wagon, with Jan then continuing alone to his own wagon. He smelled food cooking, coming from the wagons as he was passing and wondered, *What are Mom and Rebecca cooking for dinner?* The two of them had taken on the job of cooking for the nine people on their wagon. Buz was usually helping the hunters now, spotting, with Jan's pistol or rifle on him. He would be late to dinner.

Chapter Twenty

The Road Home

he caravan continued for the next two days, and the people did find fresh water along the way. They followed the twisting "path" between the lower hills east-southeast. The hunters had their routine down, and very few predators could get near the caravan without becoming dinner. The path became rather narrow at parts, and the occasional blog would be able to hop speedily into a wagon. Even the wild ones were not particularly dangerous unless cornered — they were after the food they smelled. The blogs out here were bigger than the ones used as pets or fed to the contisses back in the NOV. When standing upright, blogs were almost four feet tall. They made a racket when any predator would come close, so the caravan started to allow them in, to trap them. They began to keep blogs on leashes as alarms at night. Being the primates of D'otians, they were remarkably intelligent, and became somewhat tamer by the day, as they were fed and kept safe.

It was the middle of the day now, and the people were plugging away at their trek with rising anticipation.

"Look at this!" Dr. Kalep cried out. He had been walking in front of the wagons with the lead hunters, anxious to see any signs of the city. Far in front of them and to the right was an aboveground mansion, sitting on the side of a small hill they were just rounding. "It's magnificent!" he exclaimed, as he ran ahead of the hunters, continuing until he reached it.

"Hold on there," one of the hunters hollered. "We don't have time to clear it!"

"I want it! I want to live here!" Dr. Kalep gasped, as he was enormously excited at the discovery. The building had one westerly long curved edge going up, like the front of a boat, except that the sides along the edge were initially concave, and it was four stories high. It came to a pyramidal peak at the top. The winds coming from the west kept the gleaming metal surfaces polished like glass. The edge split the westerly wind as a big cleaver would split a gendra thighbone. The thick windows were still intact, albeit hazy and translucent. Dr. Kalep went up the hillside to the building, and put his hand to the gleaming metal. He looked at the others standing around the wagons that had arrived now, astonished. "It's cool to the touch!" he yelled to the others. They started murmuring about it, because it should have been very warm if not hot, with the sun out in the clear sky.

"We must move on! Mark it, and if we are close enough to the city, you can decide then what you want to do!" said Nugen, the lead hunter.

Kalep knew he could not stop the whole caravan. He looked around while he had the time. From where he was, up the hill a ways, he could see in the immediate surrounding landscape that there were underground homes scattered about, buried in sand, silt, and rocks. He returned to the others, and they continued.

About three hours later, they all knew they were coming up upon something important. The path they were traveling was becoming wider, flatter, and straighter. Dr. Kalep had become quite adept at spotting homes which to others looked like ordinary mounds of sand and such. These mounds were fast becoming more numerous and the "path" would eventually lead them straight towards a yet-to-be discovered big circular road. Before they could see the road-circle ahead, they noticed the outline of something up in the distance there, stretching high up from the ground, and it was very intriguing. In about fifteen minutes or so, they were close enough to not only see the tall object, but the circle around it as well.

"We've hit a crossroads!" the hunters up ahead shouted.

As the caravan arrived, they all gathered the wagons on what looked like what once was a circular road, now covered with sand. What they were goggling at was in the least, unexpected. In the center of this three hundred-foot road-circle stood a huge round metallic object that looked like an giant umbrella on a pedestal. Most of them ran towards the center to look up at it, to be completely under it. The sculpture had ornate designs high above them. The designs were done in relief, and it was unlike anything that Aletian imaginations had created in the NOV artwork that existed. The golden lines up above them were flowing from their own centers, gently curving, multiplying, and ending in big tips that looked like arrowheads. Its circumference shadowed the eastern part of the circular road beneath. Looking up at it from below, it had round depressions near its perimeter, appearing to have possibly held lights at one time.

"That thing must be over two hundred feet high!" Jasma exclaimed, "How beautiful!"

Dr. Kalep was temporarily absent as he had a digestive emergency upon seeing the structure.

They walked around underneath the 'umbrella', and observed the crossroads. The roads that joined the circle to the right and left were similar to the one by which they had arrived. The apparent road straight ahead however was wider than the rest, straight and relatively flat. In fact, it looked like it could have been a highway that one would see in the main capital of the NOV. It was an easy choice to take that way.

They continued, and Jan's wagon companions were all out walking along side the caravan, taking in the curious surroundings. They could see the outlines of what had once been streets, because the depressions in the sand were so uniform and straight, coming off their path at right angles. These were all lined with the ups and downs in the terrain that Dr. Kalep said were homes.

Jan was talking with Buz, saying, "It's going to get dark, soon."

Rebecca chimed in, "We need to keep going! We need to — get to the city center. I just know it's up ahead. I have to see it. Tonight!"

Even Martha, who had been subdued for most of the month-long journey, was beginning to become animated as she exclaimed, "All my life I have been waiting for this!"

"How do you know there *is* a city center? If there is, how do you know it's not in some other direction?" Buz commented.

Jan could feel that Rebecca was right. They were going the right way, still — "You've been acting a bit off today," Jan said to Rebecca, "What's up?"

Rebecca *was* feeling strangely. She said, perplexed, "I don't know." She looked around them. "It's all these homes. There were people here, and we killed them all. It's strange, and I — I guess I'm affected by it, that's all."

"Well, we didn't kill them — the NOV did, one hundred years ago. As far as I'm concerned this is payback for us, for all our suffering. A reward!" Rachel gushed, as she walked along with Martha, holding Martha's arm. She looked at Martha with a big smile on her face, and Martha contentedly smiled right back.

"Let's get the biggest, nicest house for all of us!" Rachel said to Martha. "We can clean it out, decorate it. Oh! I wonder what the artwork and sculptures are like in these homes? — and they must have had theaters! Big, beautiful theaters! I can't wait! I want to keep going, even if we go all night."

"The hunters have protected us so far, haven't they?" said Rebecca, joining Rachel in the debate.

Martha did not join in the conversation further. She was still digesting the long-withheld news that she was going to be a grandmother. *I sure feel like a grandmother,* she thought to herself. She was physically drained, and her knees were barking. Martha was thirty-eight now. She was getting older, but still had a good nine years left. She could live longer than the average, but those ones who dragged on often suffered greatly with sores and any number of diseases until the end. Yesterday, Martha was in shock upon hearing of Rachel's pregnancy, but since then she was able to digest the news. The rules had all changed. As far as anyone knew, there were no rules, yet. She was musing about what the others would say. *If anyone speaks of unapproved pregnancy, I'll tell them to piss off!* Martha mused about it some more — *they really should get married, though.* She glanced at Rebecca, who had seemed to be astonishingly OK with the pregnancy of Rachel. *What about Rebecca? I have seen for years now how she loves Jan. She has nobody else she wants. Jan should marry both of them. After all, out here, who is here to tell him he isn't wealthy enough?*

Jan wasn't talking much now. He and Buz decided to walk up to the front to see what the leaders may be cooking up.

On the way, Buz broke the silence, "I saw Sak today, sleeping under Winoni's wagon."

Jan stiffened at the mention of Sak. "I hope he got covered in pladises," he replied. "I never see him, unless it's from a distance. I think he's hiding from me. He may be smarter than I thought."

"Well, there are always the predators," Buz said, enjoying Jan's look of satisfaction at the thought. "Hey, I thought you love-lovers were supposed to love everyone."

"I'm still a D'otian," Jan replied dryly. "He just — doesn't belong here. No, that's wrong. He doesn't *deserve* to be here. My dad should be here." Then Jan went silent again, as they continued to walk more quickly to the front of the moving caravan.

Buz thought about Huto, and also his own mother and father and brother. They were fast becoming a distant memory. He never had developed any feelings for them, or anyone for that matter. He was a relatively successful product of the NOV. Up until now, Jan's importance had been more as an ally. He liked him well enough though. To Buz, love was an alien concept, and he perceived the love circles they did every week as freaky. He wondered though, as he lived among all these people over the last month, what was really so bad about love? They all seemed normal. In fact, they treated him better than anyone ever did at home.

"You guys are OK," Buz said, and when Jan gave him a quizzical look, he elaborated, "LERN, your group, you're OK by me," and he sounded like he really meant it. There was a feeling growing inside Buz that he not felt before. It felt good and happy. It felt like freedom was expanding, and would not stop now for anything. Buz smiled to himself.

Tama had begun to accept him as safe, and he melted every time she would talk with him.

When they reached the front of the caravan, the leaders had indeed decided to go on into and through the night. Excitement was in the air, and some wagons had broken out the tuba for an early celebration. Jasma was with Ziba, as usual, and they always welcomed Jan when he visited.

"Oh Jan," called Jasma, "Look ahead — well, what do you think?" she asked, smiling broadly.

Directly up ahead, Jan saw what looked like more iron shafts, but they were short, and perpendicular to the ground.

"That's the city!" exclaimed Jasma before Jan could answer. "I can't wait!" In spite of her age, which was about five years older than Martha, she seemed to rise above her worn out body, and she still had a youthful way about her. Ziba, on the other hand, was at the age that most D'otians began to break down with disease. She was tired looking now, but had great stamina and usually marched on with the rest. When she would get exhausted, she would ride in her wagon.

"I guess that means that we are going to continue in the dark then," Jan said.

Ziba answered, "The hunters are quite confident that the road is so wide, and the area so open that they will be able to protect us."

Jan was starting to feel the excitement, and he decided, "Why not?" He smiled at Buz and said, "We need to celebrate." He turned to Ziba who was enjoying a glass of tuba and asked, "Where'd you get that?"

Jasma chimed in and said, "Go to Winoni's wagon. They still have a great deal of tuba concentrate, and they've been brewing it for the past few days with water they had set aside. They were able to make much more when we found water the other day."

On the way back to Winoni's wagon, Jan heard an unusual noise coming from the wagon in front of Winoni's. "Something sounds wrong," he said to Buz. They went around in back, and Jan opened the doors. Inside were Asa, five of Asa's buddies, and Sak. Sak was holding his hand over a girl's mouth, while Asa was just beginning to disrobe her. Jan recognized the girl as Ghina, a girl that had arrived without her family, as they had been captured in the escape.

"What the hell is this?" Jan bellowed, as he and Buz jumped up into the wagon. Asa quickly turned, his hanging headdress flying about his shoulders and retorted, "It's cool — she's with us, right, Ghina?"

Ghina looked very groggy, and Jan demanded, "Get your hands off of her!" to Sak, who was now wide-eyed and scared. They all looked frightened now, even Asa. Nobody wanted a scene with so many witnesses walking around outside the wagon.

Sak immediately released Ghina, who clumsily started buttoning her blouse, "It's all right," she said while walking towards Jan, and then she tripped over and passed out right there in front of him.

Jan jumped to stop her fall, and Asa moved forward toward him and said, "See, she said it's all right, give her back!"

Asa was moving as if he were going to take her from Jan, and Buz barked, "Fuck off! We're taking her back to her wagon." Then he said, "And we're reporting you!"

Asa laughed a fake laugh, "To who?" He laughed some more, looking to his posse of rough looking scoundrels, who followed his lead. He looked at Jan and Buz, sneering, and spat on the floor, saying, "Silly little commoners. Go — take her!" Then he gave Jan his evil eye.

Jan looked past him to Sak. "You! You're like a fucking magnet to shit! This is your first fuck-up. You'll pay for your next one," Jan was now growling with extreme rancor as he turned with the girl, Buzz at his back.

They left, carrying Ghina, and discussing what to do about the gang they saw forming. Jan was talking, "I wanted to kill Sak before, and I think I might put Asa on that list as well."

"I don't think killing is allowed here," Buz replied thoughtfully.

"We're going to wish we had," Jan responded. After dropping Ghina off at her wagon to sleep it off, they went back to Winoni's spot for the tuba, and brought some back for the girls.

The caravan continued into the night, and they finally stopped in pitch black caused by dense cloud cover. There were no moons out tonight. The contisses were tired and complaining. Nobody could see much, unless they shined a light out, and they were trying to save electricity, so lights were used only for security. They finally decided to stop where they were, and to continue in the morning.

Back at Jan's wagon they all stayed up for a while longer, drinking, talking and planning as usual. They eventually crawled wearily into the wagon, finally going to sleep.

The night was punctuated by gunfire. It had become rather easy to sleep through it by now though.

The next morning, Rachel, who had risen early and was now outside the wagon, awakened the others. She came to the back doors, and opened them wide. She was going on and on about the city. The sky was now clear, and sunlight came blazing in. Those in the wagon got up and out to see.

What they viewed was amazing. Although they weren't sure where the center of the city was, they could see structures not far from them that were bigger than any the NOV ever had, other than the NOV capital temple. These structures were very different, though. Like the mansion that Dr. Kalep coveted, many had long, slowly sloping graceful lines, stretching upwards for up to eight stories or more. One looked like a gigantic elongated screw. They had never seen so much elaborate architecture. Back in the NOV, everything built aboveground was square and plain — nothing like this. There appeared to be brass designs inlaid into some of the buildings, and most had some type of artistic lean to them.

"Dr. Kalep must feel like he's died and gone to heaven," Jan exclaimed. He smiled broadly, as he surveyed the surrounding network of roads and structures. They were still not truly visible because of the all the sand accumulation, but he had developed an eye for it, along with others.

Jan had been a bit sullen the past couple of days, and Martha was happy to see him smiling for more than his usual short moments. She did not know that something was nagging at him.

Jan had not been able put his finger on the feeling, but it was there. Fear and foreboding was on him for no good reason — but then again, *the NOV. That's what's probably bugging me,* he realized. *I feel like they'll come after us. I don't feel like I'll ever be able to shake it.*

Lep had told him that eighty percent of the population would likely die within three years. *Lep said The NOV may never recover. There's a good chance that they will leave us be, but I just can't accept that, yet.*

Everyone was beginning to mill around, waiting on word of what was next. The planning committee had decided that the safest way to start was to move into a few big buildings as soon as possible, all neighboring each other. They prepared to send out two groups of scouts, mostly hunters, to canvass the area and report back, with maps and photographs of their travels.

Drs. Kalep and Brader would be with the group scouting eastward. Dr. Scrib went with the scouts going west-southwest. The east of their position led towards the river mouth and the ocean, while the southwest-ward direction went into the western part of the city and south from there. Winoni assisted with Kalep's group and brought a few miners along with some equipment that would help dig out the way to the entrances of structures of interest. They all rode on contisses or in wagons.

Everyone else just stayed where they were and waited. The area had been secured well the night before. After doing his or her respective chores, most settled down for an early evening. The ones remaining in Winoni's wagons broke out the tuba again. They all had a very nice day and evening, singing, dancing, and there were the stirrings of romance in the air. Buz and Tama spent a few hours together, and Jan saw Jasma with a bottle of yama wine in her hand, cornering a hunter that was taking a break.

When it was beginning to get dark, Dr. Scrib's group came back first from the southwest, bringing photos of a well-laid road structure. The most remarkable thing they found was a magnificent temple. Its peak was made of solid gold, and it was structured like a tall, narrow four-sided pyramid, but once again had the sloping, inward-leaning concave lines on the westward edge. It had multiple smaller duplicate outbuildings attached around it, asymmetrically placed, with pointed tops of varying heights, which peaked out lower than the primary peak of the central pyramidal structure.

Shortly thereafter, Dr. Kalep's group returned from the eastern area. They brought with them a wonderful surprise — the skeleton crews that had been waiting in the three boats that had indeed made it safely all the way down to the river's mouth. Those boats would certainly be useful, and they made plans to go back and get the rest. Everyone was happy to see them back safely.

Kalep's group was stirred with tales of fantastic structures. "We were able to enter one, and it went up high enough to see the ocean!" he said enthusiastically. "We have so many places to choose from, I can't decide!" He was now laughing hysterically.

Decide they did, though. After careful descriptions and study of the maps, they all decided that they would go east, toward the ocean, to a section of city that the hunters said would be easy to defend. Animals would not be so much of a problem as thought, because they had been unable to penetrate the predator-proof construction of the Platacs. Once inside the few buildings they had entered, Kalep's group found they were relatively clear of debris and sand.

Like everyone, Ziba was enchanted by the photos and descriptions. "Let us thank God for our new lives in — New Aletia!" The ones around her joined in, shouting, "God bless New Aletia!" and the chorus spread down the line to the very end of the caravan. New Aletia was born on this day.

Chapter Twenty-One

New Aletia

The New Aletians worked very hard, and the days passed quickly. They had chosen to occupy three buildings adjacent to one another, relatively close to the ocean. One had been a grand office building at one time. Next to that sat what once was a tall luxury hotel, and they also dug into an outstanding colossal underground apartment building for the families to use.

With a little tweaking, Winoni's crews were able to connect generators they brought with them to the wiring in the apartment building first, for the families. Then Winoni did the same for the other buildings. The sewage system was simple and relatively intact. Plumbing was a big problem, but they were able to take advantage of a water main that came straight from a defunct reservoir next to the river. It took two months to clear and clean it all, but they now had water. The water pipes in the buildings were made of almost pure agrist — they had not cracked or corroded, but connections were a problem. The few plumbers they had worked around the clock, repairing leaks as they arose. Winoni was able to have his people recondition the fixtures and toilets. The parts needed were being made in the machine shop he had set up in the office building. In about three months, most units had electricity and water available, with working bathrooms. The storage areas were found, and revealed stocks of many necessities, light bulbs in particular being happily discovered. Half of the bulbs did not work, but rather than divert Winoni's resources to the task of manufacturing them, teams of scouts were chosen to dig into the neighboring buildings, scavenging what they could.

At first, the colonists were awestruck by the beauty of the decorative walls inside the hotel and office building, along with the wondrous arched hallways filled with remarkable paintings and other works of art. In time, however, most folks seemed not to notice the art as much, and some youngsters had written graffiti on a few pieces, which others took down to try to restore.

It took about six months to reach the point that they possessed an oversized perimeter cleared of most dangerous animals that inhabited it. They used the blogs they captured, their "predator alarms," on not only the trip, but also here in the city as well. The people divided up the chores, which they fulfilled for the most part. Digging out streets and such was a never-ending task.

In the beginning, the yama fields in the ocean were easy to harvest. The overgrowth of yama, unharvested for one hundred years, had crept up to the shoreline from a crevice that ran miles out into the ocean. This yama field was not far to the south of where the river met the ocean. By the time that six months had passed, they saw that they were using it up quickly, and would eventually need to go out to deeper into the ocean to harvest yama.

Winoni had his mini-smelter working. He had found an old mineral processing plant near the southern end of the city, and set it up there. It would take time to get it up and going, so in the meantime they melted down scavenged metals — this was much easier than mining and processing raw ore. He still needed raw ores though, chromium and nickel for certain, in order to produce the best alloys for the particular job. Winoni needed these ores to refine, smelt and machine certain parts needed to get the grinders and such at the plant going.

A group of hunters found old mines not far from the plant, but they remained unexcavated for now. New Aletia had few skilled miners in the group. Nothing along those lines was operational yet, and Winoni had expected to be the master hero when it came to providing invaluable devices, parts, and machines here. Instead, he had become the master 'bitcher', due to his unending frustration with what he felt was close to zero production. He spent all his time telling newbies what they were doing wrong. Martha joined in with Winoni's team, having more mining experience than most, but the starting was still very slow.

Jan was standing outside one day, in the courtyard that was set before the apartment building. He was scratching at his leg. His sores were becoming more numerous, and Dr. Bilge, the one health-care doctor that had survived thus far only stocked a basic antibiotic ointment for sores. Everyone was getting more sores. The doctor said that it was because there were different strains of organisms in the city, for which their immune systems needed to adjust.

In addition, many people needed enzymes. Enzyme extracts from yama were difficult to produce, and required sophisticated resources. Winoni did not yet have the time to build a laboratory to manufacture such. Therefore, stomach and other digestive problems were abounding. Dr. Kalep had finished the last of his enzymes months ago, and was in pain daily. He had succumbed to adding raw splint bile to his daily regimen, but it was harsh, and gave an aftertaste like vomit.

Jan had lately been helping Dr. Kalep's surveying team. He found it interesting to see the varieties of architecture, and with Dr. Kalep's input, he got a lot out of it, and developed a high appreciation of the Platac culture.

He was now thinking about what Rebecca had said about the yama. They were finishing their stock of the old dried yama they had brought along with them. The fresh yama needed to be cured, dried, and processed properly, which took time. Winoni was also consuming the fresh yama for use in the hydrogen generators. These were huge aquariums filled with yama. The hydrogen they produced was collected and cooled to a liquid for storage. They needed it for the electrical generators, stoves, and the vaccine module's temperature control system.

The clouds of oxygen bubbles released by the concentration of yama in the ocean served to help somewhat with sores for those who dared to go in and bathe there. Nobody had seen a molick yet, but there were many hazards besides that ocean creature.

Pladises had started to infiltrate the apartment complex somehow, causing nasty red stripes of infection on the residents. For now, they focused on filling whatever cracks there were in the walls of the underground complex.

Jan looked in the direction of the ocean and thought again how warm, clean, and clear it was when he was up close. It was not at all like his family's trips to the dirty beaches and seawater that bordered the NOV. He scratched another sore.

He was supposed to meet Rachel and Rebecca this afternoon, and was waiting for them to come up from the apartment, along with Jo, Jan's one-month-old baby boy.

Rebecca came up alone with the baby, saying, "Rachel is still with Dr. Kalep's crew helping with the city mapping." It was Rachels's first day assisting out in that capacity.

Rebecca continued, "They still haven't found a theater yet, and she's obsessed with finding one," she said.

"She's homesick," Jan replied. Rachel had been in a funk, even before the baby was born. "If I have to hear her say, 'There's nothing to do' again, I'm going to volunteer her into the mines," Jan joked, chuckling.

Other than assisting Dr. Bilge for the occasional emergency, Rachel had been staying at home with Jo. If someone was home, she was able to go out for awhile.

Rebecca cooed into the baby's face, and giggled at the baby's reaction. "Who's a good boy?" she said, over and over.

Jan looked at her and smiled, thinking, *she's a gem. She loves Jo as much as Rachel does.* For a moment he regretted Rebecca did not have her own baby now, but quickly put that thought out of his mind.

"What's Mom doing in the apartment?" Jan asked Rebecca.

"Scratching and bitching, as usual," Rebecca replied, as the thought caused her to scratch at one on the side of her neck. "Everybody's complaining about these damn sores. I think it's starting to really get them down."

"You know, you're right," said Jan. "Even Jasma's been in a foul mood lately. She not only has more sores now, there's something that's eating away at the scales and skin of her left foot."

Rebecca agreed, "I know. Since she and Ziba had that falling out last month, they both look miserable. I haven't seen them together at the love circles."

Jan and Rebecca started their way towards the beach, which was about a thirty-minute walk away. They took turns holding Jo. Along the way, Jan mentioned the meetings. "Why are so many people skipping the love-circles? It's only once a week, but some folks haven't been there for months now."

"I don't know," said Rebecca.

"I think it's because there's no NOV here," Jan said.

"What do you mean?" Rebecca asked.

Jan felt that he could see it, easily, "Now that they believe there's no enemy of love, they're not compelled to practice it. They've become less interested in the love-circles because they don't need them as a defense anymore."

He heard the Guide. *"They don't know that their need to channel love is greater than ever here,"* and continuing, *"Enemies can be invisible as well as visible. There would be no NOV without the dragon, and each person here has brought the dragon with them — everybody."*

Jan felt a sudden chill, knowing the Guide meant him, too. He said to Rebecca, "We need to push now, to keep the love-circles going, and it's time to try to talk the non-LERN people here into attending, if not to just watch. We must keep this routine. It's our way, and it is because of our way that everyone here was saved. It is because of this discipline that we are the kind of people we are."

Rebecca turned her head to Jan and said, "That sounds a little like the NOV to me, I'm sure it'll sound that way to the people you want to force, and others. Maybe you should talk to Ziba about it."

They were heading for the yama fields. Rebecca had become a quick expert in yama. Although he had passed by briefly before, this was Jan's first opportunity to spend some time close up. When they got to the beach, Rebecca handed Jo to Jan, and ran ahead of them in the dazzling fine white sand to the water. When Jan got there, she was knee deep in the salty water. There was a steady breeze from the west, blowing much of the hyper-oxygenated air seaward. The waves were gentle. Fortunately, the water was pristine. With the white sand under the water, one could see if a "bad" fish was coming from a distance. They were just on the edge of the yama field. It coated this part of the bottom of the ocean in a relatively thin strip that grew thicker the further it was from the beach, following and dropping into the ocean's crevice from which it came. One could see that Winoni and company had already harvested big sections. Here, it was about six inches thick. Rebecca knew it would be low tide now, which made it unbelievably easy to grab with one's hands.

Rebecca waded into the yama, bent down into the water, and came up with her hands cupped, full of fresh stuff she just pulled from the bottom. The water was bubbling all around her with oxygen from the yama she was standing in. She came up out of the water grinning from ear to ear. "Here," she said, sticking out her hands, "Smell this!"

Jan did the obligatory smell, and realized, "It smells wonderful! That's what fresh yama smells like? It smells like, what?" He took another sniff and said, "It smells like when it rains or something. There's a little fishy smell in there too, I think."

Rebecca held the spongy substance to her face, and then just sunk her face into it, smelling it up, and going, "Mmmmmmmmm." She looked up at Jan, and asked, "Doesn't it smell 'healthy'?"

Jan asked, "What's fresh raw yama taste like?"

Rebecca said, "Not too bad, it is kind of fishy. Want to try?" She held out her hands again. The yama was very white, but had dark speckles imbedded in it.

"Why not?" Jan said and he plucked off a good-sized piece. He took a bite of it, and quickly spit it out, making an awful face.

Rebecca was holding a blank expression hard when Jan bit into it, but not now. She started laughing, and said, "I did the same thing!" Then she noticed the baby that Jan was holding. "Jo's turning red!"

Jo was indeed turning red. Jan had noticed a different feeling, and Rebecca, with a flash of insight said, "It's the oxygen! It's really high here."

Jo's scales had not taken on color yet, and his hyper-oxygenated blood was showing through them. "We need to leave," she said, concerned.

"He *seems* OK," replied Jan, "But you're right, we should go. I think it makes me feel good, actually."

Rebecca brought the double handful of yama home to play with in the kitchen. Jan carried Jo as they walked back to the apartment. When they entered, Martha was there, listening to Rachel, who had also just returned. Rachel was talking about a new move by Dr. Kalep to start expanding the population to outlying areas.

"He really wants that mansion we saw coming into New Aletia," Jan said. "Kalep is OK, but he seems used to getting his own way."

The earlier conversation on his mind, Jan said, "Mom, I'm thinking about talking to Ziba about promoting more participation in the love-circles."

Martha perked up and exclaimed, "I'm so glad you brought that up! What I've seen over the past few months concerns me. Nobody's going to the meetings! Do you know that there was another murder last night? Tas was drunk and beat Jerba over some stupid thing, and she shot him in his sleep!"

Rebecca was shocked, and Rachel just shook her head. Rebecca said, "Now that they have an unlimited supply of yama, tuba costs nothing. I keep seeing more and more people drunk all the time."

Jan said, "Me too. We need to stay centered on something, and it's LERN that got us here. I believe that the love-circles keep us practicing what we would otherwise forget. These things won't happen as often or as much!" He looked determined and said, "I'll discuss this with Jasma first, and try to get her back talking to Ziba again."

After a while, Jan left for the hotel next door, and climbed the stairs past the seventh floor, where Ziba had taken over half the floor for herself and her staff. Winoni had not been able to make the parts needed for the elevator, which he said were low on a long list of needed items. Jasma, her son and her staff occupied the entire top tenth floor.

When Jan reached the top floor, he went to her suite and knocked on the door. Jasma's son Asa answered it. "What are *you* doing here?" he sneered.

Jan's thoughts instantly went from promoting love to seeing this keesh on the floor bleeding. He intuitively put his foot in the way, as Asa tried to slam the door on him.

"Who's there, Asa?" Jasma called out.

With no easy option, Asa stopped his effort, and reluctantly opened the door. "Him," he said disdainfully, showing her the open door.

"Oh Jan, how nice of you to stop by, please come in," Jasma cooed. She had a glass of yama wine, and an inviting smile. She gave a stern look to her son, "Asa!"

Asa got out of the way, and let Jan in. He then left for his own suite down the hall, closing the door not too quietly behind him.

"Please, Jan, have a seat." Jasma motioned to the couch beside her.

Jan could see that she was a little drunk, and figured it could get ugly. He walked over to her and said, "Jasma, I don't have a lot of time —"

"Don't be silly, dear," Jasma interrupted, "We have all the time in the world," and she looked like she really meant it.

Jan smiled. Then his expression turned to the serious, "We need to talk, and you have the power to make this happen."

Jasma was a bit surprised at Jan's bluntness, and his complement caused her to start paying attention to what he had to say. She listened to him as he made his case about promoting the weekly meetings, and in the end, she agreed completely. She got up, and walked towards her one cleared big window. Jan followed.

"It's Dr. Kalep, she said with exasperation, "If we make any attempt to create any rules, or organize, he gets angry. He always says, "Once you start with rules and laws, there is no end! We all become prisoners again!" She tried to imitate his theatrically aggravated voice, and did a cracking good job at it. It struck Jan as hilarious, and they both laughed hard, and then settled down.

"Well, it seems to me, we need Ziba," Jan said, testing Jasma, while she was in a light mood. He really did not know what the fallout was over, but he was about to find out.

Jasma's face became stern. Then her expression softened, and she said, "Ziba and I don't see eye to eye on things." She apparently thought that statement settled it, but she was dead wrong. She looked again at Jan, and could see he wanted more.

Jasma sighed and said, "She insulted me, in front of my guests! She said I was drunk, and acting, well — improperly." Now Jasma looked hurt.

"Maybe *she* was drunk, and didn't know what she was saying," Jan offered.

Jasma drew a deep breath, and slowly let it out, gazing out the window, into the horizon that held the glittering blue ocean below it. "Perhaps," she said, lost in some thought. She snapped out of it, and said thoughtfully, "It would be helpful if she *were* on our side in this," and she turned and came closer to Jan, taking his arm.

Jan put his hand on hers and said, "Let me talk with her, and see if she'll be willing to meet with you, to discuss this."

The thought of actually meeting with someone of Ziba's lower class after such an insult was anathema to Jasma, and Jan could see it.

"Do it for LERN," he said, with utmost earnestness, and Jasma gazed off again. The thought triggered her loyalty to LERN, which had been so well developed that she found herself automatically saying, "Yes," and she looked at Jan with tender eyes, "I must forgive — for love's epiphany." Her eyes widened, and she looked past Jan, and said, "It's been too long." Then she stared off again.

"I think you've had too much wine," Jan grinned, and he gave her a peck on the cheek, "I'll go talk with Ziba and try to arrange something."

Jasma glanced out the window again, and her expression changed to one of shock, "Oh my God! Hunters!"

"So what?" Jan said as he went to the window and looked. "What's the probl —" His words were cut short, and he said the same thing — "Hunters!"

They weren't LERN's hunters, who were mostly sports hunters. These ones were definitely not LERN. They were professionals, from the NOV's Hunter Stations. They were decked out in full wildlands suits, poison proof. Their respirator air filters would be reliable for a month at best, and they could have a stockpile of them.

"They're waving a white flag!" Jasma observed.

Jan said, "I've got to go." Then he said, "If you see Ziba, try to ignore her attitude until I get back, OK?"

Jasma made a face for an instant, but then quickly focused on the Hunters again. "It looks like there are two or three hundred of them! There are a lot of little ones too!"

Jan made a quick exit, and ran down the long stairway to the lobby. Others in the hotel who had a high enough view to have seen the Hunters had spread the word already. They were gathering in the lobby and everyone there was terrified. Ziba was already down there as well. Jan saw Ziba, and said, "I have to go!" Then he remembered, and said, "I was talking to Jasma about something that we need LERN to do, and she said we needed you."

Ziba's face went tense the instant that Jan mentioned "Jasma", but dropped to confusion when she heard the last part of Jan's statement.

"I'll talk to you later," Jan said, mind racing, and he ran out the front door. *They have a white flag, and they have brought children, what's going on?* He was wondering. *Maybe —*

"They want to join you," the Guide said.

"They want to join us!" Jan exclaimed, realizing what was happening. The hunters were walking up from the river mouth, and their guns were down.

It took Jan about ten minutes of sprinting to meet up with them. Word had spread back at the city — everyone there was very alarmed and frightened. "The NOV is here!" became the quick spin. Many of them squeezed into the hotel's upper rooms to be able to see as they watched Jan make his way to out the Hunters.

Sak was with Asa at the time. They were grudgingly impressed by Jan's seeming bravery, watching out of Asa's window in the hotel. It would be good for both of them if Jan was taken out by the Hunters, but would be a dire foreboding of what was now upon them all.

Jan's heart was pounding from the run — it would have been racing anyway. He could see them clearly now, and he believed strongly that they would not fire at him. One of them, the one holding the white flag, handed the flag to another, and ran up to meet Jan.

"So you're alive!" the Hunter exclaimed as he was running, "How many survived?"

Jan responded with, "What are you doing here? What do you want?"

The Hunter slowed his pace towards Jan. They were close enough now. "We want to join you! My name is Palatu." His hands were outstretched, as if begging.

The others were coming up now, as they had increased their pace. It was a bit disconcerting to Jan as the fully armed group started to arrive where he and Palatu were standing and talking.

"How can we trust you?" Jan asked.

Palatu replied, "This was a suicide trip for us. We are desperate."

Another joined in, "We have brought our families, and we can't go back. The NOV is in chaos. Everyone knows that there is no more vaccine production, and there have been riots, home invasions, and the police have been terrorizing us, looking for any hidden doses of vaccine."

This time, a female voice was heard within her wildlands suit, "It was only a matter of time before most of us died, along with our children. We decided that if we were going to die, we should die trying to survive. You have the vaccines — we had the suits to get out here. Do the math."

"Why didn't you send scouts?" Jan asked. "They would have been able to come here, change filters, and go back to report."

"You don't understand," the female Hunter replied, "You don't know how bad it is back there. The NOV's National Police are torturing any one they think might have any knowledge of hidden vaccines. The NOV leaders are desperate for it, and will kill everyone trying to find more. Their reasoning is that those sacrificed are going to die anyway."

"They are succeeding," said another Hunter, they are saving it for themselves, along with their protectors, the troopers and police."

Jan believed what they were saying and said, "Come with me now — my people are scared to death of you. They believe you were sent by the NOV. If I go back alone to report, there will be some who will argue and make it complicated." Then he smiled, and said, "Welcome. Welcome to New Aletia."

The hunters were overjoyed, and started cheering. "We made it! We made it!"

Jan had a thought, "There is one thing though, that you must agree to."

"What?" asked Palatu, as they all became quickly quiet. They had come from a life of rules, and this sounded like the first one here.

"You have asked to join us," Jan replied, "That means you must agree to attend our weekly LERN meetings."

There was groaning from half of the males there, one said to another, "See? I told you! They want to turn us into love-lovers!" There was more moaning and grumbling.

Jan responded, "We won't force you to join, but you must attend, to learn about us, and understand us. This is *our* colony." Then he said, "There are six hundred of us, and many are watching from that building right up there," and Jan turned and pointed to the top of the hotel, poking up in the distance above the buildings between them. "We have many hunters of our own, and the rest of us have become quite proficient in the use of firearms in the past eight months, as you can imagine. We are survivors, and I can guarantee you that all of them are armed, right now, and they are waiting to see what happens."

Palatu turned and yelled to the others, "He said we don't have to become love-lovers! He just wants us to learn about them."

One Hunter, Gast, the one that was complaining the most, said, "Let's take him as a hostage, and negotiate that!"

Palatu turned, and emptied a number of bullets into Gast, who fell to the ground. He looked around at the others. "Anyone else?" he challenged. "This was supposed to be settled before we left! If I think anyone will mess this up, I will mess *you* up!"

They all became quiet after that. They then all walked into the city — into New Aletia.

When they arrived with Jan, nobody was outside but the snipers hidden on rooftops and around buildings. As they came close to the hotel, Jan went inside the huge lobby and explained to everyone about the situation. Just about everybody really was armed by now.

Dr. Kalep was upset about the NOV's influence on their new free world, but quickly saw the Hunters' value in expanding their "safe zone", free of predators. The LERN hunters had mixed feelings as well. They could use the help of these experts and their superior weaponry, but they had developed their own level of pride in their accomplishments. They did not want to give up the respected place that they had earned in this journey. They would certainly refuse anyone taking over, and that was the classic NOV style to be expected.

"They said that they would agree to attend weekly LERN meetings." Jan offered.

"No!" exclaimed Cush, "I can't believe it!" Cush had never had attended a meeting himself, and to think that these NOV Hunters would submit to such superstition was inconceivable to him.

Jasma could see the possibilities of getting the meetings jump-started using this angle. "Excellent!" she exclaimed. "This will greatly expand the call to meetings! Jan and I were just discussing the idea of increasing participation. We can all teach them!"

The ones standing there were murmuring, and Jan said, "Listen, they are right outside. What else are we going to do, really?"

There was no good answer. Nobody wanted a war, which they could have if they so chose, at any moment.

Dom chimed up, "Listen, I wasn't a LERN member, but I've learned a lot, and you guys are OK. I think they'll come around."

"Me, too," exclaimed Buz. "I wasn't one of you, and it's worked out great. If they have to go to the meetings, they'll learn that it isn't such a big deal."

Jasma and Jan looked at each other. Jasma saw her opportunity, and said, "We must all give a good example, and make every effort to come to the meetings every week. We must show solidarity!"

Jan smiled at her. Jasma was a pro, and he was beginning to truly appreciate her. *What the hell went wrong with her son?* he thought, looking at Asa, who was scowling about another unwelcome change in his life happening again.

Jan looked at Jasma, then at Ziba, and said, "Do you want to meet them?"

"Yes, most definitely!" Ziba replied. She liked what Jasma and Jan were cooking up, and wanted to support it.

"Wait! What about us?" said Dr. Kalep and Cush.

Ziba looked at them and asked, "Do you want to go out there?"

They both looked down. They did not trust the NOV Hunters that much, yet.

Jasma glanced at Ziba and smiled. Then she directed her attention again to Jan and Jasma and said, "Let's go then," and the three of them went out to meet with the Hunters, who were now sitting or standing around outside, waiting for what was next. They met, talked and when convinced, they called the others out of the hotel to come and meet the Hunters.

Jan retrieved Dom and they then ran over to the vaccine lab, which was in the office building, and met with Lep. Lep was still stuck there by the responsibility to keep almost constant watch on, and make adjustments to the vaccine module. Winoni had been finding and machining parts for Lep as well. The parts were destined for a custom vaccine-producing unit Lep and Dom were assembling. This would be useful, as well as provide a critical back-up if the first module failed for some reason. Lep was of course unaware of the arrival of the Hunters, and was shocked when Jan told him of why he needed enough vaccine for three hundred people now. Lep told Dom to watch over the lab, and left with Jan, bringing the supplies they needed.

After vaccinating the Hunters, Lep told them that being as deep as they were in the wildlands they needed to keep using their suits and respirators for another two weeks before they could safely take them off.

Five months had passed since the Hunters arrived. It had now been a year since New Aletia was born. Population: 926. They all had a raucous first anniversary party, and the Hunters were fitting in surprisingly well.

The huge rise in attendance of the meetings after the Hunters had first arrived was slowly waning now. Due to an agreement that Palatu signed as their leader, they still had to attend, even if the attendance of LERN members had diminished. About half of them, mostly the females and children, were now joining in on the love-circles.

Still, there was a negative element rising. More fights were breaking out. In the last month alone there had been two rapes, and another murder. The LERN leadership handled each of these cases individually. A miniature jail was set up in the office building.

Everyone was miserable with the ever-increasing sores, along with growing stomach and intestinal problems. Dr. Kalep's chronic stomach was becoming increasingly vexing, to the point that he had cut his workload in half. Dr. Bilge was unable to help him very much, giving the same explanation for one year now — there were different varieties of bacteria and viruses in New Aletia, and immunity would take time.

Increasing power struggles had been occurring in both LERN and especially amongst the Hunters, who had taken up residence with the others. The Hunters generally kept conflicts private within their peers. Considering the hotel, apartment building, and the office building, there was plenty of room for the Hunters and their families to live. LERN leaders had wisely decided to intermix the Hunters among their own, thus splitting them up. Still, Jan and Martha were distressed about the increase in violence. They were worried that perhaps you could take the D'otian out of the NOV, but you couldn't take the NOV out of the D'otian.

Chapter Twenty-Two

The Hidden Temple

Jan was riding his contiss Karot out to the river to do some solitary fishing. She had been awarded to Jan because he had been promoted to LERN's executive board, much to the consternation of Dr. Kalep and Cush. Cush was not a board member, so he had his wife Ushu do his bidding. In spite of this, the other primary members, Ziba, Jasma, along with Drs. Scrib and Hendy, won the vote for Jan. This all happened seven months after New Aletia's first anniversary.

When Jan arrived at his special fishing hole, he dismounted the contiss. He gave Karot a couple of tacks he had brought with him, to keep her quiet. He then sat down on the edge of the wide stream to try his luck under a whitish rock that jutted out from the opposite side of the stream, a feeder to the river.

"C'mon," he said to himself. "I know you're under there. I got your cousin last time!" He smiled, thinking about it. That last fish he had caught here had put up an amazing fight.

It is so nice to get away from the arguing. Jan thought to himself.

Dr. Kalep and his supporters had been stopping every effort to produce any kinds of rules or laws. Things were becoming more and more

289

disorganized. People were shirking their workload in the developing mines. They had plenty of hunters, but miners needed training, and they also needed to show up. It was at the point where many people weren't appearing for work at all.

The easy yama harvesting was over. They found that they needed to go ever deeper into the ocean to get to it. Winoni was developing different methods, but all were risky. They had been attracting molicks in the water more often, and other big sea creatures could be seen habitually gathering in the distance.

The people were becoming increasingly negative and complaining. Even Rachel obsessed about renovating a newly found theater on the outskirts of town, and complained to Jan continually about it. He could not understand why people were finding ways to be so unhappy in paradise.

"They always want more, and it's as if they need to be angry about something," he said to himself, sighing, reeling in his line for another cast. He continued talking to himself saying, "It's not just the complaining. It's the violence. It's as if their dragons are always raised, even here."

Time passed, and the sky started getting cloudy. Jan looked up behind himself and said, "Well Karot, I think it's time to go home."

"Not quite," he heard the Guide say. *"There is something here that you will want to see."*

Jan vision was directed to a path that went between two big boulders that had rolled down the nearby hill, and settled a long time ago. He walked over between them.

"Keep going," the Guide said.

"Where am I going?" asked Jan. "What do you want me to see?" He was now walking along the bottom of the hill, towards the river.

"You are looking for answers, you will find some today. Walk over there, to your right," the Guide told Jan, *"Yes, down there."*

Jan saw the depression in the ground. It looked like a sinkhole. "Are you sure?" he asked, knowing that the Guide was always sure.

He made his way into it, looking for whatever he was supposed to be finding, when — *Crack!* — Jan suddenly fell into — "Water!" he yelled, as he plunged deeply into a rapidly moving underground river. He swam frantically, trying to get his equilibrium as he spun around like a rag doll in the torrent of water. He determined the way up, and came hard against the rock "ceiling" of the water-filled tunnel. *No!* His mind screamed as his lungs were beginning to ache for air. He continued with the flow for a few moments, bouncing along the top, hoping for an exit, or maybe an air bubble. After a couple of minutes his rational mind gave way to the animal, and Jan found himself clawing at the ceiling kicking frantically, whipping his tail to push forward, when his head finally popped up into an air pocket. There were some big crystals poking out from the rock, and Jan grabbed hold of one, gasping for air. His legs were being pulled by the rapid current, but he was holding on for dear life.

"What am I going to do?" he called out into the blackness. The Guide did not answer. Jan could never hear the Guide in times of stress. If Jan had any anxiety about a question, he could not hear the Guide's answer — and it sucked.

"Well," Jan said to himself, as he considered his situation, "The Guide didn't bring me here to die." *That wouldn't make any sense.* "Should I try to swim back?" Jan asked himself, as he was still gasping for air. He tried to pull his legs and feet against the current. "It's impossible," he said to himself.

After he caught his breath, Jan decided that he could not just stay there. "I found one air bubble, there must be more," he said. Then he hyperventilated for another minute or so, and in pitch darkness, let go of the crystal he had held onto, and let the water take him again, swimming for his life.

Jan swam for another two or three minutes, bouncing along the top looking for air, and found himself in the same state as he just was twenty minutes ago. He was losing it, and he had to fight the impulse to inhale water as his lungs were burning for air. He missed two air bubbles because he couldn't hold on to anything. The base of his tail was aching from the use of it to propel himself through the water. Thirty more seconds later he was scratching wildly at the water and the ceiling again. His hands kept clawing upwards for the search for a bubble, he felt himself blacking out — and then there was suddenly no ceiling, and no weight to his body.

Jan was forcibly pissed out into the air of an underground cavern containing a small lake within it. *What the hell now* — he grabbed what breath he could as he fell twenty feet and smacked the water hard, plunging into it deeply. He immediately swam upwards, gasping for air as he surfaced, his spastic throat making a rasping noise as he choked to bring air in through it. Jan was able to gain some composure after a few breaths, and started swimming for the edge of the water. *I have to get out of this water.*

There were two strange glows to the space, one red and the other blue. They were coming from a large open area that was above the water and was dry. Jan swam to the edge and weakly pulled himself out of the water, still gasping and choking. He collapsed on his back on the smooth hard cool floor, seeing a high ceiling above, panting heavily. He closed his eyes and laid there for twenty minutes, breathing, recovering, and feeling as though his exhausted body was so heavy it was sinking through the marble floor on which he was lying.

While lying there, Jan eventually opened his eyes again. As they adjusted, he saw that the ceiling was covered with ornate designs from what looked like miniature tiles. They formed pictures of D'otians. He recognized the designs of long, gently curving lines that all had a common center. The artwork had the same round things at the end of the lines, pointed at the tips.

"Platacs!" he said in amazement, as he recognized them by their lighter scale coloring. There were various scenes portrayed of apparent historical events. Jan wondered about the many cryptic symbols. There were other scenes on the ceiling. These ones displayed other kinds of D'otians that did not have the lighter scales of the Platacs. Some were easily recognizable as Aletians, due to their gray coloring and tall crests. The crests on the Aletians were a bit wider, dark gray, and had half-inch peaks along the top of them that were more pointed than the Platacs. The Platac crests had smoothed-out points on their crests, and the equally tall Platac crests had colors — orange, gray, and white.

There were pictures of other D'otians. Strange wide ones with double crests on their heads and tails, and their whole bodies were orange-red.

They looked fierce. Jan also saw others that were short and brown, and they had dark brown wide crests. Those ones looked pretty tough, too.

"What *is* this place?" he asked himself, in wonder, forgetting his situation for a moment.

When he felt ready to move, Jan got up and walked over to the source of the lights. He saw hundreds of containers set and stacked around in a big area that lay between two large dormant iron shafts that were about two hundred feet apart. Jan remarked to himself, "I know these shafts!" The shafts continued straight through the ceiling thirty feet above. He always passed that pair of iron shafts on his way to his fishing spot. "I know where I am!" he said with some comfort. "Now I need to figure out how to get out of here." *But first, I need to check out this glow.*

The red glow emanated from the direction of the iron shaft to his right, and the blue came from the shaft on his left. There was no real source to the light, it was just hanging there. There was a webbing made of some type of metal suspended above the container-holding area, forming a ceiling of sorts, about twelve feet high. The same webbing also lined the floor, as well as the wall behind the containers. The webbing stopped when it contacted the iron shafts on both sides of it. There was a large container placed among the others, and Jan went to examine it. He looked through the glass enclosure, and saw a Platac male, dead, laying in it. He had a headdress on, and was adorned in strange clothing made from materials Jan had not seen before. It was a gown, and had beautiful gold thread designs sewn throughout, once again, similar to designs they had on the walls of the hotel, and on the tiled ceiling here. There was a panel on the dead D'otian's container, which displayed various buttons and lights.

"What *is* this?" Jan asked aloud as he walked among the containers, and he came across a containerized bookcase with scores of books. He pulled on the latch, and saw the electronic panel for the bookcase start blinking. He pulled a book out and opened it. It had Platac writing, which Jan could not read, as all the Platac writings he had read thus far were translations. "Dr. Scrib will know what's in these," he muttered, as he thumbed through the pages. "What kind of paper is this?" he asked, and then continued, "It's — what is it? There's no agrist, no metal —" Any paper he had ever seen was always made of thin sheets of agrist alloy.

This amazed him. These pages were light — very light. He pulled on a corner of a page, and it tore. "Wow, I'd better be careful with this." He kept the book, but closed the bookcase door, and the lights on the panel settled back down.

Jan started to notice that he felt different when he was standing on the metal webbing under his feet, in the glowing field of light that was within the space that the webbing outlined. He experienced a warm feeling throughout his body. "I feel good!" he exclaimed. He looked over many of the round canisters, all of which had similar electronic buttons and lights. Some had glass tops, and he could see what looked like thousands of very tiny stones inside.

Then he noticed a large canister that was cubical. When he looked into it, he saw something astonishing through the glass top. Inside were four of the biggest eggs he had ever seen. "What *is* this?" he repeatedly asked himself.

Jan looked around, surveying the cavern. "I need to find a way out of here!" He kept the book with him, and started searching for a way out. He peered out across the water, but the wall on that far side was difficult to see, considering the general darkness of the place. Jan kept looking across the water, along every inch of the opposite wall that was above water. "Since the water seems to stay at this level, there must be an exit for it underwater," he said to himself. He also said, shaking his head after considering it, "I don't want to do *that* again."

Jan sat down at the edge of the floor near the water. As his eyes adjusted to the darkness he was looking into, he could see variations on the opposite wall that may have been shadows.

"Maybe that wall isn't so smooth after all," he said to himself. After much self-talk, Jan decided to swim to the other side, and see what may be over there. He took the book with him.

When he arrived at the opposite wall, he found a well-constructed ledge along it. He climbed onto the ledge, and went to his right, walking in the direction of the water that was spilling out of the hole he had arrived through. *Nothing*, Jan thought despairingly.

The only thing left to do then was to walk in the opposite direction along the wall to the other end of the ledge. As he was walking that way, he saw something coming into view in the darkness at the far end. It was a rectangular hole in the wall. *Yes!* Jan had to duck a bit to get through the opening, and attempted to see what was in there.

Chapter Twenty-Three

The Resurrection of the Cathaws

tairs!" Jan cried loudly. He started singing, "Stairs, stairs, stairs, stairs!" He was sure that this would get him out of here. Peering further up the curved stairway, he saw that it was absolutely black up there.

"I have to go," he thought. He looked back at the cavern and the glowing platform across the way, trying to think of anything he may bring as a weapon. *Nothing.*

Jan had no choice. He had to go up that narrow, low-ceilinged stone-cut stairway in pitch black. He slowly made his way up the stairway. He stopped and listened for any noises ahead, and there were none. *That's a good thing.* Step by step he went up. After twenty minutes of climbing, he wanted to stop and catch his breath, but could not.

"I've got to see how this ends," he said to himself. He continued, and found that the spiral stairway was no longer rock.

"This smells like iron," Jan said. It was iron, he realized, as he dragged his weight ever upwards. About ten minutes later, he saw a dim light coming from above him in the staircase. "Light!"

Jan's pace quickened and in no time he found himself looking out from an iron shaft, and he was over two hundred feet from the ground.

"Hello!" he yelled, hoping for the remote chance that someone might be out there. He hollered for a while, and stopped to listen. *Do I hear something? My contiss!*

"Karot!" he yelled, "Karot!" He definitely heard contiss footsteps down below coming his way.

"Jan!" he heard from the other side of the iron shaft.

It's Buz! What's he doing here? "Buz!" Jan shouted, "I'm up here!"

Buz came riding around the corner of the iron shaft, and Jan started laughing. "He has no idea! Nobody ever looks up," Jan chuckled to himself. He looked and found little loose pieces of the shaft sitting beside him. He picked one up and threw it towards Buz. It was a great shot, beaning Karot on the back of her hind end, and Karot reared up, throwing Buz off her.

Himself startled, Jan yelled out, "Hey, I didn't mean to do that buddy."

Buz got up, and looked around again. He was OK.

Jan laughed some more. "Buz, I'm up here!"

Buz finally started looking upwards, and after a moment spotted Jan's arm waving out of the iron shaft above.

"What the hell are you doing up there?" Buz hollered. Then Buz followed with, "*How* the hell did you get up there?"

"I came up from inside it! Listen, I'll tell you later," Jan yelled back. "Go ask Winoni to come here. He's got a big ladder to build!" Then he remembered the book he had been carrying. It had become wet, and when he opened it now, the pages were much more fragile, and tore easily. "Wait!"

Buz stopped his actions to mount the contiss, and looked up.

Jan hollered, "Be careful with this! Give it to Dr. Scrib, and tell him and Jasma to come down here. Bring Ziba, too!" Jan tossed the book down to Buz, and it bounced hard off the ground. The cover and a few pages came off, but it was otherwise intact.

Buz mounted the contiss, and he heard, "Wait!" once again from above. He looked up. "What?" he yelled.

"Bring flashlights and be ready to swim!" Jan shouted.

Buz thought about asking why, but he wanted to get up there and see this himself. He couldn't do it without Winoni. "OK," he yelled back, and left in a hurry.

Buz rode Karot back to town, and found Winoni and the others. He showed the book to Dr. Scrib, who declared that the book was an exceedingly ancient treasure.

Since Dr. Kalep was with him at the time, he came along, too. They both appeared to be very excited.

After Buz described the lean of the shaft and how high Jan was in the shaft, Winoni gathered his main crew, and loaded up a wagon with the equipment and supplies they would need to build a ladder of sorts. Rebecca and Jasma came along too. Martha was out helping with the developing mines, and did not know what was happening. Rachel stayed home with Jo.

It took a couple of hours to fabricate the ladder on site. It required braces because of its height. When completed, they all climbed it to the entry in which Jan was waiting.

They followed Jan down the staircase, but this time they were carrying lights.

On the way down, Jan asked Buz, "Why were you out here in the first place?"

Buz answered, "Karot came to town without you, and when I asked Rachel, she said you went fishing. I know you fish out this way, but Karot pretty much led the way."

Jan smiled to himself, "Good old Karot, she's a keeper."

As they continued down the staircase, Jan described the cavern and the containers. The people with him could not contain their excitement.

"A well-preserved Platac!" Dr. Kalep exclaimed with glee, "This is wonderful!"

Dr. Scrib almost fell down the stairs a number of times because he was trying to read the book Buz had delivered.

Once they arrived at the bottom of the stairs, those with Jan quickly realized that Jan was not kidding about the swim. Nothing was going to stop any of them now, and they all went into the water to swim across to the dry area.

Rebecca froze. She just stood there on the ledge, looking. She had become silent as they descended the stairs, and now, seemed to be in some kind of shock.

"What's the matter?" asked Jan, as he stood there with her, watching the others swim across.

"I don't — I don't know," Rebecca stammered. She had a look of fear on her face. "This place makes me feel so sad." She looked at Jan and asked, "Why?" with a searching look on her face. "Why do I feel this way? It's so weird. It's the way I felt when we first entered the city."

"Just come over and look," said Jan. "It's OK, there's nothing down here to hurt us."

Rebecca reluctantly followed the others, swimming with Jan. When they got to the other side, Dr. Scrib was already surveying the bookstand, and Dr. Kalep was studying the sarcophagus.

Winoni and his crew were marveling at the technology. "Don't touch any buttons!" Winoni barked to everyone there. "This is some kind of suspended animation system. These items have not aged one bit!" After studying the magnetic iron shafts, he said, "I think these folks found a way to power all this from these shafts! The energy field gives off this light here."

"Come here!" Dr. Kalep called to Jasma, "You've got to see this!"

Jan and Rebecca went over to the sarcophagus as well, Jan saying, "Look at this guy," to Rebecca.

As they approached the sarcophagus, Rebecca took hold of Jan's arm, digging her fingers into it. As they looked into the glass top, Rebecca shrieked, and fell on the sarcophagus, crying uncontrollably. She looked at the corpse in the sarcophagus one more time, then turned and ran away, and started vomiting at the water's edge.

Jasma and Jan followed Rebecca, perplexed at what had happened. So was Rebecca. She sat down at the edge of the water, shaking with emotion. Jan sat next to her and put his arm around her, "It's all right, nothing's wrong here, Rebecca. What's happening? Why are you like this?"

"I don't know," Rebecca howled. "I have to get out of here!" She gritted her teeth. "I can't stay here."

"OK," said Jan. "We're not going to stay for that long."

Rebecca twisted around to look at the sarcophagus again, and looking at Jan, she replied, "I've got to leave, *now*." She then dove into the water, and started swimming.

Jan stood up, looking at her. "What was that all about?' he asked himself, and then looked at Jasma, who was standing there perplexed as well.

Jasma shrugged her shoulders, shaking her head. "I don't know, but she'll be OK, this place *is* a bit spooky."

Jan watched as Rebecca made her way across the small, trapped lake. She got out onto the ledge, waved to them and said, "I'll see you when you come back!" and made her way up the stairs.

Jan abruptly turned his attention to Dr. Kalep who had suddenly shouted, "Scrib! Get over here!"

He also went over to see what Dr. Kalep had found.

Sitting there were two thick notebooks in their own container, completely made of glass — the top book was larger than the one beneath it. Their container was sitting upon another much larger container, about waist-high. Dr. Scrib came over, and they opened the top container that held the books. Dr. Scrib removed the top book, opened it, and started translating it aloud for the others there —

"Whoever finds this book, in this temple, is blessed. I am Natchu, King and Chief Priest of the Platac Nation. Our faith is in the order of Milchexidike of the Cathaws. This sacred temple has always remained hidden from the world of death above. Everything you see in this room has been, or soon will be, eliminated from the surface of D'ot by the Mortiks..."

Dr. Kalep interrupted Scrib, apparently disturbed, "The Mortiks were us, the Aletians, about five or six thousand years ago. They also had another race in the Mortik nation then, the Tomaks."

Dr. Scrib looked at Kalep as if, "Are you done?" then continued —

"I Natchu, seeing what has happened, and having been shown what is to come, have prepared and preserved these creations for the return of the El'j — the White Dragon. It has been given for me to see, and the El'j will bring this treasure to the surface again."

Dr. Scrib stopped, and said, "What does that mean?"

Jasma gave Jan a curious look, and said to Dr. Scrib, "We can find out much more about the White Dragon in the bookcase, I'm sure. Please continue, Dr. Scrib."

"You will be ignorant about these items in this room. Do not open any — life units — until you read this entire book, unless directed to do so."

Dr. Scrib looked at those around him, and read on —

"This book's container is sitting upon another, much larger container. You may now open that container, and observe what is in it. It is something that the violent and oppressed ones in our world can use in order to break through the negative, and begin to learn peace. It is a means, not an end. As a medicine for many ailments, it will become indispensible. As a plentiful, renewable source of clothing, building materials, and papyr, it is unequaled. As a supplemental food, it has no match.

"As a brain-altering substance, this one is physically forgiving to leave when the lesson is learned.

"This is Kana Bosm — it opens the way of peace and love to those who know it not, those who fear it, avoid it, and those who have forgotten it. It is not necessary for those few who have already found peace, but helpful for the many who have not. It quiets the reptile, leaving trapped minds open to expand for a while. Always remember, it is a means, not an end. A clear mind that chooses peace, truth, and harmony with our Creator, this is the end. God is sober, and He is the standard.

"The more unbalanced or self-destructive souls will not be satisfied with kana bosm. Such a personality will be overtly drawn to sedation, such as excessive alcohol or the death march of n'o, and that person will abuse the kana bosm. Because of its perceived innocence, kana bosm may become a habitual part of one's life, which is not the goal.

These issues are most properly addressed in the 'Parenting Laws', which our people have refined over many generations. I have outlined them here in their entirety. We could not escape these problems, and you will not either. We must however confront them correctly in order to have expanding lives available for all of us, without endless, repressive laws and penalties.

I have placed this here to be demonstrated first, so that you may know the value of this room, and so that you will pay utmost attention to the following instructions in this book.

This will begin to help to overcome your reptilian nature, and see another way. The violence will decrease among those people who do not listen to anything else. This gift confuses the dragon for a short time, and that is why it is I place it first before you."

They were all looking at the container with the kana bosm in it, in wonder.

"I've never seen anything like this before," Dr. Kalep stated, as he peered into the glass top with the lights and buttons on the upper panel on it.

Dr. Scrib continued translating once again.

"You may consume kana bosm in food, but this limited quantity can be used most efficiently by burning a tiny amount, and inhaling the smoke."

"What?" Jasma exclaimed. "What's he talking about? Breathing in smoke? These people were very primitive."

"How can you say that?" barked Dr. Kalep, "Look around you! Does this technology look crude?"

"Still," Jasma retorted, "I've never heard of such a thing, we have plenty of drugs to help us relax."

"And they are all physically addictive!" Kalep retorted.

"I'll try!" offered Buz.

Jan looked at Buz, and said to Dr. Kalep, "Why don't we open the container?"

Dr. Scrip interrupted and said, "Let me finish with this part," and he went on.

"The two jars that you find inside the larger container of kana bosm 'kynds' are to be used as medicines. The larger jar has 'pikas' that were freshly placed. Please remove that jar, open it, and pull out a pika."

They removed the container that held the two books from the top of the large main one it was sitting on. Then they opened the top of the main container holding the kana bosm, to get at the big jar referred to in the book. Inside, and underneath the two jars, the main container was full of round, fluffy-looking green things, about two to three inches long, and over one inch around. Those standing there all gasped as the fragrance of something amazingly rich and wonderful filled their nostrils.

303

Jasma looked like she was in a trance. "That is the most beautiful —
it's, it's — a perfume from heaven!" and she bent down, close to the open
canister in order to inhale the aroma wholly. Tears came to her eyes, "I
have never smelled anything — anything —" She couldn't finish. Jasma
turned, and looked at the others pleadingly, "We can't burn this!"

As the fragrance filled the area, one of the machinists with Winoni
snickered, "That smells like a skint!" A few of the other fellows started
laughing and nodding their heads in agreement.

After a few more remarks, they removed the big jar sitting upon the
kana bosm, and opened it. It had layers of thin green pikas, about three to
five inches long. They were thin, flexible, and obviously had moisture in
them. They were sticky. Their smell was different from the odiferous
dried lighter green things that filled the rest of the huge container. The
pikas had jagged edges and each pika came to a point on one end, and on
the opposite end became a firm thin little rod. After handling them, their
fingers smelled strongly of them.

Once they examined these, Dr. Scrib continued.

*"These should be in the same state as when they were harvested, and
should be fresh. They are useful for healing stomach ailments, and for
treating other digestive problems which are prevalent in our world."*

"You can say that again," said Dr. Kalep, whose old stomach was
rotting away.

Dr, Scrib looked up, and said, "It says, *"Chew on five pekas per day."*

Dr. Kalep popped one in his mouth immediately, and started chewing
on it. "It is — very tingly — hot, like nako, and well, I've never tasted
anything like it." He continued chewing, and said, "It's, it's — disgusting!"
He started laughing, and the others did as well. But he didn't spit it out.

Dr. Scrib then continued —

*"Now, remove the smaller jar from the container. This is an ointment,
extracted from the kana bosm kynds. This is a great helper with the scale
diseases that our people often experience. There are many different types
of peta 'sipas' in this temple that will grow into healthy, disease-
preventing foods, which will help prevent sores from forming at all."*

They all looked at each other in astonishment, and most started reflexively scratching their sores.

THE RESURRECTION OF THE CATHAWS

"A cure for these sores?" asked Winoni, skeptically.

Jasma said, "Dr. Scrib, please continue."

"The last thing in the container, which fills most of it, comes from the top of the kana bosm peta. These we call 'kynds'. These are what you make smoke, medicines, teas, and ointments from."

Dr. Scrib continued —

"The sipas in this room are all labeled on their containers. A container of kana bosm sipas is to the left of the kana bosm container."

Jan was standing in that spot, and said, "He must have meant this container of little stones," and they all looked. Jan said, "These stones must be the 'sipas'. They look the pretty much the same as what's in most the other containers in here."

Dr. Scrib went on reading.

"In the rest of this book, I will tell you exactly how to do this for yourselves. I have supplied you with sipas for many different petas. I will instruct on you how to prepare the ground. You will put these sipas in the specially prepared ground, give them water, and they will all grow into tall green petas. There is a limited supply here, and you must not make mistakes".

"This container is just a sample of the rewards awaiting you if you follow my instructions, with no deviation from them."

Dr. Scrib stopped, and looked around him at everyone. "I think he's talking about raising green animals — from the ground! From these little stones! That's crazy! These must be pieces of those animals." He was becoming a little woozy, dropping his head and shaking it.

Winoni chimed in, "Maybe they're eggs!"

Dr. Scrib was a thin, bespeckled, private fellow. All this attention and the bewildering information were getting to be too much for him. "Why don't we take a break?" Dr. Scrib suggested. "I can take this book back with me to the city, before it becomes dark, and my secretary can type it out as I translate it to her there." He looked at the big book in his hands, and lightly ran his fingers along the top of it. "Let me spend some time with this, and do it right."

305

Winoni spoke up, "He's absolutely correct. That 'Natchu' priest was right on target, too. We should read everything and touch nothing without knowing what it is."

"He told us about the kana bosm!" Buz piped up.

Nobody said anything.

"Let's take it with us!" Buz persuaded, and Dr. Kalep said, "Well, Natchu gave us permission to go this far, we should be able to take some of it back with us, along with the book."

They all agreed, and then they discussed the 'peace' spoken of. The mention of love was equally intriguing. They decided to leave for the day, taking samples of the kynd, the jar of ointment, and some fresh pikas. These items and the book would stay in the safekeeping of the LERN leadership.

Since Dr. Scrib saw the water damage to the fragile first book Buz had come to town with, he had brought a watertight container in order to safely bring more books out. They were able to put all the items into the same container, with the exception of the sizeable jar of ointment, which was already well sealed when closed again.

After swimming across the water, they all made their way up the stairs, then back down the stairs outside. Aware of the treasure in the temple, Winoni was concerned about looters. He had the supplies there to have his crew fabricate a heavy door for the entrance to the iron shaft at the top of the stairs. He would put a lock on later. They all agreed to keep this information confidential for now and then left for the city.

The top floors of the hotel had the most security, as each floor had their own network of supporters of the particular LERN leader. They decided that one of the upper floors was the safest place for their bounty. Jan was the only LERN leader that lived outside of the hotel.

Jan and Buz said goodbye to the others, and as they went back to the apartment building, Buz pulled a big kynd out of his pocket, grinned at Jan, and holding it out in his hand said, "Hey brother, want some peace?"

Jan turned his head, and saw the kynd that Buz had managed to snag from the container. He smiled, surprised, but unexpectedly happy that Buz had done it.

"I need some peace, brother," Jan responded with a grin, and they both went down to Jan's apartment. They passed by some people on the way home, and heard one say, "Does you smell a skint?" They both started laughing their tails off.

Once down in Jan's apartment, they found all three of the females in the living room. They had been sitting there and talking about the newly discovered temple. The baby was sleeping in Rachel's room.

"What's that smell?" Martha asked, not long after they entered the living room.

Jan and Buz filled the girls in on what had happened after Rebecca left. They got to the subject of the kana bosm, and the kynd they had, and Rachel said, "Well, what are you waiting for? Let's try it!"

Buz pulled the kynd out of his pocket, and the girls were amazed at the pungent odor emitted by such a thing.

Martha was concerned, "It might be poisonous. What an alien odor!"

"No," Rebecca said, "It's not poisonous."

"How can you be so sure?" Martha asked, mainly because Rebecca was not usually sure of anything.

"Because — I — I was there!" Rebecca said. Rebecca then faded again towards the condition she was in when she first came back from the temple.

Martha shook her head. After seeing the state Rebecca returned in, she was distrustful of the "temple" they were talking about.

"We're going to try it," Jan said, much to the relief of Buz.

Jan, Buz, and Rachel went over to the stove. They discussed it for a bit, and decided to crush some on a pan, heat it over the stove, and see what happened. They did this and eventually smoke started rising, and they pulled the pan off the stove. They took turns, putting their heads over the smoke that was rising, inhaling it, and they heard Rebecca say, "That smells wonderful!" from where she and Martha were now standing, watching from the kitchen's entrance.

After a few turns, Rebecca and Martha saw the other three grinning at each other, and observing them, Rebecca looked at Martha and said, "I want to try! You try too!"

Martha sighed, and asked, "Jan, what do you feel like?"

Jan looked at her and smiled and said, "I feel like —" and his eyes stared at hers as he was looking for the right words. "I feel like I want to daydream."

"Well, daydreaming is not good!" Martha retorted.

Jan looked at her with a bit of surprise, and said, "That's the NOV talking. This is — this is good, I think. Come over here and let me know what you think. I don't feel bad, do you two?"

Rachel had lost the point of the conversation, and Buz just shook his head in agreement because he wanted to see Jan's mom get high. He never thought about it until now, but Jan's mom was pretty hot.

Martha shrugged her shoulders and said to Rebecca, "What the hell, they don't seem to be suffering," and they joined the other three as they were getting another batch ready for their new takers.

After passing around the smoking pan with the Martha and Rebecca now, Rachel came up with the idea of playing some music. Martha got it going, and then she brought out some splint cheese that she had procured from the successfully expanding splint farm. Along with bread, it served for something quick to eat. Then they ended up dancing, with Buz paying almost too much attention to Martha.

In the midst of this, Jan had the urge to go upstairs and outdoors. The elevator that Winoni recently had operating was broken down again, so he had to walk up four flights of stairs. When he arrived outside, there was a cool breeze blowing from the west as usual, but it felt different. Everything felt different. Jan's perspective was different. For now, different was better. *It feels as if I've just finished a love-circle — except that I didn't have to work for it.*

Jan walked towards the courtyard that was outside the apartment building. He saw Dr. Kalep who had recently stepped out of the hotel with Ziba.

Dr. Kalep waved, and hollered, "Great job Jan!" He was grinning like Jan had never seen before, and laughing with Ziba about something.

Jan continued into the courtyard and had a seat on a bench.

"Look at the moons tonight," he said to himself. Both moons on this clear night were full, and it was as if it were a heaven-lit night. His vision was drawn to them as if they were pulling his eyes.

Someone who was coming his way drew Jan's gaze away from the moons. It was Ziba, by herself now. She waved and continued in his direction. When she came over, she took a seat beside Jan.

Ziba exclaimed, "Oh! I wish I had been there when everyone went over to the Platac temple. I can't wait to see it!" She had a dreamy look, and her eyes were sleepy looking and red.

Jan was looking at her and laughed. "You tried the kynd, didn't you? The kana bosm!"

Ziba looked at Jan, and asked, "How did you know?"

Jan simply replied, "We tried it tonight too." He was still smiling at her.

Ziba looked confused, and said, "How?" Then, before Jan could answer, she said while flipping her hand, "Oh, I don't want to know!" and they both chuckled about it. She then said, "Dr. Brader did a quick test on a pika, and said the enzyme spectral activity is off the charts! Dr. Kalep is ecstatic." Ziba was also then drawn to the moons that Jan had gone back to staring at.

"Have you ever seen such a beautiful night?" Ziba sighed.

"No. not really," Jan replied. They sat there together, not saying another word. Just existing, absorbing it all, feeling the increase of appreciation for the beautiful evening around them. Happiness, gratitude's evidence, was in the air as well.

For a moment, Jan forgot Ziba was even there. He was thinking, thinking, thinking — as he always did. They both were staring at the moons, each pondering their own visions of the future here. Jan recalled how upset he was yesterday about the reports of the increasing in-fighting and violence — the return of the NOV-like behavior. That feeling was gone to him for the moment, very distant.

Jan envisioned a potential — a brand new world. He was starting to have some faith in the book of the dead Platac in the temple. *With Natchu's teachings of how to live and love — the medicines, and the new foods — maybe, maybe, we really can have our paradise.*

For the first time since childhood, Jan felt genuinely hopeful and happy. Only peace remained. Something released deep inside, as if a forgotten spasm had freed. His physical center opened, and warmth flowed like a river within his heart and abdomen. Then he farted.

Ziba tilted her head and looked at Jan, who was now grinning at her, "Bringing me back down to D'ot, eh?" ::-)

The End.

CMF: Want more? I want more. I got more. Five more — cooking in the pot.

What I need you to do is go to Amazon right now, and give this baby the five star review that you know you want to give it. OK, less, if you want — but do it! Do it.

Only you can pave the way for this escape by voting before you forget for some reason —

Do not fear the NOV.

I want to find out what happens too, you know… ::-)

Vote Here >>> http://www.amazon.com/review/create-review/

Also available at: Smashwords.com and other retailers.

About the Author

Rorschach Test

Chris M. Finkelstein was born in the woods and raised by Christian wolves that had become secular Jews by two thousand years of refinement, the first half quite dark.

Prequel to Book 4

*hat's that smell?*

Dr. Jason Ata, a sandy-haired young professor, was scuttling down the freshly scrubbed hall towards the cafeteria. Considering his girth, some would say he was waddling. *I have to be ready for this talk. They must see all of this.* Jason was focusing on the upload of his latest information — from the MU he held in his hand to the ship's central communications databank. Not a difficult task, but with the hallway, the people, the tardiness, and the coffee — Dooosshhh*! No!*

The man in front of him had suddenly stopped. Jason looked down and saw his disposable coffee cup squished and mostly emptied, between his chest and the dark suited back of the man in front of him — and yes, it was hot.

Jason rebounded backwards. The woman behind him yelped as the back of his elbow hit her folded arms, forcing them to release the armful of papers she was holding, now scattering about on the floor.

Before Jason could look to see what had just happened to her, the man in front of him twisted around to see who did what, and — *Shit!* It was Survival Marshal North, in the flesh. *Of all people* — Jason gave a weak smile, said a quick, "Sorry, Marshal North," and quickly turned to see who else was involved in this pile-up.

It was Deborah, North's secretary. Although Jason recognized her, he did not know her name. *Cute,* he thought. *She's with North's group?* Her hair was dark brown, and this close up, he was able to observe her intelligent green eyes. *She still has some outstanding African lines,* he thought. She had an elegance of motion that captured Jason's attention the day before, while boarding the behemoth interplanetary cargo ship within which they were now hurtling through space.

Deborah was gathering the papers from the newly re-carpeted hallway floor. He bent to help her, although she was reaching for the last of them.

Jason said, "Sorry," again, this time to her. He squatted with her, picking up the remaining papers, as others bustled past them.

Deborah brushed it off, saying, "No problem, it's not the first time." She gave him a sweet smile, which was pleasantly surprising for Jason. It only took a few more seconds to pick up the notes. She then centered a worried look in North's direction. "Thanks for the help — we'd better get going," she said, and Jason readily agreed.

They started for the cafeteria, again. As they neared its entrance, they saw that North's deputies were wiping the coffee off his back with towels. *Where did they get those towels?* Jason wondered, looking down at his own shirt. His nice white shirt now had a big coffee stain on the front of it, running down to his belt line. He glanced up to see a deputy watching him, and with a scornful look, he tossed Jason a towel, which landed a few feet short.

Jason went for it, and heard the deputy bark authoritatively, "Pick that up!"

As Jason was picking up the towel, he felt his cheeks redden. *What a dick.* He started wiping himself off as he looked for the deputy who had insulted him. That deputy had moved ahead of North and was entering the cafeteria.

North turned a couple of times, looking at Jason and shaking his head. North stood at six feet and five inches, and was an imposing figure in any right. It was his chin — always sticking out.

Aggressive, Jason thought.

North's face did have a distinctive profile. Along with his protruding forehead, he had a razor straight nose angling down at forty-five degrees, coming to a point before cutting back and up to the upper philtrum above his lip. He had squared off nostrils, which matched his wide rectangular mouth and that equally wide protruding chin.

Jason, at six feet and two inches, weighing in at three hundred and ten pounds, was not small, yet he had the look of an academic-for-life. Pudding-like cheeks lent him a childish look for a man of thirty-four years. His longer hair was unkempt, compared to North's salt and pepper, tight military cut.

Look at that expression on his face, Jason thought. *He looks like trouble. What's he have against me?* After a bit of thought, Jason decided that North didn't have anything against him personally. North simply did not like Jason's *kind.* Jason was old school Guild, and North was connected with that part of the Guild that was more "practical". Jason then let those thoughts go, and focused on the impending lectures.

All the attendees made their way into the white and lavender lit cafeteria, and took their seats. The ship's cafeteria still had the pleasing aroma of freshly grilled garlic, onions and butter. Jason heard earlier that lunch had been quite good. He had skipped it, having plenty of snacks in his office, where he had been preparing for this presentation. There was the spirit of "freshness" in the room that always seemed to go with a new adventure. The people attending the meeting numbered about two hundred twenty-five, although the cafeteria could hold over one thousand. They were all sitting in groups at the long lunch tables there. The Social Director, Rini Hay, was making her way to the podium, as Jason hastily joined five other speakers sitting to the right of the podium.

Since Jason was the mission's Director of Soul-Typing and Guidance, he was slated to follow Survival Marshal North, and so they were seated next to each other. North ignored Jason, his eyes studying the audience.

Jason turned his attention to the audience as well. He recognized many of the directors, managers and supervisors of three thousand, one hundred and twenty-eight breeding couples, specially selected and prepared to re-inhabit the planet D'ot8. As Dr. Jason Ata, soul-type-psycho-physiologist, he would explain his part of the mission. More importantly, he would cover what it was that made this one different from other missions. In the meantime, he was loving-up the blend of aromas of the cafeteria.

What is that smell? Sniff. *Well, certainly garlic and onions — but what else?* As he considered the possibilities, Social Director Hay arrived at the podium. The briefing was being broadcast to all members aboard the S&H Interplanetary cargo ship, Excelsior. The cafeteria was clean, but very plain, as was the rest of the ship. From the outside, the ship looked like a big orange blimp. S&H never was that fancy.

Rini started, "This is the last briefing you will receive before we enter hyposleep. Much of this information you already know. I realize you have all trained diligently, and many of you could be lecturing up here as well. Still, please pay attention. In another two hours, you are going into hyposleep, and what we are presenting here will be the last thing imprinted on your memory before you go under. You will need all of this information at the ready when we awaken in three years at Wormhole B9. I want to remind you that it takes a few days to reorient yourselves at that time, also."

Maybe it's burnt sugar. Caramelized.

Rini was a short and stubby woman, sporting a new hairstyle for the trip. Her light-brown hair had accents of red and gold. It was shorter now, and had been teased into a rounded appearance. She straightened her too-tight dark gray and sky blue dress a bit, and shifted herself to a more upright stance. "So let's get on with it! It is my pleasure and honor to introduce our Survival Marshal, whom, as you know, has complete authority in matters he deems to be critical to our survival in our new home. Survival Marshal North has commanded the settlement of four previous planets, quite successfully. It is our great honor and pleasure to have him watching out for us during the brief few years he will be with us on D'ot8. Marshal James North, please speak to us of your thoughts and observations. Everyone give him a warm welcome!"

North, a private man who did not relish speaking in public, motioned with his hands as if to say, "Please. That's enough applause." His body language said that he did not like the attention at all. He walked up to the podium. North was tall, but not lean, and he obviously paid close attention to his conservative grooming and the maintenance of his uniform. He made an impression on most Guild-trained members that his was a soul-type that expressed love through duty. He was not the type to express love overtly or intimately, unless the situation demanded it. He usually avoided such, though it was relatively common in the Guild.

Clearing his throat, and accepting a glass of water brought by one of the crew, he paused, and took a drink. He looked around, with his usual detachment, very much different from those around him who were waiting to hear what he had to say.

"Ladies and gentlemen, you have been trained to be the finest, most advanced settlers the Guild has ever sent to re-inhabit a dead planet. Your genetics were specially chosen for their tendency to produce calm, non-aggressive offspring — for this mission in particular. The reason for this is that we will attract the more peaceful D'otian souls to the families you will be building. Another benefit is that the more negative souls attracted will be governed by your stable genetics."

Jason was paying attention now. *If you only knew, brother.*

North continued, "If you only knew the wealth that this mission will bring to our beloved Guild, you would know this is a very exciting time for us all." His detached tone did little to rouse his audience, and he continued to read his speech, "The trade that typically develops over time with a new planet is just one part of the total package of benefits we receive."

North paused for another sip of water, put the glass down with a hand that could have passed for a thick glove, and continued, "With each dead planet that we colonize, we learn more. Of course, you know that by "dead", we mean that humanoids became extinct there. Other than that, these planets are usually far from dead. The Guild learns more about systems and approaches to life in each new world. This, in turn, has helped us on our home planet."

The Guild was a centralized church, which allowed and promoted only the positive elements of all religions on Earth. It began as a response to animosity between religions, and had its birth in the Philippines. It was a simple concept: Anyone who wished to join could bring his or her own religion along, but it had to be "stripped" of all negativity. Any parts of scriptures that were primarily negative were removed from the original scriptures, and what remained stayed in the Guild. The Guild was born on the island of Mindanao, in the southeastern Philippines. A good number of the ever-warring locals agreed to build a single church that all in the area could safely attend. They had hope of forming some kind of communication between the Catholics and the Muslims. Each member was considered an ambassador of the religion he or she came from. The local Muslim chieftains and Catholic Church leaders agreed to not attack the first Guild church, nor their members. They did this because their own religious doctrines would not allow peace, and they were very, very, tired of war. The first Guild church had both Catholic priests and Muslim clergy running the services.

By the end of its third century, the Guild had gained worldwide acceptance. The members thrived, spiritually and materially. The Guild and its members had invested well, and had uncanny fortune in their undertakings. Over the centuries, they grew a network of Guild-based worldwide jobs. Because of this, many naturally joined, with all being welcome. Now, over one thousand years since inception, it was the largest religious body on Earth. The Guild had given rise to numerous political parties throughout Earth.

The bishops and cardinals of the Church, by tradition, elected a new High Priest of the Guild when the reigning high priest died or aged to incompetency. The High Priest was typically a Pilipino. His holiness Jose Rizal Aquino VI was the current High Priest of the Guild.

The Guild had sponsored many interplanetary missions. In cases of planetary colonization and harvesting of natural resources, the Guild leased enormous cargo ships. They usually contracted the services of the shipping behemoth, S&H Interplanetary Logistics, for their missions. It was not because their ships were always fluorescent orange, (which in fact was the best color to repel space radiation,) it was because S&H provided predictable outcomes, based on their massive logistics capabilities.

"I have been chosen by the Guild to command this mission because this planet is so unlike any we have settled to date," North said, and then he paused.

Jason very quietly muttered to himself, "Hmmm. I can certainly agree with that."

North went on, "Granted, even though inhabitable, planets are of course very different from one another. This one seems *more* so. The temperature extremes throughout each day, the creatures, the unstable sun, and even the time structure are all unique. One year on D'ot8 takes five hundred and ninety-three days to complete. A day there is thirty-three hours long.

"The Guild will only approve a planet for re-inhabitation if the atmosphere is breathable, without the need for masks. Some of you may be given drugs formulated to compensate for imbalances in the atmosphere, although that seems unlikely for now.

"The planet D'ot8 has an atmosphere which is generated from beneath the ocean. It is a truly unique ecosystem. There is no plant life on this entire planet, and yet there is an atmosphere not much different from ours. All life there appears to be predatory. Although we have never sent a manned mission to D'ot8, we have delivered over one hundred highly sophisticated robots there. They have given us all the information we need to move forward."

Jason smiled at North's self-assured attitude. *You've looked at, but haven't really seen my information.* Jason became a bit concerned. *I've got to be careful how I present this. I shouldn't hit them with too much too fast.*

North continued, some evidence of excitement creeping into his voice. "Our robots have discovered a large, well-preserved library. Through them, we have poured over wonderfully preserved documents and recordings. It is as though we have a massive encyclopedia of this world. We have thousands of photographs. In spite of their rather advanced technology, there is no evidence that these D'otians ever achieved motorized transportation. They had no internal combustion engine technology, from what we have seen. However, they were very advanced in the sciences and engineering. They were well-versed in subjects such as biology, microbiology, chemistry, genetics, metallurgy, mining, processing, and refining the many metallic ores of this outstandingly mineral-rich planet."

Survival Marshal North paused, and pointed to the display monitor screen to his left. An image appeared, and then another. They were microscopic pictures of one-celled organisms imbedded in their own matrix.

He continued, "On D'ot8, mass quantities of this microorganism cover millions of crevices found on the ocean floor. We have named them 'Hydrosplitters'. The D'otians called these hydrosplitters, 'yama'. Based on our data, there are trillions of tons of this valuable resource available to be harvested. As far as we know, they are the only non-predatory species on D'ot8. These organisms make up the bottom of the food chain. Hydrosplitters have the unique ability to split the H^2O water molecule into hydrogen and oxygen. They utilize the split hydrogen to saturate carbon compounds they manufacture from the raw elements of the sea and the sea floor. They do this to make saturated fat, which they both use, and also release, into the ocean. These tiny protein-coated fat globules slowly float to the surface of the ocean, but they usually do not make it to the surface. Smaller ocean creatures are attracted to these globules as high caloric food. The rest of the food chain develops above the yama fields. Larger creatures arrive, and they all leave their droppings at the bottom of the ocean on top of the hydrosplitters below. It is then utilized by the hydrosplitters, completing the cycle of this particular ecosystem, and maintaining it.

"The hydrosplitters release the split oxygen which provides the planet's livable atmosphere. From those countless fissures throughout the ocean floor, massive amounts of oxygen bubble up to the surface of the ocean, and into the atmosphere."

The audience was starting to show more interest. They all knew what this meant. If humans transplanted these organisms on Earth, perhaps in isolated lakes, it could help solve the problem of decreasing amounts of oxygen in the air there due to deforestation. There were no plans to grow the hydrosplitters in the oceans, due to threat of ecosystem imbalances. Most of the audience was unaware that hydrosplitters required a much higher level of salinity in the water than that of the Earth's oceans. Indeed, measures were already in place to quarantine the first emigrations of this unique microorganism to Earth. The Great Salt Lake in Salt Lake

City, Utah, United Continents of America — was the obvious first choice, and planning was currently taking place for the first new "guests," which would be arriving in about seven years.

"The amount of life that inhabits these oxygen-rich plumes is vast. They not only feed on the hydrosplitters and their fat globules, but also on the minerals of the ocean and its floor as well. Moreover, they feed on each other. Cannibalism is common, with many species eating their own young. All things combined, this releases nitrogen into the ocean, and from there, into the atmosphere, giving us an atmospherically near-perfect balance. It is a fragile atmosphere. With no plant life filtering it, the air can quickly become poisoned.

"This ocean has most of the same minerals we have on our own planet, in sometimes highly different ratios. Every colonist will receive my D'ot8 survival manual. This will outline in detail what I am about to tell you briefly here."

Marshal North looked slowly and with great authority into his audience, forcing many of them to look him in the eyes. This was abnormal behavior in this society, if only because life had become so — well, pleasant. The expression of human intensity was unusual. The people listening were just agreeable, sane, intelligent, hard-working humans. Wars and strife were merely distant history for them. They knew that challenges were always ahead, but they were prepared for that. The network of the Guild was always there to catch them. His audience, having nothing to relate to his intense demeanor, simply looked at him, waiting for him to continue.

Jason Ata was also noticing North's expression. For an instant, Jason imagined that North might have some knowledge of what was potentially going to happen.

Look at Marshal North, Jason told himself as he put his hand on his unshaved chin, chubby fingers rubbing his lips. *He may actually have some knowledge of what we really face there. Oh, here it comes.* Jason felt a surge of a bittersweet emotion as he surveyed the group of team leaders gathered there. *You lovely people don't have a clue. If you did, many of you may not have come along. God bless you.* He thought a moment. *Maybe I should give it to them straight — not sugar coat it.*

That may not be the wisest choice, the inner voice said.

Jason wasn't listening — the Marshal distracted him.

Survival Marshal North was talking about the animals. "The life forms on this planet have been surviving and evolving for millions of years. Because there is no plant life, they all appear to be predators. It is interesting that we have found no flying animals, just a few small flying insects.

"We have vast experience clearing out such animals on other planets, and these should be no significant problem here. However, because of the unknown, you must all know that it may be some time before we can breed them for domestication. We bring a good, healthy mix of livestock to the planet for the interim period. In the meantime, I would like to cover a few of the creatures we expect to run into. If you please, look at the screen again."

North proceeded to discuss some of the strange and interesting creatures found on D'ot8. The newly discovered underground library had everything the robot probes needed to learn a language called "Aletian". Sound recording archives allowed them to learn the pronunciations of the words. As he showed pictures of each of the creatures he wanted to illustrate, he talked in detail about them.

He started with the primary creatures of his concern, the "trachnas". These were similar to spiders on Earth, except that they were about twelve inches around. Their legs had exoskeletons, like crabs on Earth, so that the muscle was inside the shell-like leg sections. The shell itself was a chrome alloy that the trachnas could utilize and grow from chrome deposits where they would nest. They used their legs to tear and rip into their prey until it was dead. There they would remain, staying for as long as the carcass lasted, sharpening their claws against one another for the next attack. They traveled in packs. They were one of the few creatures that could kill an "ela".

North went on to the elas saying, "The ela is a snake-like creature that holds poison in its tail. It can grow over one hundred feet in length, but most are less than fifty. It attaches to its prey using its large jaws, and then it raises its tail, curling back on itself, kind of like a scorpion I would say." North looked around, and then went on, "The poison tip of its tail curls from above, pointed down at its prey, and immediately penetrates the prey, injecting it with the poison. The prey dies instantly."

North stopped and looked around the room. "I hope we are not getting bored yet," he said with a smile.

Someone gave a snoring sound from the middle of the room, and the folks laughed a bit.

North continued, saying, "I did also want to go over some of the domesticated beasts they used as pets, and for transportation and hauling." He changed pictures on the monitor screen. "These animals are also still surviving there. They called this one, an 'emui'. It reminds me of our cats. It has a bigger cousin, the 'crantic', which had not been domesticated, and can be compared to our tigers. These creatures are among the few that have fur.

"Another was one they called a 'gendra', and it is a huge, stegosaurus-like creature. It, however, is four times bigger than our stegosaurus ever was. They walk into the water to spear, screen and feed on fish with their long claws. They had been able to domesticate gendras in the past, and they apparently were not dangerous as long as they were well fed, typically with fish. They were able to haul heavy equipment. They have very pointy scales, and weigh over twenty thousand pounds. They can grow up to twenty feet high, thirty feet wide, and seventy-five feet long."

North went on, "Although there are many animals to review, I am only going to mention one more. These quite interesting animals exist on the planet now, just like the others I have shown you. They called them 'contisses'. The D'otians used contisses as we used horses in our ancient history. They have leathery scales similar to an armadillo — however they have elastic properties, and can stretch. A contiss has loose skin between its front and hind legs, like our flying squirrel. This enables it to leap great distances. When alone, it can land by rolling into a ball. They were fed live 'tacks' and 'blogs', along with hydrosplitters. Tacks are like our rats, except that they are reptilian. The blogs were primates of the D'otians. Blogs have both mammal and reptile characteristics, as the D'otians themselves had."

North was busy trying to get the monitor to show the pictures of each animal as he mentioned them. He went back to the contisses. "Here we are with the contiss again. We have learned that these animals were considered to be very intelligent and great protectors of their owners. They could even defend against the spider-like trachnas. They did this by rolling on them, biting them, and by stomping them. There was also a separate breed, which they called 'guard contisses'. D'otians could not ride them, but they were fiercely territorial, and provided protection.

"We have located areas amenable to farming, and have brought twice as much soil starter as we need. This will rapidly break down the specific minerals and other nutrients from the planet's soil and make them available for our vegetables. The hydrosplitters and animal life will provide food for us as well. Our robots have found that the hydrosplitters were the major source of carbohydrates, essential amino acids and vitamins for the inhabitants of D'ot8. D'ot was the name that the inhabitants called their planet. We add the '8' because this is our eighth colonization mission, in accordance with the Guild's Planetary Naming Conventions.

"We have successfully farmed on each of our planets, and since the rate of farmland production will be faster than the growth of the colony, there will be an ample amount of vegetables for us. As farmers, we know we are hostage to the weather. The closest sun lies between D'ot8 and Black Hole 17C. This black hole is a relatively close one. It appears to have significant effects on the planet's sun, which causes quite large solar flares that have significant effects on the weather of D'ot8. There is nothing good about a black hole. They cause problems with communication, as well as throwing off our navigation.

"The reason we are starting this mission now is because D'ot8 may only have one thousand years or so before the planet becomes uninhabitable. This will be because of these tremendous solar flares, which also have 'tides'. These tides can become amplified because of the harmonic convergence with the pulsations coming from the black hole. One thousand years is shorter than you may think. The Guild needs the resources on that planet, and the souls bound to it need recycling. Although one thousand years is not enough for that, it is better to be late than never," he said with a sour grin.

North motioned to the monitor screen again, and displayed new photographs of the interiors of homes and buildings.

The audience started up with excited chatter. This was the first time they had seen pictures like this.

The rooms in the photographs appeared quite large, and they were beautifully ordained with various metallic designs, which were quite elaborate in some rooms. D'otians had a simple design for underground building. The entrances that descended into the occupied areas had a "trap" connected to them that kept water from being able to gather in the living quarters. They apparently had sewage systems that drained into common containing areas, then into the ocean or rivers or lakes. There were obvious lighting fixtures — however there was no active electricity. The robots taking the photographs supplied their own lighting. The corners and edges of the rooms were rounded, and thresholds were curved, and smoothed-out. Kitchens were the central rooms of most homes. D'otians had stoves, ovens, and refrigerators. The living quarters often had a radio in them. The robots had found some recording devices in the homes as well, and it appears they played music with them.

Marshal North went on, "Although we have brought building supplies, D'otians built most of their living and working structures underground, in well-designed architecture which you can see here. We believe these structures to be very usable even now, although we won't know for sure until we actually arrive.

"Regarding our exports to Earth, there is a natural compound on the planet called 'agrist' which is in plentiful supply, and it is very expensive to produce on Earth. When added to metal in the AOD, it increases the volume of that metal by over eight hundred times. In other words, it will make virtually any metal seventy-eight percent lighter, while retaining ninety percent of that metal's hardness and strength. It can make a 'metal foam' by combining it with almost any metal. When added to the alloy films we already use, this provides a low mass, tough outer shield. This helps to make space ships almost impervious to space dust erosion. Erosion is the main reason our ships end up decommissioned. The company that we lease these ships from gave us a very good deal on this mission, just to be the first to be able to buy this compound from us.

"We have two nuclear power sources; one will be activated upon our arrival at D'ot8, and one will stay in hibernation for any unforeseen need in the future. Since so many things are dependent on plentiful electricity, we want multiple redundancies here. Both the hydrosplitters and the agrist will be important exports for this planet to develop. Mining and harvesting equipment is on board to develop these resources."

Marshal North continued, "The microorganisms on any prospective planet are typically a concern to incoming colonists. Unknown viruses, pepotads, fungi, and viro-bacillus can be unpredictable, no matter how much probe research we have done. As you know, we always seem to lose a few colonists to a new disease, until we come up with a solution. We have always come up with an answer, although, you all know about Omegon, and what happened there — the first colonists were completely wiped out. Other than Omegon, we have only lost three percent at most, to disease. This is why we all wear masks until we know for sure. This is a three-month requirement, and it is for your own safety.

"Please read your manuals before you go to sleep. Keep this important mission in your uppermost thoughts. Thank you for your time."

Here we go. Jason suddenly longed for the day he could purely work and not be required to speak in front of people.

There was brief applause, and Survival Marshal North took his seat.

Social Director Hay took the podium once again, and said, "Thank you, Marshal North, for your exciting picture of our future home!" She paused while those in attendance gave another round of applause. Then she asked Dr. Jason Ata, Director of Soul-Typing and Guidance, to take the podium. "Now everybody, please give a warm welcome to our Soul-Typing and Guidance Director, Dr. Jason Ata!" There was polite applause as he rose from his chair.

Jason quickly forgot his butterflies on the way to the podium. He paused, took it all in with a deep breath. As he took his place at the podium, he looked at the audience, and overflowed with a tremendous surge of love for them. He had been Guild-trained, and this was habit by now. Jason did not appreciate how aware he was of that state as compared to others. It extended into them and he could feel them returning it. It felt good. It always did. He took another deep breath. *Thank you.*

Jason began to speak. "Where do I begin? Well, I believe this mission will be a challenging one. With challenges come opportunities." He paused for a moment. "You will need to practice your faith every day, for everyone around you." Jason continued, "I have reason to believe that the soul-types we will be receiving will be beyond the genetic harmonics you carry. I don't want to alarm you, but we need to be prepared for the arrival of very violent and difficult newborns."

"What do you mean?" A member of the audience blurted out.

Someone else yelled, "I never heard of this!" The room was now alive with motion and murmurs.

Alarmed by the audience's reaction to Jason's words, the social director stood up and addressed him, "Dr. Ata, please excuse me. I have heard about your team's research into the dissociative soul-mind. Does that have something to do with this?"

Dr. Ata looked at her, unmoved by the sudden onset of fear in her eyes. He was not unmoved because he didn't care. He was unmoved because his mind was always focused on one thing: *Stay connected.* Connection with the tranquil Source was habitually fixed in Jason's mind. Social Director Hay waited, continuing to stare at him. She became placated by his quiet confidence, and she relaxed some.

Looking at Social Director Hay, he softly said, "In our world, the Guild trains parents trying to conceive a baby to 'call' to the soul-type they believe they can help in the world. As you know, we accomplish this with specific meditations and prayer. When the baby is born, my department's job is to analyze the baby for its soul-type, and fashion the best guidance we can for the development of that particular soul. A soul is categorized as one of three primary types. A Type I baby is easy to raise and love. Type I babies are very responsive to love, and when loved, they return the love. They learn to use love, and it blends in with most of their efforts as they grow and mature."

Jason accepted a drink of water brought to him, and then continued. "Type II children have a tendency to *repress* love. They don't respond as well to love, and do not return it as easily. However, they can recognize love and respond, if they are in the mood. These ones will need more love, because they as they grow older they don't recognize or appreciate love, and they waste it. They waver in their ability to grow love intentionally until they are past their teens. Much depends on the skill and love of the parents. Eventually, we can guide Type II babies to give and receive love as well as Type Is can. Type II babies are the largest category, and most of us were primarily Type II babies, with both Type I and Type III characteristics in varying degrees."

Jason continued, "The III babies are those souls that have completely *dissociated* love from their awareness, resembling someone with the split personality variety of schizophrenia. One side does not know what the other side is doing. These are the most difficult to overcome. They cannot recognize love. They have a defense mechanism in their subconscious that actively *avoids and rejects* any recognition of love. This is hidden in a part of the invisible soul-mind — the 'blind spot', if you will. It hides a savage distrust and hate of love. If conscious recognition of love comes to the surface, they will mentally 'run' in the opposite direction. They will shrink from love, or, if they cannot escape, attack the source of the love — covertly, or overtly. Whereas a Type II child may use love, and manipulate a parent's love to the child's advantage, a Type III child would not think to use love for anything, love being taboo. As adults, they can learn to develop a social persona, but behind it is something very cold."

The audience was getting confused with these classifications, and Jason could tell that his description of Type IIIs was not getting through well enough, so he plainly said, "Type IIIs are where sociopathic killers originate."

The group before him seemed to get that, so, going on, he said, "Although a pure Type III baby is rare, we are all a blend of the three types. That is where we try to narrow down the soul-typing of the baby. We do this in order to provide customized training to overcome the negatives, and grow on the positives each child has."

Jason paused, and looked down at the lightly stained natural oak grain on the podium. *Should I?* He asked silently. *Tread lightly*, the voice said. Jason took another deep breath, and went on speaking, "I am a specialist in what some others call "devils". These children are always Type III. They usually have a background of childhood trauma, but a surprising number do not. When we eliminate genetic, nutritional, and environmental factors as causes, we are left with one conclusion — these are some seriously retarded souls, and all effort must be made to avoid irritation of these souls, from childbirth on."

Jason gave an example, "Think about a puppy or a kitten. We tell our children, 'don't play rough' with them, because the pet will start biting or scratching too easily. That 'button' can be 'turned on' in older pet, even though years of gentleness have kept the pet peaceful. They will become 'bitey', or 'scratchy', when simply trying to pet them. That is how it is with Type IIIs, except that they can wait to bite. They rarely appear these days, and my team has developed our own classifications of them. The wheels of research turn slowly. Although these theoretical ideas have not yet been fully embraced, I obviously believe that we may be correct in our hypothesis. I am actually here because my superiors want me to prove these theories or shut up about them. In any case, since this is a lifetime mission, they won't have to face me anymore if they don't want to." Jason gave a wry grin, "Perhaps they chose me for this mission, if only for that reason."

He paused.

No laughter. Nothing.

"I have a very strong feeling that we will need to use these theories on this planet, if we are to be successful. It will also help us to refine our guidance of these dissociative souls, and broaden our understanding of our own souls as well."

"I don't understand your reason for negativity," another person in the audience complained.

"Please let me explain further," said Jason. "Everything about this planet is unkind. It is like a very nasty jungle, without the jungle. The humanoids that lived here before must have had those predatory traits. God only knows what kind of lives they lived there. The souls still there have been bound to that planet for thousands of years, held as if by gravity, exactly like the other dead planets we have colonized. They are burning with the desire to do something to move on — but are imprisoned. When we arrive, I believe the hungriest souls will force their way into our newborns, regardless of the parent's genetic phenotypical passive harmonics. Our first generation of offspring will be their first avenue for incarnation in one hundred thousand years."

Jason continued, "Please look to the screen to my left. There you can see anatomic illustrations of the D'ot8 humanoids, generated after medic-robotic dissection of one of two well-preserved bodies recently discovered. These bodies were found in containers and appeared to be in suspended animation. The containers were still powered, after all these millennia, and I find that amazing."

The audience started talking among themselves. This was the first they had seen of the anatomy of the D'otians.

Jason went on, "You see that they had scales, and also had bodies similar in shape to ours, but about fifty percent larger and heavier. Their faces were amazingly humanoid, considering their reptilian roots. This specimen was almost nine feet tall. They have what appears to be a nuchal crest on the tops of their heads, similar to our lizards. The two we've seen in suspended animation had different colors of nuchal crests.

"We have found some remarkable things in our robotic dissections of one of the bodies. To understand what I am about to say, please look to the diagrams on the screen." He showed a picture of something that looked like three vertical tubes, side by side, each with a bulge in the center. "These are diagrams of three brainstems. The first one on the left, with a small bump in the middle is a lizard brainstem, a reptile. The second one, the one in the middle, is a dog's brainstem. It has another layer over the bump in the center, making it thicker. This is what is associated with a mammal's ability to fear and love, and it is what allows a mammal behave differently from a reptile. A reptile is only interested in basic body functions, but it does understand pecking order, and can follow certain animal behaviors we would call 'ritualistic.' It follows 'routines'. What the reptile does not understand are emotions like fear or love. If you were to call someone cold-blooded, you are saying that he or she is emotionally cold like a reptile." Jason took a Freudian glance at North, who was looking in Jason's direction with a blank face.

Jason went on, "Let us go on to the third brainstem on the far right. It is a human brainstem. It has another layer making the central bulge even bigger. It also has a more complex limbic system, and a huge cortex, compared to the first two illustrations. We have studied the medical illustrations of the D'otians' central nervous system anatomy. We can see in this next illustration that they had the roughly the same size cortex as humans. However, the thicker, emotional layer of the brainstem is very thin, compared to ours."

He stopped. *What's the best way to say this?* He went on, "I have consulted with a number of anatomical experts, and they agree that their limbic system appears to be vestigial. What they mean is that these humanoids once had a well-developed, human-like brain stem, limbic system and neo-cortex. Something happened over a long period of time to cause some sort of devolution. Not only did their limbic systems regress to something more like the reptilian brainstem, their female breasts had become vestigial as well, and ceased to function. This probably happened because although they were mammals, they retained many reptile-like characteristics, such as their scales, nuchal crests, and their tails, which also had caudal crests."

He looked at their blank faces. *I've lost them.* Jason elaborated, saying, "Form follows function. Evolution follows function, and so does devolution. If you don't use it, you lose it. We believe the growth of that middle bulge on the brainstem in humans is a *result*, not a cause. It is a result of their growth in channeling love over many millennia."

Now that he had completely bewildered most of the listeners, Jason nonetheless continued to make his case. "What I am trying to say is that I believe that it looks like the D'otians' brainstems regressed because they stopped using love — love 'left' their society. They devolved emotionally. We know from the library records that constant warring among themselves eventually caused their extinction. I fear that these are the souls we will be receiving on D'ot8, and I need to get you be prepared, for this mission to succeed.

"Your mission is my mission: To spend the rest of our lives organizing the recycling of the souls bound to this planet so that they may help us re-inhabit the planet, bringing it back to life for humanoid souls. We provide avenues for their minds to evolve and remember their soul's purpose, just as we are doing for ourselves.

"Our section of the universe will have another world to love and learn from, trade with, and according to the teaching of the Guild, bring more balance and harmony to the dimension of time. History has shown that the salvaging of a dead planet brings good fortune to not only the colonists there, but to our home planet as well.

"In psychology, classic dissociation happens when a person has a part of their mind split off. This dissociated part is unknown by the conscious mind, yet is given a will, and operates from the subconscious.

"The Guild postulates that we have all dissociated from love, and that is why we need to 'swim' towards love. When we swim towards love, we swim towards our deepest eternal home, which is invisible to those who find their soul drawn to the dimension of time.

"Our team takes it a step further: All soul-types, including myself, must dissociate, split, if you will, from awareness of part of our spiritual minds in order to find ourselves in the dimension of time. Time is a non-real temporary arena for souls to learn that 'one thing'. You all know that the Guild professes that the dimension of time was allowed to be made, or better, temporarily exist, by our eternal Author, the Source. The Author did allow this because souls have the free will to direct their attention as they please. There is a safety control here, based on free will. We are free to wander, although that is not our creative purpose. However, you cannot walk away from the light without walking into the dark. Eventually, the dark becomes so painful and fearful that we turn around. Unfortunately, the deeper one is in time, the less they can see or hear the light of spiritual sanity. Our spiritual minds become blinded by the physical senses. It can take thousands of years and many lifetimes to for the prodigal son to get a solid footing on his way home."

Jason paused, and took a drink of water. *They are listening*. He continued, "That is where we come in. Even though we are learning our way back, we are also the brothers to those who are more lost, but can communicate with us. They learn our ways, and we speak to them of the Author of life, peace, happiness and love. By doing so, we perfect the lesson ourselves."

He waited for a moment to let the thought sink in, then continued, "Guild dogma says that our wandering souls formed dissociations within dissociations in the dimension of time. This considerably complicated the problem, with further splits from love on various mental levels we made. Our memory of our true home in the dimension of eternity was lost, buried in the darkness of time. That memory resides in a part of our invisible subconscious, which we fear to look into. It is like the child who is skipping school, and is afraid to face the schoolteacher, who ironically is waiting in concern for the child's return. Through the Guild's teaching, we have learned how to reverse this. We did this by using love in every way and action. We discovered, and have now proven, that love actually affects time, similar to speed or gravity. We have tremendous agreement among top physicists on this subject, and are very close to proving the theory with the Guild's new orbiting gyroscopic particle collider."

Jason noticed the Love by Duty people, mostly Survival deputies, crossing their arms, and shaking their heads in disagreement ever so slightly.

It disturbed him that they were so firmly set against love's potential as a real, measurable entity. He took a breath, shrugged it off and continued.

"Re-inhabitation of planets has been done enough times that some experts feel that it has been perfected. Each of us does his or her job because our society developed us by properly elevating our minds and souls. Our society, guided by the Guild, promoted the obvious answer. We promoted the swimming against the tide of time, swimming, if you will, in the opposite direction. The love we use and carry attracts thoughts that harmonize with order, happiness, and keep us pointed us in the direction of eternity. This keeps us on the path, swimming against the river of time, with success! Harmonizing our thoughts with the love that extends from eternity brings truly natural order and peace to all those living in time.

"Let us swim!" Jason pronounced the familiar blessing loudly, and the audience reflexively chanted back: "We travel to love together, or not at all!"

This ritual broke the boredom in the room. After all, they had been going to the temple classes all their lives. This was rudimentary soul science. Still, Dr. Ata had added a new twist to their perspective. In the end, his theory said that the destination they were all "swimming" to spiritually was not just heaven alone. It was the other hidden side of their own eternal selves, which resided in the home of the Author, the dimension of eternity.

Jason continued, "A dissociative patient is brought to wellness by breaking through the dissociation and joining the separate parts, so that the unreal may be left behind.

"We know in psychology that the more severe the dissociation, the split, the more difficult the case. An interesting observation is that when the split is great, the other side relegated to the sub-conscious will usually expose itself in a less frequent, but more exaggerated way. This expression can be loving or not.

"I find it fascinating that these people were so advanced in studying themselves, and their world, through microscopes. The paradox is that they had almost no science in looking around themselves, in reaching outward through better travel technologies, or flight. Their historical records indicate that when they did travel afar, they did so for purposes of conquest and war.

"We have seen a trend in past re-inhabitations of other planets. We know from past planetary expeditions that if most of the creatures are generally plant-eaters, the souls from that planet make for happy babies. The higher percentage of predators always appears to correlate with experiencing more problems with the babies. The ones born on such planets take more work, and never quite make it to their parent's level. It will take those planets a few generations before the babies make for good citizens. Still, we have never had a planet quite like D'ot8. *Soften it up.* If I believed we could not succeed, I would have tried to stop this mission. However, nobody would have listened anyway, because of the enormous profit potential of the hydrosplitters and the agrist."

The room started laughing at that, which surprised Jason. He smiled and looked around. He caught a glimpse of Marshal North. He wished he hadn't when he saw a look that would burn a hole in his head of it could. Jason had an unusual flash of apprehension, and quickly looked down. *What was that look about?*

He was about to continue, when North unexpectedly got up out of his seat, laughing with the rest of the people. As he was moving toward the podium, North said, "That was great, thank you, Dr. Ata, but we must be moving on now. We have nap-time ahead!" He came over to Jason and firmly took hold of his arm, and guided him away from the podium. He was laughing as if Jason himself was joking the whole time.

Jason was caught off-guard, but he still wanted to make a good impression. *This is embarrassing,* he thought. He was not happy about having his authority undermined so callously. Jason looked at the Social Director, who was to handle the transitions of speakers.

Social Director Rini Hay appeared flustered and confused — and before she could step in, North just took over her job by introducing the mission's Medical Director, and now *she* looked insulted. "We had better move along. Dr. Reiter, would you please take the podium?" North said this as he was "helping" Jason from the podium. They took the first steps away from the podium.

Jason figured he had to interrupt North's public control of him, and so with North still holding his arm, he stopped, like a rock. North did not want to make it *too* obvious he was forcing Jason, so he had to stop, too. North looked frustrated now, having assumed he had the situation controlled.

Jason turned to the Social Director, nodded and thanked her. He then concluded with his recognition to the audience. "I want to thank you for your kind attention, and I encourage you all to read the manuals I have provided to you and your teams."

After Jason finished his parting words, he left North standing there as he returned to his seat. The Medical Director was just rising, confused as well at the break of protocol. Jason thought, *North is a "Love by Duty" party member. Jesus, those guys assume they are so right in their ways — they should control those who aren't just like them.*

After Jason sat back down, he had a daydream/flashback of a class he once lectured:

"The Guild asks us to invest love in all thoughts and actions, whenever we can remember. Not to do so is not a negative, in as much as it is simply a reflection of the level of value placed on the goal of love. In the first century of the Guild, a certain number of members in the Guild agreed that they could not accept the concept that love extends from our Author from the dimension of eternity - and is channeled by humans. However, they did acknowledge the value of the emotion of love in society. Indeed, it was difficult to refute. Over the centuries, the research had shown this fact was indisputable. The active teaching and support of remembering a continual awareness of love in the homes and workplaces of Guild members increased productivity in the long run. Yes, there was a limit to love's productivity, because love rejects slavery. However, the quality of life in a loving society is so elevated that the bit of productivity that is lost is not important. In any case this group, which has grown, and is now called the 'Love by Duty" party, accepts that love should be a major goal in society, but they choose not to express love with intimacy and words, but rather by work and duty. They have the motto, 'Actions Speak Louder Than Words.'"

Jason broke out of his daydream of that classroom experience, and resumed his attention to the proceedings — well, for a minute or two anyway. Sniff. *Definitely caramelized.*

Dr. Hans Reiter was speaking now, but Jason's mind was on other things — many things. Once again, because of pure habit, love came to his consciousness, and he could look at the people there without worrying. He thought about it. *They'll be able to handle it. Sure, they don't know now, but they will learn. They will be up to the task.*

Jason was concerned about regression. Regression would yet occur on earth in various groups of people who lived in non-Guild areas that still had high populations per square mile. Harsh environments and the resulting stress were common predictors of regression as well. When you put those two elements together, the percentage grew. Regression into primitive human traits like possessiveness and obsessive control of things and people, along with the disharmony and violence that followed, had become fairly easy to re-direct, if caught quickly within Guild areas. Unfortunately, the ones involved in the regression had to be separated and re-located in order to be successful. It could take years before the regressed parties could come together again for successful release and closure.

When first re-inhabiting a planet, however, there was no infallible way to totally separate those who had regressed into negative relationships or behavior. A "re-integration" was necessary with different work and living groups, with as much separation as possible between the individuals caught in the regression. Re-integration was an answer that worked, but it was not perfect. There had been revenge-related physical attacks among some of the "separated" colonists on other planets. Jason was concerned that it could be much worse on this planet.

With his attention drawn to his thoughts, Jason politely watched each following speaker. He applauded when appropriate, but did not hear much of what they were saying. The meeting went on for another hour, and then it was over.

Afterwards, most of the people there just hanged around, talking shop, planning. They had been on route for one day. In two more hours, they would be going to the hyposleep units and slumber in them for the next three years. Jason wished they had the new Brashier B2010 sleep units. He had heard that one woke up very quickly from those. The units on this ship were the standard fare Ebson 50's. They were very reliable, but the wake up period took a few days. *I wonder if they could just let us sleep during the wake up phase?* Jason thought this to himself, and then chuckled at the absurdity of the idea.

There was really nothing left to do now, except think of any number of challenges on D'ot8 and the arising issues down the chains of possible events there.

He decided to have a snack while still in the cafeteria. All food eaten since on board contained an additive that would be converting the eaten food into a slow acting paste. This would provide balance to the intravenous solution he would be using while in hyposleep.

A cranberry muffin and skim milk smoothed with carrageenan seemed to be the right choice for now. He sat down at one of the long faux cherry grain laminate lunch tables with a few of the team leaders. Trained to confront disturbing situations by joining in reason, they engaged him.

"Are you really convinced it will be as bad as you say with the new-borns?" A redheaded gal, Brenda was asking, (she was head chef of the bakery, and her huge frame said that she was loving it there.) Brenda's life-partner Amanda was with her, looking very concerned. Some non-child producing colonists were "on-call" to receive children that would inevitably end up available for adoption. This would happen because of a parent's disability, disease, death, or simply parents that decided that they were wrong about their goals. Whatever the reason, the system — the safety net, was there.

"Don't worry so much as prepare," Jason responded. "You have been trained thoroughly for anything that comes your way. It just means more work. You must give the children much love, no matter what. You know that is the way to build well-developed souls. Love lasts. Anything true is always revealed in the end. You just need to remember to recharge. Go to home-base, meditate, let your soul visit your Source and be refreshed. Your minds will become very well developed at D'ot8. You will be swimming harder than you have ever swum before, but you can do it. You are perfect for this mission."

Marshal North came walking towards the table. He leaned forward across the table and said quietly, but within earshot of the others, "I am in charge of survival. Frightening these people with unproven theories, and creating uncertainty is something that threatens their moral. Low moral threatens survival. Keep your concerns to yourself when we arrive." He then leaned in across the lunch table more closely — so close that his nose was just a few inches from Jason's face.

His tone was low, but gained intensity as he said, "I am disgusted that the Guild put you in such a position of authority. When we get to D'ot8, every mistake you make, every blunder you trip over will be recorded by my team. Then I am shipping you the hell out of here!" North's voice continued to rise, and Jason started to back his face away from the spray from North's mouth. "You just keep your muffin-hole shut about your bullshit, do you hear me?"

He thinks I can fear. Jason thought to himself. *I give no obedience to fear.* "I care about them and want them to be prepared." Jason countered, in a friendly way.

"That's an order!" yelled North.

Jason sighed. "Well an order from the Survival Marshal is indeed an order, and protocol is protocol. I will abide by your request."

"It was not a request!" North was clearly frustrated by Jason's lack of interest in his drama. "I would love to just slap you and wake your ass up," North said under his breath.

"I can hear you." Jason said, with a slight smirk. Then he got serious. "I *can hear* you," he sincerely said, moving his head gently forward for emphasis. "I'll be very careful of what I say, for your sake, and the sake of all the people on this ship."

North could see that Jason's Guild training would automatically try to calm North by Jason's "seeing" peace in North. North was not having any of that. He straightened himself up, preparing to leave. "This is a potentially critical problem, and as Survival Marshal I am responsible for those things I perceive as vitally important to our survival. Things that can be seen and heard and felt, *these* are what are essential!" he barked.

North turned to his waiting deputy on the way out, and said quietly, "The invisible world of Dr. Jason Ata and the rest of the Guild's old guard certainly are *not* essential." He could say this privately to his deputy, but would not dare to say it aloud in front of them all.

North left in a huff for his quarters. He and his squad would be among those sleeping normally for the next three years, not like ones in hyposleep. They would take turns at watch while the rest slept. They would also be the only ones coming back to earth after their usefulness was over at the new planet. That usually took a few years. They would go into hyposleep on the way back to Earth.

He was relieved to see North leave, and decided to settle in early himself. Jason felt he handled the Survival Marshal rather well, considering. He had resisted North's attempt to drag him down to the lower disharmonic thought realm.

With three long hallways, two stairways, and one elevator, it took Jason almost ten minutes to get to his sleep unit. It had the same exterior as the rest of the sleep units in his section — orange plastic composite with yellow horizontal stripes wrapping around it. He looked at his watch. *I've got thirty-five minutes before lights out. I think I'll listen to some classical music for a bit.*

Jason scrolled through his MU, and decided to start with "Rock n' Roll Pain Train" by Kid Rock. He thought it queer, the way he often did, that this harsh music had become so popular in recent years. An elementary soul-explanation would be that it was simple yin-yang balancing taking place. Life had become so organically ordered and pleasant for most people that aggressive competitiveness was rare. One could fleetingly see it in the elderly, or in movies and such. The time-related desire to compete was smoothly re-directed through schooling into increased productivity on earth now.

The mix of rage, love, and ego that Kid Rock put forth over one thousand years ago was the diametric opposite of life on earth now. He chuckled. *Kid Rock would have considered Earth to be hell now.* He thought about the history of this man. *I know Kid Rock was a persona. The human behind the persona — that's the question. He was a musical genius, which involves a solid connection with higher harmonics. On the other hand, he carried a great deal of the lower disharmonic realm into his music and his life. Typically, such an individual's world would have become quickly trapped, and sink towards self-destruction, with an eventual early death.* Jason thought about it some more.

"A well-connected soul," Jason muttered to himself, "When love and life bursts through extreme negativity, as opposed to being watered down, trickling through a stable culture, it is indeed a colorful thing to behold." He sighed. He wondered where that soul was now.

How far we have come, he mused. *Yet we are still learning.* He thought about that, and spontaneously said aloud, "Still, I think I've learned more about the touching the truth."

"Yes you have," said the Guide. Jason could hear him clearly now.

As per Guild dogma, the Guide was in touch with both eternity and the sub-dimension of time. All members sought the Guide, but few could hear him clearly or consistently, much less be able to channel him.

Jason had become an exceptional listener, but was spotty on the channeling. *Letting go is hard to do,* he often thought. He could connect well, unless he really wanted to hear something intensely. Then the connection would break. He knew that it was his own subconscious that broke the connection. The Guide was always ready when Jason was, if he bothered to think of him. The Guide had told Jason that he had a gift, but he had yet to appreciate it in this life. The Guide had never said anything condemning to Jason about himself, or anyone else, for that matter.

Jason knew why the conventionally accepted yin-yang explanation of Kid Rock's current popularity among classical music fans was incomplete. He had been beyond yin-yang too many times, to a *state* where there was *no* yin and *no* yang. Yin-yang was time-based: true enough in the sub-dimension of time, but there was more going on. Yin-yang was a good simple explanation for the conflicts and schizoid nature of life in this dimension, but that was all. It did not provide the ultimate answer. It was still two hands clapping, not one.

His mind wandered to another class, many years ago, "We now know with mathematical certainty that the end of time will come. Time is a temporary phenomenon. The end of time does not mean you run out of time to do things, and then you are left with time and nothing you can do," he remembered telling his class. "It does not mean that. It means that the entire dimension of time has been erased, along with everything that happened while our minds were focused and anchored in it. It no longer exists in any dimension, because there was always only the one dimension of eternity. All that is left is the truth, and it is very good. It tells of the dimension of eternity, the home of the Holy Author of our eternal souls, blesser of minds made holy again by choice. We hear the song of peace, love, and happiness. We join in intercourse and expansion, and that is the good news. The closer we come home to truth, the more we love her, and wings are lent from heaven itself to speed our return, that the prodigal child and father meet in truth at long last."

Jason recalled that classroom scene often. He smiled to himself because he remembered every word and still liked the way he had said it. Whenever Jason recalled that moment, he wondered if he channeled the last part. Since it was an area of frustration for him, when he would ask the Guide about it, he would find himself blocking the answer. He had given up asking.

He shook his head. Three minutes left. Jason removed his earpieces, got comfortable in his sleep chamber, laid back, eyes open, and waited for the sleep chamber technician to initiate the hyposleep sequence. A way-overdue crap would be waiting in three years. *Kid Rock,* he thought. He chuckled again.

As he felt the cryogenic mix of sedative gases take effect, Jason fell into a dream. His dream began with his co-travelers in it. It was as if he was a ghost, floating through recently visited areas in the ship, and then he found himself floating through the walls of the ship, and out into space itself. It seemed so weird because he fell into a state of perpetual déjà vu.

"Why do I remember this? This was so long ago — how do I know?" He found himself speaking aloud in the darkness of space. The stars were outstandingly bright, so that it was not so dark as usual. *So strange.*

His dreaming led him into a planetary approach to D'ot8. "I can see a planet. That looks like D'ot8. Is that D'ot8? That's D'ot8!" Jason said with surprise. His mind was racing. *What a dream! Is my body here? It is. Then it's not a vision, I think. Where am I going?* He flew down into and through a city. *I'm landing on D'ot8! No, I am still flying. What's guiding me? Why do I feel like I've been here before? What is that short building, and why am I going into there? It seems familiar, too. There's no one leading me, I think —*

Jason found himself floating down through a hospital, and into a plainly decorated room in which some D'otians were attending a birthing class. His journey came to rest at the location of a young couple listening to the teacher of the class. He found himself drawn to the mother's abdomen, slightly bulging with the baby it held. He heard himself say, "I know this. How do I know this?" He looked at the mother's finely scaled face. Her green eyes and her perfectly polished scales mesmerized him. *She's beautiful!* Her face then began to fade, and Jason's remaining dream slowly sank, through the twilight zone and then into the unseen realm of the cold long sleep ahead.